The Great Ideas

Suzanne Cleminshaw was born in Boston, Massachusetts, and grew up in Ohio. She moved to England in 1990 and now lives in London.

The Great Ideas

SUZANNE CLEMINSHAW

FOURTH ESTATE • London

This paperback edition first published in 2000
First published in Great Britain in 1999 by
Fourth Estate Limited
6 Salem Road
London W2 4BU
www.4thestate.co.uk

Copyright © Suzanne Cleminshaw 1999

1 3 5 7 9 10 8 6 4 2

The right of Suzanne Cleminshaw to be identified as the author of this
work has been asserted by her in accordance with the Copyright,
Designs and Patents Act 1988.

A catalogue record for this book is available from the
British Library.

ISBN 1-85702-909-7

All rights reserved. No part of this publication may be reproduced,
transmitted, or stored in a retrieval system, in any form or by any means,
without permission in writing from Fourth Estate Limited.

Typeset by Avon Dataset Ltd, Bidford on Avon B50 4JH
Printed in Great Britain by Cox & Wyman Ltd, London & Reading

To my parents, John and Helen Cleminshaw, my first teachers

ACKNOWLEDGEMENTS

My most special thanks goes to Jon Cook, who has been both my mentor and muse on this book and a most dear and cherished friend.

Secondly, I want to thank my editor, Nicholas Pearson, for his brilliant editing and unwavering faith in my writing.

Next, I would like to thank the following family, friends and colleagues: Malcolm Bradbury, John David, Trixie, Nicole and Courtney Cleminshaw, Claudia Closman, Vivien Green and the Sheil Land Agency, Rolf Gullstrom-Hughes, Russell Celyn Jones, David Kirkup, Steve Kovack, Fred and Helen Kronseder, Clare Morgan, Andrew Motion, Rose Tremain, and all the supportive and creative staff at Fourth Estate.

Lastly, I would like to thank three very important teachers: Dr Paul Wild, Dr Dave Gullette, and Dr Lowry Pei.

For living is one thing and knowing is another and as we shall see, perhaps there is such an opposition between the two that we may say that everything vital is anti-rational, not merely irrational, and that everything rational is anti-vital, and this is the basis of the tragic sense of life.

Miguel de Unamuno, *Tragic Sense of Life*

Avon Heights Tribunal,
20 February, 1999

A partially clothed skeleton was found last Thursday in the Blue Hole, a lake located on the outskirts of Avon Heights. Divers discovered the remains, trapped within a cave, one hundred and seventy feet below the lake's surface. The preliminary autopsy has revealed that the body belongs to a person who drowned at least twenty-five years ago. Medical examiners are currently working to make an identification of the deceased.

The Blue Hole was closed to the public decades ago, due to its dangerous swimming conditions. It is fed by strong underground springs, which create unpredictable currents. The temperatures in the deepest parts of the lake are extremely cold. The lowest floor of the lake has never been sounded; it is known locally as the Bottomless Lake.

PART I

THE ANCIENT AGE

When you look closely at something, like the palm of your hand, or the grain in a table, you lose yourself. It can also happen when you look up at the stars. Maybe that's what vertigo is. When you feel yourself disappear.

Across the street from where I live is a house that has been abandoned for as long as I can remember. It is large, and made of stone, painted white, with odd-shaped windows in places you wouldn't expect. The story is that back in the fifties this big family, the Monroes, moved in there – eight children, two parents, housekeeper, an uncle with a wooden leg, wolfhounds and a tame cheetah. Mr Monroe was a film producer–director, and he inherited the cheetah from a jungle movie done at MGM. He moved his family to Ohio because he didn't want his children to grow up in the louche environment of Hollywood. He installed a tennis court, fish ponds, a fountain, a grape arbor, and a swimming pool in the basement. Anyway, the family left abruptly because it was beset by tragedy. A girl was found dead on the flagstone path, just below their third-story playroom windows. A deliveryman found her body, along with a three-year-old boy, who was sitting beside her, making circles with her blood on the cold gray slate. My friend Louis Lewis swears you can still see the lines of those circles on the path, but it may be the veins of iron in the rock or the stains of ancient lichen.

The third-story windows are long and narrow. I often imagine the girl's specter at the glass, pensive, staring off into the distance. Louis and I have tried to look in other windows but they are all heavily draped. Except for a window in the door to the kitchen, through which you can see a yellow cupboard, a large white tea urn standing on a stainless-steel counter and one of those twenties-style metal spigots at the sink. If you crane your neck far enough you can make out the edge of a huge fireplace in a room at the end of a dark hallway. Through a basement window you can glimpse a corner of the swimming pool. It is a nursery-rhyme blue and just as unbelievable. We would have tried to see more – Louis would have no qualms about breaking in – but the Rent-a-Cop who patrols our neighborhood has some twisted interest in the Monroe house. Louis once climbed up a tree equipped with binoculars to look in the playroom window. He was able to see the children's names, painted in black, winding all along the top of yellow walls – Montgomery, Megan, Monroe . . . eerie and sad as the passenger list of a missing ship. Then Rent-a-Cop's nightstick brought him and a bunch of branches collapsing to the ground. I've spent a lot of time daydreaming about what is inside that house. Even though they say it is empty except for curtains and carpets, I picture dead palm trees and ice buckets and cufflinks, pale lilac gloves with a hat to match, and closets full of spare wooden legs and cheetah leashes and suitcases plastered with labels saying Timbuktu and Constantinople.

*

4

My parents are away. My father has a lot of business in Europe and my mother always goes with him at this time of year because she can't bear being here in the summer. Leonora, our cleaning lady, is staying with me. The kids in the neighborhood are afraid of Leonora. She drives an old Continental she calls her 'green hornet' and keeps an ax on the back seat. She tells me she will use it if one of her dozen boyfriends gets fresh before she is ready. Any of the kids in the neighborhood who don't believe the part about the dozen boyfriends are shown pictures in Leonora's wallet. My favorite is one of Leonora wearing a blonde wig and a long green dress that barely makes it over her hips. In it, Leonora stands next to Shane, smiling so wide that the fake pink gums of her dentures show. Leonora tells me that her daddy pulled out all her teeth himself when she was twenty. 'That's what kissing too many sweet talkers gets you!' she says and laughs so long and hard I have to hit her on the back.

Leonora spends most of her time with her dozen boyfriends. 'Bye, Sugar – if you can't be good be *careful*!' she yells as she rushes out the door. I have a lot of time to myself.

AESCHYLUS invented Greek tragedy. Which are these plays about characters who are blind to the net of fate they are caught in. And while they are struggling to get free of what they cannot see, a chorus watching on the sidelines sings verses about how the characters should never have been born in the first place. ARCHE is a Greek word for beginning, or origin. It is the invisible principle which maintains itself, while at the same time metamorphosing into the changing phenomenon of the visible world. ARCHIMEDES invented the lever and said: 'Give me a point on which to stand and I will move the earth.'

I rediscovered the *Encyclopaedia Britannica*s in my father's study. Nothing is on television this summer but Watergate. And I like accumulating facts. When you feel as though you are neither here nor there, but falling or floating off to an elsewhere, they are these immovable, heavy things that have a force like gravity, like the hand of God palm down upon you. They are points you can stand on. And each fact has its own weight, texture, taste. You can roll them around in your mouth and two together make a new flavor.

It was my sister who was found dead on the Monroes' flagstone path. This happened before I was born. No one is sure whether she fell from a tree, the grape trellis, the terrace off the third-story playroom, or perhaps even the roof. No one is sure why she fell. The police didn't rule out foul play, but they closed the case due to lack of any motive or evidence. The charm bracelet she always wore was missing. From the red marks on her wrist, it appeared to have been pulled off. It could have been caught on a branch, the trellis, or a roof tile and ripped off as she fell. But the grounds and the house were searched and the bracelet was never found.

My sister was thirteen. She was quite beautiful. They say Mr Monroe was waiting for her to grow up so she could play the part of Scheherazade in his movie version of *One Thousand and One Nights*.

ALCMAEON says we die because we cannot join the beginning to the end.

In the beginning was the word, they say, but I think it was much more likely to be a question mark. The ancients saw the world as a question to be answered. And they asked a lot of questions about beginnings. Beginnings are magical. If you start anything with 'Once upon a time' it becomes enchanted. And when you ask a question of something it changes it – it can even bewitch it. For instance, if you ask a stone, 'Are you comfortable?' it changes the way you look at the stone. Apparently, before the Greeks came into the picture, people were always asking inanimate objects questions about the future. Stones, stars, tealeaves, numbers. But then the Greeks decided to turn things upside-down. They decided that instead of listening to the inanimate objects tell them about their future, they would figure out the future of the inanimate objects.

'I grew up in Alabama, and Alabama is just a land of miracles where you can't help believing in all sorts of things,' Leonora says when I ask her if she believes in fate. 'For instance, my mother had this apron, and whenever she took it off, no matter where she hung it or flung it, the folds ended up in the exact likeness of the face of the Blessed Virgin Mary.' Leonora strikes a beatific pose to illustrate.

'Then there was this man named Old Moses who lived in a boat with a hen named Fate and a cat named Prophecy. And if you had a question about your future, you just went down to his boat, about the time of day when the sun is looking sad sitting all alone behind the trees. And Moses would draw a chalk circle on the deck with a line running through the middle. Then he threw seed in the circle and stuck Fate in the center. If she ate seed from the north side your answer was yes. If she ate from the south it was no. And if you weren't too happy with that answer you went on home and got yourself some liver and brought it back to Moses. He put the liver in a special bowl and he stuck it just outside his cabin door. Then you'd wait and you'd watch. Old Moses's eyes would go pop-eyed like a goldfish watching.' Leonora bulges her eyes at me. 'If Prophecy put his right forepaw out the door first your answer was yes, the left meant no. That's how I knew I would marry Harry. Old Moses just laughed like a kookaburra in a tree because he knew what would happen. Because prophecies linger in doorways.'

'Does it matter which doorways?'

'Nope. You just have to be aware of those in-between places – where the outside meets the inside. That's what fortunetelling's all about, pussycat. The important thing is to know what questions you want answered, and you have to want them answered real bad, before you go through the doorway.'

Mr Monroe drove his car off the Golden Gate Bridge. This was several years after he moved his family back to California. They say there was an earthquake that day. Mr Monroe drove a silver Mercedes, very fast and reckless. They say that the speed and the quake must have made him lose control. Leonora told me he always had a look in his eyes that said Emergency Room. He told everyone he was struck by lightning on a golf course and that he willed it to happen. He saw the black thunderclouds rolling in, and he yelled to the sky: 'If there is a God, prove it!' And in a brilliant flash of light he was struck, and it turned his straight reddish-blond hair wavy, and his blue eyes brown. He told a lot of stories. One of his stories was about the lucky silver dollar he always carried in the inside pocket of his English-tailored suit jackets. Whenever he had to make a big decision, he would toss it high into the air, calling out 'heads' or 'tails' as it fell, and his judgment was determined upon whichever way it landed. It made people whom his decisions could affect crazy. They say he even drove one actor to the asylum.

I see the shot from above. The camera pans along a cliffside highway where a silver car is speeding on its heart-lurching curves. I see the Golden Gate that day, swaying in the wind like coral under the sea. Mr Monroe throws his coin into the air. He asks: 'Will I die, or will I die not?' and watches its slow silver spin in the air. His body was never recovered.

Once upon a time there was a House of ATREUS and it was cursed. It had a curse that was endless and intertwined lives, like the curse of that famous diamond that made people get torn apart by wolves on the steppes of Russia or run their race cars off cliffs in Monte Carlo. But instead of a diamond this house was cursed by Fate. First of all, Atreus, the head of the household, was murdered by a whole slew of relatives, because he cooked up some of them for a banquet. Then Atreus's son Agamemnon was murdered by his wife because he murdered their daughter, so his son murdered his mother because she murdered his father and then a gang of wild women who weren't even part of the Atreus family were going to kill the son, but at this point Athena, the goddess of wisdom, stepped in and said, whoah, hold your horses, this has gone just about Far Enough.

Thought travels at 150 miles per hour. The earth moves at eight times the speed of a bullet. If we weren't held down by the force of gravity, we would go flying off at 1000 miles per hour. My friend Louis Lewis says Archimedes would never find his point because space is continually expanding.

Louis is sixteen, three years older than me. He reads about a hundred books a year, but he keeps flunking grades because he's a skeptic and never reads the books in school that he's supposed to. About two years ago he read the entire series of the Harvard Classics. He was completely obsessed by it. And when he finished, you'd see him standing in the middle of town, watching the traffic lights change from green to red to green again, for hours on end. Or you'd find him in an aisle of the drugstore, staring at a package of Bandaids, dumbstruck. Only recently when you are talking to him does he look at you, rather than something over your shoulder about a thousand miles away.

Leonora calls him a Chapter of Accidents. My parents say that he is a *Bad Influence*. I suppose he is in a way, but I don't like people who are good influences. I never learn very much from them. Louis is always teaching me things: How to make wine, how to write odes about various parts of the human body, how to develop insouciance. Once he taught me how to be a cat burglar. We both dressed completely in black and climbed around the roofs of a few houses. It ended in catastrophe. Louis fell through the Burtons' skylight and nearly killed himself. We got our pictures in the paper. In it, Louis's head is all wrapped up in bandages. I'm standing a little behind him, wearing my black turtleneck and a knit hat. I still had some charcoal on my face, which, in the picture, makes me look like I have a skin disease. Louis, on the other hand, looks like Charles Boyer in the film where he loses his memory and all these Marcel-waved blondes who use cigarette holders try to help him get it back.

'Put your left foot out, put your left foot in, put your left foot out and twirl it all about – you do the hokey-pokey and you turn around – that's what it's all about!'

We are doing the hokey-pokey at Charm School. We are learning to be graceful under pressure. The instructions are coming from a record that is playing on one of those beige classroom players. It is scratchy, and you can barely make out what the instructor is saying. That and the heat of the June sun coming in through the window makes the atmosphere fuzzy. Like the grainy print of an old movie. The tempo keeps getting faster and faster, and you have to keep up, the anaconda voice of the instructor winding faster and tightening with each beat. Besides sticking your left and right foot out on the proper beat you have to whirl left and then right. 'Pick a point to concentrate on!' Mrs Lewis, Louis Lewis's mother calls out to us through the din. She's one of the teachers at Charm School. I try to focus on the door, but I still get incredibly dizzy. I used to love making myself dizzy when I was little. Dizziness is a gilded misery – there is a certain voluptuousness about it. Halfway through the song I start thinking too much about my right and my left, and I trip over my right foot and fall to the ground. Sometimes you feel as though your body owns you more than you own your body.

Louis Lewis calls it '*tomber des nuages*' – falling from the clouds. Or '*dans la lune*' – going to the moon. I think I first started getting these vertigo attacks last fall. It was at the beginning of the school year, and we had to take all of these tests. There was a Personality Test with questions like: Would being a hermit come (a) easily or (b) with difficulty to you? Would you rather be (a) alive and a coward or (b) dead and a hero ? When doing things, do you choose to hide from others the motives behind them? Are you aware of the beauty surrounding you? Would you like to be an astronaut? Do you feel sorry for injured birds? And IQ tests with fill-in-the-blanks and pi diagrams and spatial shapes. At first I thought I was unbalanced from all the concentrating, and the hot Indian summer sun shining through

11

the big windows and filling in all those little circles and wondering if I would rather be (a) intelligent and neurotic or (b) simple-minded and well-adjusted.

But when the tests were over, I started feeling dizzy, all of a sudden, at other times. I'd be sitting at my desk, and the room would tilt sideways, as if the building were a ship suddenly hit broadside by a tidal wave. Or my pencil would seem to get larger and larger and then smaller and smaller – it would become like something in a dream – I had the odd sense that it was heavy as a feather and then light as a mountain. Or I'd look at my hand, lying on the desk, and I suddenly felt as if I didn't know what it *meant* any more – it is hard to describe – but it didn't seem to have anything to do with me, it was this thing, a hand – and then there would be a swarm of black dots like tsetse flies in front of my eyes and I'd have to blink rapidly and roll my head back and forth to focus properly again.

However, one day I discovered something that will cure these attacks. In the middle of one, I heard my geography teacher say: 'Asunción is the capital of Paraguay.' The room immediately righted itself and my head cleared. I found out that my dizzy spells also go away if I read facts in books. When I got to thinking about it, I realized that I have these huge gaps in my education – it is probably more my fault than the school system – I don't think I've ever paid enough attention, I've always been a daydreamer. If I could draw a picture graph of what I know, it would probably look like one of those South American swinging jungle bridges. With dozens of slats missing where you are supposed to put your feet in order to walk across. And I keep falling through those spaces. But if I fill in the gaps, then there will be nowhere left to fall.

Since I have basically lost the plot, I've decided that the way to find it is to start at the beginning and follow the time-line of hard facts to the end. Then I'll have a blueprint of information, a viewpoint from above, so I'll know where to fill in the blanks of what I have been missing. If I can see what is on the road ahead of and behind me, then maybe I'll stop tripping over the huge loopholes between Logic and my Life.

My grandmother disagrees. She says there is no such thing as truth, and that everything has one thousand meanings, and each of those meanings has one thousand meanings, and thinking about those meanings is the root of all confusion. She says I should learn Zen meditation. That my problem is, being thirteen, I am not a child and not an adult, but somewhere in between. So I am crossing this dream bridge that doesn't exist. But this is a perfect time for me to experience satori, to be awakened. And I should allow myself to fall through the luminous emptiness of my being.

When people talk about Great Ideas they seem possessed by gods. Their shoulders draw back, their voices deepen, they start to talk in Capital Letters. The Greeks didn't have small letters — all their words were completely capitalized. Maybe that's why they had such lofty thoughts. And they didn't have zeros. I guess this makes sense because they were very interested in whether things were changing or unchanging, One or Many. And zero is neither One nor Many. It is nothing. But it can cause change. It is somewhere between real things and imaginary things. It is a line drawn around a mystery.

'All I hear is shhhhh,' Louis says. He has a stethoscope up against my head. AUSCULATE means to listen to internal sounds. We are trying to hear each other's thoughts. The Greeks said you should 'know thyself' in order to be knowledgeable about the rest of the universe.

'Maybe it's because my mind is a still forest pool,' I say. I've been practicing Zen meditation with my grandmother. I take the stethoscope and place it against Louis's forehead. His eyes are very dark, with little gold flecks about the iris. Like wishing wells with wet coins glittering at the bottom. I close my eyes and listen. Shhhhh. I imagine his secrets spinning in stately circles. The most secret hiding place is the skull. Leonora used to listen to her first husband's lies by pressing her ear against his while he was sleeping. Sometimes they sounded like a knife sliding along a diddley-bow string.

Suddenly I hear a noise in Louis's head. 'Louis! I think I heard a thought! What were you just thinking?' I yell.

Louis pushes me and the stethoscope away. 'You're such a freak – I just scratched my head.'

I wonder what the connection is between your mind and your movements. ANAXAGORAS says that Mind is the source of all motion. And that it tumbles everything around because all is mixed up with all and It is trying to sort it all out.

If the earth moved slower, do you think our thoughts would be different? The way you move definitely changes the way you think. If I tilt my head sideways I feel more contemplative. And when I tiptoe I feel covert. And when I spin in circles my mind seems to spill outside its boundaries as crazy and nervous as a full glass of water.

My sister, before she died, when she was about twelve, had a walk-on part in one of Mr Monroe's movies. It was a film version of the *Odyssey*. My sister played a nymph. Which, I think, was a perfect part for her. In all the pictures I've seen of her there is an ambiguous quality to her. She seems elusive, shape-shifting. Almost like those drawings that change from a white vase to two black profiles depending on how you look at it. In the same picture her brown eyes can look soft and gentle, and then suddenly seem to have a false depth, like highly polished wooden tables. One of her upper lids was wider than the other. Which at one moment makes her look as though she is half winking, alluding to some secret she might decide never to reveal to you – and in the next minute like a sleepy child halfway into a dream. She usually poses with her head tilted toward her right shoulder – which makes her look like she is thinking of something strictly taboo and, at the same time, like an innocent ingenue. Whenever I look at those vase–profile pictures, I always wonder which one is more real – the vase, or the profile. Or if there is some completely different picture, that you keep missing, in between the two.

I am a kouros. My left foot is slightly in front of my right foot, my legs are straight and my arms are at my side, my fists are clenched, thumbs resting on top, pointing outward. My head is held high. My forehead, eyes, nose and mouth are Golden Section symmetrical. My hair is curled and heavy upon my shoulders. On my lips is a slight, strange smile. I am proud as the arch, noble as the lofty roofed temple. And I am in a sacred grove. There is the smell of wild thyme and the drone of honeybees. An Aeolian zephyr moves, 'ah', the laurel leaves over my head, stirring 'Cypris alas!', honeysoft 'lovely Adonis is dead' lamentations. My marble eyes are staring across olive-laden hills haunted by the cry of nymphs, over the wine-dark sea toward Ilium. But I do not see the foaming billows, the rosy-fingered dawn, for my eyes are stone. They are cold as the pebbles at the bottom of a clear spring. I can hear Leonora coming into the room. She is flat-footed, and walks around on our hardwood floors barefoot. Her feet sound like the triumphant slaps of winning cards on a table. She comes and stands in front of me, her hands on her hips. 'What on earth are you doing, petunia?'

'I am a kouros, an ancient Greek statue,' I say, trying to hold the pose. 'I'm trying to see what they were thinking by posing like them.' My grandmother told me that in order to know the path, you must become the path.

Leonora pouts, tilts her head to the side and watches me for a few minutes. It is quite distracting. Finally she says, 'You better watch yourself. My habit of stepping into other people's shoes eventually weakened my moral fiber.'

This sentence is false. The arrow is at rest. All Cretans are liars, and I am a Cretan. Does someone who says he is now lying speak truly? What is what is not? Louis tells me that thinking about paradoxes gives you an *à corps perdu, mise en abîme* frisson kind of feeling. So if I ruminate on them enough the powerful vertigo of the paradox might cancel out my own vertigo – a negative multiplied by a negative equaling a positive.

'ALETHEIA' was a poem Parmenides wrote, in which he talks about being led down a polyphemous road and left at the gates of heaven. Where he found out what is, is, and what is not, is not. Because we cannot think about what does not exist. And there can't be change, because this is coming to be, which isn't true existence. So all is One, and 'thus It hovers: bounded, finished, immobile, everywhere in balance, equally perfect at each point, like a globe . . .'

Stones seem intelligent. But sad. There is a certain melancholy to mute and motionless things. I always wonder how rocks got where they are. It's not like they can move themselves. So if you pick a rock up, you might be picking up something that has been sitting in that one spot for millions of years. It's a heavy responsibility. What would it feel like to be inanimate? A stone must think it is the center of the universe. It can't see anything around it, so it must think it is *it*.

At Charm School we have to practice being demure. A cordial, quiet manner is best. We breathe evenly. We are self-possessed. We do not fidget. We are at ease, with a philosophical in-difference. When we practice being demure at Charm School I pretend I am a stone. Stones are the most demure of all things. They are self-possessed and at ease and completely composed. They have a philosophical indifference. Maybe it is because they are immortal.

Mrs Lewis drives me to Charm School. She smells of lilac and sometimes when she drives she holds her fingers splayed outward, just the heels of her hands touching the wheel, and gazes at her fingernails. They are perfect pink ovals and the tips are very white. Sometimes I am afraid she will run a red light.

Mrs Lewis is French. Her first name is Monique. Mrs Lewis doesn't like it when her son calls her Monique, but, when he does, for an instant she is much younger. I always picture Mrs Lewis's mind full of moving walls, secret staircases, hidden rooms, her other language slumbering behind the doors like a mythical creature. I've always figured this is why Louis has the stupid name he does, that maybe in France alliterative, repetitive rhyming names are considered jaunty, full of Gallic charm. Sometimes it sounds like a dirty secret, like those French throaty accented songs full of *double entendre* I never quite get. Anyway,

I'm sure Mr Lewis had no part in the naming of his son. He probably wasn't even there. He is forever away. He owns a large company and has to be in the Orient a lot. He is a very big person. Not just in size. He enters a room with the air of a performer entering a sold-out hall. I always picture him just having arrived off an airplane, its engines still throttling down in a darkened field. Louis is certain his father wasn't even around for his conception. That he is a *enfant de l'amour* – a love child. And he says a love child invariably ends up becoming an *enfant terrible*.

Louis and his mother get along just fine without Mr Lewis. Sometimes they seem like a married couple. When they are alone they speak French to each other, and it always sounds like they are angry. They'll yell an arrogant French '*Non!*' at each other, and shake imaginary dirt from their hand with the flick of a wrist. They hit a shrill note when you are least expecting it and they growl and choke on their words as if all those accents and circumflexes are chicken bones caught in their throats. Louis says they sound this way because the French are both highly rational and highly emotional, and this makes them unpredictable in speech and action. Anyway, Louis is always sighing 'I am just a martyr to my name', but he also says it gives him more gravity. He says your name is an ultimate Noun that you gather all the pieces of yourself around, and while the rest of us are split into two, or three names, his name is basically one.

ANONYMOUS is a name which is withheld, or unknown. I used to think Anonymous and Ibid were real people. That they were both incredibly old and extremely prolific. It was very disappointing to find out that, like Santa Claus and the Easter Bunny, they weren't One Being, but a large number of people in secret collusion.

18

I have the same name as my sister. Her name was Haddie Constance Ashton. My mother was pregnant with me when my sister died. And when I was born they named me Haddie Constance Ashton. My sister was thirteen when she died. I am thirteen now. Leonora told me that a child should never be named after a brother or sister who has already died in the family; otherwise, that child will be struck down by a similar fate. She warned me to watch my step this year. Of course, not knowing exactly how my sister died, I cannot be certain what steps I am supposed to be watching for.

Imagine Achilles and a tortoise having a race. The tortoise is given a head start. Achilles will never pass the tortoise, for he will first have to reach the point where the tortoise started, and then the next point the tortoise reached. Thus the tortoise will always hold the lead. Imagine Achilles's baneful wrath resounding.

Mrs Lewis is standing in the center of the Charm School classroom yawning. The sun glints off a silver filling in one of her back teeth. We are all seated in a long line of chairs in front of her, our legs crossed at the ankle. Ms Phillips, our other instructor, is walking behind us, chanting: 'Yawn, yawn, oh yawn. I am yawning.' This is truly excruciating. Etiquette is knowing how to yawn with your mouth closed. One should keep one's mouth closed unless one needs to open it for a purpose. An open mouth expresses a weak and unstable character. We swallow hard like snakes gulping mice. Charm has a lot to do with taking responsibility for your involuntary reflexes.

The gods caused the Greeks to sneeze and yawn and hiccup. It was one of their ways of delivering messages of fortune. ARETE is the Greek word for excellence of character. The gods had a hand in this as well, because if you were inspired, it was Apollo's crash of loud lyres entering your head, and black rages were induced by Zeus, and Athena picked up spears you dropped. And if you were being completely hopeless, Aphrodite would pluck you up out of your messed-up situation and pop you into a fragrant, perfumed chamber.

ALEATORY means depending on chance. I found a silver dollar in my father's desk drawer. I'm going to try tossing it instead of making up my own mind about everything. Leonora said another way to let the Mississippi marbles play with your luck is to take a number, any number, and let *it* give the nod to all your choices. For example, take the seventh turning, read the seventh book on the shelf, buy the seventh item you find in the seventh aisle of the seventh store.

Louis Lewis has a talent for stealing. He has a talent for stealing the way others have a talent for music, or poetry. In a sense it is a rhythm, like anything else. And the thing is, if someone has a talent, you can't stop them from expressing it. It's like a raging river. So Louis is stealing all the time. He keeps his cache in the ravine behind the Monroe house, in a huge metal box under a patch of ferns, because his mother periodically searches his room for loot. And if she finds any she'll send him to the psychiatrist again. Whom Louis only spoke to in French. And since the psychiatrist didn't speak any French, he had to use a French–English phrase book to communicate with Louis. He had a theory that the French and the stealing had some dubious connection. Americans are real suspicious of anything French. It has something to do with all those moody tenses and sexy genders. Too cagey and coy. Americans like things straightforward. Like Manifest Destiny.

'Why do you steal,' the psychiatrist would ask Louis in strangled French.

And Louis would answer in French proverbs and poetry. '*Mais je suis une âme perdue*', '*Je suis un autre*' or, '*La chair est triste, hélas! et j'ai lu tous les livres.*' Sometimes he was driven in frustration to political slogans: '*Agent provocateur! Après nous le déluge! Ecrasez l'infamie!*' Then he would sit in silence, gazing off into the middle distance, while the psychiatrist flipped desperately through his handbook. 'If he couldn't understand the subjunctive how could he ever know my true feelings?' Louis sighed to me in an overdone accent.

You should see all the stuff Louis has stolen. He could open a museum. I'm serious. It could be the museum of Avon Heights because he doesn't travel far to pillage. For example, there is a silver protractor he stole from Bertrand Boomfield. Louis is sure this will be a valuable part of Avon Heights history as Bertrand is a Genius, and will one day come up with a Great Theory of the Universe. Bertrand always has pink magic marker stains on his hands, and his hair is parted down the left side in a straight line, strict as a theorem. And when he gets excited about something, like Fermat's Last Theorem, his saliva gets excited with him. It bubbles and pops all about his lips. So it is evident he is a genius. Louis stole the protractor off Bertrand's lunch tray when I distracted Bertrand by offering him my bowl of stewed prunes. I often act as an accomplice. Bertrand eats everyone's stewed prunes. Further evidence of his genius.

Then there is Miss Penny's book of Emily Dickinson poems. She makes me think of a song that you hum but can't quite remember. She is red-haired and wispy. She looks like a carrot. A julienned carrot. She recites her own poems at the library on Emily Dickinson's birthday. They all end with the refrain, 'And then she died.' In the flyleaf of her first edition of Dickinson are all these words that rhyme with died and dead: dread and youth's head, like roses bled and springtime's bed, to Orpheus wed and honor fled. She was showing Louis this list when he asked her about her method of composition, and he said, 'How about, she gave great head?' She dropped the book and fluttered off to get some tea and Louis pocketed it.

And there is Mr Jarrold Knox's baccarat crystal decanter half full of one-hundred-year-old Scotch. Mr Knox is usually ensconced in an impressive leather armchair, but you'll hear a sudden caboom of laughter and he'll rise from it as suddenly as a hippopotamus emerging from a savannah pool. Louis calls Mrs Knox the Dugong. She is tremendously ugly, yet able to exude a certain breasty sensuality. Louis stole the decanter when he was baby-sitting for their malevolent mastiff George the Second. George the First died due to a surfeit of neighborhood cats. George the Second sits behind a gate, depressed, looking like the tragic result of the coupling between a hippopotamus and a dugong.

Anyway, Louis's stealing is what led us to walk through a lot of doors. He said that if I want to know what it is like to ask questions like the ancient Greeks I should live the experience. And that opening doors is a lot like asking questions – sometimes the creaking swing of a door even sounds like a question. So that's why we are making a point of going through as many 'Employees Only' and 'Do Not Enter' and 'Do Not Disturb' doors as possible. It does give you a scary vertigo sensation just before you open it. An 'I shouldn't be here – maybe I don't want to know' feeling. Which I guess is what the Greeks must have felt asking all those questions about what the world is made of. They were probably asking themselves: Is this a door I *really* want to go through?

My grandmother told me about an aristocratic Japanese woman who kept lists of everything on pieces of paper in a drawer under her pillow. This was a long time ago, and Japanese women had elaborate hairdos back then, so they didn't sleep on normal pillows, but had wooden head-rests to perch their heads on at night so they wouldn't mess up their hair. There were usually drawers under the head-rests in which they kept poems written to them on lotus petals by lovers. But this particular woman was given a ream of fine paper by someone in the court which she used to write lists of everything she saw and everything she liked and disliked. I'm going to do this. I realized that I don't remember a lot of what I have seen. I even don't remember sometimes what I like and what I dislike. And when you think about it, what you believe has a lot to do with the things you have seen and what you like and what you dislike. And remembering it.

LIST OF DOORS: Glass doors of detectives' offices, egg-white laboratory doors, swanky hotel bell-boyed doors, doors seen from moving trains, murder mystery doors, Bluebeard's door, the open-sesame door of Ali Baba, bulging white-stomached cartoon doors, ruined-tower doors, doors that actresses lean languidly against, Italian doors of the dead, dinging drugstore doors, thorn-choked palace doors, boudoir doors, baby-blue fifties car doors, double saloon doors, dungeon doors, stainless-steel elevator doors, hidden doors leading to secret passageways, doors in bedtime stories that swing open onto other worlds.

APOLLO is the god of reason. His arrows are the sun's rays, whose refulgent beams grant clarity, individuality and order to all they touch. He is in constant struggle against his half-brother Dionysus, the god of unrestrained forces, mystery, anonymity and excess. Dionysus was twice-born, so he had to go around persuading people that he was really a god, which led to all sorts of upsets. Like sailors turning into dolphins and mothers tearing their sons to pieces and the walls of palaces falling down. From Apollo's head flow blazes of full-orbed light, and he plays celestial songs on his golden lyre. Dionysus wears a crown of grapeleaves and carries a pine-tipped thyrsus that taps wells of milk and wine. He rides in a chariot pulled by panthers, leopards and satyrs, and is surrounded by lusty women he drives wild with his frenzied music. Apollo is the god of light, who stops the flux of nature and separates it out into perfect symmetry. Dionysus is the god of dark, and opener of strange vistas, who blends all into all in a rapturous One.

There is a door on our second floor which is always locked. Behind it is the room that used to belong to my sister Haddie. It could be empty, or full of furniture. I've never been inside. On some days, at sunset, you see a band of light under the door – an eerie living red – the color of your hand when you shine a flashlight under it. Sometimes I'll press my ear against the door and listen. If I wait long enough I hear a faint humming. But it could just be the whirring of seconds passing.

'Pilgrims in China climb holy snow-covered mountains, enveloped in mists. They climb for days, sometimes weeks to reach the summit, chanting so-shi-sai-rai-i. At the top are temples lit by candles. Conches are blown at dawn and choirs of prayers sung all day long.' My grandmother stops her story to stir tea so that she can read the leaves at the bottom. We drink from thin teacups that have pictures of Chinese priests walking over gilded bridges. Cherry blossom trees are reflected in the jade water beneath them. I imagine myself sitting on the bridge, gazing into the water, watching minnows sparkling beneath the blossom shadows. I listen to the wooden clogs of priests – so-shi-sai-rai-i.

'Why are they chanting and praying all the time?' I ask my grandmother.

She looks up from the leaves. 'To lose themselves,' she says, 'they wanted to lose themselves and become one with the universe.'

Louis Lewis went off to the bathroom but he's been gone an awfully long time. Probably stealing things. Or looking for my grandmother's Art of the Bedchamber books which illustrate how the jade stalk enters the golden lotus, and how the dragon pillar meets the cherry cleft. I hear the creaking of floorboards upstairs. Louis is suddenly back in the room. He is agitated. He shifts his weight from one foot to the other, then reaches for a fortune cookie. He breaks it open and eats some and reads the little piece of paper with his mouth full of cookie. 'Be someone on which nothing is lost,' he says, spitting dry cookie all over my lap. For the son of a Charm School teacher he is extraordinarily ill-mannered. He crumples the paper into a tiny round ball. 'When the fortune is good you should eat it. Like a pill,' he says, and pops it into his mouth and swallows. My grandmother looks up from the leaves. 'Louis, you will meet someone in the future who will cause you to forget your true self.'

'Really? Fantastic! I hope it all ends in a duel. I've always wanted a dueling scar. So debonair.'

When we are out on the street heading home I turn to Louis. 'So, what did you steal?'

Louis smiles widely. 'Something of inestimable value.' He opens his jacket to reveal a small jade-handled revolver tucked in his belt.

'Where'd you get *that*?' I ask, feeling panicky, as Louis pulls it from his belt, twirls it by its handle and points it at a tree, squinting, legs apart, Jack Palance.

'From your grandmother's bedside drawer. She could hurt herself. Say sayonara Buddha man,' he says, pretending to shoot a short fat tree sitting next to the sidewalk. Ever since he read that some people have themselves entombed after their death in the hollows of trees, we have noticed how many of the trees in our neighborhood resemble historical personages. There is an elm in my yard that is the spitting image of Eisenhower. 'Anyway, lighten up, Haddie,' Louis says, tucking the gun back in his belt, 'whose hands would you rather have it in, mine, or the Empress Rowing With One Oar of the Orient?'

In Tao it is asked: Name or person, which is closer? I'm trying to remember what it felt like before I knew my name. Once upon a time I didn't know what my name was. Maybe those Chinese priests should just try to forget their names instead of chanting and praying. Or they could chant their names over and over until they fell apart. I tried this and pretty soon I didn't know what Haddie meant any more. The world seemed to tilt, I felt upside down. My grandfather used to call me different names all the time – Veronica, Clementine, Margarita, Rula Lenska. It made me feel simultaneously warm and confused. Off balance. In movies, they know someone has amnesia if they don't know their name. Dr Debonair in the white lab coat asks, 'Can you tell us your name?' and the beautiful patient just gazes at him, confused, in her own Xanadu. Who knows, maybe merged with the rest of the universe.

Louis Lewis says that there is no such thing as a lie. Because we do not know what is and what is not. If we say what is when it is not, that is a lie. But we do not know what is and what is not.

ARTEMIS is the moon goddess. She is the virgin huntress associated with uncultivated places and wild animals. She is accompanied by golden-antlered, bronze-footed deer and a pack of hounds, given to her by Pan. Living in the dark and shadows, she loves solitude, and refuses to be seen. ACTAEON saw Artemis bathing in a stream, so she turned him into a stag. And as his dogs chased him through the dark wood, finally pinning him down to the ground and ripping his flesh to shreds, Actaeon tried to call out to them in the human voice that he had lost, but he could only scream silently that he was not what he seemed.

My sister's entrance in Mr Monroe's movie is accompanied by these shrill high notes, so loud you feel as though you just got the wind knocked out of you. It is the moment when she and one of Odysseus's sailors see each other in a wood. She stands quite still, yet you get the sense that the center of her body is swaying in a tight figure-of-eight shape. There is an unreal light surrounding her. There are fierce streaks of blonde in her hair. The neon-green leaves framing her naked body are so vibrant they seem poisonous. Her eyes gaze without blinking at the sailor, for several long seconds, then she closes them, opens them, turns at the waist – there is a clash of cymbals – and like a lizard that disappears in a green flicker up a wall, she is gone. The camera

27

stays focused on the spot where she had once stood. The uneasy green light is gone. There is the brown ground. The roots of trailing vines. Thick stems of plants. Tall trees. A thousand years seem to pass. Then the camera rolls up to the blue sky which becomes the sea in the next scene.

In the deep ravine that runs behind the Monroe house are huge oaks. They look like they would have ancient names, ones full of heartache and strife – Odysseus or Agamemnon. They cast long royal shadows on the ground. Tellers of tall tales say that when the Monroes moved they released their cheetah into the ravine, and the cheetah mated with the dogs and deer of the neighborhood and left all sorts of chimera creatures behind that haunt the towering upper branches of the oaks or slumber beneath the banks of wild fern. I am lying between two boulders and waiting. I breathe in the air of the boulders. They smell of moons and minerals. When you put your ear against them you can hear a distant drumming. Overhead are dead branches, caught within live ones, listing in the wind. Crows call tcha tcha tcha. If you are quiet and wait long enough, you might see a deer, or a fox. Their ears twitch. Their tails flicker. They are always in a Complete Panic.

Sometimes I wonder what is watching me. All those animal eyes. 'Oh why did I see what I saw?' being what Actaeon cried. Leonora won't come near this ravine. She says she's heard howling and wailing, and something that is a mixture of laughing and crying – noises coming from some creature she's sure she's never come across before, and hopes she never will.

My sister Haddie had a cat named Kitty. It ran away after she died. It was a black cat. Sometimes I think I see it out of the corner of my eye. 'Psst,' I say, 'Kitty.' But it is never actually there.

'Guess who?' I suddenly hear from behind me as two hands cup my breasts roughly. Louis always covers my breasts rather than my eyes when he does this.

'Roman Polanski,' I say and turn around. 'You're lucky I'm not Artemis, goddess of the hunt. She didn't like people spying on her. She'd have you ripped to little shreds by her hounds.'

'And you're lucky I'm not Zeus. I could burn you to a little gristle on the spot.' Louis stands and pulls off his shirt. 'Come on, let's go swimming. It's hot.' And he wanders down to the stream, leaving a trail of his clothes on the way. We go skinny dipping here a lot. I toss my silver dollar to decide if I want to swim. It is nice to feel your fate as the shape of a small cold coin in the palm of your hand. As I take off my clothes I wonder what it must have felt like to have sex with Zeus. A lot of plant species have to do with Zeus's rolls in the hay — these nymphs were always turning themselves into weeds or shrubs in order to avoid him. So it must not have been that pleasant. Considering you'd rather be a vegetable.

In the summer when Louis swims in chlorinated pools the ends of his blond hair turn green. When he looks at you, his left eye focuses on you more closely than his right, as if he's wearing a monocle. He says it's called a wandering eye and claims that in the past this was a sign of nobility. He wears Oxford shirts, and has a nervous habit of pulling at the cuffs with his long fingers. Sometimes you half expect him to brandish a conjurer's handkerchief from them. His knuckles are very white — they are the knuckles of someone clutching the edge of a high building. Blue veins lie close to the surface of his wrists and hands, and one blue vein runs along his left temple, sometimes prominent, sometimes faint and dreamy. I wonder if he is correct in thinking his father isn't his *real* father. At one point in the *Odyssey*

Telemachus says, 'My mother says indeed I am his; I, for my own part, do not know. Nobody really knows his own father.'

Leonora tells me that when you are running nowhere up stairs that aren't there, and you have that upside-down feeling, you just have to right yourself by doing things backward and the wrong way around for a while.

So as a treatment for vertigo, I ate dinner for breakfast, my clothes are on inside out, I've been saying 'no' when I mean 'yes', I stood on my head for half an hour. It made me realize that our hands were formerly feet. Reading sentences backward, from right to left, makes them sound choppy and puzzling as Chinese fortune cookies: 'River same the into twice step cannot you.'

Now I am walking backward around our neighborhood. Instead of passing things by, which then disappear, what you pass by remains. What is behind you is what is beyond you. It's like one of those magical voyages in a story-book – bushes, trees, houses, mailboxes – all bolt out of the blue from behind.

The Greeks thought sight was a kind of touch, that you see objects because they exhale fiery rays. Seeing in reverse does make the unexpected flash out at you in bright, bristling colors. Leonora says magic is about jinxing time in order to get it to reveal unforeseen things to you. I suddenly trip over the curb and fall flat on my back. I look up at the sky and think about how we are always upside down. Standing on a globe with our heads dangling out into space. No one has completely explained how gravity keeps us from falling off. The more I concentrate on it, the more awful it seems. We're all spinning and rolling, holding on by some principle we can't even understand.

*

Heraclitus said that the way up and the way down are one and the same.

Louis Lewis and I are floating paper boats down the stream in the Monroe ravine. We rip out pages from a poetry book and fold the pages into little boats and set them in the water. 'Float away, purple passages,' Louis says and gives one a push from shore. 'Float away, most Sanguine Hopes of Youthful Ambition in the Spirit of Sacrifice.' Then we watch them move off, little Ships Bound to Distant Climes, our chins resting on our knees. This stream winds through the ravine for a couple of miles, and ends at the Blue Hole, a big, bottomless lake. There are billboards all along the highway, advertising it for miles – BOTTOMLESS spelled out in chilly blue capital letters, with frost capping the 'T's. It gives you this feeling of thirst that a tall glass of ice-cold water would go nowhere near relieving. The lake is closed to the public now. Because a couple of kids drowned in it one summer. They say that way down deep are freezing currents and springs, phosphorescent sea creatures that glow in the black depths, and a network of underwater caverns and caves that lead downward for miles toward the very center of the earth.

The stream's current carries some of our paper boats out of sight. One gets lampooned on a branch. Another is drawn into an eddy and starts twirling around and around. One of my shipwrecks is quite beautiful, however. It is collapsed against a mossy pebble at the bottom. It moves up and down, panting like a runover animal. Then it starts to fall apart. Bits of it drift downstream. A small fragment with 'hectic cheek' on it sticks to a rock. I break off some green reeds from the bank and toss them in the water and watch them sink. They ripple gently like the hair of mermaids.

'Why is it that anything is more beautiful underwater?' I ask Louis.

'Because it is like magic. It dissolves things. And it has a different gravity – things float up – it's kind of like an upside-down world – just look at the world reflected in it.'

'I turned my name upside down yesterday,' I say, looking into the stream at the upside-down reflected trees. 'Haddie Ashton becomes Eiddah Nothsa. Sounds like a prophet, doesn't it?'

'No. It sounds like a fundamentalist.'

'You're just mad, Siuol Siwel, because yours sounds like a product for blocked drains,' I say, lying back on the bank. I look up into the sky and imagine that I am underwater. The grass I throw will float up and away from me. Then with a push I will float up as well, above the trees, somersaulting over roofs, paddling upward higher and higher until I am out of the atmosphere. The dark of outer space will feel like a dive to the deep cold spot of a bottomless pool.

ANAXIMANDER wrote in fragments and said that everything arises from the apeiron which is indefinite and infinite, but which creates water, air, fire and earth, and from these arise hot and cold and wet and dry, and basically make up nature as we know it. The encyclopedia says the most important contribution Anaximander made, however, was to introduce the concept of going beyond the visible and perceptible world to a more fundamental imperceptible world to dig up his ideas. I think it's great that all these old philosophers wrote in fragments. Philosophy and fragments go well together – all those isms and ologies are like hummingbirds buzzing through the hot Aegean air, things bright and blue you only see out of the corner of your eye.

Laws of nature are like minnows you try to catch in a stream. Sometimes they are real and you can feel them moving through your fingers like slivers of ice, and other times they are just shadows from the trees moving overhead.

Mrs Lewis receives lots of letters from France. They are airmail letters, light and blue, and the handwriting is strange. She leaves a trail of opened letters around the house – on the entrance table, in kitchen cabinets, in between sofa cushions, among stacks of records. Once Louis and I found one tucked under the breast of a stone swan in the garden. Sometimes I'll find bits of letters she has torn apart, with fragments of sentences written on them: '*n'oubliez pas*', '*c'est rien*', '*l'espérance est*', '*idée fixe*', '*couleur du temps*', and '*souvenir, mon amour*'. I always wonder if these letters are from Louis's real father. Once I found a whole sentence, that looked as though it had been cut from a letter with scissors. Written in block capital letters was: ETRE ET PARAITRE SONT DEUX. I showed it to Louis and asked him what it meant. 'Things are not always what they seem,' he translated, then folded the paper into an airplane, lifted himself up on his toes and deftly sailed the plane into a waste basket.

Inhale. Exhale. Inhale. Exhale. This is the breathing meditation. We are not breathing but being breathed. We are completely detached. We are unmoved centers. We are in a primordial state of awareness. I'm not quite making it to the groundlessness of my being. I keep noticing things. The sun at the window. The unplayed piano. And remembering things. A teacher who told us that every breath you take contains atoms of the first breath you ever took. And I keep thinking of this crazy red-haired girl at school who I wouldn't be friends with, because she was crazy, and she wrote me a note in purple crayon that said: 'You have met your dawn.' Then I keep hearing the ticks of the big clock in my grandmother's hallway. Ping. Ping. Ping. Words ending in 'ing' usually mean something being done in the present moment. Walking, talking, swimming, breathing. 'Inging' would be a good word for the Buddhist present. It even sounds Oriental. I used to think that if you didn't blink, time would stand still. Time does seem to hold its breath if you don't blink. We probably got the idea for seconds from blinks. If we didn't have eyelids maybe we wouldn't have seconds, minutes, hours. Maybe this is what Parmenides did. Stopped blinking.

Sometimes I think about the moment just after my sister fell. It was a June afternoon. How strange the sound of a car must have been, passing on the street. How utterly strange the sound of a blackbird in a tree. Of a dog barking.

The arrow in flight is actually, at each point of its flight, at rest.

AETHER is the divine substance of which the heavens are composed. Its motion is circular, and it is the lightest element, purer than fire, transparent. I used to try to capture the blue of the sky on the bluest of blue days. I'd go outside and scoop up some in my hands and close them tight. Then I would go to my secret hiding place under the bushes and open my fingers real slow and peek inside. I expected to see a luminous blue puddled in my palm, glowing like an underground lake. 'Where does the blue in the sky go when you cup it in your hands?' I asked Leonora one day when I was completely frustrated. 'It is blue up in the heavens, Junebug,' she answered. 'It is blue from all the whispering of the angels; but the minute it touches your human hands – whoosh! – the blue goes home to heaven.'

Anaximander said that coming into being is a flaw in the Indefinite – that assuming form is a tragic estrangement from
Being.

'Papayas, prisms, papas, prunes.' We all purse our lips, saying
these words to ourselves as we walk through the Higbee's
ballroom door. It gives the proper pout to our mouths.

Entrances are vitally important. Exits and entrances are
the most glamorous of movements. I have a volume of the
encyclopedia balanced on my head. In my right hand I hold a
fine bone china cup and saucer. It is filled with tea and a thin
slice of lemon. Most of the girls' hands are shaking and you can
hear a dozen teacups rattling in their saucers. We have to
concentrate on our center of gravity in order to issue forth an
ease of deportment. It is a straight line of white light running
through our bodies. We move slowly through the doorway and
walk towards Mrs Lewis. Haste is vulgar. When we reach her
we curtsy.

Mrs Lewis reminds me of a zebra, or one of those creatures
that look like small deer and seem to be wearing high heels. Mrs
Lewis always wears high heels. She walks across the highly
polished wood floors of her house and her heels make the sound
of martinis being stirred in a tall pitcher. The Lewises' house
used to be a hunting lodge. Mrs Lewis suddenly snatches away
the silver dollar I've been tossing, while it is still in midair. She
seems very angry. I think she is going to yell at me because I am
committing the three 'l's of bad behavior: listlessness, languor
and leaning. But instead she asks, 'Why are you doing that?' and
before I can reply, she shakes her head and then says in an

extremely irritated voice, 'It is a crude, boorish habit – like a crooked card-sharp.' I think she is going to give the coin back to me, but she doesn't.

Our forays into Employees Only and Do Not Disturb worlds have revealed dusty adding machines and cardboard boxes, a slow man in a baseball cap dancing to the Bee Gees and a nasty woman in bifocals who hissed at us. Today behind the 'Do Not Enter' door of Mr Watson's Watch Shop we found Mr Watson standing over his work-table, looking through his big lighted magnifying glass. The thing was, under the magnifying glass was a woman in nothing but pearls and pink mules and a beauty-parlor hairdo. She saw us first and cried 'Oh!' and one of her pink mules dropped to the floor like an exotic bird killed in midair by the gunshot of her voice. Then Mr Watson screamed something unspeakable to us. As we left, Louis took several Timexes off their revolving showcase and slipped them, one, two, three, onto his left wrist. 'I don't think he'll report the theft, do you?' Louis asks me breezily as he sashays out the front door.

'When nervous in social situations, the kangaroo licks its fore-arms, the octopus eats its tentacles, the African horned beetle stands on its head. Dogs greet each other by sniffing extremities. When the giant petrel of Antarctica meets a strange bird in its neighborhood, it squirts a jet of oil from its nostrils with a force great enough to knock the other creature down. Ladies, it is etiquette which differentiates us from the animal world.'

LIST OF ENVIABLE ANIMAL ATTRIBUTES: Being able to purr, lick your chops, turn your head in a complete circle, raise your hair at will, break off a leg and grow a new one, swing from trees, rub your legs together to make music, secrete a shell, blend into the background or look like a stick when you want some privacy, change your color and shape at will, having a tail, eyes that swivel on stalks, a stomach with a pouch, playing dead, secreting poison, roaring, undulating.

'A black cat can mean all sorts of things – depending on where and when you see it.' Leonora gets a look in her eyes like she is concentrating on messages she is receiving from the other side. 'If you hear one miaowing at midnight, it is an omen of death. Sometimes human spirits will enter a black cat, and if you meet one on a crossroads at three a.m. on the first day of summer, it will talk to you and tell you all about the hereafter. Then, of course, they say that if the cat in your house is black, of lovers you will have no lack.'

'Is that why my sister had a black cat as a pet?'

Leonora blinks her eyes at me, returning to this world. 'Telling the Bible, honey, I think she got that cat to *bother* me. That child was a real Calamity Jane. She liked to tease me about what she called my "misimpressions". She would lay the table with the knives pointing toward the chairs, leave hats on the bed for me to find, walk under ladders on purpose while I was looking. Once she even broke a mirror right in front of me when she was in a bad temper. She put me in some *anxious* states.' Leonora bites her bottom lip. 'Mr Monroe – he threw a birthday party for her. It was a costume party. So your sister decided to dress as a black cat. Because it was her thirteenth birthday. She got dressed up early in her black velvet ears and long silk tail. Started rehearsing her in-the-groove pussycat moves – slinking about like a Siamese in her black slippers, arching her back, twitching that tail. Then she started following me around, crossing my path whenever she

37

could, and growling: "Watch out for bad luck, Leo!" ' Leonora laughs, but her eyes look sad.

'Do you think her death was an accident?'

'Honey, they say it was an accident. But I don't believe there are any accidents in this world. I think all that devilment might have caught up with her. I told her she should straighten up and fly right. You don't mess around with fortune – otherwise, sooner or later, fortune's going to start messing around with *you*.'

My grandmother and I are out moon-viewing. She says that haiku masters used to travel for days, even weeks, just to see the full moon of autumn through the branches of a certain tree. We're just walking a few blocks to a big pine that sits on a small hill.

'In the Orient, the moon evokes memories of the past and people far away . . . what *are* you doing, sweetheart?' My grandmother stops and looks at me. I've got a huge bottle of Elmer's glue and a shaker of glitter. As we walk I squeeze a trail of glue and glitter along the sidewalk. In the moonlight it looks like a giant snail trail.

'I'm proving that I've moved,' I say, a little annoyed that we've stopped as the smooth line has now ended in a large birdshit lump. That arrow paradox has become as annoying as a mosquito buzzing in my ear.

'But of course you are moving, darling. Everything is moving. The earth, the moon, the stars.' She raises her hands up and the sleeves of her silk kimono fall to her elbows. I think of hundreds of silk worms spinning. I wonder where I could get a silk worm – forget this glue and glitter mess.

'Yeah, well . . .' I trail off, too tired and frustrated to explain myself. 'It's a school project.' This always shuts them right up. School is a religion they don't question. But I put the glue and glitter away because I have enough evidence. Let Parmenides explain away this visible trail of movement.

We start walking again and my grandmother recites a poem full of green hills, temple bells and blue plums. I'm only half listening because I'm trying to knock on as many trees as possible. The ancients knocked on trees to contact sky gods. I'm not sure which ones you are supposed to knock on so I'm covering my bases by knocking on every one we pass. You can see how the ancients got their ideas for temples from groves of trees. When you walk through their shadows it's like entering a secret. Trees seem more alive at night, more conscious of you. During the day they are all involved with the sun, but at night they seem to bend forward and *listen*.

Most things are different at night. Even words. If you say the word 'moon' at noon it is different from saying it at midnight. Even a simple word like 'lilac' changes with night. People would probably believe in different things if we didn't have night, if it never got dark. Just an endless blue. A lot of what people believe has to do with night.

My grandmother and I get to the foot of the hill. The pine and the moon look like the lines out of a haiku – each involved in its own stillness. We lie on our backs halfway up the hill. My grandmother turns to me. 'Now, remember,' she whispers.

'Leonora told me that my sister dressed as a black cat for her thirteenth birthday party,' I say to her after a few minutes.

'Yes, your sister was quite a minx.' My grandmother seems to be talking to the moon rather than me. '*Gateado* is the Spanish word for the movement of a cat. And your sister had it down to a tee. She even lapped up her Shirley Temples with her tongue that night. Of course, Mrs Lewis is the one who taught her all about feline deportment.'

39

'Mrs Lewis?' I am so surprised that I sit up and stare at her. 'I didn't even know that they knew each other.'

'Oh yes. They were quite close. Don't ever tell Louis this, but I think she always wished she had had a daughter.'

'So my sister went to Charm School too?'

'No. Mrs Lewis did not teach etiquette classes back then. She took your sister out to lunch quite a bit. Out shopping. She taught her how to dress, and walk – "*frétillement*" I believe it is called – a certain wiggle to the hips. Overnight, it seemed, your sister changed from a gawky child to a kind of "*jeune fille fatale*". One day she was bouncing along – she always had a lot of energy – her walk interrupted by hops, skips and twirls, and the next she was a graceful young lady – her arms brushing just so against her sides, her feet following a perfect line in front of her. I think Mrs Lewis even taught her how to pout. And how to give a Look.' My grandmother sits up and glances upward at me with her eyes while her chin points down. She looks sexy and girlish and shy. 'It was all very fun and French. But I found the change a bit too sudden. Perhaps I didn't want her to grow up . . .' my grandmother trails off.

'Why do you think she died?' I ask carefully. My family doesn't talk about this. You can't even mention my sister around my parents.

'Darling, your sister had a wild streak in her. She loved dares – despite Mrs Lewis's lessons in refinement and grace, she remained rash and heedless. She must have been doing something dangerous, and . . . for heaven's sake do not speak about this to Mrs Lewis. She fainted at the funeral. You would have thought it was her own child who died. I do not think she would like to be reminded of . . . to remember.'

*

LIST OF CHILDHOOD MOVEMENTS: Dangling your feet in midair, climbing four stairs at a time, turning in dizzy circles, tiptoeing, skipping, hopping on one foot, jumping cracks so you don't break your mother's back, hopscotching, hula-hooping, tightrope-balancing on top of fences.

AEOLUS was the god of wind. He rolled a stone to one side of the mouth of a cave, where all the winds of the world were kept, and depending on how far he rolled the rock, different winds would escape. Leonora told me that if you are alone and walking on a windy day the breeze will tell you secrets. I can hear its punctuation marks – sometimes it speaks in italics, sometimes in exclamation marks. Often it sounds as if it is murmuring 'tomorrow, tomorrow'. The wind seems to point to the future – it rushes past you, toward the horizon, pointing, over there! – though you can't actually see the wind. It is like a verb with no noun to pin it down. It is this ultimate Verb, on the loose.

'I think that I shall never see, a poem lovely as a tree . . .' I am wandering through our backyard, wondering about movement, when I hear the upper branches of the oak reciting this poetry. At this point I could believe that trees talk. I look back at the path I have just walked down. At each point I was actually still. I feel like one of those mysterious moving stones of the desert. I look up into the tree. Louis Lewis is stretched like a lazy leopard on a high, thick branch. The setting sun casts an orange halo around his head – the color you see through closed eyelids on a hot summer day.

'Remember Mrs Payne with the wooden leg in third grade?' he calls down. 'Remember how she used to cry at that poem?'

'She didn't have a *wooden* leg. It was prosthetic – it was

made of plastic or something *industrial*.' She used to wear flesh-colored stockings so her leg color matched. When she walked she creaked. Once I went to a doll hospital to get one of my dolls fixed. There were plump pink arms and legs and torsos, and at one point a small blue eye rolled across the floor and stopped at my feet. A dozen leaves descend on me from above. Louis is shaking the branches. I look up at him. There is a green bowl of light under his face. 'And *you* were a cruel kid,' I call up to him. 'You always chose to recite that poem because you knew it would make her cry.'

'I have always had an affinity with trees. It truly *moved* me.'

'Speaking of movement, Louis,' I say as I flop down under the tree, 'did I or did I not just move from the front yard to the backyard?'

'Is all an illusion. What is is. Come on up here. There is going to be a soirée next door and I want to watch – observe *la règle du jeu*.'

Louis and I find some branches that hang directly over my next-door neighbor's backyard and lie down. It feels like the warm, muscular arm of a giant. 'Ah the Indolence of Warm Climes,' Louis says, stretching. 'Lingering is a lost art.'

'Plants are extremely languorous. What do you think photosynthesis *feels* like?' I ask, pulling a leaf apart. 'If we had chlorophyll do you think we'd just lie out in the sun for lunch?'

'Like basking Roman senators.' Louis sighs. 'And I bet the sun is delicious just soaking through your pores – you'd get it direct – like the gods.'

A squirrel stops on its trip down the tree trunk to stare at us, its tail twitching like a reprimand. 'I'd like to be arboreal and nocturnal, and hang by my tail all night and eat persimmons.' I yawn.

'Swallow that yawn. I'll report you to the Charm Authorities.' Louis swings off his branch and hangs by his legs. He has no fear of heights. 'If you had a tail you'd never have a headache. It has something to do with relaxing tension.' He pulls himself back up. 'But I'd rather have a sticky tongue several feet long.' He sticks his tongue out at me. 'A foolproof way to steal jewels.'

We hear the tinkling of glasses. We look down and see one of the servers bringing out a big box. It is already getting dark and the neighbors have lit torches. A honeyed smell drifts up into the tree. On white cloth-covered tables the servers have set out bottles of gin, vodka, whiskey, sherry, tonics. Olives and lemon slices and pistachios. Champagne is chilling on ice in large silver buckets. There are silver cocktail sticks, stirrers, ice tongs and caviar bowls. And martini glasses, champagne glasses, wine glasses, tall glasses with clear throats waiting for long cool drinks. Camembert and brie are sitting on plates with grapes and figs, kumquats and pomegranates. Shrimp on ice. Bowls of raspberries and strawberries. Petit fours, meringues, frosted fruit. And dark rich things: pâté and walnuts and stuffed dates and chocolates.

Apparently, the Monroes had lots of parties. I've heard they were like Mr Monroe – overflowing, excessive. That there was a certain giddiness to them – as if at any moment they would whirl out of control. Mr Monroe would invent special cocktails for each party, mixing together brandies and liqueurs he had sampled in exotic locations and then had shipped in cases to Ohio. It is said that some contained South American coco leaves or Indonesian herbs that had hallucinogenic properties. And there was a lot of dancing. Mr Monroe loved to teach women dances he had learned from his trips around the world. He even claimed he saw a small Italian town in the throes of a tarantella epidemic, and at one of his inebriated affairs he got the whole besotted group to imitate its wild reelings. On some summer nights, when you walk past his house, it smells like one of his parties has just ended. In the east corner of the property is a grove of plum trees, and all the fallen fruit gives off a heavy, hungover aroma, like someone has spilled vats of punch all across the lawns.

Below us I see Mrs Parker, the hostess, come out to check how the servers are getting on. She has set hair, scrolled and white. A few seconds later her husband emerges and says something to her we can't hear. She seems angered by what he's said. Her white hairdo trembles. Mrs Parker is angry a lot. Mr Parker is the cad of the neighborhood. He corners young women and stares at them with his harem eyes.

We suddenly hear Mr Knox's majestic voice booming from the street. 'Ah, it's the Pendulous-Breasted Esther and the Stentorian-Voiced Oscar,' says Louis. 'Where's the rest of the Ilk? I'd love to become part of an ilk. How do you become part of an ilk?'

'Improve your personality,' I answer, and as I do the rest of the ilk start arriving.

It is interesting to watch etiquette in action. People are shaking hands and kissing cheeks. I wish they used island manners. Then the men would be kissing the women's left breasts or blowing in each other's ears or pinching each other's buttocks. Or used some old-fashioned courtesies: bowing, kowtowing, curtsying, salaaming. I can hear endearments floating up like stray bubbles popping at the surface of champagne: dear, darling, darling, dear. And there are introductions: Robert, Elizabeth, John, Lillian, Bertrand, Edie. There are compliments bobbing around: lovely to see you, marvelous dress, terrific tan! Toasts are made. The sound of clinking glasses. Swanky chignons. Proud foreheads. Debonair hands. Polished shoes on damp grass. Dangerous pauses in conversation. Smiles like flat ginger ale. In Emily Post's *Blue Book of Social Usage*, Elmer Boresome and Cissy Chatter, Mrs Upright Eyebrows and the Richard Vulgars, Sir Benjamin Backbite and Miss Cravin Praise are always getting together at some mixer, and an 'unseemly social situation' always inevitably evolves.

'My thorax is sore,' Louis says an hour later, sitting up and rubbing his stomach. I'm getting pretty sore too. My branch is cold as cold hands. But the party is starting to get intriguing.

'Thorax?' I ask Louis.

'The insect belly. I've been thinking – it wouldn't be all that bad to be an insect. I've been composing an essay: "Ethics and Insects". Want to hear it?'

'Okay,' I say warily.

'They have none. The end.' Louis nearly falls off the branch laughing. 'Seriously, though – wouldn't it be great to have a poison stinger? If anyone annoyed you you could start twitching it. It could be sexy too. Watch out or I'll *sting* you.' Louis takes my grandmother's revolver out of his back pocket and lassoes it over his head. Then he lies back down on the branch and starts targeting it at people.

'Watch it, Louis. You could hurt someone,' I say nervously.

'Isn't loaded. Do you know that that parterre below us is full of bats?'

I look down, but instead of bats I see Mrs Perkins cornered by the host at the bottom of our tree. She usually stays very close to her husband's side, as if she's afraid someone will pull her ponytail. The host says 'Don't accept any wooden nickels' in a suggestive voice. Mrs Perkins is still and nervous. I imagine her toes in their pink summer slingbacks turning to roots, her fingers sprouting leaves. And suddenly the whole party rolls toward maddening revelry. Mr Lawson lets out a huge lion's roar laugh and then someone else's voice boomerangs from a corner, 'You old rogue!' There is women's eighteen-carat laughter. The servers come out with a huge flaming Baked Alaska and everyone starts singing 'When the Saints Go Marching In'. It is hard to understand what is going on in the general conversational din – it rises and falls in rolls. You hear: mumble mumble 'I did not!' mumble purple innuendo 'Magnificent!' Laughter like cymbals. 'I don't think that's funny George – Ouch!' 'Meet someone? Why? I know someone.' Trumpet blare of Brazilian jazz: 'Oh ho not me baby – I got some in Cape Cod.' Whistles as a couple starts to tango. 'Am I boring you?' a voice asks, furry as a fox. 'Remember them?' 'What? What?' 'Can I tell you a secret?' someone yells above the music.

Then there is the sound of an explosion in the parterre beneath us and a dozen or more bats come flying out. Everyone starts screaming and waving their hands. Glasses break. Baked Alaska gets trampled in the grass. The hostess crouches under a table, squawking like a bird.

'Gun went off by accident,' Louis whispers to me and swings down through the branches and lands softly on the ground below. Then he strolls over to the drinks table, takes a champagne bucket filled with three bottles of champagne and saunters home. No one sees him. You may wonder why no one noticed us up in the tree, hanging tigerishly a few feet over their heads, and this is why: People never look up.

ANIMISM is one of the oldest religions and suggests that all objects have two aspects. One that is external, objective and real in the sense that it can be perceived by the usual senses; the other imperceptible, the spiritual force or soul, the animus.

I am woken by Leonora's voice. 'For Lawd's sake stop trampling my petunias!' she yells. I stand up on my bed and look out my window. I think I see a dark figure crossing the street, or is it my imagination?

The next day Leonora practices shots in the front yard with her ax, mumbling about robbers, until one of the neighbors asks her to stop.

There is a painting of my sister Haddie. It is in one of the bedrooms of my grandmother's house. There are no pictures of her in our house. In the painting, she is sitting on a chaise longue. One eyebrow is raised slightly higher than the other. There is a beauty mark at her left temple, just below her eyebrow, that at one moment makes her look Oriental and inscrutable, like she might beckon you from under the shadows of a Moorish arch and draw you into some diabolical *noir* plot. But then, in the next, it looks like a sideways naive question mark. On her wrist is the charm bracelet. It is made up of miniature silver dollars. My grandmother told me it was given to her by Mr Monroe as a lucky talisman, on her thirteenth birthday. An AMULET is a thing worn as a charm against evil. She wears highly polished patent leather pumps. She looks as though she would tap her foot impatiently if kept waiting. Cross her fingers behind her back when lying. When exasperated, her hand mimes the shape of a pistol and fires it at you. She mouths silently: Bang, you're dead.

Greek philosophers' lives were full of tragedy. They were constantly being taught mathematics by Arabs, and getting shipwrecked, and being captured by pirates who didn't use any vowels.

If you see Pan by daylight you will be struck dead as if from a lightning bolt. But if you see him at night, you will receive all his vast powers to cast spells over people. Pan is the Arcadian god, often considered to be the illegitimate son of Penelope. Louis Lewis and I are out looking for Pan in the ravine behind the Monroe house. I am trying to make as little noise as possible as we walk so we will hear the pipe and the hooves. Louis is stampeding through the underbrush in front of me like an elephant in must.

'Will you be quiet, Louis? You'll scare him off.'

'Even if Pan existed – which, by the way, he doesn't – you couldn't scare him. He's a god, or something like a god, for chrissakes.' Louis stops at the stream and dips his hands in. He pulls out a champagne bottle and pops it open. 'Of course,' he says, taking a swig, 'I wouldn't mind receiving his powers. Then I could exact revenge on people. And revenge is so beautiful. It is the order of nature. I told my psychiatrist' – he takes another swig – 'that he should quit shrinkdom and start a business – Revenge Incorporated. Its motto could be: "Don't get over it. Get even." Instead of talking about their problems – yadda, yadda, yadda – people could really *do* something about them. Therapy schmerapy.' He hands me the bottle. 'Here, have some of this. This will bring you closer to a mystical oneness with nature than some old nympho goat.'

'You have to say a libation first.' I raise the bottle skyward and intone, 'With thy wine cup held on high, with maddening revelry, in an Eleusinian flowery vale, Come Bacchus, Paean, Hail!' I drink from the bottle and pass it back to Louis.

'Yo ho ho and a bottle of rum,' he says and tilts back his head to drink. His throat is long and pale and thin. Perfect for strangling.

We have finished the second bottle of champagne. Louis was right. I am definitely feeling one with nature. We are lying in a bed of ferns. There is a full moon out. The ancients believed that certain spots in the landscape had their own guardian nymphs – dryads of the trees and naiads of the spring – and that these spots were holy. My grandmother said, when I asked about him, that the little boy found sitting next to my sister on the flagstone path that day moved away with his family to another part of the country. But sometimes I imagine him still here, laughing and crying in this wood, his little body light as blown milkweed. I pretend the champagne is nectar and pour some on the ferns as a blessing. 'The wine is poured, invoke the god,' I whisper, and a big garter snake flickers out like a ripple of water. We both jump up, and the snake slides away and disappears. 'Someone should do a documentary on drunken animals,' Louis says and finishes off the bottle and throws it in the stream. 'Just souse up a bunch of them – gnus, dromedaries, yaks – the humorous ruminating ones. Then turn the camera on and watch them gambol.'

'Speaking of gamboling,' I say, my head reeling a bit, 'let's dithyramb or have a pagan dance under the moon. Throw our throats back in the green joy of the rich, dapple-shadowed tresses of the forest.' I jiggle my hips a little and almost fall back down in the ferns.

Louis catches me around the waist before I do. 'I think it is time you learn the cha-cha.' He pulls me toward him and our hips lock together. One of his legs is between mine. His hips rotate in a fast circle and mine follow. He pulls my arms up over my head and presses close to me, moving his hips slower now.

49

Then he guides my hands down and moves our joined hands up and down the sides of our bodies. 'Cha-cha,' he whispers near my neck.

'Is this the cha-cha?' I say into his hair that covers my face.

Suddenly he pushes me away. 'No, we need music for that,' he says brusquely and goes down to the stream and gets another bottle.

'It would be great to have a Greek chorus follow you around, singing of your deeds. "What we have waited for does not come to pass – O shame on earth! Apollo!" ' I sing off-key, and then sit down in one of the heroic shadows cast by an oak. Once, Louis and I found a small sparrow hopping awkwardly along the ground. When I scooped it up, I saw that one of its legs was mangled. Its body weighed the same as a peach stone. I stroked its russet head. Louis took it from me, and it pecked sharply at his hand, drawing blood. Louis went into a fit of rage. He crushed its body in his hand and threw it to the ground. I screamed. Louis kicked the bird into the underbrush and shrugged his shoulders. 'It would have died anyway,' he said nonchalantly. 'I did it a favor.'

Louis opens another bottle of champagne. Then hiccups loudly. 'Spit on a rock and turn it over,' I advise him. 'That's what Leonora . . .'

'Shh!' Louis whispers sharply. There is a high whistle and the faint sound of drums beating in the distance. The sound gets louder. In a flash two greyhounds run past us, with such grace they seem to be moving in slow motion. Then Louis is running after them and I am running after him. Ahead of us the greyhounds are up and over the incline of the ravine. We follow them and see them racing across the Monroe yard and toward the house, more gray shades than dogs. A light is on at the back door of the Monroe house. A tall dark figure stands there and the dogs run past him into the house. The door shuts. The light goes out. Louis and I stop at the edge of the lawn, catching our breath. There are huge shadows, cast by the house upon the lawn, purple and deep as dreams. When I was little I thought that if you fell into a shadow you'd never stop falling.

PART II

THE CLASSICAL AGE

Antigone said that nothing vast enters a life without a curse.

I am standing behind a large fir tree outside one of the ground-floor windows of the Monroe house. The curtains to them are miraculously open now, so I am investigating. Louis Lewis was going to come with me, but when I went over to his house to get him, he and his mother were in the car, leaving for the psychiatrist's office. Louis Lewis had the claws-bared look of a cat being dragged to the vet. Mrs Lewis rolled down her window. 'Monkey Boy has a doctor's appointment, Haddie,' she said, handed me a newspaper and peeled out of the driveway. I looked at the paper and almost fell over. Louis Lewis is always thinking of ways to become ubiquitous. He says this is what differentiates us from the gods – that we are mortal and only in one place at a time, whereas gods are immortal and all over the place all the time. And celebrities are the closest things to gods because their names live on after their deaths and they are in many minds, magazines and television sets all the time while they are alive. Actually I've always wanted to be in the encyclopedia. I wanted to be a queen, because then it wouldn't matter if the boundaries changed on veiny maps, I would already be recorded as queen of whatever country I was queen of, and the dates of my birth and death would be printed year after year, and distributed worldwide. Louis Lewis is taking a more unusual route on his road toward becoming a *nouveau* god. He's always sending his picture in to the *National Enquirer*, printed with different captions. Once he rolled in some dirt, had me take his picture, and typed under it, 'I was raised by wolves in Pennsylvania!' Another one had a halo backlighting his chef's-hatted head with 'My grandmother gives me recipes from the grave!' under it. Sometimes he'll use other people's pictures. He once published a picture of a neighbor at a garden party with her mouth full of cake, and the caption, 'I ate my baby!'

The latest one is a picture of Louis in a shaggy brown wig, fake ears, and an orange rind stuck under his upper lip, hanging by one arm on a branch in his front yard. Under the picture the newspaper has printed: 'Monkey Boy – Amazing offspring of Suburban Wife and Lovelorn Chimpanzee!' Below the picture of Louis is one of Mrs Lewis in a strapless black gown, and Coconuts, a sexually deviant chimpanzee who lives at our local zoo. He's always playing with himself, or humping a rock. Mothers are forever rushing their kids away from Chimp Island – you hear their little cries of 'What's Coconuts doing?' trailing behind them. Louis has superimposed the picture of Mrs Lewis and Coconuts, so it looks as if his arm is hanging over her bare shoulder. Unfortunately the photo of Louis is kind of fuzzy, you can't really recognize him. But Mrs Lewis and her simian lover are clear as a bell. So Lewis has bequeathed to mother nationwide notoriety. And landed his still-anonymous self in the snakepit.

Through the ground-floor window of the Monroe house I see a large, high-ceilinged room. Everything is covered in sheets. It looks like an arctic landscape of polar herds – the two covered chandeliers like snowy cormorants frozen in midair. In the far left corner is a television set on a stand. It is turned on. From what I can see it looks like Watergate. Watergate is on all the time this summer. It is on all day, and sometimes at night, too. You can hear it droning out through open windows. It is starting to put my teeth on edge. I hear a doorbell ring and creep around the side of the house to see who it is. It's Rent-a-Cop, standing on the top step, trying to look upright and official.

I hear the front door open and crane my neck as far as I can, but can't see the person who's opened it. Hellos all around. The man in the house has a twangy voice. He doesn't introduce himself. Rent-a-Cop asks if everything is all right. Yes. (Friendly, but short and concise.) How are the wife and children? There aren't any. I live alone. A bachelor? Well, not too many late nights, loud parties – harharhar. The bachelor doesn't join the laughter. No need to worry on that account. Thank you for stopping by. The door closes. Rent-a-Cop stands facing the closed front door for a moment, and then turns and leaves, touching the gun on his hip every few steps, as though he expects highwaymen to jump him from the bushes.

I inch back along the wall to the open-curtained window. One of the doors along its opposite wall is ajar and through it, in the dark, I can see a staircase. I imagine it leading up to the third floor, down a for-decades-untrodden corridor. At its end is the unplayed-in-for-decades playroom, still and hushed. A morose black daisy chain of children's names chase each other's tails endlessly around the room.

The bachelor comes through a door on the opposite side of the room I am looking into. The greyhounds follow him, their nailed paws clicking against the hardwood floors. He is tall, with a crewcut, and looks scientific. He gazes out the window. I *think* he sees me, but his eyes aren't really focused. It's like he's not there, in the room, but thinking about what is going on in some large and dangerous and gleaming laboratory. I follow his gaze as he looks absently around the room. Suddenly he jumps back and his mouth opens for a second as if to scream. But he doesn't. He is staring at large Oxford shoes, with a newly polished gleam, peeping out halfway from beneath one of the closed curtains on the far wall. I have to keep myself from screaming, and just as I am wondering whether I should call for help, or run home and phone the police, the bachelor, now completely composed, walks over to the television set and stands in front of it, arms crossed, watching Watergate, ignoring the burglar shoes. I creep around to the back of the house and look in the window whose curtains the robber seems to be standing behind. I see the empty back half of the shoes.

I return to the window with the open curtains. The bachelor is still standing in front of the television. I think of the carved wooden monkey my grandfather got for me in Bali when I was five, sitting on my dresser at home, its monkey hands clasped about its monkey feet. It is foreign and strange, and has a smooth mahogany philosophy about its face, like the bachelor who has the same calm detachment about him, as if he is rotating around his own axis, apart from this world.

ARISTOTLE said that to live alone one must be either a beast or a god.

We are introducing ourselves to ourselves at Charm School. We stand in front of the long mirrors. We do this so we can check our poise and expression. Leonora says that when you look into a mirror your soul looks back at you. She says that babies in Alabama aren't allowed to see themselves in a mirror until they are three years old, because before that they are unable to bear the shock of seeing their own soul.

When you are being polite, it is like you are mirroring the other person – their smiles and gestures. Buddha once performed a miracle of courtesy. It was a bright, hot, sunny day. Thirty-three different gods each gave the Buddha a parasol to shade himself from the sun. And in order not to offend any of the gods, Buddha divided himself into thirty-three Buddhas carrying thirty-three parasols.

Mrs Lewis comes up behind me. 'Hello,' she says, 'I'm Mrs Lewis.' I turn and introduce myself. Which makes me feel really stupid since I've known her for over a decade. But she looks at me as if she doesn't know me, which I suddenly realize is probably true. She gazes at me with these *pourquoi* eyes she often has – as if she's been taken from a gentle old country to this rough frontier land and is wondering why, looking at you for an answer. There is something about her that seems old, older even than her centuries-old Continental country. I imagine walking into a dark cave, one that has been untouched for thousands of years, and seeing her painted on the walls with the juice of berries and the blood of animals.

The ACADEMY was a school of philosophy founded by the Greek philosopher Plato. It was located near Athens in a grove said to belong to Academus, a hero of the Trojan War. Plato based his ideas on the teachings of Socrates who, through a conversational method, searched for truth by reasoning from particular facts to general concepts, from vague assumptions to universal definitions. These dialogues often proved that many things we positively believe to be true are, upon closer examination, completely false.

'From where have you come and where are you going?' Socrates is always nosing into other people's business, wanting to dredge up their pasts and corner them about their futures. I wouldn't want to get into a conversation with Socrates. Louis Lewis and I are trying to figure out from where the bachelor has come. And how long it took him to get here. Aristotle said everything has an indwelling impulse that moves it from its potential to its actual. And things move because they are returning to their natural place of origin, that rocks accelerate as they fall because they are happy to be getting home.

Louis Lewis has this theory that the bachelor is Mr Monroe, returning to his tragic ancestral home. He says he heard that Mr Monroe made a movie version of the *Odyssey* because he believed he had a lot in common with the hero Odysseus – being cunning, larger than life, and a spellbinding story-teller. That perhaps he was involved in some shady Hollywood business – they say he had connections with the Mafia – and he faked his death in order to avert trouble, with the police, creditors, or the mob. He says there are dozens of cases where a person will park by the side of a cliff, leave a suicide note in their car, drop their wallet and watch over the edge, and then disappear from their previous life. Louis says we should spy on the bachelor and see if his theory is true. But we shouldn't mention our suspicions to anyone. Otherwise, our Odysseus *manqué* may once again flee.

I am not too convinced. 'But Mr Monroe had reddish-blond wavy hair – this man's hair is brown, and straight. And wouldn't he figure people here would recognize him?'

'Dyed his hair and straightened it,' Louis answers as if this is an assured fact. 'And a person can change a lot in fourteen years, especially if they've made it a point to be undercover all that time. Hell, some parents don't even recognize their own runaway children once they've been recovered. It is uncanny what a change of hair, clothing, weight and voice will do. He could even have had help from the Federal Witness Protection and Relocation Progam.'

'So why would he want to come back?'

'Some kind of unfinished business. They say that sometimes the person who goes missing will return to his home, undetected – for the same reasons that a murderer might return to the scene of the crime, or a ghost comes back to haunt the place where it once lived.'

There is a Cadillac in the Monroe driveway, big as a boat, and from all the maps in the back seat and crumpled in side pockets it looks as though he has sailed away for a year and a day. The windows are open, and there is a new-car smell rising off its hot seats. Louis Lewis says that new-car smell is the ultimate musk that drives men wild. He says they should bottle it, as a woman's fragrance, and call it Back-Seat.

I wonder what would happen if Odysseus met Socrates. I bet if Odysseus were around today he would drive a Cadillac. He'd probably be a cowboy, yeehawing down the long highways. I picture the bachelor in his car, wanderlusting from sea to shining sea. Vist-O-Vision vistas. Telephone poles, tumbleweeds, hotels, vacancy signs, albino-pink, blinking in the brown desert sky. Hot Alabama billboards advertising anticipation in miles. Ice-cold Beer – 3 Miles; Air-conditioned Hotel, Cool Pool – 5 Miles.

That question of Socrates is incredibly irritating. I'm never too sure about my past or my future. I can't see my past any more and I can't see my future yet – you're supposed to be this arrow whizzing in some set direction, but I can never even tell if I am actually moving or not. I wish I could feel my indwelling impulse. Maybe it feels like growing pains.

They say the earth is moving at 64,800 miles per hour on its course toward Hercules. But you can't feel it. I think it would be better to calculate time in miles rather than hours. Because then, even if you hadn't done anything for a few hours, you could say, well, at least I've traveled 129,600 miles. And that's nothing to sneeze at. You'd always be on this Big Trip.

You cannot cross a field. You cannot move across an infinite number of points in a finite amount of time. You must cross half of a given distance before you can cross the whole, then half of that half, and then half of the half of that half. This will continue *ad infinitum*. For it is impossible to finish the infinite.

Over the entrances to monasteries is the sign 'Watch your step'. It is there to remind you to be mindful while walking. I am following my grandmother in circles around her living room. This is kinhin – the walking meditation. Your head is balanced on top of your spine. Your feet converse with the floor. Your breath is a wind that moves you from the inside and the outside. The walker cannot walk without breath, just as the bird cannot fly without sky. Each step forward is falling within the orbit of the earth around the sun – you need to find this path of gravity and flow within it like a river in its bed. The walker becomes the walk.

My grandmother is her walk. It has something to do with a spring to her foot and the tilt of her chin. You can almost see her line of chi – the indwelling force – flowing from the floor up her spine and out the top of her head to the ceiling. She says you can tell an enlightened person by their walk because their head does not seem attached to their body – it floats and sways above the stem of their neck.

Sometimes your mind has a walking rhythm to it. But if you are remembering, your mind is backstroking into the past while your body is forward marching into the future. And when you are imagining something your mind zooms off ahead of your body – it moves the way you moved when you were little – skipping and hopping. Maybe that's why you are so full of questions as a kid – because your equilibrium is always slightly off.

What's the most romantic form of ambulation? Snails swim through the liquid they secrete. One-celled protozoa slowly, graciously glide. Brachiation is swinging through trees. It is probably most elegant to have others do the ambulating for you – being borne on a litter by eunuchs, carried in a howdah on the back of a painted elephant, or lifted on a sedan chair by porters. Sometimes I recite poetry while I walk, which, I guess, is a kind of arcadian ambulation. I like to find the perfect poems for paths, sonnets for streets. The steps of porches are good for haikus. I memorized all this poetry when I had an English teacher I found particularly interesting. He said words like 'swoon' and 'unguent', 'verdure' and 'troth' with conviction – they sounded like Bengal tigers, fierce and almost extinct. He would lisp and stutter and when he drank, the words sounded like drunken gold doubloons in an undertow. All those Romantic poets had distinctive defects – a limp or a tic or a cough. I practiced having a tic for a few weeks. I twitched my left cheek sporadically. I thought it made me glamorous but instead it made me a pariah. Americans prefer you to be A–OK.

'What was Mr Monroe like?' I ask my grandmother when we stop walking. 'Was he handsome?'

My grandmother tilts her perfectly balanced head to one side, looking at me. 'Why this sudden interest in that time?'

I shrug. 'Don't know. I'm just curious.' I haven't told her about Leonora's superstitious warning – Leonora said that my parents and my grandmother would probably get angry with her if they found out she mentioned it. And I promised Louis Lewis I wouldn't tell anyone that we think the bachelor might be Mr Monroe.

'Well, it is hard to remember precisely.' My grandmother gazes past me and out the window, as though his apparition might appear there. 'He was quite tall. I have the distinct impression of him stooping his head as he went through doors. Yes, it always made me think of an upright British explorer entering a savage's hut.' She gives a little laugh, then sighs. She sits down on the couch and signals me to do the same. 'He was a gentleman. Completely charming. He always stood up when a woman entered the room. Lit their cigarettes, opened doors for them, complimented them. But his conduct sometimes seemed contrived, even outdated. I would not have been surprised to see him step off the curb and make an elaborate sweeping bow to a woman on the street.' My grandmother pantomimes the gesture, sweeping the air in front of her with an invisible hat. 'It was as if he learned correct behavior from a textbook – that gracious acts did not come naturally to him.'

My grandmother pauses a moment to think, and then continues, 'There were two sides to him – one impulsive, spontaneous, and the other deliberately restrained, as though he was trying to suppress something . . . I don't know – I did not know him well. But I do not think anyone did. He seemed to be hiding something. And continually improvising – his character. I have no idea where he came from originally. Sometimes he would affect a type of stutter. Other times he spoke with the wide-open vowels you only hear in prairie towns out West. And those huge epic movies of his – I had the feeling he was trying to make up for something . . . something lacking. "Tanha" is the Buddhist word for it – an overwhelming desire to become something. The fear of being nothing.'

Leonora is sick in bed with yellow dog bad temper. One of her boyfriends stood her up last night. She is lying against a bunch of pillows, with a big black hat perched between her toes. Jelly Roll Morton is on her record player, telling God all his troubles. Leonora is drinking from a bottle of brandy. 'When I see two hats,' she says, 'I'll be cured.' I tell her about the bachelor. About how Louis and I are trying to figure out who he is. I don't mention the Mr Monroe theory. 'Maybe you don't want to *know*,' Leonora says, her voice slippery as the peel of a banana. 'Everybody's after mystery, baby, and the saddest ones are those who have it explained to them. Facts ruin everything.'

The Sophists said that it is impossible to inquire into what one knows, since one knows it and therefore there is no point to the inquiry, nor into what one does not know, since then one cannot know what the object of the inquiry is.

'Penis. Gun. Penis. Penis. Gun. Gun. Penis. Penis. Penis. Beets. Gun. Penis.' Louis Lewis is reciting his list of answers for the Rorschach test he took yesterday.

'Beets?' I ask.

'Well, I didn't want to make his job *too* easy. Anyway, he said

I have problems with sex and aggression. Give the man a Nobel Prize.'

'Maybe he'll publish some research on you and you'll be as famous as Little Hans. Describe some interesting dreams to him.'

'Great idea! Fornicate and Destroy!' he yells and marches off ahead of me.

We reach a grove of apple trees next to the Monroe house. Legend has it that Johnny Appleseed planted them. He must have been drinking the ferment of apples when he planted these – they are sown in haphazard rows. Sometimes a new one sprouts up, as if Johnny Appleseed is still around, skipping and whistling 'Dixie' or some folksy nomad tune. A lot of trees around here have stories like songs, ringing in their rings. There is a pine in the ravine, that Davy Crockett climbed all the way up and then slid down, over and over, all night, so he wouldn't freeze to death. And there is a stump of maple whose wood was used for George Washington's teeth. Leonora says trees have treealities the way people have personalities because tree spirits live in them. Some spirits are evil, and cast spells on all the birds that nest in them, some can tell your fate, some bless all who walk underneath them.

Louis Lewis and I are hiding behind the apple trees, waiting for the bachelor to come out of his house. About a year ago, we took to reading hard-boiled detective novels and watching Charlie Chan movies. Our heads filled up with accomplices and alibis. We started eavesdropping and tailing people. We became quite good at it. We lie on our stomachs and peer out from behind some small saplings. There is the ripe bordello smell of rotting fruit. Wind blows through the trees and the leaves shuffle their green thoughts. Trees thinking the green idea of Tree. A few apples fall to the ground, soft thuds of Aristotle happiness to be getting home.

Louis has a pair of binoculars focused on the front door of the Monroe house. He hands them to me. I look through them, and as if my gaze is an open sesame, the bachelor appears on the front step. He walks down the steps, across the drive and out onto the street. 'Ah, the Eleatic Stranger descends from his *garçonnière*,' Louis says, and we start following him, taking cover every few feet behind the large elms that line the street on either side. The bachelor is wearing a black suit, white shirt, dark tie and dark sunglasses. He looks like an FBI agent. He walks all straight and stiff, but you get the feeling that at any moment he could keel over, his jacket opening to reveal a huge gaping bullet wound. I wonder why he hasn't taken his car. Americans never walk anywhere. Maybe he's a foreigner.

Louis thinks he is Montgomery Monroe. The name thumps in my throat. It seems to follow behind the bachelor in two irregular black heartbeats. If the bachelor is Mr Monroe, where has he been all these years since his car went over that bridge? Perhaps he lived in hotels, renting penthouse suites that overlooked sooty parks in which he walked, slowly, his long shadow sliding behind him. Or maybe he just drove aimlessly on highways, from St Louis to Joplin, Missouri to Oklahoma City, all his money stashed in a black briefcase in his trunk. The type service station attendants might eye suspiciously, memorizing his features, just in case they're shown the man's snapshot in the future by dark-suited detectives. 'You're not from around here –' the attendant comments while wiping the car's dusty windscreen. Silence from behind the flipped-down visor. 'Going far?' the attendant asks, as he counts the new, stiff bills the man hands him.

'Not far,' the bachelor says in a voice that might sing sadly to a guitar.

It's weird following someone. You start noticing things you

never noticed before. The color of bricks, the peeling of paint, a weathervane, telephone wires, the pitch of a roof. Everything becomes convoluted as a plot, significant as a drop-off point. Everything glows and glimmers with mirages of suspense.

We have come to the end of the road. The bachelor turns right and goes up the hill into town. Halfway up the hill is a graveyard. The grave of my sister Haddie is there. I let a line from the poem I memorized for this stretch of road – 'And from his fords and shallows sent a voice, That flowed along my dreams' – carry me past it and then we are crossing a field and enter into town.

We pass Davis Academy. It is a prep school. All the parents in Avon Heights send their children there so they'll get into good colleges out East. And once their children are settled in the Ivy League, their mothers go into a kind of daze. You see them around town, their eyes are slightly out of focus. They remind you of the bees you find trapped on your windowsill in winter.

Beyond the Academy is the Town Hall. Our amateur theatre company puts on plays there. When I was about four I had a pivotal role in *The Emperor's New Clothes*. My one line was: 'But he doesn't have anything on!' Next to the Town Hall is Dr Cavern's office, with tonsil-pink geraniums planted in the windowboxes. All the kids in town go there for their penicillin shots and strep throat tests. Dr Cavern has a limp from a bout with polio he had as a child, which makes us look in awe at our vaccination scars. Next is the Episcopal church, simple and white, where Mr Noble our Sunday school teacher with the huge Adam's apple protruding from his throat told us that Jesus didn't write the Bible. The bachelor walks up the steps of the church and looks at the calendar of events posted next to the door.

We can hear 'El Gato the Spanish Cat' dirge swelling from

the large ante-bellum house across the street. It is the home of Mary Carnegie Lodge School for Young Ladies and Gentlemen. It is basically a nursery school, but Mary Carnegie Lodge, the proprietress, greets the children at the door with a 'Miss' or 'Master' before their names. It gives you a false sense of the respect you'll receive later on in life. Anyway, she had us sing 'El Gato was a Spanish Cat' after lunch every day, and she must be carrying on the tradition, for we can hear children singing: 'El Gato was a Spanish cat, On a high red roof. El Gato sat, He went there to read a letter, miaow, miaow, miaow . . .' The song ends in this feline tragedy of El Gato throwing himself from a high Seville rooftop because his sweetheart met a tomcat from Toledo. We never sang 'Farmer in the Dell' or 'Old MacDonald'. Just this same sad lovelorn lament. I think she must have been unlucky in love.

The bachelor has stopped in front of the statue of George Washington standing in the middle of our town square. The first president of our country is about fifteen feet tall and wearing a toga that slips off his shoulder. Apparently the sculptor wanted to represent him as some sort of Athenian statesman. He is tight-lipped. As if he is keeping his marble morals from slipping out of his mouth and rolling away to some irretrievable place. He is also missing his nose. A few years ago Louis went through a phase where he wanted to be President of the United States. He scaled up the statue of Washington one midnight and sawed off its nose with a carrot grater. Because he had read about some Ur-ruler who cut off all the noses of his carved-in-stone pre-decessors – I guess so they'd look stupid. Well it works. Our George Washington does look stupid. He looks kind of cross-eyed. Like someone just slipped a frog down his drapery.

The bachelor looks for a moment like he might salute the

statue, but he doesn't, and instead crosses to the library and goes inside. Louis and I shadow in behind him. The library has the smell of old school buildings. The librarian is this man with long fingernails. You can hear him flipping through the card catalog. Clip. Clip. Clip. He has unnatural skin color because he is never out in the sun. He reminds me of those phosphorescent jelly-like things you find under old piers at night that no one knows the name of. But I like him. There is something foreign about him, even though he's American. It's interesting to watch him move – the cuffs on his trousers lift up to cling to his socks for a moment, and then drop down against his shoes. It is funny how a detail like that can make you feel for a person.

Louis Lewis and I creep behind the Dewey Decimal rows, peering through gaps in bookshelves for the bachelor. I find him, sitting at a yellow table in front of a window. The light behind him makes his ears glow pink and see-throughish with the delicacy of a newborn animal. He has a pile of books laid out in front of him. I turn to signal Louis, but he is gone. Probably off to look at his favorite books. *Ejaculating Ducts* by Dr Wallop Brabazon. *Every Frenchman Has One* by Olivia de Havilland. *How to Shave Yourself* by 'An Expert'. He has a real penchant for 'how-to' books: *Creative Poodle Grooming*, *The Joy of Chickens*, *You Too Can Make a Stradivarius Violin!*, *Practical Embalmer*, and *The Great Pantyhose Crafts Book* that shows you how to make lampshades, cacti and evening purses out of old runny nylons. But most likely he is memorizing disgusting passages from books that he stores up to recite to me while I'm eating. His preferred choices are from *Why Bring That Up? A Guide To and From Seasickness*, and something written by a French marquis in which these two lovers vomit into each other's mouths for kicks. It's a real fairy-tale romance.

The bachelor is looking up from his books now. At first I thought he had spotted me, but then I realize he is just gazing off into space. He seems to do this a lot. I put my face in the same position as his. Eyes tilted upward. Lips pressed together in a thin line. Jaw clenched tight. It makes me feel as though I am trying to answer a difficult question on a test.

'Fnu Lnu' is police report shorthand for 'first name unknown, last name unknown'. It sounds like someone evil and inscrutable. Someone who would know how to kill you instantly with one quick karate chop to your neck. How does someone go missing, lose their identity? I can see the bachelor emerging from the bay, cold and wet, and getting into a long black limousine waiting beneath the bridge for him. 'So,' says a fat man slowly, while lighting a cigar, 'who was murdered?' 'I was,' says Mr Monroe, laughing softly. They drive to the Desert Inn in Las Vegas. Mr Monroe emerges from the hotel bathroom, and stands in front of a long mirror. He takes a towel from his head, says to the strange, new, brown-haired reflection: 'My name is John Doe.'

Something about the bachelor does seem quite covert. You do get the sense that he's hiding something. However, Mrs Lewis can often seem furtive and secretive, but I think she's just basically kind of shy due to English not being her first language.

He goes back to flipping through his books. I can't tell what kind of books they are, but they are thick, with small print. He looks like he is going to be there for a while, so I sit down cross-legged in the aisle and browse at the books in front of me. There is a row of 'I See All' encyclopedias. I pull out Book A.

THE WORLD'S FIRST PICTURE ENCYCLOPEDIA it exclaims on the front cover. I open it and read the introduction. It is written in that loopy, enthusiastic style that makes you think of scientists in other eras, wild-eyed among bubbling flasks and

71

body parts. 'There have been many attempts to put all knowledge in a single work, and there still waits, for some pioneer in a more fortunate age, the glorious opportunity of putting all essential knowledge in a single volume!' I flip through it. There are pictures of aphids and Antwerp, the Antipodes, anklets, amulets and angels, the Andromeda Nebula and amethyst and alligators and altar pieces, alpine plants and alpha rays. Andalusians who are 'witty, handsome and good-tempered', Androcles pulling a thorn out of a lion's foot, Alexander the Great with a proud forehead and nostrils swelling in anger. The Allegheny Mountains, Aztec art, Asoka's column, the Azores which are the 'halfway house in the Atlantic for flying men', a huge auk attacking a man with upraised hands on a cliff, Ariadne helping Theseus escape from the labyrinth, Augean stables, an aviary, the auditory canal, the Atlantosaurus whose thighbone is shown towering over the man standing next to it, Aladdin rubbing a lamp, the Alexandrian library with columns and scrolls, the Adoration of the Magi, an asylum, an albatross, the abdomen, the aardvark, arms akimbo, attar of roses which shows flipped-out happy peasants tramping on flowers, alleluia illustrated by a crowd with heaven-bound eyes and open mouths, amorphous has a picture of a puzzling lumpy bump.

I look up Aristotle. It is a picture of a statue of him. His right hand is supporting his head, which is large, with prominent ears. He has the same bowl-cut hairdo as Willard Watkins, the fifty-year-old in town who walks around holding hands with his mother.

When I look up from the encyclopedia to check out the bachelor, he is gone. The books are still there. I get up and wander along the stacks, out past the circulation desk and through the doors into the street. He is nowhere to be seen. I find Louis in the children's section. He's probably been asked to baby-sit again. And I'm sure the people who asked him are new in town. Mrs Lewis wanted him to baby-sit to learn the value of money, so Louis got books from the library for bedtime reading, and was never asked back to his first assignation, or anywhere else. Word spreads. I look through the pile of children's books in front of him: *How Nell Scored*, *Come Before Mother is Up*, *Every Inch a Sailor*, *Dumps: The Story of a Plain Girl*, and *I Wasn't a Bit Like a Boy*.

I tell Louis we've lost the bachelor and we wander back to the table he was sitting at to see if we can pick up any clues. We look at the books left there. Avicenna's *Book of Salvation*, Averroës's *The Incoherence of Incoherence*, Boethius's *The Consolation of Philosophy*, Abelard's *Sic et Non*, Meister Eckhart's *On Detachment*.

'Must have become a Jesus freak,' Louis mutters as he looks through them.

One is still open. Underlined in green ink in the middle of the page is this line: 'You can know something you are not aware you know.'

AGORAZONTA is walking while philosophizing. Just the word gives you visions of agorazontizers swishing and swanking down the street, deluding themselves with grandeur. But apparently, Socrates walked more like a cowboy. I see him, entering the agora, in his wide, majestic, silver-screen strides. In Westerns, a lone man entering a town is either good or evil, and you can tell which by the way he walks. So there must be good movement and evil movement. Plato says there are two kinds of movement – the change in place, and the change in being. Maybe movement is evil when your change in place isn't in harmony with your change in being.

Sometimes I'll shadow myself. I leave my room, and an hour later, I enter it again. And search for clues to myself, my whereabouts. As though I pulled a fast one. Copped a Sunday. The voice in my head starts sounding slick and cynical as a paranoid private eye. My room has the tawdry atmosphere of a fleabag motel seen through the bottom of a bottle of bourbon. I start snooping for evidence I might have left behind that will later trip me up. If the bed is unmade, I study the shape left on the sheets. I browse through the bookshelves, picking books out at random: Who would read this? Check the clothes in the closet, their colors, cut: What kind of person would wear these? In a drawer is a notebook. Handwriting is an important index to character. The low crosses on my 't's denote insecurity. The long loops of my 'y's mean 'unhinged'. From a brush I pluck a long brown hair. On the bedside table is a glass. I dust it for fingerprints. Still, on the dresser, sits the wooden monkey, who sees no evil. Still, on the wall, is a picture, caught within its frame. Still are the lines of my writing, my fingerprints, my shape on the sheets. A still life. Like Zeno's arrow, you are still and you are in motion. You will never know where you are. You will never know if you have been moving, or if you have been still.

I often get this sense I am being followed. I stop, wheel around quickly, but no one is there. Yet, as I start walking again I feel most sure of footfalls behind me, stepping in each place I have stepped, mirroring my movements, echoing my trail. Mocking me, or in pursuit.

'He had a head of hair like a frizzly chicken and a face like a run-down porch but you can be sure as seven comes eleven he had a line of women a mile long crying a river over him,' Leonora tells me when I ask her about Mr Monroe. 'I don't quite know how he made their ding a ling – I would have told him to take it right back to the place where he got it.'

'Then what do you think they liked about him?' I ask her.

'Oh, because he was in love with himself, I suppose. That always gets everyone wondering what they're missing. Being that most people aren't too fond of themselves. And he was funny – always making people laugh and telling crazy stories. His voice was deep, but sad too – there was definitely a trumpet sounding in that man's soul. And that is probably what got the ladies the most. We're all suckers for the ones born to be blue. A man starts singing that baa baa black sheep song and we come fluttering like moths to the flame. And that's what he made you think of – some bad old black sheep of a family from god knows where who hit the road and never looked back, but who looked long gone and nowhere lonely in the middle of that crowd of children and women and movie stars.'

'You know how his body was never found? Do you think he might have just wanted to disappear?'

'He'd certainly be the type. Back home, every five years or so there'd be a man who would walk straight out the door of his house and never come back. And they were usually the ones that suffered mood indigos and shipwrecked more women than they could count.' Leonora shakes her head. 'Actually, there was a night here that was very strange. Your parents were giving a dinner party. And Mr Monroe, he got drunk as a skunk. Some man said something to this lady that he didn't like, thought it was downright impolite. So Mr Monroe yelled to me, "Leonora! Get me your Bible, honey!" And when I came back with the Book, Mr Monroe was hanging this man by his coat collar on a hook high up on the wall. The man's legs and arms were dangling.'

Leonora mimes the movements of a puppet. 'Mr Monroe opened up the Bible and started to read that man his last rites. I got scared out of my wits. I've seen two grown men in Alabama kill each other because they were arguing over which came first: the chicken or the egg.' She points to opposite corners of the room, as if said chicken and egg are here, in a face-off. 'Who knows.' Leonora sighs. 'He might have gotten himself into trouble. He had that lynx-eyed look in his eyes, like Louis does – he was always plotting something, you could see it in his pupils, flicking sharp as switchblades. Some folks just have that off-beat syncopation in their heart that brings them trouble here, and trouble down the road.'

One way to cure vertigo could be to follow directions on how to do something. Just the words – How-to-do – have a clean, new, one-two-three, on-your-mark, get-set, go rhythm to them. Setting you on the simple, straight and narrow path home.

Socrates was always pestering people to define their terms. I wonder what he would think of dictionaries. I looked up 'believe' in the dictionary, and it was defined as 'a principle accepted as true'. Then I looked up 'true' and it said 'in accordance with facts'. Facts are events or things known to have existed. Existence is having being. Being is something that exists. Which is something that has being. I started to feel like I was Socrates and the dictionary was one of those know-it-all dolts he's always questioning.

Words that you look up in dictionaries are called entries. But you enter them, and before you know it, instead of coming to an end you enter another entry. Aristotle thought the world was round because the horizon always retreats when one walks or rides toward it. I think that's the feeling you would get if you could walk through the dictionary. Or it might be like one of those labyrinths people in Greece were always getting lost in – the words standing in tall, black rows, silent as unplayed instruments. You would think you were walking toward the lair of meaning at the center, but each druggy and demented path would lead you to yet another entrance.

Apparently the first dictionary was written by a couple of madmen. One was an opium addict who hunted for definitions in drug dens and the other one wrote entries from inside an insane asylum, because he had suffered from sunstroke, thought he was pursued by Irishmen and shot an innocent man. So I guess it's no wonder the dictionary itself seems pretty unhinged, with all its psychedelic passages and smoky mirages of meaning and definitions of definitions of definitions spiraling in endless circles.

HOW TO FIND YOUR WAY OUT OF A MAZE: Enter and start walking. Whenever you have a choice, take the right branching. If you come to a dead end, retrace your steps to the last branching and take any right turn not yet visited. The best way to adhere to this rule is to keep your right hand touching the right hedge throughout the journey. Never skip a turning to the right.

Mrs Lewis is very religious. She's Catholic. She goes to church a lot. She also has insomnia. The word 'insomnia' sounds mystical, and otherworldly. Louis Lewis says that sometimes in the middle of the night, he'll hear his mother's soft steps wandering through the house, and if he gets up he will invariably find her walking back and forth, a rosary in her hands, her mouth moving in silent prayer.

'Was Mr Monroe very religious?' I ask Mrs Lewis. I'm thinking about the bachelor and his books in the library. We are in her car, on the way to Charm School. I think Mrs Lewis hasn't heard me, because she doesn't answer. She flips her visor down as if to shield her eyes against the sun, even though it is raining.

'We were not well acquainted,' she finally says stiffly. She says it in the formal tone she uses when she is speaking about some aspect of American life she finds tacky and shabby. The rain is falling faster now – the windshield wipers can hardly keep the car window clear. Then I realize that Mrs Lewis is driving much faster. I look over at the gauge – it moves from seventy to seventy-five, eighty. Mrs Lewis drives fast and is always getting pulled over by cops, but they never give her a ticket. I was with her once when she was stopped. She transformed before my eyes. 'How horr-ee-ball – I'm so sorry,' she said so softly the officer had to lean forward to listen. The officer blushed. It's funny how words can be like a force of gravity, the way they pull and push on you, cause chemical changes, blushes, yawns, shivers.

In French almost all the words have a sex to them. Maybe that's why the 'r's sound like a mixture of rattlers rattling and forked tongues flickering, and French 'n's make the whole front of your face vibrate. Anyway, by the end of their little tête-à-tête, with Mrs Lewis laughing and lightly touching the policeman's sleeve, and swaying her keys in a kind of hypnotic motion, the officer ended up apologizing profusely for stopping her. I think of her teaching my sister how to be a coquette. And then I suddenly realize that I shouldn't have asked her about Mr Monroe. That the memory of him probably triggered in her a memory of my sister, of that time. I wonder if Mr Monroe was at the funeral. Perhaps he caught Mrs Lewis when she fainted. Gentlemen in movies are always swift and assured around swooning women. First, there was the sound of her falling rosary, clattering upon the stone path. And before her black-veiled head could hit the ground, his strong arms are underneath her, lifting her as easily as if she were a small child, her feet in her high-heeled pumps dangling in the air like the long black notes at the end of a song.

When we get to Charm School, Mrs Lewis and Ms Phillips start acting out scenes which illustrate how to steer away from unpleasant themes, such as politics, religion, sex and age, which might be brought into the discussion by those unfortunate guests who are lacking in lessons of propriety. Which makes me feel pretty self-conscious and uncomfortable considering that I just brought up an unpleasant theme with Mrs Lewis in the car. Methods of delicacy on these occasions include diversion, misconstruing, introducing another person into the conversation, and if all else fails, excusing yourself. Mrs Lewis and Ms Phillips's examples seem mainly to use digressive forays into the topic of horticulture.

DIVERSION: 'Who did you vote for in the last election? We really need to run those ruthless Republicans out of Washington . . .'

'Washington . . . have you been there in spring? The cherry blossoms along the Delaware – simply sublime!'

MISCONSTRUING: 'I've just had my face done for the third time. Have you gone under the knife yet? I'm sure I couldn't guess – how many autumn seasons have *you* seen?'

'I really haven't been able to see as many shows as I'd like – but last fall there was a lovely display of a Japanese stone garden – here, do try the stuffed celery –'

INTRODUCING ANOTHER PERSON: 'Before I discovered Jesus, I was spending all my money at the races –'

'Then you must definitely meet Mrs Blickering – she is the head of the Church Charity Floral Show – Mrs Blickering?'

EXCUSING YOURSELF: 'So I said, Harry, if you are going to use yourself up on your mistresses, I am certainly not going to go stone cold when there are all those tennis instruct—'

'Oh, please do excuse me, my vase of carnations seems to be drooping –'

Now we are practicing saying 'How are you?', 'Thank you' and 'I'm sorry' with the proper intonation to convey the most sincerity. Plato wrote a dialogue called the 'Apology'. But Socrates never once says he's sorry in it – instead, he speaks to his friends about how he'll be happy to be dead, because then he'll finally have some interesting people to talk to.

Socrates is kind of rude. He seeks out unpleasant themes rather than veering away from them. And his questions are sprung traps set to snare the other person by their own replies. Their answers are torn to tatters, their definitions collapse in a puff of smoke, they end up seeming shifty as snakes. Socrates reminds me of a detective interrogating The Bartender, The Stripper, The Smart-Cracking Dame, The Pampered Playboy, The Drifter – suspects who at first are talking fast, punchy words, jeering 'Say, what's the idea, wiseguy?', repartee stiff as arithmetic. But once they get a dose of the detective's straight talk, they're up against the wall with no alibi; their future's all used up.

Zen masters aren't very polite conversationalists either. They'll ask someone a deliberately bewildering question, and when the person gets the answer wrong, the master twists their nose, or hits them over the head with a big stick. And then he reveals the answer, which invariably is some proverb you can't figure out – Logic Without a Cause.

There are certain people who like to quote proverbs about

how the wise man asks more questions than he gives answers, but you can tell by the way these people talk that they think in exclamation points rather than question marks. I wonder if there is some ur-question, and the way you answer it would completely define who you are: Does a rolling stone gather no moss? Is fact stranger than fiction? Does what goes around come around? Is a word to the wise enough?

Every day is pretty much the same. The bachelor leaves his house, wearing his dark suit and sunglasses. He walks up the street, turns right up the hill and walks alongside the fence of my sister's cemetery. Once he wandered between the humpy grass graves, reading some of the names on the stones. He reminded me of one of those mysterious people in black who leave birthday roses at the graves of the famous. Then he walks across the field into town, past the Academy, the doctor and the church. He crosses the square, passing by our Simple Simon statue. Up the steps and into the library, where he reads books on religion and underlines passages in green ink, and then copies them into his notebook. 'Nothing moves into the past, all is present' and 'I believe because it is impossible'. Sometimes I hear the lines he underlines in my dreams at night.

We've discovered that after he leaves the library he goes to the Town Hall for an hour or so. He sits there with his head resting against a wall, his eyes closed. Just before five o'clock he gets up and goes over to the cinema for an early evening show, before slowly walking back home again. The movie showing is *The Third Man*. Louis and I sit in the cool back row. The opening scene begins with the narration: 'I never knew the old Vienna, before the war, with its Strauss music, its glamor . . .' We have now seen this movie five times. I am starting to pick up Orson

Welles's sly mannerisms, his slow smile, his sideways glance. And the voices buzz in my ears all day: 'What am I to do, old man? I'm dead, aren't I?' and 'Haven't got a sensible name, Calloway'.

On the way out of the movie the last time, the ticket seller said to the bachelor, 'Must like that movie!' and the bachelor stopped, tipped his head to one side, looking at the man. Then he said very slowly, with that banjo-twanging voice, 'Yes. Yes I do. I never used to see a movie twice. But then you realize that you are always missing something.' He put his finger to his forehead as if he was touching the brim of a hat, except that he wasn't wearing one.

Mr Monroe changed Homer's ending to the *Odyssey*. In his version, Odysseus never returns. When he lands on the beach at Ithaca, and lies to the goddess Athena about his identity, instead of smiling and calling him a crafty rogue, she is angry at his deception, and is worried that he will bring back with him the old violent ways of the warrior hero, and therefore tells him that he is in a strange land. That his real home is that way, to the east, and the movie ends with him sailing off once again, over the horizon.

I've always liked movies about lone men who suddenly appear somewhere three days from anywhere. They are usually running from some kind of trouble, but then, in this new place, they discover something about themselves they didn't know, something good, when all along they had thought they were completely morally corrupt.

Socrates liked to ask people: 'Who are you?' Because he realized that most people don't know. And this is what gets them into the most trouble.

Louis's nostrils twitch when he tells a lie. He is left-handed and uses a fountain pen, and the ink often leaves blue smudges along the side of his hand and wrist. Sometimes when you see him, before he even opens his mouth, you know his head is full of new ideas and they are wobbling like plates set on top of sticks, out of control and about to fall. There is a picture in a story-book I had when I was little. A boy with a knapsack on a stick is running through backyards. There are long shadows on moonlit porches, dark and deep as memories. It was a story about a boy who belonged to himself, and that describes Louis perfectly. He belongs to himself.

Louis Lewis doesn't act, or look, anything like his father. He always has different theories going as to who his real father is. Some days he's an existentialist race car driver. Other days he's a debased marquis. When Louis used to mention these conjectures to his mother she would get extremely angry – she would shout 'Nonsense!' and 'Enough!' at him, and have this look in her eyes like she detested him. So Louis has pretty much dropped the subject with her. But sometimes I've caught her looking at Louis as if she doesn't understand who he is, as if he's some impostor posing as her son. At these times she seems sad; there is a longing in her eyes – as if she wishes Louis would return the son he switched places with. And when they are fighting in French, she often gives him glares of pure hatred. Agamemnon's son says that the mother is always a stranger to the child.

Mr Lewis never learned any French. And he forbids Louis and his mother to speak any around him. Probably because their heated conversations can get to be a bit unsettling.

Mr Lewis uses the word 'magnificent' all the time. 'Magnificent!' he says when he sees Mrs Lewis. 'Magnificent!' he comments when he puts down a book. 'Magnificent!' when he sees a sunset. He says it in a voice that makes it seem as if he's just invented Mrs Lewis, the book, the sunset. When you see him walking down his driveway it makes you think of one of those Captains of Industry in another century, striding off to check out one of his shipyards. His laugh is abrupt and surprising. And he has heavy, capable hands, the type that hold passports and hail taxis.

He usually just appears all of a sudden, smelling of jumbo jets and big hotels, spilling strange and slightly dangerous-looking coins out of his pockets and unpacking presents from his suitcase, wrapped in Chinese newspapers or pieces of colored silk. He often brings me little wooden idols that embarrass me because they are usually squatting women with drooping breasts the shape of zucchinis. I have about ten of them. Frankly, I really couldn't bear looking at them any more, so I stuck them in my closet. They sit on an upper shelf, bristling with bare breasts. They chant sexy spells into all my shoes. Sometimes I wonder if I should get rid of them.

It is hard to define a person. Plato believed in Timeless Being. That the most real things are still and unchanging, outside Time and Space. This is where the Universal Form of Man resides, which all particular men partake in, by possessing Its Qualities. But Aristotle said if all men participate in the Form of Man, then between the particular man and the Form of Man you could place a Third Man, which is less particular. Louis Lewis said that they both forgot the category of the sub-quasi-demi-hemi forms, which are forms that have gone Horribly Wrong, because where else do you classify chihuahuas and fruit bats, cedar souvenirs and candle art, bubble perms and Miss America emcees?

For half an hour, everyone was once a single cell. I sit very still for thirty minutes, trying to remember what it was like to be just one cell. The scientists say that DNA is what makes you grow and change. They say that if you stretched it, a single strand of DNA would be three feet long. I wish they could pull a strand out of you and stretch it out. It would be the ultimate accoutrement. You could wrap it around your neck as the most bewitching of boas. You could keep it coiled about your throat and wave its tips in little come-hither swirls. Or you could unwind it with a flourish, hold it in front of you like a banner and say, 'This is me!' Then everyone would know right away where you came from and where you are going. It would save a lot of small talk.

'Inadvertent phantoms' are what they call people whose current documented identity is not the one they started out with at birth. In order to obtain a new identity, these phantoms will cruise through graveyards, looking for headstones that have a date of birth similar to their own, or scan obituaries for people who have died in disasters that took place outside the country. Sometimes they will take on the name of a brother who died at birth, or in early childhood. They obtain a copy of the birth certificate of the person they have chosen to become, and with this in hand, acquire a new social security number, a driver's license, and line of credit. They memorize pertinent details – such as the dead person's place of birth, and mother's maiden name. They give up all past interests – even a simple hobby could be enough for someone to finger them. They are on constant alert for trails – checking their rear-view mirrors and pulling into parking lots and behind buildings. Some phantoms keep a length of rope next to their bedroom windows. They must remember their new name and respond to its call. They must forget their old name. It must be as though that person has ceased to exist, or never existed at all.

What strikes me most about Greek literature is people not recognizing each other. 'Orestes?' Electra asks, blinking. 'Odysseus?' Penelope wonders, blushing. 'Junior?' Jocasta says, a heavy stone thrown in deep water. I suppose you might be able to tell a lot about a person's character according to how they react in the moment of a surprising recognition. ANAGNORISIS is the Greek word for recognition, a sudden clearing of vision, which usually comes too late to help the characters in a tragedy. Socrates got extremely piqued by the Sophists because they were always messing around with the verb 'to be'. Which blurred everyone's sense of themselves and others. Louis said that Freud wrote about how what seems completely incomprehensible to us is usually something that is actually extremely familiar to us. He called it 'the uncanny'.

Beauty is a combination of qualities that give pleasure to the sight or other senses or to the mind. Plato said that love moves up the ladder of Beauty so that we may behold the Truth. So maybe contained in my sister's beauty is the truth of what happened to her.

What does it mean to be beautiful? When I look at that portrait of my sister, there is a quality beyond the perfect geometry of her features. Actually, there is something unsettling about it. It swings from drawing you in toward it, like the cadence of the first line of a poem you had to memorize by heart, to rebuffing you, warning you not to get too close.

Mrs Lewis is beautiful. And sometimes when I'm with her I feel as if she is both pulling me toward her and pushing me away at the same time. I used to think she wasn't sure whether she liked me or not. But now I wonder if it is because I have the same name as my sister. I must be an ever-present reminder of a sadness in her life.

'Do you ever find the beauty of things disturbing?' I ask my grandmother.

She looks at me, perplexed. Maybe she's thinking I'm 'disturbed'. But then she says 'Aware' softly, pronouncing it a-wahr-ray. 'It is a Japanese word,' she says, pointing to a vase of flowers, as though the word is printed on their petals, 'meaning the combined essence of beauty, and mortality. Beautiful things bring with them a consciousness of death, for through them we are reminded that nothing remains the same from moment to moment. Death and beauty are bitter-sweet rhymes that remind us that nothing is real.'

I think I saw the bachelor *in* the movie *The Third Man*. In that scene where everyone is chasing Harry Lime through the underground sewers of Vienna. The bachelor was one of the men pursuing him. He looked different in black and white, as most people do. But he had the same measured poise, manner. His shadow preceded him on the concrete, longer than life. And then he ran across the screen and into the darkness, disappearing, except for the sound of his running footsteps.

HOW TO BE A HEROIC CHARACTER: Make a lot of exits. Speak of yourself in the third person. Have 'the' as your middle name. Display overwhelming emotions so they can be the source of poetic inspiration. Be extremely inflexible. Have a tragic flaw. Follow your Fate, which will lead you toward a Glamorous Death.

LIST OF GLAMOROUS DEATHS: Being chained to a rock and

having your liver eaten out by eagles. Jumping into a live volcano. Being shot through the heart by a golden bullet at a blackjack table in Monte Carlo. Tossing in a fever bed under mosquito netting in the tropics. Coughing delicately into a lace handkerchief while composing your last line on death and roses. Swallowing two lumps of opium and a swig of brandy. Being crucified. Being bitten by an asp. Being sacrificed to the Aztec sun god. Crashing your Ferrari into a tree in the Bois de Bologne. Being strangled by a man who wears black gloves and hums a mysterious tune. Being found sprawled in a pool of blood on a flagstone path.

A copy of the *Arabian Nights* was found under the dead body of my sister. Was she reading the book before she fell? Practicing for her part in the movie? Scheherazade stayed alive by never finishing any of the stories that she started.

ANAMNESIS is mystical memory. Plato thought that all knowledge and truth is already inside you, but it's locked away in a memory chamber you have from a past life, and the key to opening it is to ask a whole lot of questions.

'Do you know anything about mystical memory?' I ask Leonora. We are in the bathroom. I am watching her get ready to go out. She has on a blonde wig and a red dress.

'Sure, baby, you're looking right at it.' She points to the mirror over the sink. 'Mirrors are full of everyone who ever looked in them. They hold memories best because they aren't liquid and they aren't solid, but both, flowing and whole. So they've got *soul*.' When she says 'soul' her voice dips low and rolls, like an echo inside a bowl. 'And the reason you have bad luck when you break them is because the memories should stay there and not be

88

let loose into the world – we have enough problems with all the ones locked up in our thinkbox.' She taps her finger to her forehead. 'I have a mirror at home that used to be in my daddy's house. Whenever I look in it, I can see my wicked Aunt Esther cackling at me from the right-hand corner.'

'Why don't you put it away – in a closet or something?'

'That', Leonora says, as she sprays herself liberally with Tigress perfume, 'would be giving in.'

LIST OF BAD LUCK SUPERSTITIONS: Do not break a mirror. Do not place shoes on a table. Do not lean a broom against a bed. Sneeze on a Friday, sneeze for sorrow. You will die soon if your shadow is cast without a head. Do not sail when the horns of the moon are tipped to the side. Do not walk a counterclockwise path. A white bird flying into your house brings catastrophe. Ill-fated are the sounds of howling dogs and whistling women. Do not sleep in the light of the full moon. Do not leave a chair rocking when you stand up. Meeting a hare on a May morning means calamity. Red skies at morning, sailors take warning. Do not start a journey and then turn back. Do not look at the moon over your left shoulder. Do not name the Scottish play. Do not kill an albatross. Watch out for black cats that cross your path.

I couldn't wait to see *The Third Man* today. But the bachelor was no longer there, in the movie. Another man had taken his place. Another man's shadow stretched along the sewer wall. Another man ran across the screen. Another man disappeared into the darkness.

The apparent motion of the film image is illusory and relies upon the physiology of the AFTER-IMAGE. Each frame in a film is still, yet the retina of the human eye holds this image for a fraction of a second, and so sees all the frames as one continuous whole.

I have seen pictures of places where the sky and the water meet at a perfect blue ruler line along the horizon, places where a band of yellow road winds through flat brown earth, where white hills descend to a black sea – everything primary-shaped and simple-colored as a child's painting. People's memories in a place like that must be pure as the elements in the Periodic Table. It's hard to think philosophic thoughts in our town. What you need is a clean fall of vertical light on everything – clean blue, clean white, clean curves, clean angles. In our town there is too much bric-à-brac. There are cupolas and shutters and fences and flowers. Tons of flowers. Did the Greeks have flowerbeds? I can't imagine it. Geraniums are like caged animals. Geraniums are a hindrance to the mind.

To have knowledge in the fullest sense is to know the causes of things. Aristotle said that there is a Logos to the Cosmos – that Nature does nothing by chance or accident. And that if we observe things with our senses we will discover all causes. But to understand any event, we must comprehend its ultimate End, or purpose. I try to apply his 'four causes' to my sister: Of what is it made? A girl. What is its form? Beauty. Who made it? My parents, and Mrs Lewis. What was it made for? Movies, or death?

'Lord I hate to hear that lonesome whistle blow . . .' That's a railway song Leonora used to sing to me at night. There are a lot of songs about railroads. They mainly have to do with un-happiness and destination. The word 'destination' sounds like it is made up of railway cars, or a caravan of camels. There is no word for that which is both a beginning and an end.

'What do you think my sister's destiny would have been, had she lived?' I ask Leonora. We are putting pots and pans, bowls and glasses out in the brick courtyard behind our house. There are big thunderclouds rolling in, and we like to hear the rain falling on them.

'Oh, she had the world in a jug, and she walked around with her chin high in the air, like she was balancing it on top of her head.' Leonora struts, doing a short little cakewalk in front of me. 'She knew that everyone she passed by went "ah". That she was The End.' There is a low rumble of thunder and Leonora comes and sits down next to me on a step under the eaves. 'But you know,' she continues, 'several months, maybe half a year before she died, she changed her chord from major to minor. She stopped laughing. Started crying a lot. Of course, sometimes it was hard to tell if she was acting – doing some fake boohooing. A lot of the things she did were made up out of the air. But I could feel it in my funny bones that this wasn't. One night she woke up screaming. I don't know – maybe something happened to her while she was making that movie. That Hollywood crowd is bad news – that's the whole reason the Monroes moved here – to keep their children away from that lot.' Leonora wags her head as though she's smelled something bad. 'But maybe she was sick. That might have been why she fell. She was walking around those last few months like an old woman – stooped over, looked like her hinges were creaking. And she stopped seeing her friends – at least the ones her own age.'

'Who were her friends?'

'Mr Monroe's daughter – Mathilde – was her best friend. They grew up together. I used to call them a couple of flummadiddle flibbogibbets. They were always together – they wore the same identical hats all one summer. Straw fishing hats. Big, wide brims – you could keep a whole family *and* their first cousins out of the rain under one of them. I kept mixing the two of those girls up. But then your sister blossomed, and Mathilde, she didn't. She was plain vanilla. So Mathilde got real jealous of all the attention your sister got. Especially from her father – Mr Monroe. She got mean-spirited. Started acting like she's lost a few cards out of her deck. She'd look at your sister like she was a cat about to pounce on a mouse. Still, I felt kind of sorry for her. Like the Divine Miss Holiday told us – them that's got shall have, them that's not shall lose –'

The rain comes down in a sudden downpour, hitting like hard pellets against the aluminum pans and binging on the glasses. Leonora says that we are allowing the pots' and glasses' celestial voices to sing and scare the evil spirits of the storm away. She says that 'things' are silent because they'll speak only to God.

ACTING is the performing art in which, by movement and gesture, a fictional characterization is realized. It is an ephemeral craft. Acting raises many puzzling questions, such as, can a performer create emotions without actually feeling them? Can an audience watch a spectacle without becoming a part of it? See MASKS, SACRIFICE RITUALS, THEATER.

If you look at anything and say 'I can't believe my eyes!' the thing loses its 'whatness'. A chair suddenly doesn't have any chairness. A table stops tabling. A lamp loses all lampality. Aristotle said everything is made up of matter and form, and you can figure out how the two come together in something by looking at all its causes, categories, accidents and essences. When you look in surprise at a thing, maybe it shocks the 'thisness' and 'thatness' out of it for a second, and its matter is startled loose from its form. And when you stare at it long enough its matter falls to pieces, you just see a fuzzy swirl of earth, air, fire and water.

I stare at the Steinway in the corner of the library. It bears the inscription: 'Played by Sir Robert Winston on his visit to the United States, April 1940.' Some people can tell the history of an object just by touching it. I wonder if their fingers would feel all the etudes, mazurkas and chopsticks played on the piano's keys, and its wood being varnished and its chords being strung, and if their hand pressed harder, the black of ebony trees in tropical forests, the trembling ivory tusks of great elephants on a plain.

I think this piano is haunted. It is made of cherry wood and, depending on the light, I can see different figures traced in the grain – Oriental men pulling carts, and plum trees with laughing branches. They move like clouds. Because it is humid, the piano gives off a deep brown smell. Plants can signal to each other through smell – they can warn each other of poison and insects. I wonder if inanimate objects can do the same – hot rocks in summer, the insides of old pianos, suitcases stacked in closets, books packed together tight. I wonder if everything is haunted, if everything is telling secrets behind our backs.

ADUMBRATION means to foreshadow. To remember and to foresee at the same time.

The bachelor lets the greyhounds run free at night. When they are running in the dark, you can't distinguish their bodies from their shadows. Their eyes look red. Like rubies set in the sockets of mummy shrouds. It is usually at dusk that I see that black cat out of the corner of my eye. The one my sister owned named

Kitty, that ran away. A shadow is the shade cast by a body intercepting light. The Sphinx was born out of the mating of the sun and moon during an eclipse. It posed deathly riddles to wanderers passing by: What trails a man at sunrise, sleeps at noon, walks ahead of him at sunset?

LIST OF SHADOWS: Cool shadows in temples, shadows under bridges, under a red rock, shadows of sound, shadows of camel caravans stretching across singing sands, shadows of time on sundials, me and my shadow, shadow-boxing, shadows under the eyes of debauched men, shadows of clouds on hilltops, shadows of *film noir* electric fans, shadows cast by statues in deserted city squares, shadows of eclipses, shadows sold and folded into a pocket.

One day, instead of following the bachelor to the Town Hall and the cinema, Louis and I stay at the library to look up articles in the archives on the Monroes in the local newspaper. There are two. One is about a famous movie star who visited the Monroes, about a year before my sister died. The movie star's name is Emmalou de Cherraglio.

'I wonder what it must feel like to have a name like that,' I say to Louis.

'Spare me. She should have cut the coy act and called herself Immaluv de Fellatio. That would have gotten her into the Hollywood haciendas faster than those hundreds of French postcards she's no doubt featured in.'

There is a picture of Emmalou, posing with the Monroe family. She is definitely the first one you notice. She stands out, larger than life among them, as though she alone is standing under a kleig light. She is cello-shaped, wearing an evening gown.

There are insinuating, concubine curves to her shoulders and hips. She has big Theda Bara eyes and spiky eyelashes. She looks dangerous as a big blackjack bet. In movies, men would hire thugs to kill for her. One of her slender arms is raised in a gesture of hello! or goodbye! Wafture is the name for that movement. I wonder why we wave hello and goodbye – who first lifted their arm and swayed their hand to let you know they were coming or going. I look at the movie star and think of how this is what my sister might have become. Then I focus on Mr Monroe. Unfortunately, the shadow of a tree blocks his face, so all you can see is a tall figure with broad shoulders. He could be the bachelor. But, then, he could be anyone. I match the names underneath the photo from left to right – Megan, Matthew, Mercedes, Manfred, Mason, Mathilde. Mathilde is long-legged and thin, with short hair, parted to the side. She could get lost in a crowd. Her eyes are large and dark as closets. I wonder if, at the time of this picture, she had already started hating my sister.

The second article is about the death of my sister. It doesn't say anything I don't already know. Although it does give me a funny jolt to read: 'Haddie Constance Ashton fell to her death . . .' – as if I'm one of those characters in movies attending their own funeral: 'But we thought you were –' the tearful relatives say, choking on their words. 'Dead?' I answer for them, raising one eyebrow. And then it makes me think of how you fall. Either it is an accident, you are pushed, or you jump on purpose. But in all three cases there have to be reasons before the final cause of the fall. If you jump on purpose, there has to be a reason why you would – something very upsetting had to have happened to you that would make you want to take your own life. If a person pushed you, then something had to have happened previously that made them want to push you. And even an accident has to have some event precede it that causes it. Did someone dare my sister to go up on the roof, walk upon the ledge of the third-story window, climb to the highest branches of the tree? Could someone have purposely loosened roof tiles, broken branches?

The picture of the Monroe house accompanying the article is gray and grainy. In the sky above the house is a formation of birds. The Greeks read their futures by watching birds in the sky. If you could read auguries, maybe you could have detected in the bird pattern over the Monroe house the spelling of my sister's doom.

Leonora says that when your parents name you, you immediately become linked to all the other people who have the same name as you, throughout all time, and across all distances. So if your name is Joe Schmoe, you have invisible strings attaching you to all the other Joe Schmoes everywhere in the world and down in history. And all those strings keep you upright, they're like stays on a mast. But if your name is a bit eccentric, you don't have as many strings attached to you, so you are easily tippable and end up on a scale somewhere between peculiar and screwball. For instance, Leonora knew these two women. One was named Hepsa Arngrin Apathy and the other was called Venerable Violet Organ, and both of them were mad as March hares. But you shouldn't change your name. Even if you have one that puts you off your stroke. Because if you deny your name you will succumb to witchcraft.

In Plato's dialogue 'Cratylus', Socrates says that the universe is like a great bell, and every object in the world has its own special ring. So if you strike an object, the sound that you hear should be the natural name of it.

What is the sound of yourself? When you look at things, you see their form on the outside, but if you strike them, you hear the sound-shadows of their insides. I read that violin makers look for trees that are crooked and gnarled, because these shapes show that they have suffered a difficult life. And that angst is trapped in the wood, and echoes bitter-sweet waves through the music. Pain must make the body a better instrument because the best singers have the blues so bad it hurts their feet to walk. Instead of letters, we should have notes of music make up our names. Then you would sing or hum someone's name instead of saying it. And that sound would be closer to their soul.

I wouldn't call a cat Kitty. It is a stupid name for a cat. I would call it Minnaloushe, Clovis, Crazy Jane or the Count. Perhaps Captain Cat, Pangur Ban, Mr Kid, Max von Mayerling. If that cat had had the right name, maybe it would not have run away.

'If you have to climb into an attic, even if you are wearing tights, the polite male goes first, saying "follow me" rather than "after you" and always comes down last.'

Now Mrs Lewis is demonstrating how to take a seat at a restaurant. I am wondering how many opportunities there are for the young lady and her polite male to go up and down attic stairs. Mrs Lewis's peach blossom lipstick is bleeding around the corners. She leans engagingly toward Ms Phillips, her polite male companion at the dinner table. I picture her on dark attic stairs. A man with shiny hair like Dean Martin is on a stair below her. The air smells like peach blossom lipstick and the garlic of a spaghetti dinner. 'Follow me,' Mrs Lewis whispers.

If you pretend a blindfold has just been whipped off your eyes after you have been shanghaied from a dark alley, thrown into the trunk of a car, driven long black miles, then taken out and tied to a chair, you'd perceive the piano sitting in front of you differently than you would if it were just a piano in a town library you are sitting looking at, of your own free will. I think frightening yourself is a good hobby. It brings your mind and body, thinking and being, together. You feel the presence of the present pressing on you, in Big Beats, like a force of evil.

Aristotle thought the heart was the seat of the soul. He said that all our thoughts were contained in it, and that the brain condensed all the vapors rising from it. I wonder if you would look at people differently if you thought their mind was in their heart. When I look into people's eyes, I feel as though I am looking through their pupils into their minds. But your head is so silent. If your thoughts were contained in your heart, you would hear them – beat by beat by beat.

We are inside the bachelor's house. He went somewhere in his car with his greyhounds today. So we have broken in. Don't ask me how. Louis did it. He shimmied up a drain-pipe and disappeared over a roof and a few minutes later he was letting me in through the back door. I hesitated for a moment, but Louis said, 'Come *on*, Haddie. The unexamined life is not worth living,' so I entered with the feeling I was falling into a picture book. That we were walking through pretend doors, down make-believe hallways.

I look out one of the long front windows of the Monroe house. It is made of old glass so everything outside – trees and grass and the slate path – undulates slightly. I say 'fourteen years ago'. And I see the cheetah on the warm path, sunning its rosetted fur. The uncle limps past, boring one of the children with tales of the

Boer War. Then I see a large, dark shadow upon the path, like that of a huge bird, then a fast, blurred shape falling. I turn quickly away from the window.

Louis calls me into the dining room where he is standing still, listening for something. It is full of large, dark furniture. Louis walks out of the room and I follow him. Across the entranceway is a closed door. The murmuring of voices seems to be coming from behind it. We stare at the doorknob. Louis skips in light bandit steps across the parquet floor, listens for a minute, then he pushes the door open. I gasp – the voices are loud now but Louis goes into the room. I edge slowly to the open door. The voices are coming from the television. Watergate. I wonder if the bachelor ever shuts it off.

The sheets have been removed from the furniture. The pieces are those kind of awkward dark antiques that look as though they've been at the scene of a murder – a sofa someone was stabbed in, a settee in which the victim was strangled. Louis suddenly stumbles backward and chokes as though he is swallowing a long sword. He points to the shoes beneath the curtain. I stroll nonchalantly over to them and lift the curtains so he can see they are empty.

'Oh,' Louis says archly, 'I thought it might be the comic valet.'

We walk through the downstairs rooms, most of them heavily draped and dark with unpacked boxes against the walls. They smell of empty old desk drawers and bowls of unlit pipes. The smell of loneliness. When I pull out the drawers of tables or desks, they are empty except for a few pens from distant businesses – 'Parker Insurance Company, Mayfield Road, Buffalo, NY' or 'Oliver, Oliver and Oliver, Princeton, NJ'. And there are matchbooks from risqué-sounding nightclubs – 'BoomBoom Room, Fontainebleau Hotel, Miami' and 'Nihilist

99

Nero's, Caesar's Palace, Las Vegas', and an ashtray with 'Capri Club' written in bamboo letters on its bottle-green bottom. I suppose a real gumshoe would piece all these bits of evidence together and puzzle out an identity, but they just make the bachelor more anonymous to me.

One of the rooms is more unpacked than the others. It is the library. Most of the shelves are filled with books, a few with edges of gilt that flash like whispered secrets. I look at some of the titles. Ray's *Ornithology*. Walpole's *Journals*. *The Herder Book of Fortunes*.

Leonora practices bibliomancy. You open a book at random, read a few lines, and the lines you read are a clue to your future. I open a book entitled *The Roads to Discovery* and read, at random, this line: 'Hope went before them, and the world was wide.'

Leonora said that she could tell that Mr Monroe was unhappy. The bachelor looks depressed. But it could be a look of loneliness, guilt, or secrecy. It's hard to tell. Leonora once told me the story of the little bird. Once upon a time, a man heard the bluebird of happiness singing high in a tree. And the song was so beautiful that he followed the bird as it flew from branch to branch. He followed it until he was clear out of the town in which he lived. And when he finally returned, he discovered that he had been away for over a hundred years, and everyone he had known was gone.

Louis Lewis is knocking on books, trying to find the entrance to a secret staircase. He says all these old houses have them. I go over to a piano near the window. On top of it is a framed black-and-white photo. A man and a woman, young, tanned and white-toothed, sitting at a leather banquette. The man could be the bachelor when he was much younger. I can't tell. Capri Club

1958 is in cursive writing at the bottom left-hand corner. The photo has that naive, unreal quality that only pictures in the fifties have.

The static twitching of the television makes me jumpy. I'm getting burglar nerves. I'm ready to get out of here. I go back to the library to get Louis and just as I enter one of the bookcases slides sideways, revealing a staircase behind it. Louis turns to me, says, '*Voila! Esprit de l'escalier!*' and climbs up it. I follow him. As usual.

The stairway is dark and creepy. A stairway a murderer would use to escape from pursuers after the crime. It leads to the nursery, which is empty, except for a paint tray and a roller and a rumpled sheet on the floor. Someone has painted over the names. But you can see them beneath the new coat of yellow paint, misty dark shapes, like weighted corpses rising to a lake's surface. I wonder if my sister climbed these secret stairs on the day of her death. Maybe she discovered them by accident and surprised someone. Or perhaps someone led the way, and she followed – 'Hurry,' Mathilde whispered to her, pulling on my sister's arm. 'I want to show you something . . .'

Louis and I walk over to the far french windows. They look out on the terrace that my sister might have fallen from. I open them and step out. The wrought-iron rail surrounding the terrace is not very high – my sister could have been sitting upon it. I lean out a little and look up at the roof. It looms at a threateningly sharp diagonal. Then I look over the railing and, even though I'm holding on tight, my stomach lurches. I thought this would scare me more – that I would suddenly feel the haunting presence of my sister, or be overwhelmed and sickened by the scene. When actually, I'm all right. But then I notice that Louis isn't next to me. I turn and see him standing at the threshold of the french doors. His face is completely white. His eyes are large with alarm. 'Louis?' I say to him, and he jumps backward into the nursery. 'It's higher than you think,' he says, wiping sweat from his forehead. I have never seen him frightened by heights before. Actually, I don't remember ever seeing him frightened by anything. But I follow him out of the room and down another staircase, to the second-floor hallway. We open doors on either side. Most are empty, with the still air of closed places. One has a single chair at its center, giving it the look of an execution room.

At the very end of the hall a door stands open. I look inside. It is a bedroom. It must be where the bachelor sleeps. It is full of furniture – bed, dressers, a large wardrobe, wing-back chairs. I walk over to the wardrobe and open it. Suits hang in soldier rows – pinstripes, navy blues, hound's-tooths – and at the far end are uniforms covered in plastic with brass insignias on the lapels. On the wall next to the wardrobe, above a trouser press, is a painting of a boy in a blue suit. He is holding a bird on a length of string in one hand, and a barking dog at bay with the other. Behind him is a pink-clouded sky. I go over to the table next to the bed. On top of it is an overturned bottle of pills. The prescription label is peeled off. I open the drawer of the table. Inside is a round leather case of cufflinks. A Bible. A large gray rock. An ivory letter opener. Some stolen soaps and sewing kits from Hotel Intercontinentals. At the back of the drawer I feel a piece of heavy paper. I pull it out. It is another black-and-white picture. A woman is gazing over the epauletted shoulder of a white-uniformed man, whose back is to the camera. It is the same woman as the one in the photograph on the piano. Who is she? A movie star? I wonder if my sister knew her. Maybe the bachelor disappeared in order to be with her. Maybe she'll arrive here, under cover of night. Or maybe she's already here – he smuggled her in in a rug, she's outside the bedroom door now, a knife between her white teeth, or a heavy lamp held high above her head. I am just about to tell Louis that we should get out of here, fast, when I hear the front door close loudly downstairs.

Louis runs over to the wardrobe and folds himself into the suits, clicking the door behind him. I'm frozen next to the bed, the photograph shaking in my hand. The wardrobe door opens.

'Hide idiot!' Louis hisses through the crack.

'Where?' I ask, helpless.

'Dumbwaiter,' Louis orders.

The dumbwaiter is next to the bedside table. I get in, and shut the door after me. It is dark, and quiet. My knees are bent up to my eyeballs. Then I hear the sound of dishes and glasses below me. Running water. The bachelor must be in the kitchen. With a jolt, the dumbwaiter begins to descend. Damn. I cross my fingers and start praying to God and cursing Louis Lewis. The dumbwaiter moves in slow creaking suspense. I see myself with a bullet hole through my forehead, the bachelor over me, stylishly blowing at the tip of a smoking pistol.

The dumbwaiter makes a jerky stop. I hear ice clinking in a glass. Silverware-stirring sounds. My heart pounding. A telephone ringing. Footsteps. A distant voice saying hello. I shift slightly, trying to decide whether I should attempt to make a break for it, when the dumbwaiter starts moving again. It seems to fall for about an hour, and then it stops. Silence. I lift the door and look out. I am in the basement. I am behind the counter of a bar. I unfold myself out of the dumbwaiter and hop down from the counter. The empty pool is in front of me. It has the otherworldly blue of planets photographed from far away.

I walk over to one of the windows. It is several feet above my head, so I pull some boxes underneath it and climb on top of them. I push at the window and miraculously, it opens. I lift myself out, softly close it, and then run like hell to the apple orchard. When I reach it I fall to the ground on my stomach and look at the house. It seems charged with the tragedy of a trapped Louis Lewis. Just as I am contemplating how to help his escape, a heavy weight falls on top of me, a hand covers my mouth and a wet tongue plunges into my ear. 'I am your Incubus,' Louis whispers moistly, 'come to steal your vestal virtue while you sleep.'

I push him off of me. 'Yeah, well, I'm awake. So go away and be somebody else's bad dream.'

'That's no way to talk to your savior,' Louis says, now lolling beside me. 'I pushed the button that sent you happily home. Now, look what I've purloined.' He pulls a huge beribboned medal from beneath his shirt. He pins it to his pocket. 'I am King of the World. You may now bow and grovel before me.' He holds out his hand to be kissed.

'You know,' I say, slapping his hand away, 'Leonora's right. You *are* a Chapter of Accidents. You have a real problem with stealing.'

'*I* don't have a problem with stealing,' Louis says, stretching out in a patch of sunlight. 'My mother has a problem with stealing. And my psychiatrist has a problem with stealing. But I personally have no problem with stealing at all. In fact, it comes quite naturally to me.' He closes his eyes. 'I am merely making my potential Actual.'

When you look at something, are you seeing what is outside of you, or what is inside of you? Or both? I am looking at a blue book. There is the book outside, in my hands, and the book inside, as a thought in my mind. What is the difference between what you see outside and what you see inside? And do you become what you have seen?

In a way, when the book enters in through my eyes, it comes to life. Because it is suddenly living, in my head, a part of me. But I become the book, because part of me becomes the book just by looking at it. I become mixed up with the book and the book becomes mixed up with me. Everything is outside of you, yet everything is also inside of you. And you can't tell where the outside ends and the inside begins.

APORIA is bewilderment caused by encountering the self-contradiction of paradox. It is an emotion of both irritation and fascination in finding out that you do not know something that you thought you knew.

LIST OF EYES: Monocled eyes, masked eyes, blank statue's eyes, furtive eyes, eyes with tics, Argus eyes, blindfolded eyes, glass eyes, solar eyes on the tombs of Egyptian kings, pince-nezed eyes, X-ray eyes, kohl-eyelined eyes, eyes on the tails of peacocks, eyes on the prows of fishing boats, eyes of the beholder, serious Iowa farmer's eyes, shifty card-player eyes, pious heaven-bound eyes, omniscient eyes.

'I like Alcibiades,' Louis says. We are lying on the side of the hill in his backyard, practicing reclining gracefully, like they did in Greek symposia. Louis is flipping through my copy of Plato's *Dialogues*. Louis says he thinks Plato is an old hippy, and who wants reality when you can have Appearance? However, he likes the idea of the Noble Lie. And he wouldn't mind being a philosopher-king. But the first thing he'd do is have the military-industrial complex manufacture a *deus ex machina* machine for him so he could be plucked out of sticky situations.

Louis also says the reason I am dizzy all the time is because I am a virgin. And, according to Plato, Eros is what thrusts us from the state of 'innocent simpleton' to 'wise sage' – it excites the sybaritic soul to move upward toward the Realm of Forms. 'Ergo, through the power of my priapus,' Louis says, one eyebrow raised, the other lowered, 'I can cure you of your dementia praecox. And via the tremors of amour, a *voyage à Cythère*, lead you to a rapturous vision of the Beautiful. Posthaste.' He snaps his fingers. 'Quicker than that trying Buddhist tedium. Besides,' he sighs, 'Zen people just live in the present because they have no future.'

He edges closer to me. Caresses my left shoulder and nuzzles me under my chin. Before I can push him away, we hear, '*Don't!*' Mrs Lewis is standing below us, at the base of the hill. The single word shouted at us appears to hang sharply above our heads like a knife. Mrs Lewis's face is red, she seems to be trembling with anger. She starts shouting at Louis in French, and he yells back at her in French. I get up and shuffle backward out of the yard, and then run all the way home. I am sure that many minutes will go by before Mrs Lewis and Louis even realize that I have gone.

The librarian spends the quiet part of the afternoon putting cellophane wrappers on new books. As you walk by him you get a whiff of their fresh, eggy smell, the pages crackling like new money. Or he cuts the pages of enormous old books you aren't allowed to take out. He uses these special little silver scissors. He looks like one of those eighteenth-century anatomists dissecting some musty relic stolen from a grave. The book's arthritic spine cracks and the pages fall open in deep bronchial dustbombs. His favorite activity is erasing the underlinings in books. There are little signs everywhere in his pointy reprimand writing. On bookshelves, over the water fountain, even in the bathroom. 'DO NOT WRITE IN BOOKS. SILENCE.' The sound of erasing on a hot afternoon is like the sound of sleep. His eraser is fat and pink, like a tongue. It makes the sound of silencing – shush, shush, shush.

The bachelor is sitting at a table. His back is straight. His hands are palm down on either side of an open book he is reading. He reminds me of one of those Zen monks who sit immobile, calm and composed while an earthquake makes the floor shake and windows break. My grandmother said that Mr Monroe was both impulsive and restrained. If the bachelor is him, it looks like his restrained side has completely taken over. Maybe after he got into some sort of trouble and had to disappear, he decided to mend his ways. He looks like the sort of man who might sit down and compose his own strict code of honor, memorize it and then never waver from it from that day onward. But Louis has a new theory that the bachelor is a 'sleeper', a secret agent who lives a completely normal humdrum life – job, wife, children – until the day he is 'activated' by his nefarious government. Louis says that most people in the film industry have bolshevik leanings and that Mr Monroe might have returned to finish some sort of shady political business here – maybe cover some tracks he left behind.

When the bachelor leaves, I go to his table with my finger-printing kit. Louis says that if his theory is correct, Mr Monroe might have had his fingerprints removed. I brush the table with powder, lay tape on top, lift it carefully and press the tape onto the card. Then I take out a magnifying glass and study the prints. They are made up of loops with pointed arches at the top. I take out a card with my own prints on it and compare the two. Fingerprints are like a red pin stuck on a chart: You are here. But as I study them, they seem more like vacant maps you'd find when you are lost, that locate you nowhere.

HOW TO SPOT A COMMUNIST: Be aware of persons who drive at alternatively low and high rates of speed. Watch for cars that go through yellow lights at intersections and make illegal U-turns. Keep an eagle eye out for those who stop at every filling station on the highway, walk around their car, always looking, and then move on.

'The wise find pleasure in water, the virtuous find pleasure in hills.' My grandmother is always sticking these fortunes in our mailbox for me. She has Chinese food sent to her house all the time. My parents try to get her to stop because the monosodium glutamate is bad for her heart. She's addicted to it, though. She carries little packets of soy sauce around with her and when my parents take her to a fancy restaurant she takes them out of her pocket and pours it all over her lobster thermidor. Sometimes when Leonora has a date, I go over and have chop suey at my grandmother's. She has a big blue Buddha on her dining-room table. He's got this placid smile and his pupils are at the outside corners of his eyes. My grandmother says this is because he is looking outward, toward eternity. I turn him away from me whenever I eat there. Those eyes make me nervous. Eternity can make you nervous. It can make you disappear.

'Now and then you meet someone who stares, whether speaking to you or not, that second too long,' Ms Phillips is saying. 'It is bad manners. Break the habit if you have it.'

Mrs Lewis is my staring partner. We are supposed to be learning by example that being stared at is uncomfortable. I can see myself in Mrs Lewis's pupils, two tiny figures standing on her irises.

'To stare is to overstep your boundaries. It intrudes on another person's privacy. It can be considered as aggressive as a cutting remark, or a slap to the face.'

Leonora says there are charms you can use to ward off the evil eye. And she knew of a man who could pop his eyeballs straight out of their sockets. She said it was a talent that made him feel safe in the dark slums of any city.

Mrs Lewis is suddenly looking at me strangely, as though something about me frightens her. Her eyes are startled, and wary, like someone who hears footsteps behind them on a dark street. Then her pupils go real small, her eyebrows draw together, as though she is angry. The corners of her mouth pull down briefly. She presses the back of her hand to her forehead, tilts her head back and closes her eyes. Then she looks at me again. 'You are wearing shadow, *non?*' She wets a finger and runs it under my brow bone. 'Cosmetics, on a girl your age, looks ridickluss,' she says sharply, and then stands up and leaves the room. When she returns, she has a wet paper towel pressed to the back of her neck. 'It is so hot,' she complains, and then takes my long hair in her hand and lifts it off my nape. I feel a cool breeze run along the back of my neck. It makes me shiver slightly. Mrs Lewis knots my hair up in a twist. 'Maybe you should cut this off,' she says. 'It doesn't suit you. There is too much of it.' She lets my hair drop abruptly, as if she is disgusted by it. I feel a pain in my head and my stomach at the same time. I've always been complimented on my hair. In fact, I think it is the one thing about me that is actually more attractive than my sister.

*

My sister Haddie's eyes were hazel, and changed color according to her mood. She tended to incline her head toward her left shoulder when listening to you. She would stand on one leg and wind the other around it. She tended to sit on the top stair and sulk. She wanted to be a warrior, after the fashion of Alexander the Great, and slept with a dagger under her pillow. She enjoyed asking people: 'What if the entire world was just first created in this very last instant?' None of this may be true.

There is an abandoned railway station in the right corner of the large field you have to cross to get into town. The bachelor is sitting on a warm bench outside it. He sits upright, his knees at hypotenuse Abe Lincoln angles to the ground. Louis and I climb through one of the station's broken windows and watch him from behind one of the columns. I can see his profile. He stares at the tracks, a muscle in his jaw twitches. He seems almost in a trance. As though he is willing a train to arrive. Then he takes a small drawstring bag, a notebook and a pen out of his inside jacket pocket. He shakes the bag, then opens it, and takes out three stones, one at a time, and lays them down on the ground in front of him. He opens his notebook, and reads, then writes something down. He looks at what he has written for several minutes, then rips the page out, crumples it up. Picks up the stones and puts them back in the bag, throws the paper in a waste bin near the bench and walks off toward town. Before following him, Louis and I take the crumpled piece of paper out of the garbage. On it, in capital letters, are the words – LOSS. CHANGE. JOY.

'Apollo! Apollo!' Cassandra was always lamenting. 'Damned, damned! O misery, misery!' She was given the powers of prophecy by Apollo, but then doomed to be disbelieved by everyone because she would not give him love back in return. She was carried off from Troy by Agamemnon, which was probably a relief to the Trojans, since after being sacked and pillaged they hardly needed Cassandra drooping around and moaning 'I told you so' about that wooden horse. And once she arrived at Agamemnon's home in Argos she saw visions of nets, and roasted human flesh and blood dripping from the walls of the palace. 'Where is this you have brought me?' she cried. 'For this house here a choir never deserts, chanting together of chance ill-destiny.'

Night falls / The bridge becomes / The stream. Haikus punctuate the space between things so you can see chi – the breath of heaven. But they also show how the edges of a crow and an autumn night, azaleas and a cuckoo's cry, loneliness and a well, bells and dusk, melons and moonlight, shiver and shimmer and in the final line you see how the space between them was just a dream.

Aristotle invented the syllogism, which is the cornerstone of all logic, and states that if A is A, then A is not not-A, and everything is either A or not-A. The harmonious balance between opposites is the Golden Mean. Haikus are a little like syllogisms. They are three lines long and they describe the 'thusness' of things by taking a leap from 'if' to 'then', from 'since' to 'therefore' to the sameness beyond difference.

It reminds me of the time Louis and I found a couple of huge wood spiders and sealed them tight in my terrarium. The next day I looked to see how they were doing, thinking I would probably let them out. But they were gone. One long brown leg was left. And a wisp of webbing in the corner. The terrarium was still sealed tight as a drum. I asked my parents and Leonora if they had let the spiders out. They hadn't. My first thought was that they ate each other. Which is, of course, impossible. Spiders can't eat each other and disappear without a trace. The more I thought about it the more frighteningly odd it seemed. The whole situation had the logic of a nursery rhyme. Of wide-open maybe spaces, where there is lots of real in the not-real, and not-real in the real.

I checked the *Arabian Nights* out of the library the other day. I thought since it was found with my sister when she died, that maybe there would be some clues in it about her death. My favorite story that I've read is about this man who dreams he will find a fortune in a distant land. He undertakes a long and difficult journey to the place of which he dreamed, and falls asleep on a patio. He is awoken by a man who asks him what he is doing there. And when he tells this man about his dream, the man laughs, and says that there is no truth to such a dream, because he has dreamed three times of a courtyard with a fountain at its center. And underneath the fountain is buried a treasure, but it is nonsense – he has never found such a courtyard. He tells the traveler to forget about his dream and to go home. But the traveler recognizes in the man's description of the courtyard that of his own, situated behind his own home. So he returns, digs under his fountain and finds riches beyond his wildest dreams.

Aristotle said a likely impossibility is always preferable to an unconvincing possibility.

Louis Lewis and I were going to dissect the brain of this dead squirrel we found, but rigor mortis made its body bowl-shaped, and hard to get a grip on, so instead we've decided to sacrifice it to the gods. We've gilded its stripes with gold paint and we've sprinkled the altar with gold glitter and thyme. We've also placed some old toys around the squirrel – a Mr Potato Head, Lite Brite, GI Joe and Malibu Barbie in an amorous embrace – because we are mourning our childhood and placing all childish things at the shrine of Artemis. My head is garlanded with a ring of dandelions. I have anointed myself with oil. I scream as loud as I can. It's called 'ololuge'. It's what Greek women did at sacrifices.

'Chill out, Haddie,' Louis says to me as he tries to light the left paw of the squirrel. We are pretending it is the fat thigh of a white she-goat. 'You don't want to deafen the gods. You want them to be able to hear our requests of them.' He lights a match to a stiff whisker.

'First you've got to rip out its heart and liver and eat them,' I tell him. 'It's called "sparagmos".'

'*You* eat its fucking heart and liver,' Louis mumbles. 'But don't blame me if you end up with some feral, lupine illness.' I was surprised at how amenable Louis was to this sacrifice idea. But then I'd forgotten that he's really into fire. He used to start fires all over the neighborhood. Sometimes, if I couldn't find him, I'd just look for smoke on the horizon. Louis gave up being a pyromaniac when he became a thief.

'I can't eat anything earthly,' I say, waving my branch of laurel. 'I only inhale the smoke and drink the water of the sacred spring. Otherwise I won't be able to tell our futures.' I close my eyes and try to go into a trance. In order to tell oracles, I think you are supposed to sit in a cave, but there aren't any caves in Avon Heights, so our garage will have to do. I wonder if there are any guardian nymphs of the garage.

We are also drinking milk and honey, the ambrosial nectar of the gods. 'This doesn't taste too heavenly,' I say, tasting mine.

'It is made from the lactation of doe-eyed creatures considered holy in the East and of the love potion made from the quivering sex organs of flowers and the intricate dance of treacherous insects in homage to their sovereign queen. Of course it's celestial,' Louis says and gulps some of his, gags, and throws the cup and its contents over his left shoulder. 'Okay, get ready to gnash your teeth and rend your tunic.' The tail of the squirrel is starting to smolder.

'Great!' I yell. 'Now dance around the altar with glad paean cries!'

Louis hula-moves around the altar, fanning the smoking tail and singing: 'A Hoki Hoki Hoki Lau . . . We're going to the Hoki Lau . . . Hula hula maiden, silvery moon, Paradise now at the Hoki Lau . . .'

I close my eyes and try to summon the deepest powers of the earth. I don't think I'm quite as close to nature as Aristotle. For instance, I've never seen salacious birds. Or a fish bursting asunder from eating too much. Or a hummingbird flying into into someone's forehead and boring a hole into their brain. Louis is always saying we should get back to our limbic system and think fierce wild animal thoughts. He usually makes this point during our country club's junior women's tennis championship, but I think it might be a good idea all round. For instance, I really enjoy all my vestigial reflexes. My favorites are yawning and sneezing. And there is a real sexy frisson to a shudder. I guess I like anything that's involuntary – where you don't have the responsibility of making a decision. So maybe I have to go back to my limbic system to summon the deep powers of the earth, since that's where all the things you've forgotten you know live.

I keep my eyes closed and rock slightly. It feels as though I am falling into a deep abyss. It is a bit hard to breathe. Maybe I've entered into trilobite time, before I had lungs. Suddenly I'm lifted up and carried away. I must be in a trance of ecstasy. Then I feel the hard thud of the ground. I open my eyes, and start coughing so hard I almost retch. I am lying in the grass outside our garage, from which billows of smoke are now rolling. Louis is collapsed, coughing, next to me. I hear a siren wailing in the distance.

'Did you meet that movie star who came and visited the Monroes?' I ask my grandmother.

'Which one?' my grandmother asks. 'Mr Monroe entertained a lot of people . . .'

'Emmalou de Cherraglio.'

My grandmother lifts her eyebrow. Then sighs. 'Yes,' she says in amused tone, 'it was an interesting evening. Actually, your sister took the spotlight from her, which did not please Ms de Cherraglio – not at all. Mr Monroe had suggested your sister take elocution lessons. And he was quite proud of her progress. So he had her give a recitation for our visiting movie star.' My grandmother laughs. 'I can still remember some of the lines – "O what can ail thee, knight-at-arms? Alone and palely loitering?" ' My grandmother's 'l's trill dramatically. 'Mr Monroe sat in an armchair, his elbows on his knees, his fingers making a steeple under his chin, listening raptly to every word. Ms de Cherraglio did not, however, obtain the same pleasure from the performance. She had an unusual sort of half-smile on her face.' My grandmother purses her lips in a line, sharp as a paper cut. 'And she kept crossing and uncrossing her legs as though she was in dire need of the ladies' room – at one point she even started drumming her fingers on the armrest. But at the end of the performance she was lavish in her praise, and kissed her fingertips and tossed them toward your sister. I'm sure she wished blown kisses could contain poison.'

'So how did the evening end?'

'I left very soon after. But as I was getting my wrap from the closet, I saw Mr Monroe and the starlet through an open door that led to the kitchen. I couldn't hear what they were saying, but through their movements I could tell they were in the midst of a fierce argument.'

'Do you think they were having an affair?'

'That could be possible. But it had been rumored that Ms de Cherraglio was often seen in the company of, oh I forget his name, but a man high up in the Mafia – if you can use such terms of scale with that organization. Apparently this man had heavily financed one of Mr Monroe's movies and, in recompense, wanted Ms de Cherraglio to be placed in some starring roles.'

'So did you see the outcome of their fight?'

'No. Not that I would have remained to eavesdrop, on any account. But just as I was turning to leave, Mrs Lewis rushed past me, into the kitchen, shutting the door closed behind her.'

'One should never assume one knows who one is,' Ms Phillips says. 'This is a world of millions of faces and one should exclude the possibility of embarrassment on another's part for not recognizing you, by always introducing yourself first.'

This reminds me of a time, a few months ago, when I went to New York City with my grandmother, and as we were walking down Fifth Avenue, my grandmother squeezed my hand and said to me: 'Look at all the faces.' It was around five o'clock and there were thousands of people on the sidewalks. And all of a sudden, my head went staticky from all those faces entering it, and I felt limp, and fainted in the middle of the street.

Yesterday, before our meditation, my grandmother asked me the question: 'What was your original face before your parents were born?' Then we sat on cushions, backs straight, legs crossed, left hands cupped in right and stared at a white wall. In front of me were two specks of black, that I started seeing as eyes, and then every second or so a different face would appear, with the specks as their pupils – hundreds of faces of people I didn't know, one after the other. And I thought that we must remember every single face we have ever seen, that there must be thousands of faces inside our heads that we aren't even aware of, because how else would we recognize the familiar face of a stranger?

'The basic problem of etiquette is that there is yourself, and there are others,' Mrs Lewis is saying. 'And you must know who you are, where your bounds of polite civility lie, and not let others cross them.'

Louis told me '*hexagone*' means the six-sided shape of France. But it also means the impenetrability of its citizens. How they are placed apart from the rest of the world by their moody, exotic peculiarities – mysterious, indefinable, *insolite*.

The bright sun coming in through the high windows makes Mrs Lewis's pupils huge. She almost looks cross-eyed. Like I-Ching, the Siamese cat that my grandmother used to have. After my grandmother told me about samsara – the succession of rebirth of all things – I used to look intensely into I-Ching's eyes and say to him, 'Who are you *really*?' and every time he would arch his back, bush out his tail and go flying out of the room. I get the feeling if you asked Mrs Lewis that same question, while looking deep into her eyes, she might have the same skittish-cat reaction.

*

One out of every 1000 strangers you encounter at random will have killed someone. 'My theory is that everyone is a potential murderer,' said Robert Walker to Farley Granger in *Strangers on a Train*. Louis and I are shadowing the bachelor down our street. All the houses are large and sunken in among elms and maples. They seem to have some sort of communion, there is something pachydermish about them. If they were alive they would be slow-moving and powerful, and unaware of what was scurrying about at their feet. The bachelor walks very slowly and methodically, as if he is counting his steps, or working out a story problem in math full of unknown x and y variables. People who purposefully 'go missing' will often change their gait. This is actually quite difficult to achieve and an orthopedic lift or a strategically placed thumbtack, pushed point down into the sole of the shoe, affects the change better than could hours of practiced walking.

The bachelor stops and pulls a leaf from the tree in front of Miss Dimmer's house. She has hair the color of flat champagne and wears silk robes out in her grape arbor all day and is pretty crazy – for instance, she can't stand the word 'succulence' and as kids Louis and I used to hide under her bushes and chant 'succulence, succulence' until she banged open her shutters and flung wineglasses of water out at us. The bachelor examines the leaf from her tree, pulls all the green flesh from it, and then holds its veined outline up to the sun as if he is reading a symbol. Then he drops it and walks on.

Next to Miss Dimmer's is Mr Lodge's house. He is old as Methuselah and lives with his white-uniformed nurse, crisp as an aspirin. As we pass by we can hear Mr Lodge calling to his nurse. It sounds like a crow calling in a rooky wood. Mr Lodge's house sits up on a slight incline off the road. All the kids say that he has a poisonous garden, that all the plants in it are toxic –

jimsonweed, nightshade, oleander, red sage, rhododendron. Belladonna is Italian for 'beautiful woman'. It has pale-blue flowers from June to September. All parts of this plant are deadly — roots, leaves, berries. One of the symptoms of belladonna poisoning is rapid heart rate. It has been reported that one can hear the victim's heartbeart from quite a distance away. If you give this poison to your victim in small doses, they will appear to have a wasting disease that cannot be properly diagnosed. Sometimes, rather than dying of the poison, the victim may have an accident, such as a fall, brought about by their enfeebled condition.

The bachelor walks past Mr Karanovsky's. He escaped from Russia during the Revolution, and the diamonds hidden in his underpants deflected the bolsheviks' bullets. He has a huge temper and lots of girlfriends. He's always making suicide pacts with them. But then the girlfriend calls the hospital and the ambulance arrives and they emerge from the house, blinking in the siren lights like celebrities arriving at an opening, and fall in sleeping-pill swoons upon the stretchers.

The bachelor pauses outside the gates of Mr Mastrioni's house. Everyone says that he works for the Mafia and his son told our class that they bury their victims face down so they can't haunt the killers, but he might have just said this to get popular. Maybe Mr Mastrioni was Emmalou de Cherraglio's boyfriend. The bachelor leans against the gate, takes off one of his shoes and taps out a small stone. Could this perhaps be a signal to someone waiting behind a window? If it was, the bachelor doesn't wait for an answer in return, but moves on down the street.

My grandmother said that no one really knew Mr Monroe. Where he came from. Maybe Montgomery Monroe wasn't his real name. Maybe he had disappeared before. People who fake their deaths and change their identities usually keep moving along, never staying long in one town. They suffer from an extreme sense of loneliness because they cannot attach themselves to or remain in one place.

At the end of the road, the bachelor sits on a whitewashed rock. He takes off his black jacket and folds it across his lap. There are sweat stains under his armpits. He runs a finger under his collar to loosen it, and then takes his notebook and pen out of his pocket and writes a few lines. He writes very quickly, then jabs a full stop. He rubs his earlobe between thumb and forefinger, gazing absently at the sky. He starts tapping his foot, as if to a song. There are long spaces between the taps, so it must be a slow song, maybe a slow song full of worrying notes, his foot taps matching the ending beats of a lost lover's name. Plato said that your true being can be revealed in the way you love, and whomsoever you choose to love.

Mrs Lewis hands me a Kleenex from her purse to wipe the lipstick off my mouth that I just learned to put on properly in Charm School. The Kleenex smells of lilac, Chanel, cigarettes. We are in the jewelry section of Higbee's department store. Mrs Lewis buys four gold chains. 'No box,' she says, and fastens each one around her neck.

Mr Lewis met Mrs Lewis in France. He was there on business. They met at a dinner of a mutual friend, were seated next to each other, got along well despite some language difficulties, he called her the next day blah, blah, blah, boring schmoring. I see her pulled down the Champs Elysées by two large and out-of-control poodles, one dyed pastel pink, the other blue. Mr Lewis is sitting outside a café, sketching a cathedral, a beret set rakishly over one eye. Out of the other eye he sees a pastel storm cloud, followed by an elegantly tapering ankle. '*Mon Dieu*!' Mrs Lewis cries. '*Zut alors*!' Mr Lewis gulps down his *citron pressé* in a shot and chases after the runaway poodle train. There is a tense moment when the poodles veer dangerously right, about to cross in front of a truck *au pain*, but Mr Lewis comes up behind them just in time, grabs the reins of the leashes from Mrs Lewis's fashionable mauve-gloved hands. 'Whoah little doggies!' he shouts. 'Naughty Booboo!' Mrs Lewis chides. 'Naughty Bonbon!' Then she looks up into Mr Lewis's wild blue yonder eyes. They kiss in the middle of the wide boulevard, Mrs Lewis's leg kicking up chic behind her.

Mrs Lewis grabs my hand when we cross Euclid Avenue to get to the car. Her rings dig into my palm. She wears rings on her pinky and on her middle finger – very savoir-faire and European. People are their faces, bodies, belongings. I try to picture Mrs Lewis with different color hair, wider hips, orange shag carpeting, and she dissolves like sugar. When you turn the word belongings inside out it becomes longing to be.

Sometimes when I look at something, a tree for example, I'll say 'black-and-white photograph', 'cartoon', 'oil painting', 'mosaic', and the tree is washed of its color, then flattens out into imaginary shapes, then thickens at the edges into impasto strokes, and finally hardens into a thousand pieces of glinting glass. When I say 'abstract' the tree turns into a pattern of arcs and lines.

The Oracle at Delphi said that Socrates was the wisest person in the world, but his daemon told him not to believe it. If you were the wisest person in the world, how would a tree look to you? You might see some of the eternal, unchanging truth it is partaking in. So within this one tree in front of me – the one next to the Monroe house, that my sister could have fallen from – I might see all the trees that have ever been – Sumerian date palms and olive trees in sacred groves and the apple tree in the Garden of Eden and the Buddha's bodhi tree and pine trees in Northern forests and oak trees filled with oracles and the Daphne-turned-laurel tree and orange trees in pots in palaces and the Yggdrasil tree and jungle trees and frontier trees and birch trees with their limbs like magic wands – all trees throughout space and time merged into one Tree.

All of a sudden I am about a hundred feet above myself, looking down. I am a little black dot on the ground. Like those specks that are supposed to be islands in the middle of blue oceans on globes. And then I fall until I hit the black dot, and in a flash of light I am back down on the ground.

HOW TO LOSE ALL SENSE OF TIME AND SPACE: Take something extremely cold, an ice cube for example, and touch it to the hollow behind your right knee, two and a half inches above the axial line. This will release reflexes which give you the illusion you are visionary. Alternatively, place the ice cube against your glabella – the space between your eyes, where the pineal gland, or third eye resides. Drill a small hole into your skull near the left temple. Dampen a wax string and snort it up through a nostril. Inhale said string with enough velocity to fish out its other end from your mouth. With both ends in hand, move the string backward and forward. Imagine yourself traveling toward a horizon of pure light. This is the light of the mind.

Numbers are infinite. And the squares of numbers are infinite. The number of squares of numbers are not less than the totality of all numbers, nor vice versa. Thus, on the infinite scale, the ideas of greater than, less than, and equal become meaningless.

ARITHOMANIA is the compulsive desire to count. I can understand how a person could get carried away with it. It's got that one-two-three 'Johnny Comes Marching Home' rhythm that makes you feel as though you are getting somewhere. A row of numbers seem to point toward the future. And they figure a lot in fortunetelling. The Greeks thought that numbers made up this timeless order beneath the surface confusion of the world. So the world was like a huge paint-by-number painting, and if you could scratch off all the colors you would see the numbers underneath. Murmuring multiplication tables, doing clandestine divisions, secret subtractions.

Numbers are the ultimate adjectives. When you put a number in front of something it really defines it. One house, one man stands alone, one life to give, one-liner, one-night stand, one-horse town, a one-track mind, two in a bush, two shakes of a lamb's tail, two peas in a pod, three Wise Men, three blind mice, three wishes, three brothers setting out to seek their fortune, four cardinal points, four elements, take five, five senses, sixth sense, the seven gates of Thebes, the seven deadly sins, seventh heaven, behind the eight-ball, nine years of war, nine orders of angels, nine lives of cats, nine planets in space, nine tollings of the bell, the whole nine yards, ten commandments, ten plagues of Egypt, twelve signs of the zodiac, the thirteenth floor, sweet sixteen, twenty-three skidoo, twenty-four hours, thirty-nine steps, forty thieves, sixty miles per hour, one hundred bottles of beer on the wall, 153 fishes, 360 degrees, 365 days, 1000 springs, 1001 nights, the 64,000-dollar question. One defines things the most though. One Acropolis. One planet Mars. One Grand Canyon. One Plato. One Aristotle. One God.

123

Leonora takes a stone out of her pocket and rubs its surface with her thumbs. It is one of her pondering rocks. She says she's got bucketfuls in her bedroom at home. Each rock contains thoughts you want to remember. And you get the rock to recollect them for you by stirring warm circles over it with your thumbs. Leonora gets a big smile on her face. 'Uh-huh, I recall this one now.' She opens one eye and looks at me with it. 'But you're too close to the cradle for me to be telling you about it,' she says, and clamps her jaw shut. Her false teeth rattle inside her mouth like a closet full of skeletons. 'You can use these to disremember too.' She holds the rock up to the light as if searching for thoughts caught in the crevices. 'If there is something you need to forget, you throw the stone in deep water.' She puts the rock back in her pocket. 'I knew a man who remembered every single thing he saw, heard and read. Every Thing. It made his head ache and his body heavy. So he started to throw his memories away, one stone at a time, off the end of a dock every day. It made all the fish start jumping.'

I go out and wander along the stream. I find stones that have singular shapes, and then rub my thumbs on them, thinking of embarrassing experiences that periodically jab me like a stitch in my side. Then I walk along the stream to the Bottomless Lake. I skim the stones and watch them skip before they disappear in ripples of water. Leonora said you throw coins in water as well, because when you wish and forget you want to untangle all the twists and turns in your trip up Salt River to Long Gone. The circles surrounding the thrown stones make me think of those stories in the *Arabian Nights*. I wonder whether my sister liked that same story about the treasure under the man's own court-yard. We have a courtyard. Maybe she hid something there.

Something secret. Something that would reveal to me a reason for why she died.

My grandmother asks me: 'A flag moves. What moves, the flag, or the wind?'

'Ethel Merman,' I answer. Lots of times, when I ask my grandmother a question, she'll give me this off-the-wall fruit-loops answer. She says she does it to transcend logic and make me realize the unreality of the world.

'No,' she says, looking at me like I'm demented. 'Neither the flag nor the wind moves. The mind moves.'

I've been walking around the courtyard, trying to figure out where my sister would bury something. We don't have a fountain, so that is ruled out. First, I examined each brick, to see if any looked loose, or tampered with. But they all look pretty much the same. Besides, at least fourteen years have passed. I try to think of what other clues there are in the story. There is a sundial, and a tree. We don't have a sundial, but there is a tree at the courtyard's center, surrounded by bricks in a sunlike pattern. I pull up each of these bricks, and then dig under them with a garden spade, but there is nothing but dark earth the color of freshly ground coffee, and then a layer of hard gray clay. Then I think of the courtyard as a grid, or a graph. Perhaps she plotted some magic number combination upon it. But the possibilities are endless. The sun beats down upon my head. Small pieces of mica in the bricks sparkle, they seem to be staring at me, with thousands of eyes, then the bricks appear to get larger and larger, and then smaller and smaller, they pound softly, then louder and louder, the lines of the design are black strings strumming shrill treble notes, I hear 'Haddie, Haddie' murmuring, low and throaty – I back away from them and fall backward down upon the grass.

'How do you search for something, Socrates, when you have no idea whatsoever it is? What sort of unknown somewhat will you propose as the object of your search? And if you are lucky enough to come across the object of your search, how will you know it is that unknown somewhat?'

What does it feel like to forget? The Asphodel Fields is a place where people who have forgotten everything wander aimlessly for eternity. I'm standing in front of a glass case at the library. There are Indian-head nickels and Mrs Maddie Cohasset's widow's ring, which is onyx and opened partway to show the piece of hair off her husband's head who was killed in the Civil War, and also an indentured servant's contract with the red seal of the king that looks like melted red licorice. And there's a big soup tureen, with painted Chinese pagodas and trees and people walking over bridges and a typewritten card under it that says: 'This soup tureen was used in the service of luncheon to Mrs Mamie Eisenhower who visited Avon Heights in 1965.' All the things encased inside have that sunken-ship grandeur of something forgotten and then remembered. One of the poems in a poetry book I had started with the line: 'I remember I remember the house where I was born . . .' Which sounds like a magic incantation to bring back memories.

I close my eyes and chant the line and try to remember my very first memory. I see the banister of a staircase. The leg of a table. The picture is clear, and then it dissolves. It reminds me of those picture games. There is a drawing, with scratchy marks itching darkly around objects, inky and full of unseen eyes. Because hidden within the drawing are all sorts of things you can't see right away – an owl in the door, a violin in the trunk of a tree, a fish in a chimney, an ax in the road. When you first look at the picture all you see is a simple drawing of a house and a tree and a road, but slowly, magically, you see the hidden objects – they rise up out of the drawing like jellyfish floating to the surface of the sea before a storm.

'Do you feel okay?' someone drawls next to me. I open my eyes. It is the bachelor. My heart pounds.

'Yes. I'm fine,' I manage to say.

'I just thought you might be ill . . .' He puts a large hand on my shoulder.

'No . . . I was only trying to see what it feels like to forget.'

'And what does it feel like?' His one eye squints, as though we are standing in bright light.

'Like losing something. Like you misplaced something and you're looking for it without the light on . . .'

'Yes. Yes. I agree.' He nods his head. 'Remembering things. And reading. They can sometimes make you feel the same way. Like you've lost something.' He winks his squinting eye at me. Then he strolls on out of the library.

A door is a door. Something being most true at the cost of saying nothing. If I stand in front of that locked door on the second floor for long enough, I start to get a prickle at the back of my neck. Then I hear a single note repeating itself inside my head, first at a slow tempo, but that gets louder and faster, ascending the scale. All is still. There is the stillness of the lock. The stillness of the wall. Still floor. The stillness of the door. Why is it that stillness can be so frightening? In horror movies the stillness is always more frightening than the attack.

*

My head is humming and my hands are shaking. It cannot be true. I cannot believe it. It does not seem possible. I stare at the photo in the encyclopedia. I blink my eyes several times. But it is him. It is a photograph of the bachelor. I recognized him immediately. The same square jaw, the same squinting eye, the same slightly lopsided smile. 'Remembering things, and reading . . .' he had said in the library, 'can make you feel the same way. As though you've lost something.' I look through the window of our study at the Monroe house across the street. Then down at the photo in the encyclopedia. It cannot be possible that he can simultaneously exist in the encyclopedia and live in the Monroe house. They are in two different realms.

I found him, by accident, under 'Astronaut'. In between the entries 'Astrology' and 'Astronomy'. He is one of the first men to have landed on the moon. He was born in 1935 in Virginia. He attended Annapolis and MIT. He married his high-school sweetheart. There is a second picture of him, standing in his space suit, the moon reflected in the glass of his helmet. These are some of the adjectives they use to describe the astronauts: extremely intelligent, supremely competent, mentally stable, physically fit, highly courageous, moral, patriotic. A man's character being his destiny, said Heraclitus. I think of him walking the roads of our town. It's as strange as those sightings of kangaroos loose on some flat field in Kansas.

He was up so high that the blue of the daytime sky turned to black. So high that he escaped the earth's pull on his body. So high up that he saw the whole of the earth, small and round, against the endless dark of space. I wonder if afterwards everything down here seemed a little unreal. He has this slightly convalescent quality to him, like someone recovering from a long and serious illness; he walks as though his head is clouded – he seems out of touch, in a sort of trance. 'Remembering things can make you feel the same way,' he had said. What memory has made him feel a loss? Nostalgia is a longing for something far away and long ago. He seems sad, lonely, even homesick. In a sense, it is as if he has not fully *returned*.

ANAGOGIC is the experience of a truth one already knows.

I am in the ravine behind the Monroe house. I see the bachelor there. From far away I thought he was Pan. I move from tree to tree, remembering the Indian steps I used when I was younger. When I am opposite him, a few yards away, I stop. His head is bowed. He reminds me of one of those lonely figures in old pen-and-ink drawings, standing at the edge of an abyss, looking down, and you can't see what he's looking at because the drawing stops short of his view. I have actually been looking for him; I wanted to see him in person in order to be certain, to have absolute confirmation and proof. But I didn't expect to find him here. I try to match his name to him. His name seems bigger than him, apart from him. The fame of his name. But then, abruptly, it fits like a key in a lock, and I can feel his aura, the space and the light surrounding him is suddenly glossy and important. The Greek heroes chose fame, rather than happiness. They knew that you could rarely have both.

I wonder what it feels like to pass over into immortality – do you sense yourself crossing over a line, from the finite to the infinite? And does that crossing feel like a step into endless, bottomless space? The tree above the bachelor sways its branches. The sun straining through the branches creates shadows over his head. I realize he is praying.

PART III

THE MEDIEVAL AGE

'Are you following me?' The bachelor's eyes are revolving doors, from curious to sad and back to curious again. My heart jumps up into my head and whirls around like a wild bird.

'Don't be afraid, sweetheart. It's just that I keep seeing something out of the corner of my eye and I think it's you.' He smiles.

'I saw you in the book.' I push my hair behind my ears. All I want to do is run, run, run, but I want to stay, too.

'Book?' He squints one eye, tilts his head to one side. 'What book?'

'The encyclopedia.' A plane passes overhead and we both watch the thin, neck-arching line it makes across the clear blue sky. The bachelor looks down at his hands, as if they don't belong to him. He puts them in his pockets. Then he takes a pack of chewing gum out of one and holds it out to me. I shake my head and he slowly pulls out a stick, unwraps it, puts it in his mouth. He chews in silence, and gazes at a mirage that dances in a dip in the road.

I think of him praying. I think of his hands – how they were clasped together. Some African tribe believes that hands have a separate soul from the body. I try to see traces of faith in his face. His jaw clenches and unclenches. I once saw a signpost in the Tennessee mountains. It said: 'Jesus Is Coming Soon.'

'Does anyone else know about me? Who I am? From the encyclopedia?'

'No.'

'Would you mind keeping it a secret? My name? Just between you and me?' He stares at me in a way that makes me feel uncomfortable. His name fills my head and pounds like a cold headache.

'No,' I say. 'I mean, yes, I'll keep it a secret.'

'People expect things.' He looks away. Then back at me. 'Have you ever heard of the Indian rope trick?' He is suddenly relaxed, almost chatty. 'A conjurer throws a rope up in the air and then climbs up it. He pulls the rope up after him and disappears.' He chews his gum, thinking. 'Vanishes into thin air.' He snaps his fingers. Then he turns and walks back to his house. I watch him as he crosses his yard, unlocks his door and steps inside. His name seems like something that belongs to another world. I think of those huge stones that stand alone in the middle of fields, or islands. And no one knows how they got there, or what they could possibly mean.

It is so very strange that the bachelor is trying to conceal his identity. But a different identity from the one Louis and I thought he was trying to conceal.

Astronaut is Greek for 'sailor to the stars'. When you look out at the farthest visible star, you are seeing four billion years into the past. Because the light from that star has been traveling, for all those years, at 186,000 miles per second, to reach you.

*

My grandmother told me about a Chinese painter who opened a little door in the mural he had just completed, entered through it, closed it after him, and was never seen again.

This is one of the koans my grandmother has asked me to puzzle out: What was your name before your parents were born?

Names are like doors. They link your inside to your outside. The gods used to have secret names and, if you could find them out, you had power over them. By reciting the incantation of their name, you could conjure them up. Leonora says this is because your name is the only part of you that *remains*.

'So why doesn't God have a name?' I ask her.

'Because, sweetie,' she answers, 'He doesn't need know *who* He is. He just *is*.'

Some of the most memorable lines in movies are when a person tells everyone their name: 'I'm Spartacus! I'm Spartacus! I'm Spartacus!' 'I am Heathcliff.' 'Call me Shane.' 'Call me Lola.' 'It took more than one man to change my name to Shanghai Lily.' 'My friends call me Renjo – nickname I had as a kid – right name's Henry.' 'Johnny is such a hard name to remember and so easy to forget.' 'Ma'am, I sure like that name – Clementine.' 'I'm Mimi – I'm dying.' 'Nosferatu rings like the cry of a bird of prey – never speak it aloud.'

I wonder if the bachelor finds it hard to hold his name within himself. And if sometimes it grows huge and round within his throat, half choking him like a hairball, and in a crazy rage he needs to shout it out. I can see him, standing at the edge of a Western canyon at night, howling his name out to the huge, dark sky, the last echoes of it still returning to where he stood, long after he is back in his car, driving in the opposite direction down the highway. And, if, like light, sound never ends, perhaps it is still moving in crested waves toward the farthest star.

AUGUSTINE wrote the *Confessions*, in which he recounts the story of his restless youth and his conversion to Christianity, at which point he entered his inward self and beheld a spiritual sun, illuminated by God. Augustine wrote that in order to understand, we must first believe – a relationship with God based on faith and prayer is more important than an intellectual encounter with ideas. For Augustine, Logos was not an impersonal mind, but a divinely personal Word – thus the most real is not what is seen in this world, but that which is invisible, and outside time, eternal.

The moon weighs eighty-one quintillion tons. It hangs 240,000 miles above us, moving at 1000 miles per hour, with no visible means of support.

I looked up 'gravity' in the dictionary. It is the pull on all bodies in the earth's sphere toward the earth's center. But we can't see it. It is an invisible attraction at a distance. Actually, I don't think anyone is completely clear what exactly it is. The Hindus thought that the earth was supported by an elephant that was standing on a tortoise, which in turn was floating in a sea contained in some sort of vessel. We can only see within a certain spectrum of light. Our eyes can see just according to certain wavelengths, so a lot of the world is invisible to us. There could be fireworks going on in the sky all day that we aren't aware of. Maybe the elephant and tortoise and the vessel full of sea water are on different wavelengths, invisible to us, like gravity.

Leonora says that she won't tell our parents about the fire in the garage if we come to the Cathedral of Tomorrow with her and pray for forgiveness. Louis Lewis is slouched in the back seat of Leonora's green hornet with a look of eternal suffering. He could learn something from the Christian martyr, Archbishop Vladimir, who had his clothes stripped off by seamen and was beaten and then showered with taunts and insults. Or the martyrs of Lyon who, after whips, many beasts and the iron chair, were thrown into a net and cast before a bull.

I've gone to the Cathedral of Tomorrow with Leonora before. Everyone there has that 'Where will *You* Spend Eternity' look in their eyes. And the music from the huge organ cartwheels around the room, and the preacher's voice boomerangs off the walls, and the whole congregation stampedes down the aisle like it is one big exclamation mark at the end of Amen. Even the building, with its turrets and steeples and buttresses, is shaped like one big Alleluia.

We pull into the parking lot and join the crowd filing into the church. Most of the ladies wear hats with plastic flowers and dresses with matching gloves. Day turns to night once we are inside the dark amphitheater. 'In the middle of the week I found myself in a dark temple where logic was lost,' Louis mumbles.

There is a quiz show excitement about the place. The choir is already singing. 'Will Thy will be unbroken?' the male choristers ask. 'By and by, Lord, by and by,' roll the answers of the women. 'There's a better home a'waiting,' the men yell to the ceiling. 'In the sky, Lord, in the sky.' The women raise their hands and swing their big boom-boom hips.

We find a seat. The place is full. 'Spirit-O-Rama.' Louis gives a low whistle. The preacher comes out onto the big stage. He walks back and forth along its edge like a caged animal. 'I talked to the Lord last night!' he yells into his microphone. 'Sweet Jesus.' The lady next to Louis sighs and slaps her thighs. 'And the Lord, he told me I have to save someone today! Is there someone in need of saving out there?' the preacher asks. 'Yes, Lord!' the whole crowd booms. 'Shall we gather at the river?' the preacher asks. 'Yes, we shall gather at the river,' the crowd answers. 'Gather the saints at the river!' the preacher yells, now stalking up the center aisle. 'That flows by the throne of the Lord!' The crowd sounds like a mighty, muddy river breaking loose over its banks. 'Go down Moses! Way down in Egypt Land! Tell old Pharaoh to let my people *go*!' The preacher runs down the aisle and leaps back onto the stage and points his finger at a tall, beautiful woman shining under a spotlight. 'I looked over Jordan and what did I see?' the woman sings. 'Coming for to carry me home,' sings the choir. 'Hot diggety.' Louis gives another low whistle.

'Has anyone out there sinned?' the preacher asks the crowd. Leonora looks over at Louis Lewis and me, giving us the snake eye. 'Raise your hands if you have sinned!' yells the preacher. Leonora pinches me and I raise my hand. 'You, too, Mr MoJo.' Leonora nudges Louis. He rolls his eyes and puts up his hand. 'Ding-a-ling,' he says, arching an eyebrow at me. Suddenly, the preacher is running up the aisle toward us. I look around and see that Louis Lewis and I are the only ones with our hands in the air. The preacher is beckoning to us. 'Come down and be saved, children. Come down and let the Lord *save you*.' Our hands drop to our laps.

'Go on, Baby Love – do what The Man tells you.' Leonora is pushing me out of my seat.

'I've got the *Devil* in me,' Louis Lewis suddenly shouts and stands up and climbs over the laps of several women, who are clapping and crying, to reach the preacher in the aisle. I sigh and look at Leonora. *Please*. But she's got tears in her eyes, and cries, 'Praise the Lord!' Sometimes she is completely irony deficient. She pushes me out of my seat. 'Don't just talk the talk, Baby.

Walk the walk!' Leonora is quite strong. 'Great,' I mumble and follow Louis, who is swashbuckling in front of me and the preacher down to the stage.

He is across it in a few strides, kneeling in front of the sexy solo singer. 'I got the Bad Breast – Give me the Good One!' he pleads to her, but a couple of guys who look like those informers in *Kojak* – amber-tinted glasses and gold bracelets – practically pick him up and lead him back to the front of the stage. Then Louis sees the cameras – they air these sermons on television – and starts mugging for them. He pulls at his collar and rolls his head, kind of swoons into the men's arms. He starts mumbo-jumboing about the Promised Land and the Baby Jesus. I'm forgotten in all the *brouhaha*. The preacher puts his hand on Louis's forehead. 'Out! Get out, demons!' he yells. Louis swoons and yells back, 'Beelzebub wants me *bad*!' The crowd yells 'Rejoice!' 'Leave me alone Old Roundfoot,' Louis screams. 'Arch Fiend, Be Gone!' The preacher presses the heel of his hand to Louis's forehead, yelling 'Out! Out!' He turns back to the audience. 'That boy had nine demons in his young body. I just released five of them, but there are four demons left. Devil, we command you in Jesus's name to Let Him Go! *Pray* for him!' There is a sound of distant thunder rising from the crowd. 'Those of you watching at home.' The preacher is talking to the camera now. 'Put your hand on the screen! Put your hand on the TV screen and pray to Jesus for this poor boy's soul!' I start inching off-stage, trying to get out of the camera's sight. 'Pray for your friend,' one of the women in the choir hisses at me. She's big.

I clasp my hands together. Bow my head. 'Lord save us,' I whisper. Then I pray that Louis will be hoisted by his own petard.

'Fuck! Asshole! Fuck! Shit! Shit! Fuck!' Louis is writhing on the floor now, shouting obscenities. Once Louis pretended that he had Tourette's Syndrome and shouted 'Fuck you, cunt!' at the principal's secretary. He got twenty Saturday detentions.

The preacher is visibly unsettled. His assistants are trying to grab Louis and shut him up, but he is an out-of-control tempest of possession. Suddenly, he sinks back down to his knees. 'I need the blood of Jesus,' he whispers. 'I saw the Messiah on the mountain. Quoth he: "Drink of My Blood! Drink a Jeroboam of My Blood – flush that Dark One out!" '

Now I see clearly the direction he is headed.

'Drink of His blood . . . Drink of His blood . . . *Drink of His Blood*' the crowd chants.

The preacher snaps his fingers and a woman comes from off-stage with a jug of wine and a glass. She pours a glass of wine and hands it to Louis, still on his knees. He drinks it down in one gulp. 'Manna from heaven.' He smiles and holds out the glass for more. He swallows a second and third glass before the *Kojak* men help him to his feet. 'Consider . . .' Louis says, the words sloshing around in his mouth, 'the lilies of the field . . .'

'Are you saved, son?' the preacher asks.

'I think there might be one more little demon left . . . right about here . . .' Louis says, pointing a finger to his forehead and holding out his other hand for the glass.

The preacher whoops and strikes Louis's forehead with his open palm. 'Do you believe that Jesus died for your sins?' he asks Louis.

'No,' Louis replies, smug. 'He did not die.'

The preacher wobbles a bit, but then he bounces right back. 'Because he was resurrected on the third day!' He turns triumphant to the camera.

'No.' Louis gets a cat's-pajamas smile on his face. 'Because' –

Louis pushes the preacher to one side and faces the camera – 'I am Jesus Christ.'

Mayhem, Kum Bay Yah and Cain are generally raised. 'Lucifer! Satan! Mephistopheles!' A few people roll down the aisles. Some try to storm the stage. The big men push Louis in front of them off toward a side door. I start to follow him, but the preacher suddenly has me by the arm. My knees are shaking. 'Gird up your loins, Miz Jezebel,' Louis shouts gaily to me before he disappears behind a door. 'Where do you think I found my soul?' the choir is trying to sing above the chaos of the crowd. 'Listen to the angels shouting!'

The preacher is staring into my eyes. 'Do you take Jesus as your Savior?' he asks me. I swallow. The preacher hits my forehead and I see *Light*. Bright white lights explode inside my head and then I am falling down, down, down a deep well. I remember spelling 'Mississippi'. I remember Eli Whitney and the cotton gin. I remember the Sumer Valley, Cradle of Civilization. I remember 'All of the Above' being the correct answer.

Smote means to be struck. With powerful effect.

There are nine principal vices to which humans are subject: Tristia, Philargyria, Fornicatio, Superbia, Cenodoxia, Gasturngia, Aredia, Ira, and Taedem Cordes. They sound like those ancient diseases that made people's faces go yellow. I picture the bachelor standing in a desert. In his eyes are reflected miles of yellow sand, stretching away into the distance. Acedia, the demons of midday, swarm about him like flies, and all becomes long and full of doom. Like a Sunday afternoon. He repeats the beautiful bell words – Kyrie eleison – over and over until they are as natural as his breathing. He wears a brown tunic tied with a rope. He clutches a gold cross in his long white fingers. Raised red holy marks cover his chest, bearing divine messages. He lives on locusts and honey, and fifteen figs at sunset. His face has gone yellow. ASCETICISM is the practice of the denial of physical desires to attain a spiritual ideal. The Desert Fathers became strangers (alienum) to the world in order to be one with the Divine.

LIST OF LIGHT: Light of the violet hour, of the rings of planets, of excommunicated comets, of votive candles, light glinting off the propeller of an airplane high in the sky, Monday morning light, the light of hallucinations, the green light of a melodious plot, the suffering light of sanatoriums, X-ray light, light on the rims of darkling plains, of the high noons of Westerns, of candles stuck to the backs of wandering tortoises in harem quarters, riddling, brillig light, tragic light of Greek ampitheaters, of the black suns of Melancholy, light of a burning bush, golden orange glows in a thicket's gloom, Dante's light of love that moves the sun and other stars.

Leonora had a religious vision when she was twelve. Her daddy worked as a porter on the Southern Pacific railroad and she was riding on the train with him, as she often did when her mama had a headache and Leonora seemed on the verge of stirring up a hornet's nest. Out the window there were rivers, bridges, trees – it became a kind of rhythm with the clicking of the train. River, bridge, trees . . . river, bridge, trees . . . river, bridge, trees. Then everything opened out onto a field of daisies and the train stopped. There was an announcement that they would be stopped there for at least an hour, so Leonora's daddy let her get off and run through the daisies. A line of trees stood at the edge of the field and Leonora said as soon as her feet hit the ground she ran toward them, they beckoned her like a song. When she reached them, she saw a stream running below them, so clear that the stones on the bottom shone like new silver nickels. Leonora climbed down to its banks, took off her socks and stood in the cold water. Schools of minnows darted around her ankles. Dragonflies buzzed nearby and since she knew they stitch your eyelids shut she closed hers tight. That was when she heard the bells. Thousands of bells tolling so loud they seemed to be inside the dome of her head, clanging at her temples. And when she opened her eyes she saw below her in the stream an enormous golden cathedral. It seemed to be a thousand feet below her in the water, but rising at each toll of the bells. The golden light began to blind her with its brilliance, and then a dozen angels swooped around her head in an iridescent glimmer and she felt herself rising out of the stream and up above the trees. The next thing she knew her daddy was carrying her back to the train. Raindrops, big as grapes, in the now darkened sky, hit her face and mixed with her ecstatic tears.

HOW TO LEVITATE: Lie flat on your stomach and feel yourself getting heavier and heavier, sinking down into the floor, further and further, until you reach the center of the earth. Now stop falling and start to float. Feel your head, arms, legs – all the cells of your body, floating. Slowly raise yourself to a standing position. Direct the vertical lines of your body upward, up, and up, further and further upward. Now bend at the knees and push your feet against the floor. Lift your body up and off the ground.

Mrs Lewis is wearing a dress the color of absinthe. She is

standing at a pew a few rows ahead of me. We are at the Sacred Heart Catholic Church. From where I am standing I can see the small brown mole on Mrs Lewis's face, high up on her right cheekbone just under her eye. Once, when she caught me staring at it, she told me that during Louis XIV's reign, women pasted fake beauty marks on their faces – *'grain de beauté'* – and according to where it was placed it had different meanings. One placed under the eye meant all-knowing and worldly. 'Makes me seem sophisticated, no?' She laughed, showing wet white teeth. They are slightly uneven, like children's teeth that have just come in and are not yet worn smooth. When I was little and didn't quite know the meaning of 'French', I thought her teeth caused her to talk differently – her 'r's rolling like coins in a gutter, her 's's sputtering firecrackers in wet grass. She stresses syllables in places you wouldn't expect it. She says, *'Je ne sais pas'* a lot – the *'sais'* hitting a high, sharp note. And she often begins questions with *qui* or *quand* or *quoi* or *que*. She calls Louis *'mon petit chou'* which means 'my little cabbage' – a term that lovers use to address each other in France. Louis gets embarrassed when she does this in public. She moves her hands when she speaks. Sometimes she holds one hand over her top lip as if she is telling you a secret. She uses her long fingers to flick back the stray strand of ash-blonde hair that continually falls over her left eye. Her hands are very elegant – you get the feeling she was born knowing how to use an oyster fork.

She does not really talk about her life, about growing up in France. What I know about her past I learned from Louis. That she wanted to be a ballerina. That she practically lived in pink tights and a black leotard, pirouetting and *grand-jetéing* in the gilt-ceilinged studio, so cold that her earlobes and fingernails turned blue. That she had an uncanny resemblance to an ancestor in a painting who was killed in the French Revolution, and for many years she would awake in the middle of the night from guillotine nightmares. That she attended a convent school where she was not allowed to look in mirrors without permission, and had to gaze at the ground when passing men on the street. She was a fallen Catholic for a long time. She fell when she met Mr Lewis, who is Episcopalian. But she returned to the faith, about a decade ago, with renewed vigor. My grandmother told me this is the case with a lot of Catholics. At some point in their life they feel something is lacking, and they come back to the Church, much more fervent than those who never left. Because they suffer from the guilt of their betrayal.

Once, when I was over at the Lewises' I saw something I am sure I was never supposed to see. Louis and I had just come into their house, and I was on my way to use one of the bathrooms, when I heard voices through its half-opened door. Louis told me that his parents fought a lot, but they never did in front of me. 'You think this . . . voodoo can absolve you of sin?' I heard Mr Lewis saying to Mrs Lewis in a disgusted tone of voice. In the reflection of the bathroom mirror I could see he was holding up her rosary. 'Give it to me,' Mrs Lewis said. I couldn't see her, but her voice sounded wet and muffled, as though she had been crying. I knew I should leave, but something in the tone of their voices riveted me to the spot. 'Come and get it,' Mr Lewis said, sneering and mean. I heard the sound of something falling in water. 'No!' Mrs Lewis gasped, and at the same time there was the flushing sound of the toilet. 'I am going back home! You can't stop me!' Mrs Lewis was screaming now, hysterical. 'How will you do that?' Mr Lewis replied, cool and measured. 'No court in the land will give you a single cent of mine.' I hid behind the stairwell as he strode out the door. I could hear Mrs Lewis crying. I wanted to go and comfort her, but then I knew that she would not want me to.

We are seated now. Men with gray hair are walking down the aisle of the church with collection plates. Their cufflinks flash beneath their dark suit jackets. Their shoulders are wide as mantelpieces. When you see them walking through town, they take long corporate strides, but here they seem to be mastering some exquisite form of balance. The Virgin Mary gazes down at us from a painting in an alcove. Behind her is a background of jagged rocks and bare trees. She has a long, slender neck and there is a beautiful and strange flare to her nostrils. She doesn't look like a very good mother. The Baby Jesus is tumbling from her lap while she gazes off toward some vanishing point.

No one knows where the soul is located. But maybe artists do. Is there a name for that white fleck painted in the dark center of eyes in paintings? In medieval times they named everything – churches, bells, walls, swords. So they probably had a name for it. Perhaps something in Italian, with an *issimo* at the end of it. Written only in italics.

A procession has started toward the altar for Communion. The priest places a wafer in each person's mouth. He moves his lips but you can't hear what he is saying. The wafer is supposed to be the body of Christ. And not just a little part of his body, but the whole thing because the divine cannot be divided. There is something secret in the act of digestion. Everything that you put in your mouth has to travel through red arches and slide down wet passages and then magically the nonliving things you eat become something living. Maybe that is why the innermost corridors of your body have such fabulous names – the palatoglossal arches, the isles of Langerhans, the ampulla of Vater, the sphincter of Oddi.

Leonora's daddy ate a page out of the Bible every Sunday and he said he could feel the righteous words running through his veins like the flaming swords of the Lord. So maybe learning feels good because it feels like eating something good. Maybe our brains evolved from the chlorophyll in plants, and that's why insight is like a light that just turned on in your head. Swedenborg was converted when he had a vision of Jesus at breakfast who said to him: 'Eat slower.'

I see the bachelor kneel at the far end of the altar. I wasn't expecting him to be here. After the priest places a wafer in his mouth, and he takes a sip of wine, the bachelor bows his head over his hands. Under his dark suit jacket you can see his back and shoulders are stiff and firm. Everyone else bows their heads for a few seconds and then stands up and makes the sign of the cross, steps down and goes back to their seat. But the bachelor stays where he is, motionless. I think of the moon, four days high in the sky and what the earth looks like from there. And darkness, centuries wide, on all sides.

Several pews of people have filed up for Communion and returned to their seats. Then I see Mrs Lewis kneel at the place next to the bachelor. Her hair is up in a chignon, and when she bows her head you can see the nape of her neck, white and vulnerable. The trees outside the church windows sway in the wind and their shadows make the edges of Mrs Lewis's dress tremble. The space between the bachelor's pressed black suit and Mrs Lewis's green dress seems to go from liquid to solid and back to liquid again. A breeze rushes in through an open door. The bachelor lifts his head as if awoken. He looks over at Mrs Lewis, her head still bowed, her bare shoulder round and soft. A chain of gold glimmers at her neck.

*

Praying seems like something strange and illegal. Like absinthe.

Louis isn't allowed in the Catholic church. One Christmas, a long time ago, we were in a live nativity scene they display every year on the lawn of the church. I didn't belong to Sacred Heart. I just tagged along with Louis, as usual. Anyway, we were a couple of sheep. We actually had the best parts because everyone else was freezing to death in their Jerusalem summerwear and we were all snug in our fleeces. We were on all fours, gazing at the Baby Jesus in His cradle, baa-ing every once in a while. And then we all started singing Christmas carols, 'Noël, Noël', etc. One of the Wise Men kicked Louis in the rump and told him sheep don't sing, idiot. So Louis got up on his hind legs and dumped the Wise Man's box of frankincense over his head and said, beware of wolves in sheep's clothing, asshole. Then the Baby Jesus, who was played by a dwarf with a five-o' clock shadow, leaped out of his cradle and started throttling Louis by his collar of bells. I could hear Louis choking, so I started kicking the Baby Jesus's back with my front hooves. The Virgin Mary, who was a burnout, but got the part because of her soulful face, long dark hair, and confessional overtime with Father Timothy, sat down on the grass and lit a cigarette. In all the hoopla, the star of Bethlehem – a big spotlight set on a ladder – fell on Joseph and knocked him unconscious. So Louis got blamed for it all and was kicked out of church forever. Louis said that it is all right because at the right moment – he might have to wait until he is thirty-five, like for the presidency – he is going to declare himself Antipope, storm the Vatican, take over the Papal throne, change his name to Innocent and ride into town in his Popemobile and excommunicate the whole congregation. Then he'll spend the rest of his infallible, supremely pontifical days issuing edicts and selling expensive indulgences.

Changing your name to Innocent would definitely alter the atmosphere of your life. Every introduction and salutation to you would be a grand, righteous moral assertion of yourself.

AQUITAINE was a court in France that was like a huge Charm School, where the queen taught everyone Ars Amandi – the rules of courtly love. For instance, the lover must pale at the sight of his beloved, his heart must palpitate, and he must always be fearful and tormented, and not eat or sleep. Love easily obtained had little value; the more difficult, the more precious the love. True love was always adulterous and a love made public rarely lasted. There were five steps to falling in love: seeing your beloved, drawing near to her, conversing with her, kissing her, and what they called the final thing – *de factum*. There were all sorts of silent, secret codes invented for the lovers. So the castle was just full of batting eyes over dinners of oysters and figs, secret messages left in bowers, demure glances from behind rose bushes, a quick tug of an earlobe from behind a fan, private duets at dawn, tossed swain cushions, hands held under tables and trembling fingers twisting a tendril of hair. Head nods and tosses, and swoons, and shrugs of shoulders and eyebrows arched and devastating grins and blushes and winks. In fact, the whole court was one big *double entendre* designed for dalliance. Roses meant ardor and lilies were yearning and half-closed curtains were flirting and doorways deceitful and colors were either expectant or enamored or enchanting. Everyone lived *contrecoeur* – by the heart rather than reason – and suffered madly for its deadly joy and happy pain, but they weren't responsible for their madness because it was usually caused by a magical love philter that made them obsessed with each other to the point that they wanted to be dissolved into one another, become one, and die.

In science class we learned that with sex came death. Before sex, things divided to produce more of themselves. What would it feel like to divide? I wonder if there is a certain frisson to it. A certain ooh la la.

LIST OF ETIQUETTE: Do not tuck your napkin under your chin. Do not drop your voice at the end of sentences – this will depress your listener. Never appear in public on horseback unless you have mastered the inelegancies attending a first appearance in the saddle. A gentleman should learn how to spring to his feet with alacrity at the approach of a fellow guest. It is best to voice subtle hints to house guests before the visit becomes too far advanced, lest, like Odysseus, the host is tempted toward violent measures. Do not ask personal questions involving insurance, money, marriage, false teeth, wooden legs or glass eyes. For the sake of one's country's international prestige, it is well not to go about ships in bizarre costume. If introduced to a king, curtsy while extending your hand – if you by chance have an objection to the institution of the curtsy, do not ask to be presented to a king. Study the sculptures of Greece for their peculiarly beautiful attitudes and superiority of mien. Do not be given unduly to introspection – it is unbecoming.

There was once a medieval queen who had thirty-four secret pockets concealed in her skirts, each containing the embalmed heart of a past lover.

Louis Lewis is teaching me how to flirt. I am winking at him. I am not getting it right. Louis is acting like one of those petulant French dance coaches. 'No, no, no!' he says, exasperated. 'Like *this*.' He tosses his wavy blond hair and winks his right eye behind a lock of it. Louis has great hair. Sometimes after he's just washed it, it looks like the hair on the Metro-Goldwyn-Mayer lion.

Who invented the wink? Who thought it would be a sexy idea to close one eye and keep the other one open? In the Sermon on the Mount it says that it is better to have one eye, because with two you will be cast into hell-fire.

I wink at Louis again. And he suddenly looks at me oddly. As though I am a stranger to him. 'Do that again,' he says slowly. His pupils are huge and black. One of the sins Augustine talks about is 'lust of the eyes'. Which, besides being sexual, can also refer to 'idle curiosity'.

'Do what?' I ask nervously.

'That,' Louis says softly, and reaches over and nudges the lid down over my left eye. He looks at me for a long moment. His face has gone all soft and angelic, like one of those cherubs in paintings that look innocent but evil too. As though they might pinch you while you were looking the other way, and then scamper off, snickering.

I tell Louis I've got to go. It makes me really uncomfortable when he looks at me like this. He didn't use to. I suddenly remember when, recently, I was with Mrs Lewis, after Charm School, walking down Euclid Avenue in Cleveland. A man walking by us said 'hello' to Mrs Lewis in an insinuating way. Then, a few moments later, we heard running footsteps behind us, and when we turned, we saw it was the same man, with a bunch of roses clutched in his hand. 'Please. You are so beautiful,' he said, thrusting them towards Mrs Lewis, and then half bowing to her. Mrs Lewis scowled, turned on her heel and walked away, so quickly that I had to run to keep up with her. She dropped the flowers in the nearest waste bin. 'I hate roses,' she said in a disgusted voice.

'But aren't you flattered', I asked her, surprised, 'that he found you so beautiful?' I thought it was utterly romantic.

Mrs Lewis did not answer me, but once we got to the car, she sat still for a moment behind the wheel. She looked as though she might start to cry. 'Don't be fooled, Haddie. You never know what it is that a man finds attractive about you. It is usually not you. It is something inside,' she jabbed at her chest with her forefinger, 'inside them that they see in you. A reflection of themselves.'

HOW TO TELL A MAN YOU ARE NOT IN LOVE WITH HIM: Twist your hankie in your left hand. Bite the tips of your gloves. Slowly lower your opened fan until the sticks are pointing to the ground, and with the back of your hand make quick, swift, brushing-away movements.

If One exists, it participates in being, and therefore there are two parts to it – being, and the one that is being. But each of these parts is one and exists, so within each of these parts is two parts, which thus enclose two more parts, which each are composed of two parts, and thus One can be divided, *ad infinitum*.

When you look at someone, you no longer completely own yourself. There is the you looking and the you in their heads. There is the you you want to be and the you they want you to be. When you think about it, it is like being in a room full of mirrors. The original you disappears among all the other yous. It seems that you can get vertigo from anything if you think about it long enough.

ASTRONAUTS had extensive training to accustom them to living in the weightless environment of space, by simulating the conditions of zero gravity. The patron saint of astronauts is St Joseph of Cupertino who, while praying, used to fly in rapture up to the high branches of trees, and the other monks would have to run and grab a ladder to get him back down.

The bachelor, however, seems weighted down. He has the slow, solemn gestures of those people in engravings of the Bible, where everything – robes, jugs, clouds, temple steps and camels – is shadowed by black cross-hatching. I once read a story about a fugue – a person who goes and lives another life somewhere else – having complete amnesia for his former life. The bachelor's rituals have the set pattern of someone who has lost something important and is combing back and forth in search of it. Or a sole survivor, who has had to make up a whole new life after having been washed ashore, memorizing through repeated movement the strange terrain. One of the sentences he under-lined in the library was: 'We seek, as it were, the center of the circle which holds the whole together.'

I picture him on the back seat of an open convertible on Fifth Avenue under the rain of a ticker tape parade. I see presidents, sheikhs and kings marching up red carpets, like diplomats in black-and-white World War One newsreels with those strange, tipping walrus steps, presenting him with medals, awards and ribbons. On the cover of *Life* magazine, standing in his space suit with the moon reflected in the glass of his helmet.

ANABASIS is the Ascent Myth. It is the journey of the hero, who travels outside the boundaries of his culture, often nature itself, to gain knowledge for his society and culture. The hero is often isolated, a rational being in an irrational world, living by a rigid, archaic code. He stands outside time and space, in an uneasy position between the human and the divine. Like Achilles, heroes are not men and not gods, but somewhere in between. While society needs heroes to grow and evolve, the hero cannot live comfortably within society. The hero is a lonely, exiled individual, both because of his superhuman characteristics, and his inability to return to a normal life after his transcendent journey.

The first time I had an attack of vertigo was at the end of last summer, just after I turned thirteen. It happened on a ride at Disneyland. The one where you go on little boats through a man-made stream inside a large amphitheater. The boats glide past moving papier mâché figures that represent all the nationalities of the world – on your right are Eskimos ice-fishing, on your left are Mexicans making tortillas, you turn a corner and head straight toward Italians stomping grapes. The ecstatic tinny tune of 'It's a Small World' was piped through enormous loudspeakers. In a little over seven minutes you had glided by the whole world and its peoples and customs. It took me the rest of the vacation to recover. Some may find it a cheerful and uplifting thought that you can enclose the whole of the world in a hot and dusty amphitheater, but I found it depressing.

Leonora told me that your soul travels at the pace of a camel. So if you fly off somewhere, your body may be at your destination when you land, but it will take your soul whole days to catch up with you.

Louis found a ring. In his mother's jewelry box. It is small and gold, with a fleur-de-lis design. Louis is sure it is a present from his 'real' father. 'Look,' he says, pointing out an engraving that winds around the inside. I squint my eyes. The words are minuscule, unreadable. 'I had to get out a magnifying glass to read it,' Louis says. 'It's in French. *On revient toujours à ses premiers amours.*' I raise my eyebrows at him.

'One always returns to one's first love,' Louis translates. There are blotches of bright pink on his cheeks. He goes through these manic phases – they blow through him like a hot sirocco wind – where he is frantic to find out about his father. He's stopped questioning his mother, but he will spend hours scanning through her bills, tax returns, her purses and pockets for clues. He pieces together her torn letters. She says they are from estranged family members. They cut her off when she married Mr Lewis. But Louis is sure they are from her one true love. I think he has that syndrome – if it is a syndrome – when a child thinks that their 'real' parents are people much more glamorous than their own – sovereigns, sultans, or suzerains of some lost dynasty. In my case, it is the other way around. My parents sometimes look at me as though they are suspicious there was some gypsy switch made at the hospital nursery.

But sometimes I feel confused about Louis's intentions. I wonder if he is actually looking for concrete evidence that his father really is his father. Although he would never admit it, he actively seeks his father's approval. I think that's why he read all those classics in one giant gulp. When Mr Lewis is around, he is always quizzing Louis on obscure information. It is practically the only way they communicate. The questions are usually about tedious ancient military and political maneuvers – pertaining to things like Xerxes, and Persian phalanxes and fleets, and the strategies of Alexander the Great, and Cicero and the Cataline conspiracy. And if Louis doesn't know an answer, he goes nuts – he won't speak to me, or anyone else until he finds it. I'll see him in the library, bent over books like Thucydides's *History of the Peloponnesian War* and Tacitus's *Historiae*. He's been sent to the principal's office for insubordination on numerous occasions, because he's been hot on the trail of an answer. Once, in algebra class, instead of listening to the lesson, he was poring through Marcus Aurelius's *Meditations*. His father had recently quizzed him on something about one of the emperor's winter marches along the Danube. The teacher asked Louis a question. He completely ignored her. She walked up to his desk, and closed the book. 'Shit,' Louis muttered, and as though she was some pesky fly, waved her away, stood up with the book, and walked out of the classroom. Another time, he turned in a mid-term exam with no answers, just diagrams of old battles drawn in the splotchy blue of his fountain pen.

Although I think Louis is caught up in some grand illusion over his recently found ring, it reminds me again about hidden, secret things. When I get home, I go and sit out in the center of our courtyard, and try to think of all the codes – twisted paths and spirals – that can be overlaid upon a grid. The sun is hot overhead. When I close my eyes I see bright orange. Augustine said our inner minds are like vast courtyards, and if you look inward and then upward you will see a spiritual sun. The 'ah' sensation of understanding is caused by your connection to the divine mind of God. I say 'holy, holy, holy'. My grandmother says the sound of the letter 'e' helps open the third eye. But instead of concentrating on solving the cipher of the courtyard, I keep thinking about Mrs Lewis. Augustine said we have a restless heart and this is what makes us wander from the eternal love of God toward the temporal love of people. He says, 'My love is my weight.' Because anything you love pulls you toward it. So if you love God, you are thrust upward, but in concentrating on the cupidity of earthly loves you are drawn downward, which makes you lose your way and follow the path of sin.

I wonder if Mr Lewis suspects that Louis isn't his son. And if he knew immediately, when Louis was born, or if he sensed it gradually. Perhaps he knew the man that Mrs Lewis had the affair with, and as each of Louis's birthdays passed, he recognized the man in the shape of Louis's eyes, the line of his jawbone, the way his hair fell about his head.

A thought nudges at the back of my mind. A memory of a picture of Louis when he was two or three years old. It is one of the few photographs Mrs Lewis has of Louis as a little boy. The Lewises don't have family photo albums. They have all their pictures on slides. In the photograph I remember, Louis is wearing red shorts. He is looking over at someone, off camera, to the right. His hair is a halo of blond-white fluff. Then I feel an icy-hot dart through the middle of my skull. The boy found next to my sister on the flagstone path, the day that she died, playing with her blood, was three years old. He would be sixteen now.

ALCHEMY is a medieval doctrine which sought to expose the hidden reality underlying all things. There is a line-drawing of a medieval alchemist – a crazed-looking man surrounded by steaming vials. The alchemists made philosopher's stones, which they believed would concentrate human thought and the structures of nature upon a single point, by dissolving body and coagulating spirit and creating a direct correspondence between the visible and invisible worlds. To the alchemist, gold represented the eternal spark in the human body. Gold was the embodiment of incorruptibility in the physical world. In trying to transmute base metal into gold, the alchemists were seeking to extract the eternal from the everyday.

'In the church of my heart the choir is on fire!' Leonora wakes me up in the middle of the night to tell me this after one of her dates.

'Leonora,' I call to her as she is about to leave my room, 'who was the little boy found sitting next to my sister the day she died?'

Leonora turns back. 'Oh, some neighbor child . . .'

'Was it Louis?' I ask, cutting her off.

Leonora pauses in the doorway, then comes and sits down on the edge of my bed. The moon is bright outside my window. Apparently, medieval virgins were always getting ravished by moonbeams.

'I wasn't here that day, honey. And they never put the boy's name in the paper. There was a reason for that. The boy was too young to know what had happened. If he did, well, you can imagine – he'd most likely have a whole lot of bats flying around in his belfry.'

'So you think it could have been Louis?'

'Louis used to walk in his sleep. Back home we call them "spirit trances". Spirits warn you of something in your dreams, and then guide you to where the trouble's at.'

'So you think Louis was sleep-walking that day – and ended up, next to my sister . . . because he dreamed she was in trouble?'

'It could be that . . . I'm not saying it *was* him.' Leonora lifts both hands up, palms toward me, like a bank teller during a robbery. Then she places her hands back down on her lap, tilts her head to one side, thinking.

'Your sister saved Louis's life once. He wandered out into the street. Was sitting smack in the center of the road. And a big delivery truck barreling down the hill toward him. Your sister ran out and grabbed him just in time. Even at that age, when Louis was around, dominoes would start falling. Mrs Lewis had her hands full. The minute she turned her back on him, he was off like a shot. So who knows which way around it was? Louis could have been climbing up a trellis, and your sister went to rescue him, and she fell. Or Louis was led by a dream of misfortune toward her. Backward or forward, whichever way around it happened, if it was Louis, he certainly doesn't remember any of it. And he doesn't need to . . .' Leonora rolls her eyes upward. The whites of them gleam in the moonlight. 'I should not have said anything, sweet potato pie. Louis is already crazy as a betsey bug without having this weasel of an idea popping off in his head.' She leans over and brushes the hair from my face. I can smell her Tigress perfume. 'So lock this notion up in your thinkbox and throw the key out to the deepest part of the sea.'

'All composite things decay. Strive diligently.' I got another fortune from my grandmother today. Sometimes she also sends me koans. You are supposed to rotate them around in your mind all week until you understand them. One goes like this: A man asked his master, 'Do dogs have Buddha souls?' And the master replies, 'Moo.' This one gave me a headache. I prefer the Bible to Buddha. There is a lot happening in the Bible all the time. There are natural disasters, and wars, and people being smote. Buddha just sits.

My grandmother and I are sitting on the floor, concentrating on this koan: 'Thinking of neither good nor evil, at this very moment, what is your Original Nature?' We recite this question internally, using bamboo breathing. You say each word with rapt attention, letting your breath out in short spurts.

If you turn the word 'evil' the wrong way around it becomes 'live'. Augustine said evil doesn't have true existence, but is rather a hole in being. The blind spot of the eye is the point which is insensitive to light. Sometimes when I'm bored I try to figure out where it is. In Mr Monroe's movie, my sister blinds the sailor who sees her. Because he saw something he was not supposed to see.

'Leonora said that the boy found next to my sister might have been Louis. She said that he used to sleep-walk . . .'

'Darling, you are becoming too morbidly absorbed in the events of that day. I adore Leonora, but she does sometimes become rather confused, doesn't she? What happened, happened. And it certainly did not involve Louis. You must not dwell on the past.'

'But did he use to sleep-walk?'

'As a matter of fact I think he did. Troubled children often do . . .' She trails off, then clears her throat. 'Sleep-walking is what most people do their entire lives. This is why you need to experience "satori", to be awakened.'

'When did you experience it?' I ask her.

'Some experience it after hearing a frog plop into a pond, or the whisk of a broom sweeping a step,' my grandmother says softly and vaguely.

'But what about you? Your experience?'

My grandmother doesn't seem to hear me. She tilts her head to one side, as though listening to distant temple bells. 'On that day, the stones in the garden were covered in spring pinks. Cool breezes were whispering in the pines. I saw your grandfather in bed with another woman. And suddenly' – she claps her hands loudly together – 'everything became very clear. I saw, in a burst of light, both inside and outside of me, that everything is one . . .' She stops speaking abruptly, and shakes her head. 'You must find your own way – in order to know what I am talking about. These things can never be explained in words.'

*

HOW TO WHIRL LIKE A DERVISH: Have someone play the reed flute. Don a tall felt hat and a full white gown. Tilt the hat to the same angle as the earth's axis, as the dance symbolizes the movement of the planetary spheres. Rotate on the left foot in short twists, using the right foot as an anchor to the ground. This movement will appease the evil stars and channel help from the good stars, and eventually lead to ecstasy and higher truth.

At Charm School they are teaching us how to cross our legs properly. We sit on the spindly ballroom chairs set in a circle on the top floor of the downtown Higbee's department store. One leg is wrapped like a snake around the calf until the toes of the top leg touch the inside ankle of the other.

Mrs Lewis unwinds herself from her chair and stands up. 'This is how you make the curtsy: Place your right foot behind your left heel. Then bend your knees, and do a quick dip. Dip down, not too far, then up again. At the moment you begin the curtsy, extend your right hand to the person you are greeting, who shakes it, as you do the dip.' Mrs Lewis curtsies, quick and exquisite. 'A lady's curtsy is a modified genuflection,' Ms Phillips adds. 'A short choreographed tribute of honor bestowed upon the other.'

After class, Mrs Lewis stops at the cosmetic counter of Higbee's to buy some night cream. The saleslady has Mrs Lewis look into a magnifying mirror after applying some of the cream to her forehead. I never noticed the little horizontal lines at the sides of her eyes, the vertical creases between her eyebrows. The lids of her eyes look slightly pink and puffy – as though, last night, she cried herself to sleep. I look in the mirror next to me and practice the Gothic smile – confined to the left corner of the mouth – which was considered an infallible way of attracting the opposite sex. I get the sense someone is looking at me, and I raise my eyes and see a man standing across from us. He is wearing a gray suit and a red tie. He smiles at me, in a way that seems to curve and warp the space between us. Without thinking, I decide to practice my 'wink', but just as I do, Mrs Lewis shouts, '*Tiens*! Stop that!' and grabs me by the arm and marches me out the door of the store.

'You are a silly girl. You will get yourself in trouble,' she says while pulling me down the street. 'You think these are games,' she says, once we are in the car. She is staring through the windshield at the line of hot cars in the parking lot in front of us. 'Many little games without any . . . goal.' She hits the side of her right hand down hard into her left palm. 'But men only play *one* game – and they play to win. You understand?' She looks over at me. I nod, even though I don't, really. Mrs Lewis looks at me for several seconds. Then she turns and puts the key in the ignition. She runs her hand through her hair. 'Why take you to these lessons if you learn nothing' – she hits the steering wheel twice: on 'no' and 'thing' – 'about how to behave as a lady?'

There is a silence between us all the way home. I feel my wrist aching, and see that there is a wide red mark like a rope burn, where Mrs Lewis grabbed it, and four faint half-moon marks from her fingernails. It reminds me of the time Louis brought her diaphragm to school for Science Show and Tell. We were studying evolution, and were supposed to bring in 'examples from the animal world around us', i.e. cocoons, snakeskins, robin's eggs. Louis still has a small white diamond scar high up on his right cheek where his mother's wedding ring clipped him when she slapped him. You could see the red mark of her hand on his face for a week.

HOW TO BE A MARTYR: Wear burlap shirts, a crown of thorns

and keep pebbles in your shoes. Sleep on a bed of broken glass. Drag a heavy cross behind you. Sit on top of a pillar. Hold your arms above your head until they wither. Do not bathe. Do not speak. Do not fornicate. Ward off dancing girls with a hot poker. Wear an iron girdle. If you are good-looking, rub quicklime and acid into your skin and gouge out your eyeballs. Lament loudly. Swoon in ecstasy. Work a miracle. Wrestle an angel. Be tortured on a rack, impaled on an iron-spiked wheel, thrown on a bonfire. Have molten lead poured down your throat. Become the patron saint of an obscure dermatological malediction. Get a symbol that means *you*. Have a body part saved and venerated in a reliquary. Do not decompose after death.

Augustine said that the good is what is most real. When you think about it, pain is the most real thing you can experience. You can never deny its existence, you never have to ask someone: Is this pain that I am feeling? Can you verify this? Maybe this is why the saints were always torturing themselves. Knowledge being suffering, we're still paying for the truth Eve discovered when she ate that apple. Actually, it is the only thing we know for certain. In a way, the saints duped the dint of death – by making their lives so miserable they probably didn't mind dying.

Medieval monks saw everything *sub specie aeternitatis* – as pointing toward eternity. Colors and trees and flowers and birds were all symbols bearing spiritual messages, fragments of God's handwriting in his Book of Life. For example, butterflies meant the resurrection and most flowers had something to do with the Virgin Mary. Trees could stand for the crucifixion or biblical knowledge or the Trinity. The color red meant hell-fire, love, the blood of martyrs, cardinals, and the whore of Babylon. I try looking at everything in the Monroe wood *sub specie aeternitatis*. Heretic vines clutch at the tall commandments of trees. Leaves fall like damned souls. Spruces stand stern as sermons. There are the dark plum sins of berries in bushes. Sunlight dapples the ground in the bright letters of a parable of good and evil. A row of clovers spells out a proverb. A woodpecker in the highest trees drums *dies irae*, *dies illa*. The whole wood is ringing with bells, bells, bells, bells, bells and underneath all the hymning and rhyming and chiming and singing is the rolling thundercloud baritone of God's Word, resonating in a major key of meaning.

I am about to climb a tree to see how things look with a view to eternity from above when I see the bachelor sitting on the other side of it, writing in a notebook. He looks up and sees me.

'What are you writing?' I ask him.

He lets the pages of the notebook leaf through his fingers. Then he stops at a page and reads it. 'I am supposed to write a book about my life.' He slips the notebook into the inside pocket of his suit jacket.

'Are you going to write about the moon?'

He stands and looks at me as if he trying to decide something. He slides his hands back into his pockets, tips forward on the balls of his feet, and then back on his heels. He stops, and listens. There is a sound of a whippoorwill and something small running under the ferns. There is a red glow behind the trees. 'I must go,' the bachelor says abruptly. Then he walks away, distracted and uptight, through the ferns toward the path. Clouds float between the trees in a psalm-colored sky. I think of the picture of him in the encyclopedia. Standing still in his space suit. A fact in a book of facts.

St Augustine said that when he didn't think about time he

understood it, but when he thought about time he didn't understand it at all. Being that the past is no more and the future is not yet. Louis Lewis says French has all these tensed verbs because time is very emotional, and full of wishes and promises, and the French are obsessive about expression and so they do it at every possible opportunity. He says one day he is going to storm the French Academy and introduce more tenses: the disappointed tense, the mocking tense, the bitter-sweet tense.

You'd probably need different words and tenses to describe something no one on earth has experienced before. Were the names given to things before the Fall different from the ones given after? Because before the Fall Adam and Eve didn't know anything about death, and they were enclosed within the wall of the Garden. So their sense of time and space must have been completely different. How strange it must have been when from the wilderness they looked back at the Garden, glowing green behind the walls of fire, with an epic darkness surrounding it on all sides. The meaning of a word like 'always', the meaning of a word like 'endless', would have to have changed.

While they orbited the earth, the astronauts saw sixteen sunrises and sixteen sunsets in a single day. A powerful telescope will be able to make out the footprints left on the moon by the astronauts. They will remain visible for over ten million years.

Sometimes I'll play this game, where I look out at the field beyond the railway station and say 'Click' and then the name of a country and a time. Click, China 1550. Click, Tunisia 1800. Click, Spain 1600. And the field changes to rice paddies or rolling plains or a stretch of pampas leading to an Armada-laden shore.

Click. This town, sixteen years ago. When the other Haddie was, and when I was not.

Augustine wrote that he could not understand all that he was, that the mind is too narrow to contain itself entirely. But, he wondered, where is that part of it which it does not contain? Could it be outside itself and not within it?

If Louis was the little boy found next to my sister, I wonder where his memory is of that event. Perhaps he lost the memory because he did not have the words to describe it. But if the memory was lost, where did it go? Was it lost in space, or time?

LIST OF TIMES: A clock striking thirteen, the hour of the monkey, the blue hour of dusk, the green hour of Paris, high noon in a Western town, the dead of night, a bullring at five o'clock in the afternoon, Aztecs blowing conch shells at dawn, Mayans mad with time, Tibetan time sticks, muezzins calling the hours, the Babylonian sixty-second minute, the time of a pregnant pause, of a slow-dawning and a double-take, of a plain brown package that ticks, of sundials and hourglasses and schoolroom clocks on hot June afternoons, of the dawning of the Age of Aquarius, the time of tenses of verbs, of cesium atoms in laboratories, of things trapped in amber, of oranges in still lifes that mean immortality, the time of epics, and proverbs, of an Egyptian solar barque on its twilight journey, of the Stone Age and Bronze Age, of monitor lizards and terrapins and stylites sitting on pillars, the time it takes a Chinese painter to draw a perfect cat in a single stroke, for a frog to snatch a fly, the Egyptian instant – the time it takes a hippo to lift its head from water and check for danger.

I am trying St Ignatius's Fifth Spiritual Exercise where you meditate on hell, by imagining yourself to be there. I shiver from the chill winds emanating from Satan's black o'erspreading wings. I smell fire and brimstone, and the filth of unclean desire. A tornado of the lustful whirl high above my head, thieves are entangled in serpents at my feet. Traitors are up to their eyeballs in ice, angry souls flail their arms in ire at passing boats on the River Styx, in the forest of suicides souls stand rooted to the black earth, their upraised arms turned to burned broomstick branches. I can hear the beating oars of Charon, harpies, doleful sighs from steamy sepulchers, tires ripping up the gravel of our driveway. I jump up from the lawn and see a red Porsche pulled up about two inches in front of me. I blink. In the driver's seat is Louis Lewis.

'Get in,' he yells from the open window. 'I am in haste!' He revs the engine a few times. I just stare at him. Louis Lewis leans over and opens the passenger side door. 'Come *on*, Haddie. We're going on a pilgrimage – God wills it!' He adjusts the rear-view mirror and looks into it. 'Did any of those pilgrims get a halo after their journey? Because I'd look really good in one. It would bring out all my gold highlights.'

'Try sackcloth and ashes, Louis,' I say, as firm as I can manage. 'They'll bring out the black demon seeds in your eyes. Take this car back where you found it, *now*.'

'Haddie, how do you think I got the keys?' Louis says real slow, like I'm a dimwit in curlers at the scene of an accident. 'I was walking along, minding my own business. And that Russian came zigzagging down his driveway. Completely blotto. Clapped me on the shoulder, gave me a fifty and the keys to his car, and asked me to go get him a bottle of scotch. Only through the Charitable Dispensations of Providence was I available to prevent my neighbor from committing carnage on our community roads.'

I just stare at him. 'Haddie, if I am lying, let the Lord cleave my tongue to the roof of my mouth.' His face is the image of piety.

I get in and close the door. 'Do you even know how to drive, Louis?'

'Honey, I am hip to this baby's funky poetry,' Louis says, grinding the gears and backing down the driveway at fifty miles per hour.

'Louis, where are we going?' I ask as we turn onto the freeway.

'To the mall. To venerate relics.' Louis shoots into a space on the highway between two semis. Then he pulls out into the speed lane and guns the engine so the trucks become tiny black specks behind us. 'I am going to show you how shopping is the ultimate religious experience.'

'What about Mr Karanovsky?' I ask.

'I helped him back into the house before I left. He passed out on the couch. He won't know how long I've been gone. Besides, I'm doing yet another good deed. I'm letting some of that alcohol in his system dilute before he tanks up again. Just call me Holy Joe.'

About twenty miles and two seconds later, we are in a jewelry store at the mall. 'Montjou!' Louis exclaims. I told him this is what pilgrims say at the sight of the holy city's spires. Louis says jewelry stores are great places to experience vertigo. All that gold does make your head spin.

The salesman asks if we need help. Louis wants to see an emerald ring. The salesman has clear polish on his fingernails and a disgusted expression on his face. Louis puts the ring up to the light. 'Caligula used to look through one of these while watching Christians being eaten by lions.' Louis looks through the stone at the salesman. 'He said it made a jaundiced experience more vibrant.'

When we are out on the highway again, Louis tosses a small ruby ring onto my lap. I stare at it. The sun hits it and it glows, red as sin.

'We . . . Have . . . To . . . Return . . . This.' I am stuttering.

'Pilgrims pillaged the Holy Land. Besides, those places have insurance up to their eyeballs, Haddie.'

'Louis, St Augustine stole one little pear and he was haunted about it his whole life. He even wrote a whole book of confessions about it.'

'Yeah, well, they didn't have TV back then. They didn't have as many ideas of how to sin properly.' Louis honks and flashes his lights at a Ferrari going about ninety miles an hour in front of us. 'Besides, he had the Brothels of Carthage, didn't he? He was way ahead of me. I should stop stealing. God save me. But not just yet. Actually, I'm thinking of dedicating each day of the week to a deadly sin. I really need to brush up on my covetousness and sloth.'

I make Louis stop at the Cathedral of Tomorrow as penance. There is a gift shop here that I want to go to. 'See if there is anything Made in Japan in there,' Louis calls out the window to me and then does some figures of eight in the parking lot. Louis collects things that are Made in Japan. He's sure that some day the whole island will go under in a huge volcanic eruption, like Atlantis, and then he'll have a corner on the market of souvenirs from the place. 'Can you imagine what a ceramic monkey with "Made in Atlantis" stamped on its bottom would be worth nowadays?' he's always asking me.

I go inside. There is a big woman standing in the corner. She has a name tag that says Sister Thelma Roosevelt. There is hymn music in the background and she is humming along to it and swaying slightly. There are lots of gold crosses, St

Christopher statues to hang from your rear-view mirror, tapes of the Cathedral of Tomorrow singers and large gilt-framed pictures of Jesus, who has flowing hair and eyes like a doe.

Then I see a plastic bas-relief of the Virgin Mary, the type you can hang on your wall. There is a lightbulb inside and an electric cord coming out of the back so you can plug it in. Mary's eyes are slanty and she wears a low-cut blue dress with great billowing folds. She looks a little like Sophia Loren. But she's about three feet tall – I don't think she'll fit in the Porsche. So Sister Thelma Roosevelt says she'll throw in the lightbulb and one of the postcards of the Cathedral of Tomorrow singers and mail it to me, free. You can tell she is used to wheeling and dealing.

Our last stop is at the Terminal Tower in downtown Cleveland. Louis says that God is the ultimate voyeur, and in order to understand Him we should try to see things from His viewpoint. It is all windy and cloudy out. There is the smell of exhaust, and sulphur from the steel factories.

'What do you think brimstone smells like?' I ask Louis.

'Probably a *fleur du mal* miasma.' He takes a deep breath. 'But what I'm interested in is the taste of the forbidden fruit. Can you imagine what the taste of pure sin would be like? Probably luscious and prickly as evil roses. Pure *nostalgie de la boue*.'

'A sin-sation,' I say, and feel a shiver down my spine. I look sideways at Louis. I am dying to ask him questions that I know I cannot. Do you remember sleep-walking? Do you remember a summer day, a day like today, thirteen years ago? Do you remember seeing a girl, the same age as me, falling? Do you remember her still form on a stone path, the feel of something sticky and warm on your fingers? The Bible says that knowledge brings suffering. If Louis did remember, how would that change him? Would he be the same person?

In order to stop myself from asking Louis these questions, I scream '*Buongiorno Roma!*' loudly into the wind. I feel like Gina Lollobrigida. Louis holds me while I lean far out over the edge. I get whirlwinds in my temples.

'Do you believe in God? That he created and runs everything?' I ask Louis while gazing fifty stories below us.

'No. But I don't think it's all complete chaos either. I think God is like a weekly cleaning lady. When everything gets overrun, He shows up and dusts and mops, takes a cigarette break and complains just loud enough for us to hear about what slobs we are, then collects the check and leaves.' Louis suddenly pulls me up so hard and fast the wind is almost knocked out of me. When I get my balance I see he is looking over the side of the building. I lean over and see a couple of police cars surrounding the red Porsche below us, their blue lights flashing. A few policemen are milling around the car, taking down the license plate number. One is jimmying the lock.

'Shit. Johnny Law,' Louis whispers. He glances over at me. 'Looks like we'll have to take the bus home.'

I stare at him. 'You . . . lied,' I screech at him.

'What's new?' Louis shrugs. 'My psychiatrist says I suffer from cognitive dissonance and moral indolence. We should probably wait up here until they leave.' Then he watches an ant crawling across the stone side of the building, with a feline intensity. 'Wanna see God?' he asks it, and then smashes it with the heel of his hand.

In almost all movies, there is the line: 'Let's get out of here!'

ANGELS are numerous benevolent spirits, divine messengers, that mediate between the realm of the sacred and the profane realm of time. They are beings of pure intelligence, unencumbered by material bodies, and their existence is aeviternal – having a beginning, but no end. Therefore, angels see all things at once, by direct intuition. Outside the element of time, they have no need for memory or reason, and recognize universal forms at a glance. They alone can imitate God. Having seen God's essence, they cannot turn away.

Some monks in the fourteenth century decided to count up all the angels. At that time they numbered 301, 655, 722. I wonder how many there are now. Leonora's always talking to herself. Except she says she's talking to angels. She calls them by different names: Sachiel, Behemiel, Shakziel. Her favorite is Nathaniel, the angel of fire. 'That's the element I feel closest to, baby!' she says, wiggling her hips. I asked her what they look like. 'They don't look like nothing, sweetie. They just *sound* you out.' She draws the word 'sound' out like it's taffy.

At night I try to listen for them. They say there are sounds too large to hear, like the earth moving, and sounds too small to hear, like your cells rotating. I wonder how big angels are. It would take you two whole weeks to count from one to a million. There are millions of stars. And you can't hear them. Large numbers can give you vertigo. APEIROPHOBIA is the fear of infinity.

Death is the godfather of the thirteenth child. My sister's mad godfather sent her a birthday card. It arrived today. I guess he forgot she was dead. I thought it was for me. It was addressed to: Haddie Ashton, Treelawn Drive, Avon Heights, Ohio. She was born on 20 June, a Gemini. Those born under its auspices have a dual nature – light and dark, heavenly and earthly, capable of extremes of love and of hate. She would have been twenty-six years old now.

Leonora's preacher says that heaven is 2000 miles up in the sky, but we've been higher than that and no one saw heaven. Unless it is invisible. Medieval peasants used to think that nests were pieces of paradise, and you could find herbs of invisibility in them. If you were invisible, would your thoughts be different? Without any outlines, you wouldn't feel you were in any particular place, but rather floating, betwixt and between. And without a body, you couldn't feel pain, so you would lose all fear – of loud noises, the dark, falling. Maybe because you were invisible you would be able to see other invisible things – time, thoughts, sounds, secrets. And you could be carried by the rushing motion of your mind toward the iridescent edges of things.

HOW TO PASS THROUGH A BRICK WALL: Bend at the waist and lean forward. Let your body be supported by your knees. Press your palms against the wall. Chant the secret formula. Plea to the powers beyond understanding.

ABELARD was a theologian and philosopher best known for his solution of the problem of universals, and for his celebrated affair with his private pupil Heloïse. He wrote the book *Sic et Non*, in which he tried to reconcile through rules the contradictions of the meanings of words. After Abelard was castrated by decree from Heloïse's enraged uncle, he fled to the Abbey of St Denis, where he wrote *The Story of my Calamities*, and received passionate letters from Heloïse, which are considered to be the most beautiful expressions of love ever written in history.

I am sitting on my bed, waiting for dusk – the hour of vespers.

My Virgin Mary light is off, and as it gets darker her face seems to shrink. I go to the closet and feel for the silk dress I am going to wear. I already have my stockings and shoes on the bed. I pull off my jeans and shirt, and carefully roll on the stockings and fasten them with the garters. Then I step into the dress and zip up the back. It has a swishing sound like those drum brushes just before the first notes of 'Volare'. The material of the dress and the stockings is so very smooth; in it, my room seems coarse and childish.

I am going to a champagne wedding reception for Missy Sabrina Carmichael and Tad Bradley Wilkins. Missy Sabrina wears monograms on everything: MSC. Louis Lewis says she should get herself branded on the forehead. He says that if there is such a thing as reincarnation, Missy will come back in her next life as a stuffed animal. One with sad eyes and a heart around its neck that says 'Huggums Wuvs You'. And he says that Tad Wilkins is the missing link between the plant and animal kingdoms, that he is in urgent need of a jejunal biopsy to remove the growth of ennui that is his head. So I guess they are the perfect match.

In my purse I have a love potion that Leonora made. She boiled orange rind and rose petals in lavender water, added a few petals of marigold, her grandfather's gold tooth and some shavings of ginger root. She says you are supposed to use mandrake root, but that it is hard to come by as you have to get someone willing to pull it from the ground and go insane from its wild screams. Then she poured it all through a sieve into a little bottle placed on a circle of red cloth and chanted: 'Har har hou hou, *danse ici*, *danse là*, har har hou hou, dance here, dance there, play here, play there,' screwed the lid on the bottle and handed it to me. She insisted that I pour a little of it into the bride's and groom's champagne because it will ensure an everlasting, mad love.

My grandmother is my date. I love the way she dresses when she goes out. At her house she's always wearing kimonos and silk pajamas, but whenever she socializes she wears suits she bought back in the fifties. They are made of fabric you only see in places like Bergdorf Goodman's, and she wears extinct perfumes like Guerlain's Sous le Vent, Bonwit Teller's 721, Worth's Imprudence. I've seen them advertised in ancient *Vogue*s my grandmother has piled in her closets. One had the word '*soigné*' written in cursive writing over an endless-necked model with a *retroussé* nose. For a long time I thought *soigné* meant angry. As the final touch my grandmother puts on her 'reds' – rubies, emeralds, diamonds, sapphires. She says that after seventy-five you can wipe vulgar from your jeweled-apparel vocabulary, because your assets turn from flesh to stone. From legs and cleavage to carats and rocks. And you should make sure they are precious – anything semi, hemi or demi is entirely inappropriate for a woman of a certain age.

When we arrive at the wedding, the Mayor corners my grandmother, telling her about all their ho-hum mutual acquaintances, so I wander over to the hors-d'oeuvre table. Louis is standing behind it, tossing olives from a formidable height into his open mouth. When he sees me he says, 'Quick! What am I?' and then drapes himself backward over the table, eyes closed, hands waggling down from the crown of his head, his tongue sticking sideways out of his mouth. I shrug, ignoring him, looking for candied almonds. 'A dead rabbit in a Dutch painting,' Louis says, still holding the pose.

'I don't think that we have met.' A woman is standing over Louis's prone body. She must be in charge of catering. She has those administration eyes, ones with timetables continually scrolling behind them.

Louis springs to his feet. 'Herr K,' he says in this obscure Baltic accent, shaking her hand and clicking his heels together. 'And this is Dora,' he adds, sweeping a dismissive hand at me. He's always introducing us to strangers as deranged patients of Freud. 'Psst,' he whispers sideways to the woman while looking at me. 'Don't mention horses,' and draws circles with his finger in the air by his ear and crosses his eyes.

'That was Little Hans, stupid,' I say, glad of a reason to call him stupid.

'Shh. No hysterics. Coax that uterus down.' Louis leans over and gives me a patronizing pat on the head. 'Well, I'm off to find a village girl in knee socks to tumble under a hedge. Tahnk heaven for leetle girls.' He sighs, and then disappears into the crowd of tuxedos and taffeta.

I walk over to the edge of the dance floor. The air is heady with the scent of lilies, which are gathered in huge bouquets in vases around the room. Some are already dying extravagantly, their stemmed necks thrown back in ecstatic agony or bowed like expiring saints. I see my grandmother dancing with the Mayor. Children run in and out among the dancing couples and a sobbing flower girl chased by the ring bearer takes hold of my grandmother's skirt and wipes her runny nose on the hem. My grandmother is elegant, glittering, aloof, and without missing a boxstep beat she slips a rose from her corsage, places it behind the little girl's ear and sends her skipping gaily away.

Missy and Tad do a turn in front of me and a whiff of Love's Baby Soft perfume hits me. Louis and his mother are dancing near the band. Mrs Lewis is wearing a dress with purple and yellow flowers on it. The fabric is see-throughish, and when she moves the flowers freeze and melt, and then freeze again. Louis is wearing a tuxedo and I have to admit he does look debonair. He wants to be a *quatorzième* when he grows up. Which is a fourteenth – a bachelor who lives in Paris and dresses in evening clothes every night at six o'clock, ready to step into any dinner party threatening to have only thirteen guests. 'A living talisman warding off occult threats of the unlucky number' is how Louis describes it. So he is always in training for his Valentino *vie manquée* as a gay lothario. He plans on circling the globe with his entourage of polo ponies, Pomeranians, Swiss valet, his own personal wet-nurse and Xavier Cugat's entire ballroom band.

Louis leads his mother surefootedly across the floor, pulls her in close, leans down to whisper something in her ear. She laughs, her white teeth glistening, her neck arching backward to reveal a long string of pearls disappearing beneath her dress. Louis dips her in a smooth movement, her long leg kicks up, and then he twirls her in tight circles.

I decide to take care of the carnal duty Leonora saddled me with. I go up to the bar. I figure I can pour a couple of glasses of champagne, slip in the mickey, and then offer them to Missy and Tad as they come off the dance floor. The uncles all hang out at the bar. Most of them are large, with shoulders like bridges, but there is always a little one like a sneeze stuck in among them. They are at that obscure stage in life – in between yelling 'hey Dude' to their friends and wearing black socks and brown shoes down to the beach. They bore each other like mad, but they try to rise above it all by acting boisterous and describing the hips of a new secretary with hand motions in the air.

I step up to the bar and am suddenly enclosed in their patriarchal musk. I dip glasses under the champagne fountain and get lots of winks and saloon cajoling, and offers of chasers to go with my double-fisted tipple. Then I am forgotten as they launch into a round of binge and bender stories, so I pour the potion into the glasses without them noticing and go back to the dance floor to wait for Missy and Tad. One of the glasses is taken swiftly from my hand, and Louis raises it in salute to me. 'Thank you, sweet thang,' he drawls, and is about to drink it, when Mrs Lewis comes up behind him and takes the glass away. 'I don't think so, darling,' she says, and takes a sip herself. Before I can say anything, Louis murmurs 'Ecce Homo', while looking over my shoulder.

I turn and see the bachelor standing just behind us at one of the open french doors that lead out to the pool. One of the drunken uncles is pulling him inside by the elbow. The bachelor is protesting, trying to turn around and leave, but the uncle keeps telling him he has to have a drink in celebaashun of a bootiful mirage. The bachelor finally assents, and they walk toward us. The uncle is walking as though the floor has stairs. His giddy eyes alight on me and he grabs the other glass of champagne from me, saying 'Tsk tsk, too young', handing it to the bachelor, and then teetering backward a few steps. Louis gets behind the uncle and leads him over to a chair. 'Come on, sugar shoes,' he says gently.

The bachelor looks sheepish, but raises his glass: 'Congratulations to . . .' He looks around for the bride and groom, but they are nowhere to be seen. 'Missy and Tad,' I say, 'but, umm, I don't know where they are.'

'Missy and Tad,' the bachelor repeats softly, and then drinks some champagne. 'I was just walking my dogs . . . on the golf course . . . I don't want to intrude . . .' He trails off, suddenly staring in a kind of trance at Mrs Lewis, who is standing next to me. Her hand is at her throat. The blood has drained from her face. She lifts her glass to her mouth, and I can see her hand is shaking. Her wedding ring chimes against the glass. Mrs Lewis can be easily startled, like a flock of birds.

'Yes . . . well . . . mm . . .' The bachelor clears his throat. There is a band of sweat on his upper lip. He looks from Mrs Lewis to me, and then back to Mrs Lewis again. I try to think of something to say because the silence is tense. Mrs Lewis is twisting her strand of pearls in knots.

The bachelor drinks some more champagne and then places the glass on a table. 'I really must . . .'

He stops mid-sentence because there is a sharp, snapping sound as Mrs Lewis's necklace breaks and the pearls fall, rolling over the floor.

'*Merde!*' Mrs Lewis whispers with a sharp intake of breath. Her face is bright red.

We all kneel down and start picking them up. We hear a loud thump behind us as a couple of dancers slide on loose pearls and fall. Mrs Lewis is biting her lip and whispering '*Pardonnez moi . . . pardonnez moi . . .*' over and over, each time someone drops a pearl into her cupped hand. The bachelor places his handful of pearls in Mrs Lewis's hands, and then curls her fingers over them, gives them a quick squeeze. He smiles at me, and nods, and turns and exits through the french doors.

A lock of hair has fallen across Mrs Lewis's left eye. There is a tiny drop of red blood on her bottom lip where she bit it. Louis strides over to her and pushes the lock of hair behind her ear, wipes the blood off her lip with his thumb and licks it. He takes the pearls from her cupped hands and shoves them in his pocket. 'Who *was* that masked man?' he asks, sarcastic. 'Dance?' Then he takes her hands and tangos her out to the center of the floor.

'Well, it looks as though Mrs Lewis has found herself a new

friend,' I hear a voice saying behind my left shoulder. I turn and see Mrs van de Bere. Louis calls her 'Old Goat Eyes' because her pupils are tiny as pinpricks. She's always saying things like: 'My, you're looking *better* dear,' or 'How *courageous* of you to wear that little dress so soon after your pregnancy!' to younger, prettier women. She makes these comments in a cloying voice that makes me think of candied apples stuck full of rusted razors.

'How nice for her,' Mrs van de Bere continues, gazing off over my head. 'Goodness but she must be lonely with her husband away so much. What is the reason for all the traveling that Mr Lewis does?'

'His work . . . he . . .'

'Of course, dear, work is the best thing to do when you are unhappy – keeping busy is the remedy for a troubled mind . . . you tell Louis not to worry . . . sometimes separations can help set a marriage back on the right track . . .'

'But the Lewises aren't separ—'

'Aren't you a good and loyal friend – of course they would not want to make a separation public information,' she says in a bright voice. 'So who is this new man in Mrs Lewis's life?' she asks, while lighting a cigarette.

'He isn't . . . she just . . . kind of . . . met him. He's the . . . a bachelor. He moved into the Monroe house . . .'

'Goodness, that is convenient,' she says, while blowing smoke out of the side of her mouth, 'and what a *coincidence!*' The word 'coincidence' rolls about in her mouth in swirls. 'I am sure she has been missing Mr Monroe horribly. As women grow older, it becomes much harder to find favorable companionship . . .'

'But . . . there is some mistake . . . Mrs Lewis said she didn't know Mr Monroe . . . that they were not well acquaint—'

'How utterly revealing.' Mrs van de Bere's small eyes that

have been darting about the room suddenly set themselves squarely on my face. 'Mrs Lewis and Mr Monroe were very congenial – perhaps more well-disposed toward each other than is quite proper for those already espoused. Of course, conjugal vows mean different things to those from different cultures . . .' Her eyes, which have started roaming again, suddenly hit upon a target. 'Missy, sweetie,' she says gaily to the bride, who has just stepped off the dance floor, 'what an absolute marvel to see you in *white*!'

Later, I see Mrs Lewis out by the pool. It is drained, I suppose because they are going to clean it. I go up to her and say hello. 'Don't you love aquamarine?' she says, looking down into the deep end. 'Yeah, I guess so.' I don't really know what to say. 'Not just the color. The word. Aquamarine.' She sits down at the edge of the pool and lets her feet dangle into it. 'Aquamarine,' she says into the pool and it echoes a bit. I sit down next to her. I try it: 'Aquamarine.' It sounds great. I realize it must be my favorite word. When you say it, you can feel yourself submerging into its turquoise depths, bubbles rising at each consonant. And I wasn't even drunk.

Mrs Lewis must have been reading my mind because she looks at me and says, 'I'm not drunk.' 'I didn't think so,' I say, even though I guess I did. She kicks her feet against the pool wall and the flowers on her dress dance around. She seems happy, which makes me realize she is usually quite sad. I wonder if what Mrs van de Bere said about Mrs Lewis knowing Mr Monroe quite well was true. And, if so, why Mrs Lewis lied to me. Perhaps, with some people, like Louis, lying is just a natural reflex. And, if so, maybe Louis inherited it from his mother.

An ABYSS is any deep place, but is especially applied to regions of the sea or waters under the earth. In general, the abyss is regarded vaguely as a place of indefinite extent, an abode of mystery, and sorrow. '*Les vertiges des grandes profondeurs*' is the vertigo of the great deeps. At certain depths, the deep-sea diver becomes influenced by the illusion that natural breathing is possible, removes his tanks, and drowns. In Hades, the abyss is where the damned fall for centuries and never hit bottom.

My grandmother and I are resting on pillows. We were just practicing a type of yoga in which you try to awaken the snake energy located in the root chakra at the base of your spine. I can still feel a soft whirring at the bottom of my back.

'Was Mrs Lewis friends with the Monroes – Mr Monroe in particular?' I ask my grandmother after a few minutes.

'Yes.' I think this one-word answer is all I am going to get out of her, but then she sits up, and sighs, saying, 'Mrs Lewis used to be much more sociable. She was friendly with a lot of people. But especially so with the Monroes. She had known them for years before they even moved here, to this town.'

I sit up in surprise. 'What? How?'

'She had met them in Paris. Mr Monroe was studying cinema there. I believe, in fact, it was Mrs Lewis who suggested that the Monroe family move here – Mr Monroe was quite concerned about his children's well-being, and Calif—'

'But Mrs Lewis told me she wasn't well acquainted with Mr Monroe.'

'I can't imagine why.' My grandmother raises her eyebrows. 'But then, Mrs Lewis can be rather odd and secretive, can't she?' My grandmother frowns. 'Yes, I had the sense they were very good friends. Mr Monroe spoke fluent French. And of course they had the experience of Paris in common. Mr Monroe was quite nostalgic about the place. I remember, one evening, reminiscing with the two of them about the Bois de Bologne at dawn, the Sacré-Coeur, the Tuileries – the usual thing.' She gets a look in her eyes, like everyone does when they talk about Paris – as though she might suddenly break out into sentimental song. But then she jerks her head back. 'You know, when someone takes their life, it is such a tremendous shock to their friends and family,' she says softly. 'Everyone reacts differently toward it – some cannot forgive that person. They come to hate – wish they had never known the person. Perhaps this is the case with Mrs Lewis . . .'

'Wait.' It feels like a piece of ice has just been dropped down the back of my shirt. 'Mr Monroe . . . commited suicide?'

'I thought you knew, dear.' My grandmother looks at me uneasily. 'I probably shouldn't have said anything . . .' She lets out a long breath, and her face becomes composed again. 'Mr Monroe drove his car off that bridge on purpose. He left a note in which he said his inspiration had dried up. I think he had too much attention too early in his career. Which can be quite damaging. Perhaps even' – my grandmother looks past me, out the window – 'this is a bit fanciful, but your sister acted as a sort of muse for him. I do not completely understand these things – but I know that some artists always use a certain model. Without whom they cannot paint. But to leave his wife and children – it is shameful.'

I yell 'O felix culpa!' and dive from a high branch into the Bottomless Lake. I am trying to see what it is like to think while you are falling. It's a voluptuous feeling, like being completely overwhelmed – in that sexy space between the yes and no of temptation. And my mind seems to separate from my body – it whooshes right out through the bottom of my feet. I wonder if, after that first bite of the fruit of the tree of knowledge, Eve felt a jolt of surprise – as if she had just accidentally walked off the edge of a high building – and then the sharp, jagged terror of time rushing by.

If my sister chose to jump from the Monroes' house, what had made her so unhappy that she would want to take her own life? And if she did, why didn't she leave a note? Maybe she did, and no one ever found it. I wonder what her last thoughts were, as the ground came looming up to meet her. Did she suddenly regret her actions? Or did she feel a wonderful peace as her beginning and her ending clashed together in a bright flash?

I wonder if the earth and the sun and Neptune and Venus are all falling and we just don't know it. If we can't feel the earth moving, we wouldn't feel it falling. When you wonder about something, it makes you catch your breath, as if a trapdoor has just opened beneath you, and you start to fall.

If a hole were drilled through the center of the earth and you were thrown into it, you would fall faster and faster, reaching a speed of 18,000 miles per hour at the center of the earth, then fall slower and slower until you stopped just to peek over the edge at a surprised Chinaman before you zoom back down again and reappear on your side. The whole trip would take eighty-four minutes. This assuming you had someone on your side waiting to hand you a rope or pluck you out with a staff. Otherwise you would bob like an olive infinitely. The way up and the way down being one and the same.

When you think about it, it is amazing how hard the universe is working just to keep you in place.

*

Louis has taken up The Brush. Because his new hero is Leonardo da Vinci. So he is an *Uomo Universale* – Universal Man. He calls people dolts and ruffians, and uses exaggerated affectations and feigns *sprezzatura* – a contemptuous indifference. And he walks, talks and eats *con brio* and *di bravura*. This is achieved in part by walking around with his arms akimbo. It seems to me that this *sprezzatura* and *con brio* are a bit at odds with each other, but when I mention this to Louis he just gives me a contemptuous look and swanks off down the street.

All of the people in his paintings look as though they have tuberculosis. He's just finished another one of me in which I have a long, yellowish face and blue, mottled hands that look as if they're not screwed on right. It's titled *Wastrel Youth*. His favorite is a painting of me as St Sebastian all stuck through with arrows. It looks more like a tubercular patient surprised by a bramble bush. Which I think is a much more original concept. But when I suggest to Louis that he change the title to *Tubercular Patient Surprised by a Bramble Bush*, he goes into a moody artistic sulk and archly comments that artists used to stab Philistines to death with poisoned daggers. And receive papal pardons for it. Because it was considered just punishment for thwarting divine inspiration.

The first crush I had was on a monk in an El Greco painting. He's at the Cleveland Museum of Art. I first saw him when I was about seven. He's in a room full of paintings of people suffering. All their mouths are open and their eyes are rolled upward and their hands look arthritic. They remind me of people in aspirin commercials.

The monk is in between two huge paintings of suffering people. He is very tall and seems to be both sitting and standing at the same time. He has long white fingers that rest on the arms of a black chair. They seem very alive. His face is long and pale and thin. He is so serene. Looking at him after seeing all those grief-stricken people is like diving underwater at an overcrowded pool. His eyes are the best part. They are brown and deep – they are like long, dark passageways into the cave where his mind lives. You can get vertigo looking into his eyes.

We've been having a heatwave. It's about 102 degrees in the shade. My grandmother and I have been doing the underwater meditation, feeling our hair undulate downstream, and little fish darting over our heads. Leonora's been sitting out on our back porch all day, complaining about how the minutes are about as long as the Mississippi, drinking hobo cocktails, which are tall glasses of water, and practicing her game of three-card monte. She says she's got dealer's hands just made for the dupe. Mrs Lewis, who always looks '*bien dans sa peau*' – feeling good in her skin – is flushed, and keeps smoothing the outlines of her clothes, and is restless, as if the music has just stopped and she's been left without a chair. 'Do not multiply epithets and adjectives. Do not be too fond of superlatives. Moderate your transports,' she tells us at Charm School, in a voice that keeps getting faster and higher with each word until my teeth are completely on edge.

The heat has gotten to the bachelor the most. He seems slightly unhinged, like he is searching everywhere for a hat that is already on his head. But he's looking less formal – he carries his black jacket slung over his left shoulder, his sleeves are rolled up, his hair sticks wet to the nape of his neck. Once I heard him whistle a sad gypsy tune. While serving tennis balls to his garage door, his morning ritual. Sometimes, when the bachelor does walk into town, he'll stop abruptly on his way, turn around, and go home, as though he is a sleep-walker who has found himself out of doors, bewildered to be awake.

I've joined Leonora out on the porch. We sit there in silence. It is too hot to talk. The yellowing grass of the lawn smells like warm hay. I close my eyes and tilt my head toward the sun. When I open them, I see Leonora looking at me, in a complicated way, as though she is trying to connect the dots between different parts of my face. 'What?' I ask her.

'Never mind,' Leonora says, shuffling her cards and laying them out in front of her.

'What?' I ask again. 'Tell me.'

Leonora gives me a long lion's stare. Several muggy seconds pass. 'You look like her.'

'Who?'

'Maybe not.' Leonora waves an indecisive hand in the air.

'Who?' I repeat.

'Your sister,' Leonora says, in a heavy way, as though the words have anchors attached to them. I have to keep myself from jumping up and immediately looking in a mirror.

'Is that bad?' I ask her. The sun is hammering on top of my head. A rivulet of sweat runs down the side of my face.

'No, butterfly, it's just strange that I didn't notice it before. Of course, I made the Change overnight myself. One day, I was some cross-eyed kid drinking Nehi sodas under the cottonwoods, scratching at chigger bites on my knees, and the next, I was bothering every man I ran into on the street. It is a *strange* business.'

I go to the bathroom and stand in front of the mirror. I look closely at my nose and eyes and mouth, and tilt my head toward my left shoulder. A sudden sweet pain runs through me. I look like her. I am beautiful. I get this overwhelming, weird feeling, where I don't know whether it is my beauty, or hers. I lean closer toward the mirror. So does she. 'Hello, Haddie,' we say at the same time. I close my eyes and have to hold onto the sink to steady myself.

Philosophers often talk about the connections between Beauty and Truth. And, in a way, both Beauty and Truth can make you feel as though you are falling.

AQUINAS wrote the *Summa Theologiae* in a question-and-answer format. It is an encyclopedic treatise which, in the spirit of the age of Scholasticism, aimed to unify the corpus of ancient knowledge and Christian theology into a single volume. Aquinas articulated the difference between natural and revealed theology, believing that our earthly intellects cannot have direct access to transcendent ideas, but rather indirectly perceive the divine by observing the visible particulars around us, which all participate in God's existence. God grants all things their existence; thus a thing's essence, its reality, is the degree to which it is a part of God's existence. For Aquinas, to gain knowledge of our world had a profound spiritual significance – using our senses to learn more about nature led us on the holy path toward the perfection of absolute Existence. Man, Aquinas stated, is 'a horizon of the spiritual and the corporeal'.

Sometimes I close my eyes and picture Leonora when she was twelve, running through the daisy field toward that sunken-cathedral stream. If I concentrate hard I can hear the wind rustling the daisies, the whispering of celestial secrets. Little green grasshoppers ping out of her path. She brushes bees from her bare arms. There is a hot yellow smell. In religious paintings there is usually a foreground of warm animal brown and distances of cool, silvery blue, the color of tomorrow. Sometimes I picture Leonora and her daisy field in the background of some religious painting. Blue train, blue daisies, blue trees, blue stream – everything inside the rarefied air of a prayer. Paintings seem to be giving you an answer to something. A painted answer. And you have to figure out the question.

'Imagine yourself as a bowl of water in the middle of the ocean. Imagine the glass of the bowl breaking, and feel yourself merging – water into water.' My grandmother has a cocktail voice, cool as ice cubes chinking against the inside of a glass. I think of how Louis likes to break things. It is one of his favorite hobbies. He says there is nothing more sublime than the sound of shattering.

'You can also enter the sound of your name, and through its vibrations, become one with all vibrations.'

I say 'Haddie, Haddie, Haddie'. But instead of entering inside it, each time I say it, it seems to get further away from me. Aquinas concentrated on questions he called quodlibets. One has to do with the incorporeality of angels. It asks: Can two things occupy the same space simultaneously?

'Do you think I look like my sister?' I ask my grandmother.

'Umm,' my grandmother murmurs noncommittally, obviously involved in her name's vibrations. Then she looks over at me. 'Outwardly, yes, I have noticed – you are looking more and more like her.' She sighs, as though this is not something she wants to admit. 'Your sister – matured – much earlier than you. Which is not necessarily a good thing. I remember the last year – she had become quite uncomfortable with her – how she looked. Your age is a difficult time. Very confusing. And your sister was suddenly the object of a lot of attention. She was put in the limelight, so to speak. Everyone expected her to become a star.' My grandmother waves her hand up high in front of her. 'She started to become ill-tempered about it. If someone commented on her beauty, she would give them a rude stare, and say, "So?" ' She puts her hands on her hips, rolls her eyes skyward like a bored teenager.

'It seemed as though your sister wanted to hide all of a sudden. The way she walked – her shoulders slumped, shuffling her feet. We had to force her to put a comb through her hair, to take a bath. She took to wearing these horrid, baggy overalls, every day – and she became stubborn and obstinate. She would go for days without speaking to anyone. She even devised her own way of saying "no". She would lift her arms up over her head, palms together, elbows pointing out, in a sort of Balinese gesture, and shake her head and waist, at the same time, from right to left.' My grandmother raises her arms and shakes her head, in said gesture. She looks petulant and spoilt. 'This is why you must be on guard against becoming too attached to your appearance. It can end up separating you off from others. But heavens!' My grandmother drops her hands heavily into her lap. 'It could just be your age. I remember Mathilde Monroe had all sorts of problems at that time.'

'What sort of problems?'

'Oh, I don't know the details. She caused her parents a lot of heartache. They ended up sending her to a psychiatrist. It may have been the same one that Louis goes to. She ran away from home several times. Actually, yes, I remember now – she ran away again before the Monroes moved. As a matter of fact, I do not know if she was found before they went away.'

My sister Haddie in that painting seems to be answering something. You get the sense of it more from her hands than her eyes. They are composed, calm, almost nonchalant. In Leonardo's *Last Supper* the hands of the disciples are all gesturing and pointing, in answer to the question: Who among you has betrayed me?

When you look at a painting you are neither outside it nor inside it, but somewhere in between. If you look at it long enough you can start to feel like you are in that hyphenated space of those vase–profile, rabbit–duck pictures. Leonardo calls the boundaries between things '*termine*'. He defines it as a part of the abutment that has no physical substance in its own right.

LIST OF SPACES: The space between parentheses, the space between your eyes, between the notes of music, of silent 'w's and 'h's, the space inside a locked locket, between elements on a chart, between lines of poetry, inside the throats of flowers, cursed spaces inside ancient tombs, spaces between the rings of a telephone, between dots to be connected, the space before a punchline, the airy space of vowels, the space of hesitation, of temptation, of an indentation, between drops of water in Chinese torture, of the blind spot, the space between a sylvan maiden and a man on a Grecian urn.

'*Voila*!' Louis tosses a manila folder down in front of me. 'It's Mathilde Monroe's file. From my psychiatrist's,' Louis says, while throwing himself into a chair next to me. I had told him what my grandmother said to me. About Mathilde's problems. And about my suspicions concerning her and my sister's death.

'How . . .' I begin to ask.

'I had a fit of hysteria,' Louis says, cutting me off. 'After Dr Schultz showed me some anatomically correct puppet. I ran screaming from his office and barricaded myself in the file room.

You should have seen him afterwards – beaming, and pleased as punch. He thinks he's made a real breakthrough. He gave me a copy of *I'm OK, You're OK.*'

I open the file. On top is a letter to Dr Schultz from the principal of our school. It talks about Mathilde's callous behavior toward others, her sudden drop in academic achievement, of how she was repeatedly caught smoking and vandalizing school property. But the main reason for the referral is an essay she turned in to her language instructor. Apparently, the students were supposed to write 500 words, in French, on their favorite hobby, and Mathilde chose to write about – and here the principal's wording becomes obviously strained and delicate – 'the various favors she bestowed upon members of the football team, under the bleachers, after home games'. I look up at Louis, open-mouthed. 'Did you read this?' I ask him.

'Uh-huh. According to that letter, she sounds perfectly sane to me. A veritable black Venus of my dreams.'

I snort, and flip the letter over. The next few pages are notes Dr Schultz made during her visits. How she was uncooperative and unresponsive. When asked what she most enjoyed doing, she replied 'sleeping'. When asked about friends at school, she said she had none (no mention of my sister). When Dr Schultz asked her why, she said, 'Because I am about a thousand years older than all of them.' There is just basically more of the same, and then after all the notes there is a letter Dr Schultz wrote to the principal. It says that due to her father's refusal to have her come to any more appointments, her therapy was terminated.

'Why do you think Mr Monroe had her therapy ended?' I ask Louis.

'Because Schultz is an asshole.' Louis waves a blasé hand in front of him. 'Here.' He takes the file from me, ruffles through the pages, and then hands me a Personality Test. The same one we had to take at school. 'This is where you get the sense she is definitely one brick short of a load – look at the Creativity Test.' I open up the booklet and flip through it. The Creativity Test is a square, cut up into eight little boxes. Each box has a line in it – half-circles, diagonals, horizontals. You are supposed to use the line already in the box as a starting point to draw a picture from. However, in Mathilde's test you can't even see the original lines. Because she has blackened in each box completely with her pencil. But what is even stranger is that she hasn't just colored them in. You can see, when you look closer, that she has written hundreds of 'M's overlapping each other, in each box, until there are no white spaces left.

Louis reaches over and turns the pages of the test to the Emotional Stability section. 'Look at some of the questions she answered "yes" to.' He runs his finger along the page – stopping once in a while at certain entries: Would you be more upset by the loss of material things than hearing about the serious illness of a friend? Do you hurt people in order to get what you want? Do you sometimes have cruel fantasies? Would you like to witness an execution? Have you ever felt the urge to kill some-one? Louis stops at this last question, underlining it with his finger, and then tracing a line over to the 'yes' she has circled. I feel a prickling at the back of my neck, and along my arms. Like the temperature in the room just dropped below freezing.

The bachelor has been spending whole days copying out parts of the Bible. He sits under a tree on his front lawn, the book propped up against a large rock, a notebook open upon his lap. When I stopped and asked him 'why', he said that books reveal things to you in a different way when you copy them out, word by word.

Hidden things, that can't be seen by the eye gazing at the page, but only flow when you mimic the movement of their letters, feel them in the muscles of your fingers, wrist and arm.

Augustine was weeping under a fig tree in his garden when he heard a child's singsong voice saying, *'tolle, lege, tolle, lege'* – take up and read – and so he picked up a Bible and read the line, 'Come, follow me . . .' The universe is God's book and the Bible is our index to understanding it, he said.

I take out our Bible and hold it at arm's length, squint my eyes and try to read the pattern of the white spaces between the black lines, which could be the silent secret language of angels.

HOW TO ACHIEVE INSTANT SALVATION: Say: 'Namu Amida Butsu,' the magical formula praising the Amida Buddha.

Monks in medieval scriptoria believed that each word they copied out of the Bible smote a devil. And they kept diaries of their encounters with angels. Nobody ever mentions there being books in heaven. Probably because limbo is where all the books are kept. People who read a lot of books have trouble making up their minds about things. I can imagine all these people in limbo wafting around, books in hand, going ah, maybe, I can see that too, perhaps, hmm . . .

Sometimes when I get that dizzy, *déjà vu* feeling, I also hear a jingling sound inside my head. Maybe it is the sound of angels, passing through, their divine messages fluttering like the thin gilt pages of bibles, making me dizzy because they are moving in the crazy sideways figure-eight shape of infinity. And their *aevum*, the eternity of angels that has a beginning but no end, halts for an instant the arrow of time, and leaves it rocking like a small boat on heavy seas.

In the 'Theology' section of the library I find a book called *The City of Angels*. Someone obviously misfiled it, because inside, on the front page, is the subtitle: 'Hollywood: Heaven or Hell?' I flip through it. There are pictures of Oriental dens of iniquity; a body shown floating face down in a huge heart-shaped pool; a couple of movie stars handcuffed outside the Bamboo Room; some actress slumped over a round table at the Brown Derby with the words 'Heroin Heroine' underneath. In a chapter entitled 'Organization Connections' I find a picture of Emmalou de Cherraglio. She is seated at a velvet banquette, with three men in dark suits. The caption says, 'Miss de Cherraglio, whose knack for acting is centered around her knockers, is shown seated at the Trocadero with male companion Eddie "Leadhead" Lumbago and two unidentified associates.' The two 'unidentified' associates look out of place – as if their natural habitats would more likely be off the highway cocktail lounges at noon, or smoky police interrogation rooms.

The chapter talks about the mob's nefarious connections with the Studios, and how their corrupt currency is the filthy lucre behind most big movie budgets. They thereby fiendishly control producers, directors, writers and actors. There are pictures of the people who did not 'cooperate'. J. J. Berman, who was found in the men's room of Beachcomber's with an ice pick driven through his heart. C. K. Price, who disappeared off his yacht and was washed ashore two weeks later on a beach in Carmel, a bullet hole in his forehead. O. K. Edwards, who choked on a hemlock salad served to him at Chasen's. A dashing Errol Flynn look-alike run over on Sunset Strip by a speeding limousine. The writer says that when the murder is not an act of revenge, instead of bullets and cement shoes, the mob will make it look like an accident. The examples the writer gives of these 'accidents' are being pushed in front of a speeding train, or haphazard falls from high places.

Louis Lewis says that if we can't experience a miracle, we might as well create one. Then our town would become a landmark, like Lourdes, and we could make all sorts of revenue selling souvenirs and relics and those religious postcards in rainbow colors of Louis and me, divine children of God.

'What', Louis muses, 'are miracles but fear and hope copulating to weird beat?' I had never thought about it this way, but I nod my head in agreement. 'And mainly what this sleepy suburb lacks is fear.' He sighs. 'Where are those hordes of invading Huns when you need them? As every schoolboy knows, a fresh influx of barbarians is what brings new life to a humdrum culture.' He looks at the copper-roofed gazebo, the white-painted century homes. 'Someone should sack our city.'

As if in answer to Louis, we hear the sound of gunshots. But it is only the fire department testing fireworks. It is the Fourth of July and we have the Independence Day firework display tonight. I've always hated our national holidays – all those pollyanna pilgrims with their buckles and corn and quilting bees, and Yankee Doodle Do or Die and Betsy Ross and her stupid flag. One Fourth of July I was wearing a stars-and-stripes bathing suit all day and I was left branded with the stigmata of patriotism. The sun went through all the white bits, so for ages there were little brown stars all up and down my belly. Louis Lewis says the best thing the Revolution produced is the Bicentennial Review in the Boom Boom Room at the Fontainebleau Hotel in Miami, Florida, which features a nude Betsy Ross and a topless Statue of Liberty doing the cancan.

'Hey, I've got a great idea!' Louis jumps to his feet. 'I could get elected to sainthood for this.' He starts pacing back and forth in front of me. 'Everyone will be at the fireworks tonight, right?' I nod. 'Even old Sulks from the Bainbridge Estate.' Old Sulks is the caretaker of the Bainbridge Mansion. It is called The Elms and is enclosed on about two dozen acres in the north-west corner of town. Charles Prescott Bainbridge died I don't know how many years ago and left the house and the grounds and his private zoo to our town as a national monument to himself. The zoo has a little petting pen full of mangy sheep and goats. And there are wild animals too, a giraffe even, a couple of rhinos, zebras, ostriches. They don't have much wildness left in them. They mainly lounge about in their *faux* exotic settings like pouty models on a shoot. Old Sulks sits on the fire engine during the Fourth of July fireworks, wearing a fireman's hat. Lord knows why. It's some vague tradition. 'So,' Louis continues, 'I think we should free all the animals in the zoo. Like Leonardo did with all the birds at the market.'

'Louis, why would you do that to all those poor animals? Where are they going to go?'

Louis looks at me as if I am half-witted. 'Haven't you ever heard of those stories about people's pet dogs and cats? The people are moving, all their furniture is in the van. They are ready to go. But, oh no! Where's Poochy? He's nowhere to be found. Finally, they have to leave, amid great wailing and weeping and gnashing of teeth. Then, months later, who shows up on the porch in California but Poochy. It's animal instinct. They can find their way home.' Louis looks satisfied with himself.

I am unconvinced. 'How do they know it's their dog?'

'They have absolutepoochyproof. There is usually a nametag

or an appendix scar. And these are animals that have been inbred for centuries. Mr Bainbridge's animals will be off like a shot, finding their way back to their ancestral African home. Have faith in instinct.'

The hormone for fear and curiosity is the same. Under a microscope its molecules seem to take the shape of a parading Chinese dragon.

Louis and I turn a corner past a grove of pines and the Bainbridge house comes into view. Louis points at it. 'Yonda lies da castle of my fadda da king!' he says, doing Tony Curtis from *The Black Shield of Falmouth*. It is very big. There isn't one particular style to it, but it has lots of turrets and gables, and a couple of towers with ivy creeping everywhere. When I was little I thought Vincent Price lived there, his frog-belly-white face illuminated only by candelabra. And hearts beat in the walls and harpsichords played at midnight, their plucked-spinal chord notes reaching the high towers where vultures nested in the eaves and a tragic princess with a gloomy childhood sat yo-yoing a spider on its string.

Louis and I are walking outside the fence that encloses the whole of the property. We know of a section that has a break in it. At intervals, the sky is lit up by fireworks. We find the break and crawl through, and then dodge dramatically from tree to tree until we reach the petting pen. The goats and sheep look forlorn against the background of the lit-up sky. Louis has a metal cutter from his garage. He snaps the lock off the pen's fence and opens it. The goats and sheep stare at us dumbly. Louis stamps the ground. '*Vive appassionamente! Vive con brio! La Dolce Vita!*' The goat chews on the wire fence. One of the sheep goes 'Baa'. Louis stamps the ground some more and tells them to live passionately and with zest again, but to no avail, and we finally have to get inside the pen and push them out.

The ostriches, zebras, rhinos, and giraffes are a bit easier. They must still have some wild blood in their veins. 'Harness my zebras, gift of the Nubian king!' Louis yells as they stripe past us. The ostriches go racing across the lawn – their bouffant feathers lit up intermittently by fireworks. The kangaroos jump in great leaps into the woods and the giraffes follow with an angular glamor. The rhinos are the most amazing to watch. They steam across the yard and then vanish like storm clouds down the drive, leaving huge billows of dust in their wake. '*Delenda est Carthago!*' Louis yells after them. Then he turns to me. '*Fait accompli!*' He has a triumphant smile on his face. 'A veritable *idée force* in action. This could be as good as a gang of marauding Mongols.'

My parents say that we are Episcopalian. But they are basically pagan. They get edgy around anything religious. Yet we go to church on Christmas Eve and Easter Sunday. Everything in our church is white. The minister's face is the color of water stains on old ceilings. He seems very depressed. And there is always a row of Daughters of the American Revolution with their First Lady hairdos standing right behind you, singing hymns in high voices like tea kettles about to go off the boil. I don't think the people in our church are true believers. They say they believe in God and the Bible, but they say they believe in the theory of evolution too. I don't think they really believe in it, though. I don't think they really believe that they are animals.

'Never kiss and tell for that is the road to hell.' It is humid in the

Charm School classroom today. Ms Phillips has opened the windows and I can see more clearly into the dance studios across the street. One dancer lifts another high into the air and spins around. Mrs Lewis is wearing fawn-colored stockings and tan suede shoes. One leg is wound perfectly around the other.

I read about Amazon anacondas this morning. This is how one attacks you. It wraps its coils around you, pins your arms to the side. It doesn't squeeze hard but tightens its grip each time you exhale, making it increasingly harder to draw the next breath. It doesn't bite, but holds its face close to yours, watching, while its forked tongue flickers around your nose. 'They watch you rather closely,' said Sir Wilbur Phillipus von Hohenheim, a nineteenth-century survivor. Ms Phillips pulls back on my shoulders. 'Don't slouch!' she hisses. 'While the man is allowed to originate the embraces,' Mrs Lewis is saying, 'the young lady has the privilege, which must be assumed sacred, to say, "Stop. No further." '

Later on, while I am waiting to leave with Mrs Lewis, I look at myself doing 'The Look' – the one my grandmother told me Mrs Lewis taught my sister, head bowed, eyes raised – in one of the mirrors that run along the back wall of the ballroom. I hear a heavy thud, and keys clattering on the polished wood floor. Suddenly, I realize Mrs Lewis is behind me, watching me. My face goes bright red. Her face is drained of all color, completely white, as if she's seen a ghost. She closes her eyes, seems to be trying to steady herself, keep herself from fainting. I take hold of her elbow. 'Are you all right?' I ask her. She has dropped her purse and keys. The contents of her purse are spilled out on the floor around her.

'*Je suis désolé*,' she murmurs, 'forgive me,' and opens her eyes. 'I'm fine,' she says in a louder voice, but shaky. Her forehead is damp with perspiration, there are beads of sweat on her upper lip. 'I . . . did not . . . eat today,' she says slowly, running her hands along the sides of her body, as though smoothing out the angles. 'We should go and get some lunch.' I bend down and pick up her comb, wallet, lipstick. I see her open Bible, face down, a few feet from us. I pick it up, and something drops from it. I think it is a used old Kleenex, but when I squat down to get it I see it is a pressed blue rose. I look at where the Bible was open to in order to replace it. It is 'The Song of Songs': 'I am the rose of Sharon, and the lily of the valleys. As the lily among the thorns, so is my love . . .' I start to read, but Mrs Lewis takes the Bible from me before I can finish and shoves it in her purse.

'Here,' I say, holding the rose out to her by its short stem, 'this fell out of it.'

Mrs Lewis jerks her head back in surprise when she sees it, as though I'm handing her a big, ugly insect. When she takes it from me, her hands are trembling slightly. 'I forgot,' she says vaguely. 'I have not used this Bible for a long while.'

'Aren't blue roses rare?' I ask her.

'Yes,' she says, crushing the rose in the palm of her hand. It crackles like fire. 'Very rare.' She brushes her hands together and pieces of blue petals float down to the floor. I smell something dusty and sweet.

In the Bible, a rose can be a symbol of the Virgin Mary, and of the passion and suffering of Christ. 'Do you believe that everything, down here, is just a symbol for what is up above?' I ask Mrs Lewis when we are driving home.

'I do not understand,' Mrs Lewis replies in a tired voice.

'Well, like these trees.' I point out to the green blur outside the car windows. 'Or a rose — they are visible things that point toward something invisible. They are all like doors, and if you have the key of faith and belief, you can open them and see what is beyond them, which binds them all together as one.'

I think I felt a divine spark of inspiration the other day, when I was reading poetry. Metaphors and similes are religious, because how else could everyone read: 'My love is like a red, red rose' or 'her eyes are like the sun' and not only get the connection, but also find it so very beautiful?

'I do not understand,' Mrs Lewis says again, in a tone that closes the conversation. She presses the fingers of one hand to her temple as though she has a headache. Then she absently rubs the cross hanging from a gold chain around her neck. Her lips move slightly, as though in silent prayer. There is a continual prayer – 'Lord Jesus Christ, Son of God, have mercy on me, a sinner' – that if you say often enough, will travel from your head down into your heart, the words beating, every second of every day, in endless joyful noise unto the Lord.

AMARANTH is an unfading flower, eternally beautiful and ever-lasting. In the *Dictionary of Symbols* it says that the blue rose is symbolic of the impossible.

HOW TO CHARM A SNAKE: Catch a king cobra. Milk it of its venom by grabbing the back of its neck and making it bite a piece of paper held over a jar. Gently squeeze the glands on either side of its head so that the poison squirts out. Put it in a basket and play the flute. The snake will stick out its head to see what is happening. Keep the flute moving at all times. The snake cannot hear the music, but will follow your movements, trying to decide when to strike.

*

Louis just finished an *Annunciation* painting of me as the Virgin Mary. He painted himself as the Angel Gabriel. We are in his bedroom. It is lit by fireflies, which he captured in glass jars and let free in his room. They are supposed to lend an atmosphere of chiaroscuro and *sfumato*, which are the misty boundaries between light and dark, the sublime luminiferous ether of vanishing points.

There is more of a headache atmosphere to Louis's painting. Our haloes look like stars around the heads of cartoon characters when they've been struck by a heavy object. I look nauseous. Like I'm kneeling and bowing my head about to vomit. Louis is hovering over me, his hands upraised, menacing rather than full of grace, as if he's about to box my ears. I tell Louis he should practice sumi-e. It is what Japanese painters do. When they are painting a pine tree, for instance, they enter the tree to share its delicate feelings. Then they raise their brush over the paper and paint the image in one swift black stroke.

'Ah, yes.' Louis muses for a moment. 'East meets West.' He looks at me strangely, his voice gets real suggestive. 'Via the Silk Route . . .' And before I know it, he is on top of me, ripping off my wimple and biting my ear. 'What animal would you most like to be bitten by?' he whispers into the hollow of my throat. I struggle with his hands that are pulling at my blue virgin robe. I get hold of his wrist and bite it. Louis jerks back and sucks on his arm, holding me down with the other hand. 'Ah, the cruel amours of the mantis,' he murmurs, arching an eyebrow at me. Then he slips his fingers under my bra straps and pulls them down.

I wriggle my shoulders to get them back up. 'Louis . . . what . . . are you . . . doing? Stop . . . it . . .'

Louis laces his fingers in mine and presses them down to the floor. I never realized how much bigger his hands are than mine. '*Droit de seigneur*.' He smiles down at me. 'The feudal rights of the lord. You *are chez moi*. Calhm to zee Cazbaahh,' he says in his Charles Boyer voice, and brings one of my hands up to his mouth and kisses my open palm, sucks the tips of my fingers.

'I am posing as a *virgin*, Louis – pure and chaste – remember?' I ask, struggling to get out of his grip.

Louis smiles and licks his lips. Something flickers in his eyes. 'Yeah . . . but the things that you're liable to read in the Bible,' he sings softly, 'aint necessarily so. Besides, you've got that cultish virgin allure. It really stirs up my moral turpitude.' He grinds his hips into mine. 'Did you know that Fra Angelico did it with the nun that posed for him?' He runs a finger down my arm, across my collarbone. His lips brush my cheekbone. He bites my lower lip. He smells of spice, and salt. 'All for art's sake. Need to know . . . body . . .' His tongue draws an invisible pattern under my chin and down my neck.

I can hear my heartbeats in my ears. Little sparks like fireflies run through my veins. 'Don't . . . Louis . . .' I say as I feel my knees tremble. A warm glow moves in waves from my ankles to my thighs.

'Commit . . . moral . . . or venial . . . sin,' Louis is saying into my hair, 'according to where you place kisses.' He sucks and kisses my earlobe. 'That is . . . probably venial.' He eases his hands under my robe, caresses the small of my back, pulls me close. 'Where do you suppose I should kiss you in order to commit a moral sin?'

I feel his hips, his chest, his heart beating. I feel as though I am going from liquid to solid and back to liquid again. 'Really . . . Louis . . . stop, okay? Louis.' I am out of breath and my mouth is dry.

Louis raises his head, flips back the blond hair that half covers his face, and looks at me through half-closed lids. His lips are very red. 'You're blushing,' he says. He puts one of his fingers in my mouth and then traces my cheeks with it. 'Here . . . and here . . . all blushes . . .' I can hear him breathing. It makes my breath catch. 'Do you know that when you blush here' – he kisses my cheek – 'other parts of your body blush at the same time?' His thumb draws circles in my palm. 'Secret parts,' he whispers into my hair.

I pull my head away. 'No . . . but Louis . . .'

Louis places his fingers over my lips. 'Shh. Should we see where else you are blushing? Do you want me to show you?' Before I can answer his hand has slipped under my bra. 'Here . . . you are blushing here.' He eases my bra down and kisses me there, while his hand moves down my stomach, across my thigh and under my knee, pulling it away from the other one. He slides his hand between my legs. 'And here . . . you are blushing here.'

I am suddenly terrified and start fighting and kicking like a wildcat. Louis rolls off me, swearing. He stands up and paces around the room, then drops to the floor, leaning against a wall, his arms draped over his knees. 'Jesus, Haddie. Do you want to castrate me?' One of his eyes wanders off.

I'm standing in the middle of the room, hugging my blue garment about myself, dizzy and hot. The fireflies' lights buzz on and off. They are like those sparkles you see after you rub your eyes really hard. 'You scared me. You . . . shouldn't have done that. It wasn't funny.' I feel like I am going to cry.

'I wasn't *trying* to be *funny*, Haddie.' Louis's voice is low and soft. The blue vein is prominent at his temple. Something makes me want to touch it. Then he cocks his head to one side, suddenly jaunty. His voice has turned sharper. 'Pure sex and pure terror are the only things that make you live completely in the present.' He stretches out languidly on the floor, propped up on one elbow.

'That is why the French call an orgasm *"le petit mort"*.' He lies down completely, puts his hands behind his head. *'Pas de deux.'* He gives me a leer and thrusts his hips up and down a few times, 'Sex is doing zee leetle danze of death together.'

HOW TO FIGHT A BULL: Shake your cape and call: *A-hah vaca!* (Hey cow!). Now made aware of your presence, the bull will drop its head and charge at you. Stand still. The bull will head straight for the cloth because of its quivering movement. As it charges through the cloth, yell *'Ole!'* Its momentum will carry it several yards beyond you before it realizes it has been fooled and comes to a stop. This is called the 'pass of death'.

Suppose an arrow is flying out toward the end of space. If we say there is an end to space, and at this end there is nothing, if the arrow stops at the end, what is stopping it if nothing is there? And if the arrow does not stop, but keeps flying, then is it not flying beyond the end?

What does God have to wonder or to think about? If He created everything, if He knows how everything works, then what does He think about all day? There's this man, Mr Forester, who comes to all my parents' cocktail parties. He knows the manufacturing process of everything – shoes, plastics, soup. And if you get stuck next to him he'll tell you about them. The whole process. From start to finish. If you could speak to God, maybe you would be disappointed. Maybe He would tell you how amoebas, giraffes, star nebulae are made. And you'd be disappointed.

An AUBADE is a love serenade sung at dawn. I'm woken up by a gentle tapping at my bedroom window. The upper branches of the elms in our front yard sometimes do this, and it usually lulls me to sleep. But this has a different sort of rhythm, like chewing. I go over to my window and lift the shade. At first I think I'm dreaming. Backlighted by the moon is the face of a giraffe, eating leaves off one of the elm trees. One of its heavily lashed and lidded eyes is looking right at me. It is huge, and doesn't seem to have a pupil – a distant liquid planet. I'm still half asleep and I feel as though I've just walked onto the page of a nursery tale. I can see the leaves slide down inside its long, printed neck. I can't believe it is still on the loose. I can't imagine it crossing continents to find its way back to the plains of Africa.

Damn Louis. I throw on some jeans, go downstairs and quietly let myself out the front door. It is almost dawn, a low mist hangs over everything. I haven't exactly planned what I am going to do about the giraffe, so when I reach its legs, standing firm and tall as trees, I stare up at its head, beanstalk-high in the elm. Then I see its tail, hanging above me like the pull on an old-fashioned dinner bell. I reach up and give it a quick yank, and before I can say 'Kalamazoo' the giraffe has wheeled itself around and run across our lawn, the street and onto the bachelor's property. It stops to sniff the air, and then disappears into the Monroe woods.

On the bachelor's tennis court I can see a large dark mound. As I walk toward it I see the greyhounds sitting on either side of it in identical positions – gray guardians – paws crossed, heads alert. Their coats gleam in the silvery dawn light. When I get closer I see that the dark mound is the bachelor, sprawled on his back, eyes closed. At first I think that he has been gored by a rhino, or stampeded by a giraffe or something, and then I see a bottle of Scotch lying on the baseline. The dogs stand and bark, and the bachelor lifts his head and squints open his eyes. He waves a vague hand at the dogs. 'Sit. Sit.' His voice is hoarse. He gets up on one elbow and looks at me through half-closed eyes, then drops his head to the ground again and puts a hand over his eyes. 'Sorry,' he mumbles, 'excuse me.'

'Are you all right?' I ask. I'm standing over him now. One of the dogs sniffs at my tennis shoes.

'Yes . . . yes. Excuse me for not getting up . . . I was out . . . I was out here looking. At stars. I must have. Gone . . . went. Fall asleep. Yes. Must have. Yes. Do please excuse . . .' He tries to get up again and then falls back.

'Can I help you? Do you want anything?' I look around nervously, thinking of the neighbors.

His eyes flutter open. He coughs, clears his throat. 'Water?' he asks, as if he is guessing the answer to a difficult question. 'I don't want . . . to impose . . . but I would appreciate . . . very much . . . a glass . . .'

'Yes,' I cut him off as I can tell he is finding speaking difficult, 'of course, I'll be right back.' I start to walk back to my house, but the bachelor calls out, 'No . . . no need to . . .' He points to the open door of his house. 'Kitchen, back, right. Thank you, thanks, very, very much oblized . . .'

I walk across the lawn and into his house, guilty that I already know where the kitchen is. As I enter I hear the television, and as I pass the living room I see Nixon's face on the screen, jowly and widow-peaked. Once I remember him saying that the moon landing was the greatest thing in history since the creation of man. The house seems different now that I know who the bachelor is. The empty shoes, the secret staircase, the room of maps, the yellow nursery, the dumbwaiter, the pool – all their mystery now swirls around one name.

Everything has become monochrome in the early morning

light. Except for the oriental carpets, with their wizard patterns in hocus-pocus colors. I go to the kitchen and run water into a glass. My hand shakes as I hand it to the bachelor. He sits up and drinks it. His knuckles are red, scraped and bleeding. There are grass stains at the knees of his trousers, and pieces of grass are stuck to his socks, his jacket, his hair. His shoes are muddy. I squat and brush a ladybug from his lapel. He takes my hand in his and kisses the tips of my fingers. 'Thank you, sweetheart,' he says, his voice now stronger, more clear, and then drops my hand. He smiles at me, uncertain and apologetic. 'I feel . . . better.' He draws in an unsteady breath. He stares intently at his grass-stained knee for several minutes. He seems to be trying to balance something delicate and precariously placed within his head. Then he straightens his shoulders and drinks down the rest of the water. 'They say water is composed . . .' The bachelor stretches his legs out in front of him and half loses his balance. I help him to sit upright again. 'That water is composed of two atoms of hydrogen . . . and one atom of ox'gen.' He looks into his empty glass. 'But it feels different . . . than that.' He looks at me, trying to focus on my face. His attention is intense, and then faraway, like a person who keeps appearing and then disappearing into a crowd. 'It is more than that. Water. We are all . . . dissolved . . . dissolved in it.' He raises his glass and one eyebrow at me as if toasting someone. 'I studied biology and physics,' he says, as if that explains something. A slight tremor moves through his whole body, and he puts the glass down and lies back on the court. 'Tennis anyone?' he asks and blandly smiles up at me. 'You could . . . sit down . . . if you like.' He pats the ground next to him.

I sit cross-legged beside him. I smell grass and mud and whiskey, and something else I can't define, something like the sea. 'I grew up down south. In Virginia.' The bachelor's voice is flat and factual. 'We lived on a farm. But my father was not a farmer. He was a scientist. A scientist.' A muscle moves at the bachelor's jaw. A vein throbs in his temple. He frowns, and rubs his neck. We sit in silence. I picture silos and a huge blue sky, a boy with a fishing pole dangling his feet in a cool green river. And a strange man in the dark part of a barn filled with flasks and Bunsen burners and microscopes and complex elements, cutting things open and blowing things up. Surrounding him is a warm farm animal silence.

'What kind of scientist was your father?' I ask.

The bachelor blinks his eyes at me as though he has forgotten I was there. 'A physicist. But he was interested in biology. I remember him telling . . . he read . . . to me that the evlushun . . . excuse . . . ev-o-lu-tion . . . tion of the eye . . . the ver-te-brae eye sent shivers down Darwin's spine. Imagine . . . ha.' He gives a short laugh. He looks down at his scraped hand, his brows draw together in concentration. 'He was alsho . . . so also interest in great explorers.' The bachelor's hand jerks abruptly outward in a wave toward the horizon. 'My father . . . was interested. Told me stories about . . . Arab . . . way-far-ers. Vikings sailing . . . sailing the unknown . . . the unknown seas. Diaz reaching stormy cape. Raleigh's search . . . his search for El Dorado. Mungo Park and the Niger. Liv'stone's last journey.'

'And then you became an astronaut.'

'Yes. But first' – he raises a finger – 'I was a scientist.' He sits up and rubs his jaw. It is covered in dark stubble. 'Do you think that you can believe your eyes?' he asks, but doesn't wait for an answer. 'Science believes this. That you can. Believe your eyes. Even though we . . . have discover other . . . discover-ed other-wise.' He watches the greyhounds chase a sparrow across the lawn. 'Going to the moon made me realize. We are always upside down.' He picks at some weeds growing through a crack in the court and lets them sift through his hands. 'It sounds ridickluss. We all know . . . know this. Gravity pulls up . . . it pulls us up. Not down. But is very over-whelm-ing to think about . . . this all the time.' He stares at the pile of weeds. 'Is different to know something and experience it.'

'What was it like on the moon?'

He raises his eyebrows at me. Then speaks quite softly. 'It was dark.' He strokes the side of his cheek with his thumb. 'And silent.' He pauses, runs his fingers through his hair. 'Most important, of course,' he continues, his voice louder now, 'was the earth. Seeing the earth. When you look out . . . over my lawn . . .' He stretches his arm out, moves it in a wide arc, pointing. 'You see several yards. Circum-ference 180 degrees. On flat field you'd see more . . . further. We saw the entire earth. I saw that all life . . . outline against . . . invisible. Dark ocean of invisible . . . on all sides. You understand . . .' He looks at me closely. 'Beyond. Beyond everything. Everything you see' – he waves his hand out toward the trees – 'is this . . . invisible . . . in-visi-bil-ity.' He shakes his head. 'I'm not making sense. But we are dissolved in it. Invisibility. Like . . . as . . . in water. We won the race . . . to find out we are not anywhere . . . in no place . . . nowhere.'

I hear footsteps and see Mr Lodge's nurse at the end of their driveway, picking up the morning paper. She has a bleak puddle of a face. The type you sometimes see looking out of bus windows. And a hairstyle without much conviction behind it. Leonardo wrote in his notebooks that 'every object that moves with speed seems to tinge its path with the semblance of its color'. Nurse Howard wears a white uniform and bustles about, and the immediate area around her does seem to have an efficient whiteness about it. She is quite a contrast to the bachelor in his grass-stained suit.

'Maybe you should go inside,' I say to him. I help him get to his feet, and pick up the empty bottle of Scotch. He sways slightly in place, so I take his arm and we walk to his house. At the door he stops and leans his head against the door-jamb. I see that dew has collected in the hollow of his throat.

He dips his head and looks into my eyes. He touches my cheek. 'I thought I had a vision.' His voice is low and controlled. 'All of it happened very slow, like a freight train going about 500 miles per hour over a cliff. And I could feel my life rushing forward to a time when I would not understand any of it.' He whistles to the dogs and they canter up the steps and past us into the house. 'You are an angel of mercy.' The bachelor kisses the top of my head. 'I think I can take care of myself now.' He winks at me and then steps inside and closes the door. And when I turn to face the street I see that it is suddenly day, all light and bright, with birds singing and the green grass shining, and the night of giraffes on the loose and drunken men passed out on lawns seems a million miles away. Fallen voluptuously off the edge of the tumbling blue earth.

PART IV

THE MODERN AGE

It is a black-and-white photograph. Of the bachelor. In the encyclopedia. It is slick and glossy and the colors aren't black and white so much as platinum, steel, zinc, his eyes are liquid mercury. Without colors you notice the angles of his face more – his jaw and forehead, the curve of his chin, and eyelids, the vertical line of his nose. The photograph is dated 1964, so it was taken before he went to the moon. He certainly looks different. Despite the metallic severity of the photo, there is a candidness about his face, he is someone open, someone who wouldn't have secrets. He looks pensive, and there is also an arrogance, he is almost jaunty. He knows he has been chosen, picked out from hundreds of others, to do something important, be someone important.

I can see him in a silver airplane, flying low over a hot Florida beach, tipping a bright wing to do illegal somersaults and spins over the surf and impress women with ivory-white smiles and teeny-weeny bikinis. Or striding confidently down the cool corridors of a laboratory, where the light glints off the stainless-steel instruments, which click and hum, measuring atomic structures and planetary atmospheres. I think of him living across the street, solitary and guarded and hesitant. St Augustine said that all sins are the same sin, the sin of a divided soul. Maybe I can help the bachelor tell his story. Maybe his salvation is *in* his story.

Achilles cannot get across the field because to cover an infinite number of points would take an infinite amount of time. Ergo, motion is impossible. Or time and space are actually not made up of separate pieces but actually One – a huge, unmoving circle. God being the splendor of eternity which is forever still, said St Augustine.

I wonder if St Augustine spent a lot of time thinking about how he could possibly cross an infinite number of points in a finite amount of time inasmuch as it is impossible to finish the infinite. And that being the cause of his wondering where that part of his mind was that didn't contain itself and thinking he knew things he wasn't aware he knew and always being quite certain exactly what time it was until someone perchance happened to ask him.

It is 14 July, Bastille Day. Louis Lewis is dressed in a purple silk shirt and black velveteen breeches, in mourning for the *ancien régime*. He says he was named after le Roi Soleil and has *sang de souverain* coursing through his imperial veins. He is lying on a chaise longue in the sun room, his leonine hair spread out on satin pillows, granting me royal audience to his soi-disant State of Despond. We go through this every year.

'You may kiss the monarchic member,' he says as I enter, pointing to his fly.

'Dream on, dauphin,' I mumble and flop into a chair opposite him.

'Peasant.' He shrugs and places a single pomegranate seed in his mouth and sucks, eyes distant and broody. Gazing off, no doubt, at the lambent glow of lost empire. 'What's not happening out there?' He sighs, and waves a languid hand at the windows. '*Quelle barbe*,' he moans before I can answer, stroking his right cheek with the back of his fingers. 'Where are all the sordid intrigues of yesteryear? No more secrets. No more scandals. No more epistolary correspondences waiting to be used to my sadistic advantage. *Son altesse!*' His eyes light up as his mother comes into the room with a tray of petit fours and orangeade. 'My whipping boy has arrived, *Maman! Commence le vice anglais!*'

'Haddie, darling.' Mrs Lewis comes over and brushes my hair back from my eyes with her long fingers and bends to kiss me on each cheek, and then looks into my eyes. 'You know Louis is only horrible to you because he likes you. Louis.' She turns to him. 'Stop. You are making Haddie sad.'

'Provincials always look sad, Mother. It is bred in their genes. In order to prompt the *jeunesse dorée* to practice *noblesse oblige*.'

Mrs Lewis blows air out of her mouth and walks over to Louis, waving her hand. He lets her sit next to him, and then lays his head down on her lap. 'You should be teaching her the French wallow at Charm School.' He points an accusing finger at me. 'One should know how to bow before the highborn.' Mrs Lewis smooths hair from his brow, then plucks a white grape from the bowl in front of them and pushes it through his lips. 'Now hush and be good,' she says softly to him. Louis opens his mouth wide for another grape. Mrs Lewis laughs and puts one on his tongue. 'Mmm. *L'état c'est moi*,' he says juicily, eyes closed. She leans over him, tut-tutting. '*Cocorico mon coq gaulois*,' she murmurs.

She always plays along with him too much, but then they are

usually in some sort of collusion. They call each other *mon minet*, or *ma tourterelle*. They have these little unspoken signals. With the flick of a wrist, the slight nod of a head, the lifting of a finger, the pursing of lips, there is immediately some unspoken agreement between them.

'Hey, you, parvenu.' Louis snaps his fingers at me. 'Time to be obsequious. I'm hungry. Go force-feed the geese. Drown the ortolans. Pluck the tongues from the peacocks.' He waves me away with a royally dismissive hand.

Mrs Lewis shrugs, with her palms out in front of her chest. 'What *would* we do if this boy were in line for the monarchy?'

'Assassinate him,' I mutter.

'*Le roi ne s'amuse point*,' Louis says, raising himself on one elbow. 'And how would you propose to do that, o scrofulous one?'

'By shoving your silver spoon down your throat.'

'No man is a hero to his valet.' Louis sniffs, and settles his head back down on his mother's lap. And then the two of them are off onto this macabre game of theirs where they cite the elegant aphorisms and pithy proverbs they would quote on their way to the scaffold.

'Haddie, are you all right?' I hear Mrs Lewis ask me, sounding concerned. I look up and at the same time realize I have been holding my head in my hands.

'Yes.' I shake my head a little, trying to focus. 'I've just been having trouble thinking clearly lately.'

Louis waves a banana at me like a scepter. 'I might be able to help you. If you are suffering from doubt, you should look to the Beautiful Country. Our land is full of melancholy misanthropes. Descartes, for instance, who couldn't decide if he was sleeping or awake. Which,' he muses, peeling the banana, 'is a great excuse for not getting out of bed in the morning. Am I awake or asleep? Asleep? Or awake? I could ponder the dilemma all day long as I lie in in my baroque bedroom. You may now behold the wondrous spectacle of my sleeping form.' He lays his head down in his mother's lap, arms crossed at his chest, and shuts his eyes.

'Well, I'm off to the barricades,' I say, getting up. '*Liberté. Fraternité. Egalité. Vive la République*, etc.' I walk across the room, open the door.

'Do look up Descartes,' Louis says, looking at me through a half-opened eye. 'He started the beautiful tradition of solitary solipsism. Of course' – he sits up – 'his vision doesn't translate well over here.' He rolls his eyes upward and screws his forefinger into his temple. 'In the United States, existential dread has been reinterpreted as the Bad Hair Day. Which would never have come about if you *arrivistes* had not overthrown the Crown. You peasants would still be tramping around, ignorantly blissful under your matted locks while we', he states grandly, as if the whole of the French royal lineage is standing in line behind him and his mother, 'would still be wearing pomaded periwigs, or, in the tradition of Catherine the Great, keeping our personal hairdressers imprisoned in iron cages to guard the secrets of the royal coiffure.' He sighs. '*Après nous, le déluge!*'

'*Where* did you find this?' Mrs Lewis suddenly asks in a high-pitched voice, holding Louis tightly by the wrist. I see that he is wearing her small gold fleur-de-lis ring – the one with the engraving that he found in her jewelry box.

Louis sits up and raises his little finger with the ring on it near his ear, tilts his head as though listening to it. 'I know your secret, little bird,' he says in a soft singsong voice.

Mrs Lewis says something under her breath I cannot

hear. Then she says, 'Give it to me.' The words are heavy. Her face is red. A muscle twitches at her jaw.

Louis moves to the other side of the couch in a swift movement, his knees drawn up to his chest. 'Not until you tell who your first love is.' He wags his little finger back and forth in the air. 'And *are* you planning on returning to him?' He takes off the ring, tosses it into the air and catches it. 'One always returns to one's first love,' he chants, tossing it again.

Mrs Lewis is sitting quite still, watching him. Her whole body is tense – the muscles in her shoulders seem to quiver and her chest moves up and down in quick, shallow breaths. Then, suddenly, she laughs. 'Silly . . . your father gave it to me. Now be a good boy and give it back to me.' She holds her hand out to him, palm up. Her eyes are pink and watery.

'I figured it was from my father. But who is that?' Louis puts the ring in his mouth, rolls it around, and when he sticks out his tongue at her, the ring is encircled on its tip. He wags his ringed tongue at her in lascivious circles.

'You *know* who your father is!' Mrs Lewis shouts, and stands up, upsetting the bowl of fruit. Grapes, strawberries and kumquats roll across the floor. Mrs Lewis stares at Louis. He has placed the ring around the tip of his index finger, which is pulling down the skin under his left eye. It is a gesture which means I don't believe you.

'If I were you,' Mrs Lewis says softly, 'I would drop these notions about your father. If I were you . . .' She doesn't finish the sentence, but turns and walks out of the room.

'If I were you . . .' Louis softly mimics his mother's voice while gazing at the door she has just exited through. Then he looks over at me. 'She was using the subjunctive tense just then. The form of the verb used in expressing what is wished or hoped for.' He puts the fleur-de-lis ring up to his left eye, looking through it at me, while closing his right. 'The realm of feeling, desire, fear and doubt.'

Humans are the only creatures that point. When you point something out to animals, they stare at your finger, rather than the imaginary line you are drawing toward the horizon. There is a full moon out tonight. I wonder why we never named it. When you point at the moon it seems to pull you toward it. My grandmother says this is because there really are no boundaries – the moon and the stars are inside of you. And oasis, mirage and hallucination are Oriental words that describe the yearning of your inside to be outside.

An ATLAS is a book of maps which emphasizes place locations, the connections between them and the relative size and significance of the places designated. The encyclopedia shows pictures from old atlases. They are full of places with storybook names: Crocodilopolis, Abyssinia, Peking, Siam, the Cape of 11,000 Virgins. And 'Where Dragons Be' and 'Here Be Lions' in the far-fetched, starry-eyed margins. I wonder what it must have been like to think the world was flat. To have monumental waterfalls of ocean endlessly cascading over the edges of your imagination.

I got a book out of the library titled *The Age of Reason: Being a Genealogy of Metaphysick and Homo Rationalis including some Digressive yet Prudent Sallies into the Apologia Pro Vita Sua of its Author* by Professor Hemholtz Gottfried von Weltschmerz.

I read about how Professor Weltschmerz met a high-born maiden Helga, who overflowed her bower and whose curves

Praxiteles could not have captured, for her Attic shape was of such a kind that caused Thaumaturgical Changes of Eleusinian Nature while in Heaven-Sprung Motion. He spends a couple of pages talking about her raven tresses and eloquent Brow. Suddenly everything is written in Latin. After flipping through ten pages of this, I find him back in English, talking about Helga meeting a poltroon of unbridled, fustian Temperament, and soon Weltschmerz realized that her charms were Cadmus-sown and *varium et mutabile semper femina*, and like Catullus he *odi et amo* and O ruins of Ilium caused by the Follies of her Sex! And like Heine's boatman he was lured to destruction by his love, and he felt the Harbinger of Oblivion's deepening veil blah, blah, blah and for twenty pages he is rowing Lethe-wards until suddenly he is reveling in the Tumescence of Ideas that *homo rationalis* got a hold of without recourse to Majick or the *odium scholasticum*, yadda, yadda, and the bright Doric order etc., etc., and basically he takes about fifty pages to say that he is leaving romance to live the life of reason.

Finally, on page 165, he has a short passage about Descartes. Who spent long stretches of time alone in Holland, next to a stove, watching wax melt. Which made him question his senses. Which led him to believe that he might not have a body and that his brain could be controlled by an evil magician. Soon he wasn't sure if he was awake or asleep. But he roused himself by realizing that since his thoughts were so deficient there must be a God that made up all the perfect geometry of the universe. And from that he concluded that his mind was separate from his body, because his body was made up of so many parts he could hardly get a handle on it, while his mind was quite singular and unique. So, therefore, animals are machines.

'So how come I've never seen a watch give birth to baby

watches?' Queen Christina asked him. She had sent for him to come to her castle in Sweden and teach her metaphysics at five in the morning and write musicals about princes who thought they were shepherds. It was the Age of Lunatic Monarchs. Queen Christina was a hermaphrodite, cursed like a sailor and liked to sit sideways on her throne with her feet dangling over the armrests. And she asked a lot of vexing questions that put Descartes in an exceedingly peevish temper because how was he supposed to teach his method to someone who couldn't follow a perfectly clear and rational line of logic?

Do you remember the first time that you knew you were waking up? That you had been asleep, drowned in dreams, and that now you were awake, in the light and air of the outside world? I wonder if you could feel the clanging of your body and mind colliding. Weltschmerz says Descartes wrote that the pineal gland is the place where the mind and body intersect. It is also called the 'third eye', and if you burst it you can see all that has ever happened from the beginning of time and all that will ever happen to the end of time. But you shouldn't try this because it will make you take permanent leave of your senses. Leonora told me that if you wake a person while they are sleep-walking, they will forget everything they had in their dreambox before you woke them.

I say, 'Holland, 1600.' And the field behind the train station turns to tidal flats smelling of herrings and the sea. There is a low white sky. A few patches of Delft blue. There could be a windmill, a church spire, a tavern in the distance. The colors are red russet and burned umber. If I walked to the tavern and peered in the window, I might see the huge slab of a wooden table. On top of it lie a large carp with dead eyes, a basket of oysters with glistening interiors, cut lemons, cerise cherries, melons with tangerine-green rinds, and peaches with blushing cheeks. Through an open door you can see another room. Black and white tiles cover the floor. There is a jug, a candlestick, a chair, a pair of slippers and a dog.

Descartes said that matter does not have mind, and therefore our minds are made of a different substance than our bodies. But all those fruits and candlesticks and slippers and jugs in the place where he lived seem to be humming with some sort of inner life and thoughts, and in a lot of portraits of that time the complex convoluted folds of fabric often seem more cerebral than the sitters.

Didn't Rembrandt paint a portrait of Descartes? He painted a lot of self-portraits. Our art teacher told us he was painting his mind, rather than his body. He used chiaroscuro a lot, which makes his paintings all fuzzy, and Descartes said that for thought to be real it should be clear and distinct. There is definitely an atmosphere of ideas to Rembrandt's paintings. But more like the slow dawning of an idea that never completely forms. This is how I would paint my portrait if I wanted to represent my mind. When my idea of myself is most real, it is usually pretty fuzzy.

Across the field I see a figure walking toward the train station. One of those smudgy inkblots that are supposed to be distant huntsmen in Dutch landscapes. I walk across the field and as I get closer I see it is the bachelor. He walks in easy, long strides, but if you were walking with him it would probably be hard to keep up. While he is athletic-looking, slender and strong, you can tell he is not a team player. If he played baseball he would probably be a lackadaisical outfielder, dreamy in the blue summer heat and acres of grass, perhaps in the listless stretches of strikeouts, knotting long strands of daisy chains, thinking about what books he would rather be reading. But if the ball came his way, I could imagine his long lazy arm lifting up and catching it as easy as taking a can of tomatoes from a high shelf, and his throw would send the ball so fast to home base that the hand of the catcher would sting and ache long into the night.

When I reach him, he is standing on the tracks, looking off toward the direction of town. When he sees me, he smiles. 'See that?' He points his finger toward the horizon. 'See where they meet?' I follow with my eyes the two black lines of tracks to where they converge, sharp as the tip of an arrow. 'It is hard to match up what you see and what you know is real.' He drops his finger but continues to gaze off at the tracks. He seems to be measuring something without the tools he needs to measure it. He turns to me. 'I like the illusion of it. It is a good illusion. An illusion that you are certain is an illusion. A good, solid, certain illusion.' He puts his hands in his pockets, contented, like a farmer after a good rain. Then he asks me if I'd like to sit with him on the bench outside the station. We walk up the steps. The creaking sounds like a hobo's harmonica. Leonora told me at night in Alabama she could hear the roustabouts holler from deep in the piny woods. Yonder come that train, red-blue lights behind. Red for troubles, blue for a worried mind.

'You never told me your name,' the bachelor says when we sit down.

'Haddie. Haddie Ashton.'

'Haddie.' He nods his head a couple of times, as if it's the name he expected. 'Haddie. I like your name.' He cocks his head sideways, looking at me. He seems to be tossing my name up like a brightly colored ball, catching it, and then tossing it up again.

'It is an unusual name. Were you named after a great-aunt, or a grandmother?'

I look down at my hands. When I asked Leonora what she thought about Descartes's notion about our bodies being machines, that don't completely belong to our heads, she told me about a man in Alabama who had Alien Hand Syndrome. His one hand would put on his hat and his alien hand would take it right off again. Or his good hand would open a door and his alien hand would slam it right in his face. She said it got him into all sorts of other mischief she won't be able to tell me about until I'm past puberty.

'I don't think I had any great-aunts or great-grandmothers with the name Haddie. My sister's name was Haddie. She died. Before I was born. So I guess I was named for . . . after her.' The field stretches out in front of us. Wasps buzz under the rotting lintels.

The bachelor leans his elbows on his knees. 'Has that been hard on you?' he asks, 'having the same name as her?'

'I don't know, really. I mean, ever since I can remember I have had her name. I don't know what it would feel like not to.' No one has ever asked me what I felt about it. They never seemed to think it really mattered. 'Sometimes, it's hard to explain, but sometimes it feels like everything's double vision or something.' I look sideways at the bachelor. His eyes listen. I never saw anyone with eyes that listened. 'The first memory I have is being at a mall with my parents. And I got lost. They had me paged. A woman kept saying over the loudspeaker, "Haddie Ashton, please meet your parents at the lost and found." And I couldn't move because I kept thinking they were calling her. You know, that they had lost her and they were calling and calling. I was sitting under this big rack of fur coats where it was warm and dark. I thought if I hid there long enough they would find her.' I stop abruptly. I don't know why I am telling him this story. He must think I'm crazy. 'You must think I'm crazy,' I say out loud.

'Not at all, sunshine,' he says, and then runs his thumb in a gentle stroke along the arch of my eyebrow. He's the kind of person who would know the technical reasons for a rainbow, the square roots of peculiar numbers, how to gather water from the cupped leaves of island plants. Someone you'd like to have with you on a lifeboat.

He clears his throat. 'People place too much importance on names. Obviously your parents placed too much importance on a name and that has caused you pain.' He pauses, seems to be reaching two steps forward in his mind and then three steps back. 'It is a word. Haddie. How many – six letters. It is not you – you did not choose it, and your parents picked it before they got to know you. It is a placemark people use for you.' A breeze blows through the station's broken windows. 'There are tribes where a person changes their name three or four times during their life, because the name they had as a child no longer fits them as an adult. They often choose their new name after returning from an adventure. The old name is buried, and not mentioned except upon sacred ground.'

'Is that why you no longer use your name?' I ask him, 'Because it didn't fit . . . any more?'

'Would you care to walk into town?' the bachelor asks, standing up. Despite the heat, his white shirt is stiff and pressed. He clenches and unclenches his fists. I'm scared my question made him angry, but I say 'sure' and we walk along the tracks toward town. The clouds have cleared and the sun shines on the rails, the nails in them gleam like gold teeth.

'When I was a college student, I worked in a laboratory.' The bachelor says this softly, watching his shoes stepping between the tracks. 'What the experiments were is not important. The work was very methodical. I would write down the numbers from one counter, reset gauges, write down those numbers. I became an extension of the apparatus. I was no one, no one in particular. Rather like a hand of a clock. I have found that by following fixed habits, a set ritual as it were, here' – he points down the tracks, there are rows of brown cattails, milkweed and Queen Anne's lace – 'it gives my days a solid pattern.'

He slows his walking. 'My father had a very odd habit. One which I have inherited.' He stops, points to his shoes. They are wingtips, and shiny like the coats of otters. 'He would place a pair of shoes under the curtains of his study. With just the tips pointing out –' He taps his shoes and little dust clouds rise around them. 'To make it look as though a burglar was standing behind them. He did it to scare himself.' The bachelor laughs and shrugs. 'He believed it helped his heart. In line with the idea that small doses of poison eventually create a strong resistance – he felt that small shocks to it would make him immune to a big attack.' I suddenly remember when I was standing outside his window, spying on him, seeing him enter the room and jump back upon seeing his shoes under a curtain. 'More importantly,' the bachelor continues, as we cross over from the tracks onto the sidewalk leading into town, 'he believed that private fears should be cultivated.' He lifts an overhanging branch for me to duck under. 'Like growing exotic orchids.'

As we are passing the library, Mrs Lewis swings through its doors with a pile of books in her arms. When she sees the bachelor and me she stops, looking slightly shocked. Mrs Lewis is easily shocked, and by things you wouldn't expect anyone to be shocked by. 'No! I am shockt!' she'll say in disbelief.

'Hi, Mrs Lewis. How are you?' I say, with a wave of my hand.

'Hello, Haddie.' Mrs Lewis adjusts the books in her arms. Her face is all set and tense. From out the library window, I can hear Miss Penny, the director of Children's Hour, reciting a nursery rhyme: 'Try as I may to find the way, I can never get back by day . . . Nor can I remember plain and clear the curious music that I hear . . .' Mrs Lewis shifts her books again. 'Well . . .' she says, and smiles at the bachelor. I suddenly realize that I should introduce them.

'Mrs Lewis, this is –' I swallow. I remember my promise to him. To keep his name a secret. Mrs Lewis and the bachelor are silent. 'Um, Mrs Lewis.' I cough, hoping the bachelor will save me, but he is still and silent as the statue of George Washington in the square beyond us. 'George . . . George Smith,' I stammer, just as the bachelor clears his throat to speak. 'George, this is my neighbor, Mrs . . . Monique Lewis.' They exchange nods and hellos, and start to chat about the books she is holding but I am not listening. I feel as though I am floating three feet above, looking down. Louis says this is why he loves to lie. He says it is a great high, better than midnight martinis. I feel the sidewalk spin. I need a drink of water. I excuse myself from them and just as I open the door to the library I hear the bachelor's laugh. I have never heard him really laugh before. It is like dark wood, and you can feel it drumming inside you.

I go to the water fountain and take a long drink. 'How many miles to Babylon?' Miss Penny asks the circle of children at her feet. 'Four score and ten,' they answer in singsong. 'Can I get there by candlelight?' 'Yes and back again.'

When I get back to the doors I can see through the panes of glass that Mrs Lewis and the bachelor are sitting on a stone bench facing the library. Mrs Lewis is wearing a sleeveless dress. Her arms lie loose upon her crossed knee, one cupped hand holding the other. Her arms are tanned, except for the insides of her elbows, which are white as shallow saucers of cream. It is strange, but seeing the two of them sitting there together makes me realize how lonely they both are. The bachelor motions with his hand as he talks. It seems out of character, a gesture he's copied from someone he admires. The secret of his name swells inside me, beating like a second heart. 'Pussycat, pussycat, where have you been?' Miss Penny asks in a high, thin voice.

When I come back out through the doors, Mrs Lewis is laughing. She looks up at me and her eyes are moist, as though she has been crying. Her eyes always water when she laughs. Louis says this is because the French see the tragic inside the comic: *Nous risons en pleurs*. Mrs Lewis gathers her books onto her lap. Her cheeks are pink. 'Thank you,' she says, looking at me, although she is speaking to the bachelor who has risen to stand next to her.

'Pleasure,' he says. The word rings deep in his throat.

'Well, I will go and check my plants,' Mrs Lewis says, looking at me again, although I have no idea what she is talking about. 'I probably don't need these gardening books after your advice.' She is still addressing me.

'Good. Good luck with it.' The bachelor has moved to stand next to me, in Mrs Lewis's line of vision.

She shifts her eyes quickly toward him, and then away. 'Goodbye,' she says, walking backward a few steps. 'Goodbye, Haddie.' Then she turns and walks up the sidewalk toward her car. The bachelor stands with his arms at his sides, watching her leave. You know she can tell she is being watched because she is walking differently from how she usually walks. I suddenly see her as she must have looked twenty years ago – in knee socks and a school uniform, walking under centuries-old chestnuts, staring at her saddle shoes and whispering 'Hail Marys' while men catcall and whistle from the windows of their zooming Citroëns.

'She reminds me,' the bachelor says while watching her car turn round the gray bend of the street and disappear from sight. He cocks his head slightly. 'Reminds me of something I had forgotten.' He looks down at me. 'When I was a boy, there was a woman who lived down our street. She used to sunbathe in her backyard every day in summer. Her kneecaps and her nose were always slightly sunburned.' He smiles and touches the tip of my nose. 'One night, after a party, she walked through all her lawn sprinklers. She walked very slowly, with her arms stretched high over her head.' He smiles, distant, and we both stand still for a minute. In a southern state on a summer night. But I am suddenly reminded of a winter. Here in Ohio. Mrs Lewis was waiting at a traffic light in her blue convertible. Its top was down. And it was snowing. Just a light snow. There was a pinkish glow to the flakes from the red light. The snow was falling gently on Mrs Lewis's bare head – almost as if someone was placing each flake there in some sort of arrangement.

'Do you still want to go to the library?' I ask the bachelor.

He drums his fingers against his thighs. 'Come with me to the court-house,' he says. 'I want you to hear something.'

The court-house is across the square and sits high on a small hill at the top of wide concrete steps. I have to half run to keep up with the bachelor who is walking in wide, fast strides, his arms swinging and his fingers snapping. We walk through the entrance into the waiting room. It is long and high-ceilinged. There are murals on the walls that depict Indians and cowboys and corn and rivers. The bachelor sits on one of the wooden benches and motions for me to sit next to him. 'Listen,' he says softly, as though we are in a church. I hear typewriters and telephones and electric pencil sharpeners, elevator doors opening and closing, the dial tone of air-conditioning.

'To me the sound of machinery is the most soothing of sounds.' The bachelor tilts his head sideways. 'The lawn mower. The electric can opener. The power saw. Music of the spheres on a small scale. It is the sound of laws. Ritual. Even planets in space have ritual. It is what keeps them afloat.' He strokes the indentation between his nose and upper lip with his thumb. You can tell by the shape of his eyes that he is tired. 'If they ceased moving in their ellipses they would fall.' He stops talking. Quiet and concentrated next to me. I listen to the dinging of the elevator doors, the ringing of telephones, the tinging of typewriters. They are clear, ringing metal sounds. Like an orchestrated chart of elements. Tinging, dinging, binging – everything seems to be saying here, now, now, here.

As we sit there I notice something else. I notice how women look at the bachelor. One stands in the middle of the room, pretending to be busy with a file, but actually doing a kind of Dance of the Seven Veils from behind all these carbon sheets. Another woman goes clicking by in a dress like a shot of tequila, and gives the bachelor an 'It's Witchcraft' look before disappearing into a room of clacking typewriters. I look at his face, and see for the first time that he is extremely handsome. Actually, he looks like Jungle Larry. Jungle Larry is a man who works at an amusement park about an hour from here. He wears khaki. He has a square jaw, and a dimple in his chin, kind of like those mounties that yodel to their lovers on mountain peaks. Jungle Larry steers a paddleboat down a windy river in the middle of the park and shoots at the Indians on the bank and the alligators surfacing at the side of the boat. He yells, 'Take cover!' and he never misses his shot. I thought he was the bravest man alive until one time Louis and I had to sit in security until our parents picked us up because Louis ran our old-fashioned car off its track and rolled it down a hill into a tree, and I saw Jungle Larry standing there smoking a cigarette with a Cherokee, and Louis told me the alligators are remote-control robots, idiot. Anyway, he's real handsome, Jungle Larry, and the bachelor looks like him. I didn't really notice before, what with his mystery and strangeness. And the sadness he carries with him all the time, pooled in his joints, or weighing on his bones.

St Augustine's *Confessions* was the first autobiography. He paved the way for all the rest because he straightened the cycle of history, which used endlessly to repeat itself, into a line. Everyone's destiny is unique. I suppose that's why people started writing stories about their lives in the first person. They suddenly realized that they were the first person ever to have their own particular life.

The encyclopedia says that autobiography comes in many different forms. One describes travels to the wilds of Tartary and what it's like to suffer ague and fever, and hear the voices of ghosts in the Gobi Desert. There is another one, by an artist, who murdered and brawled and dragged his mistress around by her hair, and escaped from castles and stole the Pope's jewels. An aging libertine wrote one, recalling all the women and men he seduced and how he wished he still could. Someone else just asked: *Que sais-je?* while sitting alone in his tower library, and his answers hopped from fleas to cannibals, thumbs to sleep. Another kept a diary in which he recorded his thoughts on Art, wearing periwigs, and pinching chambermaids. Confessions range from describing the damask rose and forgetfulness of opium dreams, to not being able to forget a first love to the unforgettable pleasure of being spanked by a nanny. In a lot of autobiographies the authors will describe the minute details of their childhood – like what a garden path looked like through the different panes of colored glass of a stairwell window, or how it felt to step upon a certain flagstone of a long-ago path, or how some once-lyrical path has become a miserable gray now that youthful bloom has passed away.

Apparently, people became interested in their youth because they started to believe that rather than being pulled from above, they were being pushed from below, and so if they could re-member all the places they had been, they might have a better idea of where they were going. And they wanted a lot of other people to know who they were and where they were heading. I suppose when everyone thought they were all on the same big vicious cycle of life, everyone could afford to be fairly anonymous. Everyone knew where you were because they were all going your way, and they all knew who you were because you were all basically in the same boat. I guess, once everyone had their own destinations to go to, they wanted to describe the passing view, even leave a map with a dotted line behind, before they were going, going, gone forever.

Leonora is always telling stories about her life. She says that when you can tell three good stories from your life about the Facts – Life, Death, Love, etc. – you're halfway to getting some cat sense in your hat rack. A lot of Leonora's stories are embarrassing, or even horrible. About drinking muddy water when the rain kept falling. But when she tells them, it's as if she is talking about someone else. She will say, 'It was a day when all the air was still and the whippoorwills sounded too blue to fly,' and just the way she says it, you know that that still air contains a mystery, and a secret. And that she is going to lead you toward that secret, but in her own good time.

'Why is it that when you admit your sins, you are forgiven?' I ask her.

'Because, Susie Q, what you are hiding isn't ever half so bad as what you'll go through to hide it.' She gives me a strange look, one you could bend spoons with. 'Besides, that's what words are for, baby. Everything you say is confessing something. They let you see all the troubles other people have seen. All the saints' – she waves her hand toward the living room, as if they are all sitting in a line on the sofa – 'their hearts were pierced by words. They told the Bible. And that's how they suffered their way back to Paradise.'

My grandmother says that all stories are about how something has gotten misplaced. A person. A thing. An action. Or even a place. And stories make you either laugh, or cry, because these are the reactions we have toward things being out of place.

'Planet' is derived from the Latin word for 'wanderer'. The word 'moon' contains the meanings for both measurer and fancy, logic and caprice.

I drew a map of the bachelor's journey from his house, into town, and back again. The still image of his movement is the shape of an elongated circle. A mathematical theorem states that the surface of a sphere is finite, yet moving over it you will never find a boundary. It will seem to go on forever.

LIST OF MOONS: Huge harvest moons, the full moon mirrored in the green, green sea, the moon the cow jumped over, moon high over highwaymen, crescent moons in black cats' eyes, moons in old atlases, moons in rolled Japanese scrolls, ghostly galleon moons, paper moons sailing over cardboard seas, moon climbing the sky with sad, silent steps, moon in the seventh house, Druid moons seen through stone monoliths, wolf-howling moon, lunatic moon, the old moon singing 'Where are you going and what do you wish?', moon like a flower in heaven's high bower, that old Devil moon in your eyes, sickle moons, moons reflected in champagne, horned moons over doldrummed seas, moon walking the night in her silver shoon, moon wandering alone among stars of a different birth, a roving moon, inconstant moon, phantom moon, blue moon.

Leonora says it is dangerous to sleep in moonlight because you could become pixilated – which means being confused as to where you are. She says the blues is the music of moonlight because it is all about people going off somewhere else and not knowing the why and wherefore of it. And blue notes are slurred, offnotes that can't even be written down, because they are in between our time and spiritual time. When you are tired of living but afraid of dying, they describe your longing to be further on up the line. A longing with a strong beat.

In the days when people suffered apoplectic fits and attacks of the spleen, and black bile of the blood, they also died of nostalgia – the deep and persistent longing for all things past and faraway. The symptoms of nostalgia were palpitations, stupor and fever, which could result in death if the patient was not returned back to their home.

'Being both a thinking non-extended thing and an extended non-thinking thing at the same time, I am bound to be misled from time to time,' said Descartes.

*

Roof, balcony, trellis or tree. Roof, balcony, trellis or tree. The places from which my sister could have fallen run over and over in my mind like a bizarre nursery rhyme. The method of Descartes involved thinking only clear and distinct thoughts, dividing them into as many parts as possible, and then ordering those parts from simple to complex.

A roof is a structure covering the top of a house. A balcony is a platform with a rail, or a parapet projecting from the outside of the upper story of a building. A trellis is a light framework of crossing wooden bars, used to support climbing plants. A tree is a perennial plant with a single stem, or trunk, with branches spreading outward some distance from the ground. Murder is the unlawful, malicious or premeditated killing of someone. The date was 21 July 1961. The time was five o'clock in the afternoon. The sun rose at 6.38 a.m. The weather was partly cloudy, with temperatures in the upper eighties. The door of the Monroe house is eighty-four steps from the door of our house. For what clear and distinct reason did my sister go over there that day?

'Haddie. Your cat's on our roof,' Mathilde says in the expressionless, monotone voice of the mad. She has a sallow face and stringy hair. She is wearing a long-sleeved black dress that runs down to her ankle bones, even though it is almost ninety degrees outside.

My sister looks up from the book she is reading. The *Arabian Nights*. A common theme in the book is the unpredictable reversal of fortune. She stands up swiftly. 'I'll call the fire department,' she says, going toward the door of our house.

'Don't be stupid,' Mathilde says drily. 'We can get it ourselves. Come with me.'

My sister follows her across the street and into the house. Up the secret staircase to the nursery room. Mathilde climbs each stair slowly, deliberately, placing each foot next to the other. She is going over her plans in her head. The cat is dead. She fed it Black Flag. Then tossed it by its tail into the Bottomless Lake.

When they get to the nursery, Mathilde opens both french doors at once, in a dramatic gesture. The black dress swirls about her slim hips. 'Stand on the railing,' she says to my sister, motioning with her thin white hand. 'I'll hold you by the ankles – you'll see it from there.' Mathilde knows my sister is reckless and heedless of danger. They used to play 'Truth or Dare' together, and my sister always picked the dare.

My sister places her book on the railing and climbs up, resting the sole of each foot squarely on the center of the rail. She holds her arms out horizontally, tipping, then balancing, wobbling to one side, then the other. Mathilde takes hold of her ankles. My sister leans out slightly to get a better view of the roof. Mathilde tightens her grip. My sister leans out a little more. 'I . . . can't . . . see,' she gasps.

'It's there,' Mathilde says in a dead voice. And then, suddenly, she lets go. She brushes my sister's book over the edge. My sister's head fills up with the wavering and suspicious sensation of Doubt. She verges right, then left – her arms start to flail wildly. The ground zooms up and then back down. Just as she starts to fall, Mathilde twists the charm bracelet violently from her wrist. 'You have met your dawn,' Mathilde whispers, and then laughs as she watches my sister fall. 'All is Allah' is a recurring phrase in the *Arabian Nights*, meaning that one's destiny is held wholly in the hands of fate.

'When did Mathilde run away?' I ask my grandmother. 'Was it just after my sister died?'

'No. It was several months later. It was after they returned.'

'Returned? Returned from where?'

'The shore. The Monroes had a house at the shore. The New Jersey shore. Mrs Monroe stayed there with the children most summers.'

'So she wasn't here . . . when . . . during my sister's accident?'

'No.' My grandmother looks at me, concerned. 'Haddie, you really must put all of this out of your mind. Accidents happen. And this accident happened over a decade ago . . .'

'But what do you think she was doing over there . . . if everyone was away?'

'Mr Monroe wasn't away. He was not supposed to join his family until later in the summer.'

'Could he have done something . . . to her?'

'Enough of this, Haddie. You have a wild imagination. Why would that man possibly want to hurt your sister? He adored her. She was like a daughter to him.'

In Amy Vanderbilt's *Complete Book of Etiquette* there is a section on 'The Bachelor's Social Problems'. The bachelor, being assumed lonely, has to fill in the numbers at dinner parties and be seated next to unwanted relatives; he runs out of money because he is expected to escort his lady friends to the to-be-seen-in restaurants; and he is often the dupe of duplicitous fortune hunters. But to the hostess, even if he is one hundred and two, penniless and lacking all faculties, he is as rare and wondrous as the Cigar Store Indian, and as wanting of collecting. When I mention this to Mrs Lewis today on the way to Charm School, after she says that she found my bachelor friend George an interesting man, she blinks rapidly several times, blushes, and then turns to *Easy Listening FM* on the car radio.

Once we arrive at Charm School we start learning how to be

demure. Which is simply the habit of harnessing inner impulsive emotion with discreet outward decorum. While at one time, a lady was able to mask her tears and feelings of anger or embarrassment by collapsing on the floor in a faint, this mode of behavior is no longer fashionable, and we have had to cultivate other rituals to hide our gaudy sentiments, which only create contempt and fear in others and therefore should be displayed solely in the private sphere.

The first thing we practice is having reposed, rational eyes. A fixed stare can denote effrontery, a wide-eyed glance imbecility, moving your eyes from side to side and up and down can implicate violence, and wandering eyes madness. One should imagine one's eyes as still waters which run deep, whose surface will not be rippled by others' impudence or ill-breeding, and should show a cast of interest in the other person's topics and well-being, yet not a gaze too inquisitive or stimulated, for this could lead to an impression of meddlesomeness, cunning or voluptuousness. There is not any advantage to be obtained by eccentricity in eye contact. Nor does one gain points with creativity in deportment. And there is little *savoir-faire* in spontaneity.

In romance novels, there is always a lot of tension in the way the hero or heroine look at each other. There is usually a woman with a full mouth and slender white neck, whose hair tumbles down her proud back with an escaping curl at her cheek, and she has ivory-white shoulders and uptilted breasts. And she is volatile by nature and broadcasts a regal certainty, and is aware of appreciative glances.

The man has an air of isolation and is tall and straight as a towering spruce with broad shoulders that the woman thinks must tire under the burden he carries and she can feel the power coiled within him when he walks. He has a firm mouth, always on the edge of laughter, and a swath of unruly hair falls casually over his forehead, and he has a commanding manner and the appearance of one who demands instant obedience; he is perhaps a bit unscrupulous, and complex and not easy to know intimately.

Soon after the man and woman meet, his rapier glance passes over her, there is a significant lift to his eyebrows, then he chuckles, a dry and cynical sound, then his laughter breaks off, his eyes smolder and glow with a savage inner fire. Her blue eyes flash with an azure flame and dart nervously back and forth. He looks up from beneath craggy brows, she observes him through lowered lashes, he gives her a conspiratorial wink, her eyes grow large and limpid, his eyes pierce the distance between them, rivet her to the spot, she blinks, feeling lightheaded, his dark eyes soften at the sight of her, she regards him with impassive coldness, his eyes flash imperiously, she shoots him a withering glance, the mystery of his eyes beckons her irresistibly, her eyes sparkle as though she is playing a game, his mercurial eyes sharpen suspiciously, darken dangerously, her eyes have a burning, faraway look, a sudden, icy contempt flashes in his eyes, her eyes are pools of appeal, his black eyes impale her, her eyes blaze with sudden anger, his dark eyes grow completely wild, her eyes widen in alarm.

After Descartes, everyone started questioning their senses. And wondering, who were they? In his book, Professor Weltschmerz says this is because Galileo said: '*Eppur si muove*', which means everything is moving even though not many people noticed it before Newton invented a law for it. And when they did, they started thinking of how strange it was that our lives revolve around a huge ball of burning gases, and how from this perspective even very ordinary things took on quite a bizarre aspect.

Which makes Weltschmerz sentimental for the Ptolemaic conception of a geocentric universe. Then he describes two gentlemen named Lyell and Lamarck who expanded geologick time to infinitudinous Dimension which delivers Weltschmerz to Torchlusspanik's door: the horror of looking into the Abyss which looks back. So these academies and salons and societies started meeting to Record Phenomenon Hitherto Unrecorded or Unobserved, basically to figure out what else we were missing out on. It was decided that everyone would be a whole lot happier if they could count on what they were seeing was the same thing that was actually happening out there. So while some were writing like mad to get down on paper everything that they knew about the world outside, others were wondering how they came to know all that stuff in the first place. And if they could still believe it.

If you take a piece of paper and tear it in half, and put one half on top of the other and tear it again, and repeat this process fifty times you will have a pile of paper 17,769 miles high. A piece of a neutron star the size of a pinhead would weigh more than one million tons. If you had a building twenty miles high, twenty miles wide and twenty miles long, one grain of sand within this building would equal the ratio of matter to empty space in the known universe. If every atom in a grain of sand were the size of a pinhead, that grain would be one mile long, one mile wide and one mile high.

My grandmother and I are kneeling at a low table in her Abode of Fancy, the little gazebo in her backyard used to house the poetic impulse. This is where we have tea ceremonies. It is small, with white walls and a little alcove where my grandmother has placed a small branch of pine to remind us of the unchanging nature of Things.

'Is the branch inside, or outside of your head?' my grandmother asks while pouring my tea. She is the host and I am the host – there is no such thing as 'guest' among enlightened people. When two such people meet, it is like 'two thieves in the night who know each other immediately'. They do not shake hands, but bow to each other to pay tribute to the godhead in all. 'It is neither,' my grandmother answers for me, as I am still dumbly transfixed by the pine branch. We are wearing white headbands wrapped around our foreheads because they intensify your concentration. They are called haki-maki. Chinese acrobats sometimes wear them. My grandmother has pictures of some, hanging from wires by their long licorice-whip hair. She says they can feel the differences in gravity each day. She also has a picture of a man she knew who was an enterologist. Which means he could displace all his sockets and fit himself into a bottle. He was also an opium addict. Our science teacher said that most of us is empty space, and if you got rid of it, the solid matter that remained would be smaller than a pinprick. And if you let the air out of the whole population of people on earth, you could fit everyone into a matchbox.

'Haddie, you are not concentrating.' My grandmother is holding up her teabowl. I pick up mine and sip some. In the Orient it is called the golden elixir. It is grown on bushes which first sprouted after the Bodhidharma tore off his eyelids and threw them to the ground because he was getting groggy. 'Notice the shape of the teapot.' My grandmother runs a finger along its spout. 'How the line and the curve are reconciled in harmony.'

'Mm. Real wabi,' I say, swallowing tea. Wabi is the loneliness and simplicity you can see in objects worn out by time.

'Now listen, watch, taste and smell.' My grandmother uses a wooden whisk to whip up the tea and water. You are supposed to watch her fluid movements, listen to the sound of the whisk and the tea as it is poured, smell its fragrance, feel of the teabowl in your hands, the taste of the tea in your mouth, with your whole mind – sensation, emotion, intuition and reason. Then you have had the whole tea experience. I have found you can do this with anything. I especially like having a book experience. You can press the cover to your forehead in reverence, open it and listen to the crack of its spine, smell the pages, feel the weight of it in your hands.

I pick up my teabowl and let it rest in the palm of my hand. It is warm. It fits the contours of my palm so perfectly, a feeling of calm breezes through my whole body. I wonder if you can feel your thoughts happening inside your head. The touch of the teabowl seems to be making an arch under my skull from one ear to the other. I look at the honey color of the tea. The thought seems warm at the back of my head, under that little valley indentation above my neck. The sound of the pouring seems to be happening at my temples.

'Each preparation of leaves has a story to tell,' my grandmother is saying. 'There is greatness in all small incidents.' Tea masters in China have black bottom teeth from tasting. Lately, when my grandmother smiles, you can see her bottom teeth more than her top teeth. She says this is always the first sign to call her plastic surgeon.

'Do you have three good stories about love, death, etc., that have happened in your life, that make you understand them?' I ask her.

My grandmother closes her eyes. She often does this before speaking. Sometimes she closes her eyes for long minutes in the middle of speaking. 'I don't know if the loves and deaths I have experienced have made me understand them,' she says slowly, opening her eyes. 'The more experience I have had, the less I have understood.' She closes her eyes again. I think she has finished speaking, but she opens them once more, takes a sip of her tea and murmurs, 'Strange.'

'What is strange?' I ask.

'About death. The first thing that came to my mind when you mentioned it was a night I left your grandfather to gamble away our money at Happy Valley and took a rickshaw home. I fell asleep, and when I awoke we were in the middle of the road with rice paddies on all sides. Green light at the horizon. The rickshaw driver had dropped dead from a heart attack.' She places her bowl back on the table. A lot of my grandmother's stories have to do with being stranded in the middle of nowhere. A broken-down Peugeot in Brittany. A bicycle with a flat tire in Bermuda.

'And I had a gentleman friend once, who was dying,' she continues, 'of an inherited disease. He heard that a tidal wave was due to hit an offshore island. When such a wave is about to hit the coastline, the water recedes all the way to the horizon.' She waves her hand toward the open door of the Abode, as if the sea is lapping at her lawn. 'If a person wanted to, he could walk out several miles before the wave comes crashing to shore. My friend went to the island. And he never returned.'

'What about Grandpa's death?'

'Oh.' She waves her hand in the air. 'I was prepared for that. In my time women endured rather than divorced. Many of us spent our marriages preparing for spectacular widowhoods. Then we spend our widowed years preparing for spectacular invalid years.' She likes to give the impression that she doesn't miss her husband. But once I walked into her house without knocking, and her voice called to me from upstairs, 'Charles?' thin and reedy, like a child lost in a dark park. And sometimes you'll hear her talking to herself in another room, and as you get closer, you realize that she is talking to him. 'Anyway,' she says, pouring me more tea, 'stories you tell about your life, and your life itself, rarely have much in common.'

The Buddhists believe that your last thought at death determines the character of your next incarnation. If my sister wrote her autobiography, the first line might be: 'I always knew I would die young.' Of course, it would be logically impossible for her to write that line. Just as authors can never reasonably write 'The End' at the conclusions of their autobiographies.

When Mrs Lewis tells you things that have happened to her, she often ends with a lilting question, or she'll pull the skin of her right cheek under her eye with her index finger, which is a French gesture of disbelief. *Incroy*able, she says, stressing the last syllable. Sometimes she begins a story with the phrase, '*Il était une fois*', which means 'there was a time', and these stories usually have to do with her growing up in the sixteenth *arrondissement* – the sad sixteenth of Paris. But she rarely tells whole stories. She'll describe sounds and smells. The sound of a gypsy fortuneteller calling '*L'avenir, l'avenir*' from a bridge. A vendor yelling '*Bière, Schweppes, Orange!*' on a beach. She will say '*oui*' while sucking in her breath, describing Camembert soft as an eyelid. Louis says the imperfect tense in French is called imperfect because emotions and atmospheres do not have definite shapes – they have the motility of clouds.

If you extend your arm out in front of you and look at your

thumbnail, this is the size of the earth from the moon. Suppose the earth is completely still. And that it is actually at the center of the universe, that it is, in fact, flat as a pancake. Suppose our beliefs that it is moving round, and at the edge of one of many galaxies, are just illusions.

LIST OF ILLUSIONS: Half-moons, bent sticks in water, the green flash of the sun, vanishing points in paintings, the mare of the night, the veil of Maya, the painted grapes of Zeuxis, black dogs on lonely English roads, gray dogs of delirium tremens, pools of water on desert highways, wagon wheels moving backwards in Westerns, eyes in paintings following you, statues that bleed, mermaids and mermen, eyes on the wings of butterflies, the roar of the ocean in seashells, palaces and palm trees in the middle of the Sahara, fata Morganas, the Flying Dutchman, codpieces, the face of Jesus in a plate of spaghetti.

I see a girl on a bus, bored, sulky. Her legs are crossed, she is wearing black patent leather pumps. She looks out the window, one eyebrow is raised higher than the other. She sees red-brick buildings, blue airplanes, churches with steeples. A boy sits next to her, singing 'Which-a-way, which-a-way does that blood red river run?' The bus stops at a train crossing. The sign over the doors – 'Watch your step' – flashes like a worn-out proverb. An entire train once disappeared completely into quicksand in Colorado in 1875. 'That's funny,' the girl hears someone behind her say. 'That plane's dusting crops where there ain't no crops.' A man in a gray sharkskin suit runs across the field. The Barrymores said that an actor needs to live a thousand lives in one moment.

*

In Volume IV, Section III, of *The Age of Reason*, Weltschmerz visits a scepter'd Isle, full of verduous Glooms where the forlorn Nightingale sings lachrymal Langors of the Lasslorn and where three men of philosophick Disposition wrote books on how dubious they were as to the Source of their Ideas. In brief, one of the philosophers, Locke, said ideas came from the fevered Emanations of Matter, and that sweet, blue, warm things weren't anywhere near as real as bulky, square, moving ones. Then the next one, Bishop Berkeley, came up with the motto: *Esse est percipi*, which meant that when you aren't looking things are purely hypothetical, but we shouldn't worry because God's mind is always around to make sure it's not all completely immaterial. The third, named Hume, said that since we have no sense of connection, everything we believe is basically a bunch of our perceptions stuck in a rut. But all three pretty much agreed that what makes you you are the ideas you have. And those ideas come from your senses. When I told Louis about this he said there was this melancholy Frenchman who decided that everyone has only three ideas in their whole life that will actually affect their life. I wonder if one of the ideas that affected the depressed Frenchman's life was the idea that we have only three ideas. I think one of the ideas that I've had, that has affected my life, is that I have No Idea.

Maybe she was dead before she fell. Maybe she was thrown, as a corpse, out the window, to make her death look like an accident.

Berkeley said: 'Being is being perceived.' In Latin it is '*Esse est percipi*'. It sounds chi-chi, glitzy – it could be the name of a Hollywood club where stars congregate in order to be seen. And Emmalou de Cherraglio was being seen – camera shutters snapped wherever she appeared – with each flash she swelled with more life. She was being Seen – larger than life.

But then a shadow, cast by my sister, passed over her, obscuring her from view. 'Hello, Haddie,' Emmalou says in a voice as phony as a counterfeit bill. 'Come in.' She moves sideways, allowing my sister into the Monroe house. 'Mr Monroe is out. I don't know when he will be back.' Emmalou is standing in the middle of the half-lit hallway. The shadow her body casts along the wall is distorted – it looks like the shadow of a raven, rather than a woman.

Haddie enters the living room. It is quiet . . . too quiet. She feels a prickle at the back of her neck and turns to face Emmalou. The shadow of a lead pipe is cast over her head. 'What . . . is . . . this?' my sister cries out. 'Murder, my sweet.' Emmalou smiles as she brings down the pipe.

Emmalou kneels next to the body. She rips off the charm bracelet and pockets it. Then she walks toward the Bakelite phone that looms in the foreground and dials a number using the end of a cigarette holder. 'Send them over. To the Monroe house. We gotta make it look like an accident,' she says and then hangs up. A shaft of light enters through a slit in one of the curtains, highlighting Emmalou's baby-blonde hair, illuminating her baby-blue eyes. Colors are not what is absorbed by an object, but rather what is reflected off of it. What you see is never what is actually there. Things are not what they seem.

Logic proves that the arrow cannot move. For it cannot fly across an infinite space in a finite time. Thus it only appears to move. If our senses prove that it moves, that proof only proves that our senses are deceptive.

'What's with the kung fu do, Lulu?' Leonora asks me, pointing to my haki-maki headband.

'I'm trying to focus my mind on clear and distinct thoughts. I think it might help me figure out what I believe.'

'Well, Confucius, just because an idea is clear and distinct doesn't mean you are going to believe it.'

Someone left flowers at my sister's grave. I cut through the graveyard on my way back from town today. I had this desire to read the inscription on her gravestone. It is a modified version of the last stanza from Landor's 'The Sea-Nymph's Parting': 'The tear for fading beauty check, / For passing glory cease to sigh; / One form shall rise above the wreck, / One name, Haddie, shall not die.'

A bouquet of summer blossoms has been carefully balanced on top of the gravestone. It must have been placed here recently, for the flowers are still fresh. In fact, the colors look inappropriately gay. Who could have possibly left them? I get a chill down my back. Nymphs are supposed to live 10,000 times longer than mortals.

I turn from the grave and run toward the ravine, where I wander aimlessly for a while on its cool dirt paths. Suddenly, a dark object darts out of the corner of my eye. I swing my head around, but there is nothing, only trees, their leaves swaying and shushing in the wind. The sun is bright and hot. If you close your eyes after staring at the sun, it appears as a black sphere. In China, the soul is thought to be a small round black object that can enter and leave the body at will. I see something flash by again. And then, between the trees I catch sight of the bachelor, in his black suit, running. He runs quickly, leaps over the stream and up the side of the ravine. I look in the direction he came from to see if there is anything chasing him. I look back to where I last saw him, but he is gone.

*

'Avoid making inappropriate noises while in the company of others,' they tell us at Charm School. 'Do not hum, whistle or whisper. Do not tap your foot or drum your fingers. Do not slurp, burp, cough or hiccup. Masticate quietly. If you suffer from any impediment to your speech, have it corrected as soon as possible inasmuch as those involving plosives and fricatives might inadvertently spoil your dining partners' appetites.'

We are driving home. 'It is extremely impolite to stare, Haddie,' Mrs Lewis says in a hard, cold voice. I didn't mean to, but I guess I was staring at her. She looks different – tired – there are blue smudges under her eyes, lines I never noticed at the sides of her mouth. Her hair is slightly tangled and dirty.

'Your sister could be very rude,' Mrs Lewis continues in a stern voice. Her lips are drawn tight against her teeth. 'Very rude indeed.'

I realize I am staring at her again, but this time in complete surprise. She has never mentioned my sister before. I wait for her to say more, but instead she changes the subject completely. 'Don't believe the things Louis tells you. About his father.' She clears her throat several times. She seems to be searching for the right words. Even though she looks quite tired, she is still very beautiful. In French, adjectives come after nouns. I wonder if it feels like more of a compliment to be called a 'woman beautiful' than a beautiful woman.

She clears her throat again. 'Haddie,' she says, and I think she is going to say something more about my sister, or Louis's father, but instead she asks me to get her pills out of her purse for her. I find the amber prescription bottle, and shake one out and hand it to her. She tosses it in her mouth and swallows. She's always taking these pills, but I never thought about what they were. I read the name of them on the label, and when I get home, I look it up in our *Family Book of Medicine*: Relieves acute anxiety attacks, prevents overstimulation of the heart.

You see, the arrow is at rest because at each point of its movement it is still, still being defined as something which occupies a space equal to itself, or in other words, fills a space exactly identical to its dimensions, and at each point in its flight the arrow is occupying a space equal to itself and therefore it is at rest at each of these points, and each of these points makes up the flight, which in actuality is not flight, but points of rest. Being a collection of perceptions succeeding each other with inconceivable rapidity. Perhaps I am not stating this clearly. One could go on endlessly. One should end things precisely.

Professor Weltschmerz writes that a French philosopher named Condillac posed this question: If you were nothing but a nose, and you were surrounded by roses, would you think you were the scent of roses? Being only being being when it is being perceived.

Weltschmerz doesn't exactly answer the question, but writes that there is a long and unfortunate History of sensitive Individuals becoming asphyxiated by the pulmonary Imposthumes of the Flower. Then he talks about the floral Harems of the Linnaean system and the priapic Pistils titillating the secret Raptures of the Stamen. He thus warns the benevolent Lector of the wild Dyspepsia of mind Substance that the heady Blossom of Spring can Occasion.

'O blessed joys of truth suddenly shining forth, what Transports of the Flesh are there to compare with you?' Louis raises an eyebrow at me. We are sitting in my father's study. He's reading

Professor Weltschmerz's exuberant discovery that the dung beetle's horns are not insensitive to finely drawn outlines. 'He's obviously opiated and unhinged,' Louis says, 'but he's clearly a person of unbounded Imagination. I'd like to go Sturm und Dranging with him, composing posthumorous epistles on Angst.'

Louis wanted to go Wandervogeling – running naked through the woods – in tribute to Weltschmerz's homeland, but since I absolutely refused we've settled upon going on a smell safari instead. 'Dispatched by the Royal Society to discover the lost tributaries of our souls' is how Louis put it. He's been reading a little bit too much Weltschmerz. Louis says we need to compose an olfactory dictionary–map of our town, that if you want to know the archeo-source of your ideas you need to define your ur-sensations.

In science class we learned that smells are the voices of flowers and plants, and that they are basically saying one of two things: 'Let's get it on' or 'Help!' Apparently, inside our nose is the vomeronasal gland, which detects fear and sex in others. And someone had a theory that our noses are getting more and more spectacular over time because our brains grew out of the olfactory stalk, and so as our brains grow, our noses grow right along with them. So, if our noses are getting bigger, then that gland must be getting bigger too. So it must follow that we are getting to know more and more about what people are attracted to, and what they are afraid of. And you can find out a lot about someone just by knowing what they find sexy and what they find scary. Sometimes it is the same thing. Just ask Dr Freud. Or Louis's favorite marquis.

'Trombipulation means using the nose as an instrument.' He gives me a lewd look. 'I wish I had a prehensile one – like an elephant. It would be perfect for inhaling the musky emanations of the bodice.' He pulls me toward him by my T-shirt and sticks his nose down inside the front of it. I pull his head back out of my shirt by his hair. 'And you'd never have to ask someone to pass the salt at a dinner party,' he adds.

'I doubt you'll be attending too many of those if you make a habit of inhaling the hostess's *décolletage.*'

'Not' – Louis raises his finger – 'if I claim it is a custom indigenous to the island culture where wild in the wood I ran.' Louis says I'm wasting a lot of time with Charm School when I could take the short cut of saying that I was weaned in the Troubriand Islands, or Papua New Guinea. Or basically any place with 'land' at the end of its name. Then it's an etiquette free-for-all where all your *faux pas* would be considered fanciful and thought-provoking. You could stuff the silverware in your pockets, lick the serving spoons, dip your head in the bowl of blancmange, and if you don't like what they're serving you can pound on the table, demanding cocoyamfufu until they bring you a peanut butter sandwich.

'If fairy tales were true you'd have a nose as long as the Nile from lying,' I tell him.

Louis shrugs. 'Honesty is rude. Isn't that what my mother has been teaching you? The elaborate art of affectation?' He sniffs the air. 'Maybe we'll educate our unlettered noses to such a pitch that we'll be able to detect lies from truth on the breath of others.'

'Or on the pages of books,' I say, lifting one off the shelf and smelling it. 'Libraries always smell alike. I wonder if there is a smell to learning.'

'I plan on perfuming my Bibliothèque Bleu. It will be the largest collection of rare engravings of *le soixante-neuf* love acts. I am going to scent each delicate sheaf with the sweat of the Abyssinian civet cat.'

'Whatever happened to Scratch and Sniff technology?' I ask him. 'Fragrance could really enhance some of those boring nineteenth-century novels. Like Sir Walter Scott. You could scratch and sniff heather and smoke. It would alleviate the boredom. And scratch smelling salts. To keep you awake.'

'I'd rather be sodomized by a bagpipe than read *Ivanhoe*,' Louis says. 'But enough of this. Let's go sniff the book of nature.'

We leave my house and wander over to the Lewises' garden. Louis snaps a rose from one of his mother's bushes. He brings it up to his nose and inhales deeply. 'Here, name this smell,' he says and hands the rose to me.

I breathe in its fragrance. No words come to mind. Just memories. I can't really describe. It's like trying to catch a mirage in a mousetrap. 'This is going to be difficult,' I say to Louis.

Louis takes the rose back from me and smells it. 'Maybe a word with "ess" at the end of it.' He drums his pen against our notepad. 'I've got an idea. Go put on a petticoat. *Sans culottes*. Then come back here and swing on that swing.' He points to the one fastened to a tree. 'Real high so that your skirts billow out. I'll loll on the ground underneath you. Come on, be a sport.' He whines, when I give him a look, 'The men of the Enlightenment always had a muse to set their quills aquiver.' He wraps his arm around my waist.

I read that coquettes used to cavort in the audacious spirit of *aude sapere* – daring to know – their bodies and minds rhymed like the vowel chimes in the closing couplets of unseemly sonnets. 'Okay,' I say, surprising myself. Louis looks at me with these big saucer eyes. 'But go get one of your mother's taffeta skirts. Weltschmerz says that taffeta has a frenzying effect. That should inspire you.' The last half of my sentence is lost to Louis who is already at the back door of his house.

Louis returns with a peacock-blue taffeta skirt, and a pair of his mother's opera glasses. He hands me the skirt. 'Everything looks even better when looked at through a lorgnette.' He gives me a salacious grin. I pull on the skirt over my shorts, fasten it at the back and then pull down my shorts underneath with what I hope is a coy wriggle, let them drop beneath me and step out of them. Louis picks them up and holds out his hand. I lick my bottom lip, pout and, while staring at him with amorously intriguing eyes, draw my panties down and hand them to him. He kisses them. 'These' – he rubs the silky material between his fingers – 'were invented so an Italian princess could ride her *cheval à l'amazone*. Side-saddle.' He shoves my shorts and panties into his pocket. 'I shall wear these under my breeches into the battlefield.'

I walk over to the swing, letting my hips sway to a silent song. Then I sit and swing higher and higher. Louis is lying beneath me, gazing up, dreamy and intense. He could be one of those eavesdropping cupids that seem always on the verge of tumbling from their pedestals and scampering off to tattle on everything they heard through the rosevine. The taffeta skirt rustles in the breeze. I feel very *vogue la galère* and *au fait*.

'Louis!' I hear Mrs Lewis's voice calling from across the yard and I screech the swing to a halt and hop off, brushing the skirt smooth. Louis is still lying on the ground.

'Yes, *Maman*,' he answers, gazing up at the sky through his lorgnette. He lifts them and looks at me. 'This is a comedy of manners,' he says and winks.

'Hello, Haddie,' Mrs Lewis says, walking up to us. 'Why are you wearing evening wear? I have one in just that color.' She points to the skirt. 'I wear it with a silk blouse, though.' She tilts her head, looking critically at my T-shirt with its red peace sign.

'Of course, your cotton shirt is much more *à la mode*.' She laughs. Her hair is windblown, her lips are full and red, her eyes bright, as if she's just stepped out of a reckless speeding convertible. 'And Louis.' She turns to him. He is looking at her through the lorgnette. 'I told you not to touch those glasses. They were my grandmother's. What are you doing with them?'

'Actually' – he stands up – 'we were navigating our world of smell.' He turns to me. 'Mother knows all about that.' He grabs his mother by the waist and pulls her toward him. 'I should define the scent of the woman who suckled me.' He nestles his head in her neck. 'I could bottle it. Call it "Après Raison".' He sniffs her neck for several long seconds. Mrs Lewis rolls her eyes and says 'Enough' and tries to push him away, but he takes her arm and smells all the way up her sleeve.

'*Where* have you been?' he says, circling around her back and sniffing her other shoulder. Mrs Lewis stands very still. 'What would you call *this* smell?' Louis asks me, pointing at his mother.

I laugh out of tension and lean over and smell her hair. At first I pick up the jasmine and ginger scent she usually wears, but underneath that there is something different. 'I don't know.' I shrug my shoulders. 'It smells like men's cologne.'

'Ooh . . . la . . . la . . .' Louis says slowly. He turns to face Mrs Lewis, looking into her eyes. 'Is the little mouse playing while the big cat's away?'

'Louis. Enough.' There are blotches of red on Mrs Lewis's cheeks. She looks as if she might strike him. 'No more teasing. Be nice.' She turns to go back to the house, but Louis grabs her hand in both of his, turns it over, kisses her open palm. Mrs Lewis relaxes a little, but she is still angry. She jerks her hand away from his. 'Come on,' she says. 'Time for dinner. Haddie, would you like to stay?'

I start backing away before she tries to persuade me. 'No thanks,' I say, and turn and half run across the yard and out into the street, the stolen skirt shushing about my legs.

It is dusk. Between the wolf and the dog, as Louis calls it. My grandmother told me that in the Orient they sometimes light long candles which are layered with different scents and as they burn down they perfume the air with a different smell each hour. Leonora says ghosts are basically odors, and that's why night smells different from day.

As I pass the Monroes' yard I smell something intriguing. I follow my nose toward it. The aroma gets stronger as I get closer to the house. It is musky and heavy and sweet. I walk along the bushes and turn the corner – and see a bush of blue roses climbing up the trellis of the house. Just as I lean over to smell, I hear 'gorgeous scent, isn't it?' – the bachelor's voice, behind me. He tilts a watering can toward the base of the shrub. 'These were dormant,' he continues, 'asleep . . . I only needed to wake them up with some pruning . . . the right soil, and water. They've just bloomed.' He takes a pair of scissors out of his back pocket, snips off a blossom and hands it to me. 'They are very unusual. Blue. They match your eyes,' he says, winking, and then walks back to the front door, whistling.

I put the rose up to my nose and breathe in its fragrance. It smells like something that would grow in the garden of an enchanted Persian palace, something happy and sad. If *déjà vu* had a smell, it would smell like this.

There is a loud hum of crickets rising from the grass. The trilling notes seem to run like an electrical current through the trunks of the trees, causing a static in their leaves. I always thought that, if you could hear it, this is what gravity would sound like. Professor Weltschmerz says that like gravity, odor is the Antediluvian spirit force of Attraction that first merged the Animalcules in a puff of smoke Osmosis, and constituted the ephemeral Bridge of sacrificial Aether between Heaven and Earth that fed the Olympian Gods. I wonder if gravity has a smell. And you don't notice it because it is always there. Like the music of the spheres that Weltschmerz says you don't hear because the Mysterium Cosmographium has been ringing in your ears forever. Each planet has its own tune, and the earth's is mi fa mi, which are the notes of misery, famine, misery. Hence our natural Disposition toward Melancholia.

The name of the smell of gravity would have to be pure breath, composed completely of vowels – aeiouy. Johnson, in his Preface to the *Dictionary*, says that when he tries to define anything, he feels like the first inhabitants of Arcadia who, when chasing the sun over the hills as it set, found that no matter how fast or how far they ran, they could never get any bit closer.

An APHRODISIAC is a substance which arouses sexual desire. The encyclopedia gives examples of natural aphrodisiacs. Certain moths release aphrodisiac perfumes from the ends of hollow hairs on their abdomens and then wave the potion over the female by fluttering their wings.

On the same page is APOPLEXY. It is the sudden inability to feel, or move.

LIST OF INTERESTING SENSATIONS: The sensation of walking through a spiderweb, of peeling dried glue from your fingertips, of the cool side of the pillow on a hot night, of laughing while lying on your belly, of writing on a banana with a ballpoint pen, the feeling on your lips when you blow through a kazoo, of saying a big word when you're unsure of its meaning, of committing a *faux pas*, of forgetting how to add, the sensation of seeing something from a vantage point, of reading a book in a canoe, of spelling Mississippi, of touching a dolphin, of shrugging your shoulders, of eating maraschino cherries, sky-blue popsicles, the sensation of surprise at seeing Marlene Dietrich emerge out of a gorilla suit to sing 'Hot Voodoo'.

'Causality' is the observation of particular concrete events in temporal succession. Hume said we never actually experience 'cause' as a sensation. We only see one thing, and then another. And we can never be sure that two things will ever happen in the same way again in the future. I wonder if coincidence is two fates colliding, head on, and sometimes the crash is so big that it convolutes the whole plot of your life.

Persistence of vision is the term used for the illusion of linked causes and motion in movies.

The establishing shot might be overhead. A bird's-eye view. You see roofs, chimneys, the tops of trees. The camera tilts down and focuses on the leaves of one of them. The tall chestnut next to the Monroe house. Cut to a black cat balanced in one of its high branches. 'Kitty! Kitty!' you hear a voice calling in the distance. The camera pans down the tree, across the yard, over the street. There is a close-up of a girl's worried eyes. My sister's face. She looks right. An empty street. Left. Silent houses. There is a low-angle view of my sister. She is holding a book. The *Arabian Nights*. Her fingers nervously fan the pages. 'Kitty,' she calls again, softly. She looks ahead. The camera, acting as her eyes, shows the view across the street. The Monroe house. The camera moves back to my sister, tracks her walking toward the house. Then it pulls back on its dolly, watching her move. Her hips in gingham shorts. Matching halter top. Brown belly.

Dimpled knees. Her hair is parted sideways, and falls over one eye. She stops. The camera zooms in on her. Follows her eyes as they move right, then left. 'Kitty?' she calls. You hear a soft mew. Her eyes move upward, following the sound. She walks toward the camera, until the gingham cloth fills the screen. An over-the-shoulder shot. She is looking up into the branches of the chestnut tree. The camera moves among the leaves, stops at a black shape. There is a slapping sound on pavement. A shot of the book of *Arabian Nights*, thrown upon the gray slate path. Then the unsteady movement of the camera in the tree – branches, leaves, rise up and fall, hit the lens. Pan back to my sister climbing up, up.

Then another sound. A heavy thump on wood. The camera moves back to show my sister, paused in her movement, in a high crook of the tree. A loud click. Her eyes move to the open window of the Monroe house, next to the tree. It is a high window, almost two and a half stories tall – my sister is parallel to the very top of it. She is looking in the window. The camera zooms into the house, hanging just below the ceiling. A deep-focus shot. In the foreground is a briefcase, full of money, on a table. Mid-ground are two men – Mr Monroe and a stranger. Mr Monroe's back is to the camera. The other man is in profile. In the background are shadows – the other windows of the room are shuttered. Shafts of light hit the banister of the stair, a brass doorknob, a black telephone, the white triangle of a handkerchief in the stranger's suit pocket, the white spots at the back of the sleeping leopard's ears.

'Felines', the stranger says in a slow, sinister voice, while scratching the leopard under its chin, 'are a jealous breed. And territorial. You are smart to strike first, Mr Monroe. Before your wife can get her claws . . .'

'Don't speak of her – ever!'

'Oh, but I won't . . . need to,' the man continues in his oily voice. He straightens his white tie. 'Once she is – gone – you will get a call. Three o'clock. Friday morning. It will ring thirteen times. Do not answer it. It is only a signal – to let you know. Did you know, Mr Monroe, that if you can make an ordinary clock ring thirteen times it will summon the devil from his slumbers?'

'The money is all there,' Mr Monroe states flatly, waving his hand at the briefcase.

The camera reverse-tracks, up and out of the room, through the window. Shot of my sister's stricken face. She is staring with disbelief at Mr Monroe's back. She sees herself, in the tree, in front of him. She is reflected in the long, tall mirror that runs over the mantelpiece of the fireplace. Just then she sees Mr Monroe watching her. His eyes turn cold and hard. 'Get her!' he shouts, pointing at my sister. Reaction shot of the stranger, looking toward the tree. His hand moves to his jacket pocket. Cut to my sister, grabbing at a branch, she hesitates, seems unsure as to whether to go up, or down. An oblique-angle shot as everything starts to tilt one way, then another. She is falling – there is a blur of green leaves, blue sky, branches and slate – she falls out of the bottom of the frame. The screen fades to black. Which you slowly realize is the huge pupil of a black cat's eye, focusing on her still, sprawled body.

If you could see a 'cause', then maybe the fact of your seeing it is actually involved in the cause itself. For instance, if someone saw the cause of my sister's death, then they were probably a part of it. Otherwise, why would they remain silent about it all these years?

'Because' is between 'becalm' and 'beckon' in the dictionary. It is like a bridge between questions and answers. And you don't have to cross it. You can sit on it and enjoy the view from either side.

ANATTA is the Buddhist doctrine that there is no such thing as a self.

'At five years old you look out at the world, but you don't see yourself,' my grandmother says. We are lying on the floor, preparing ourselves for an out-of-body experience. 'At ten you see the world and yourself in the world. At fifteen you see the world, yourself in the world and yourself seeing yourself. At twenty you see yourself seeing yourself seeing yourself seeing the world. At twenty-five . . .' I tune out at this point because I am already out of my body and spiraling up through space, and hoping one of those ancients was correct in his statement that nothing can ever fall completely out of the universe.

I don't think Emmalou de Cherraglio had anything to do with my sister's death. I just found an article about her, dated about six months before my sister died. It shows her with Lenny, her new husband. He is a carpenter. They are standing in front of their white clapboard house in Iowa. Lenny looks like he might say 'Howdy'. He looks like no one warned him of the dangers of painting in unventilated rooms with closed windows. But Emmalou looks sincerely happy, which makes me realize that in those Hollywood pictures she was just *acting* happy. I wonder how she found her way to Iowa and Lenny. Maybe she drove inland from the coast, and decided that the first guy who asked her 'What is your name?' rather than 'Can I have your autograph?' is where she would settle down for the rest of her life – nowhere in general, where she could be nobody in particular.

Is there a sensation of self? Is there a feeling whose shape you know is the feeling of you? I lie down on the ground and stretch my arms over my head and try to feel the boundaries of my body. I can't feel my shape all at once – there are just these jabs of alertness, like those beep-flashes of filmstrips – a twitch in my calf, the roundness of swallowing, a memory of snow that makes my teeth tingle. I think of how I am obeying the laws of gravity. Apparently, your body is shaped by the huge whirlpool of gravity 4000 miles deep, that surrounds the earth.

Once upon a time I knew this boy, Rupert, who one summer got hit on the head by a golfball. He went into a coma. When he came out of it, his hair had turned completely white. He used to sit on a seesaw, by himself, at recess. He had an unapproachable 'he could have died' awe about him. But one day I went up and sat on the other end of the seesaw. Without saying too much we got it to balance out straight by moving our weight forward and backward. We didn't say much, just listened to the slap of jumpropes and the whistle of a blackbird in the tree above us. We were enclosed in that heavy atmosphere that surrounds you when you're concentrating on your equilibrium.

I asked him how he was feeling. And he told me that ever since he woke up, he had had a hard time knowing where he ended. That he could be the seesaw, or the pavement, or even that line of trees over there. Or you. He pointed to me. Just then Louis Lewis came up and straddled the bench behind me, almost sending Rupert flying off his end and into another coma. And even though I acted real mad at him for throwing off our balance I was secretly glad he had. What Rupert had said gave me the heebie-jeebies. With his snow-white hair and sandman-sleepy eyes he seemed like a sprite who might suddenly vanish, leaving you with a wish granted that you didn't really want.

Professor Weltschmerz says that he suffers from Ontalagia – pains in the joints of Being. I wonder if he got it from thinking about himself too much. I can't find the shape or sensation of my self. There is always something There – a twitch, a pain, or a memory, but I can't find someone Here. If you know what I mean. You just can't get there from here. And you can start getting a headache in your soul from trying.

High noon. A gas station in the middle of a desert. Red pumps. Coke machine. A Burma Shave billboard. The sigh of airbrakes on a silver Greyhound bus. A woman steps off, opens the snap of her purse, takes out a pack of cigarettes. 'Anybody got a match?' she asks, bored, one eyebrow lifted higher than the other. She tilts her head toward her left shoulder. Her charm bracelet jangles on her arm. 'Zowie,' says the millionaire with a number at the end of his name. His chauffeur looks up from the tire he is changing. 'Say, was you ever bit by a dead bee?' the google-eyed attendant asks her, striking a match. In the bathroom she washes her face. The fan above the door. The white porcelain sink. Her shadow on the tile floor. The long bus ride makes her feel as though she is still moving even though she is standing quite still. A folded note is slipped under the door. She opens it. It asks: What have you done with her?

'You have to be the arrow. And the target,' I hear the bachelor's low voice saying behind me. I have been trying to hit this target for hours now. The bachelor takes the bow and arrow from me. He strings the arrow onto the bow and then lifts it to shoulder height. He focuses on the target. And suddenly he is pure Balance, a poised statue, filling a space exactly identical to himself. Then the arrow is in the bull's-eye – I hear the singing of the strings – his arm swiftly shifts back to release it. It all happened Backwards.

He hands me the bow. 'The arrow was flying just then, wasn't it?' I ask him, blinking.

'It was always there,' he says, pointing to the target. He turns to leave, but then stops, and reaches into the inside pocket of his suit jacket. 'I found a picture of you – I was cleaning the air ducts in the basement of my house. I found this' – he hands me a photograph – 'on top of the air-conditioning unit.'

I stare at it. It is my sister and Mr Monroe. 'This . . . isn't . . . me . . .' I stutter, still staring at the picture.

'No?' He sounds as if he doesn't believe me.

I look up at him. 'It is my sister. And Mr Monroe . . . He used to live in your house.'

The bachelor looks from the photograph to me, and then back at the photograph again. 'Uncanny,' he says softly, 'the resemblance . . .' He stands awkwardly, as if he's not sure if he should have shown me the picture.

'Thank you,' I say. 'May I keep it?'

'Of course, of course.' He seems relieved. 'Well, I . . .'

'I'll see you later,' I finish for him, and then watch him walk off.

I sit down on our porch step and look at the photo again. I get a funny jolt looking at my sister. Like you do when you see yourself unexpectedly in a mirror. We do look so very much alike. She must have been exactly my age when the picture was taken. She and Mr Monroe are standing on the deck of a boat. It must be docked, because you can see palm trees behind it. My sister is wearing a pink-and-white plaid bikini. Her hair is pulled up in a high ponytail and there is a glow to her cheekbones. Mr

Monroe's arm is around her bare waist. She is holding the wrist of one arm with the hand of the other. She is wearing the charm bracelet, and the glare of the sun on the little silver dollars casts circles of light along her brown legs. She looks as though she is tossing her head back slightly – her chin is tilted up to the right. She has a slight frown of disdain on her lips – an expression I've seen on Mrs Lewis's face. Was this something Mrs Lewis taught her? One of her lessons in allure? It does look sexy. She does look like me. But she is different from me. I can't explain it, but it is as if she *knows* something.

Mr Monroe is tall, and handsome. But not in an ordinary way. There are deep lines in his forehead, and bags under his eyes, and jowls at his chin. But he looks powerful. His head is as big as a buffalo's, and his eyes are bright. If he acted in movies, he would play Holy Roman Emperors, or explorers who name oceans and continents after themselves, or kings of Siam with 9000 wives. He would say things like: 'Don't believe in surrenders', or 'Drop the gun, Harry', or 'Let's ride', and who-ever he was speaking to would listen to him. But there is some-thing else about him I can't really define. Something familiar and strange at the same time. Like *déjà vu*. Like I've known him before.

A PRIORI is a Latin phrase meaning 'from what came before'. It is knowledge which is independent of all particular experience.

'How would you write your autobiography?' I ask Leonora.

'Well now, Sugar, you won't be seeing *that* happen in a month of Tuesdays.' Leonora throws invisible things over both her shoulders.

'Why not?'

'Because that's like driving your car without lights in reverse down a switch-back mountain highway. I don't *think* so.' She stands with her arms crossed in front of her, her lips set firm. 'Besides, anytime you do something backwards you're just asking for trouble. Backwater backsliding and that old black magic go hand in hand.'

'What about your thinking stones? That help you remember?'

'That's just thinking about a certain time and place – flash-backs. You don't heave up all of those elephant years and then, every once in a while, you get some good luck and in one of your remembers you find there is a sign of your future.' She puts a hand on her hip and points at me with the other. 'I bet a fat man somewhere put the pilot light out on that old French philosopher friend of yours, Rainy Dizzycat, but he might have a point about our heads not walking the dog with our bodies. Telling it straight, Junebug, I can often remember what my body was doing in the past, but am in a complete cross-town quandary as to what my mind was up to.'

The AMYGDALA is a nodule in the brain responsible for re-cognizing fear in others' faces. If damaged, one will not be able to tell the difference between laughter and screaming.

ANATOMY is the science of the structure of organisms. The encyclopedia has a picture of Vesalius dissecting a corpse by candle-light in his operating theater in Padua. There is also a woodcut from his book – *De Humani Corporis Fabrica* – of a skeleton leaning against a large Grecian urn, holding a skull in one of its bony hands. On the outside, the parts of your body have monosyllable names: nose, mouth, ears, arms, legs, wrists, but inside the names sound far-fetched: the Isle of Langerhans, the Demilunes of Heidenhan, the Canal of Schlemm, the

Spaces of Fontana, the Crescents of Granzuzzi, the Pyramids of Malpighi. And you'll never see them. My internal organs don't seem to be *mine*. They lead their own lives. It is said that at the center of the earth there are wild rolling rivers of volcanic fire. You can't quite believe it when you are walking across a serene green field. It's the same thing with my body. I can't quite match my inside to my outside.

It is 3 a.m. I can't sleep. I get up and dress and let myself quietly out the door. It is dark and still on the street. Everyone is asleep. I wonder what they are all dreaming about. It's strange to think of everyone going into their own private trance every night, and then resurfacing in the morning to have their coffee and get in their cars and forget about the strange place they came from, where no one else can ever go.

There is a light on at the Lewises' house. As I get closer, I see the light looks strange – it flickers and flares. The thought of fire jumps jaggedly in my head, and I start to run toward the house. When I reach the gate, I see that the light is in fact coming from the backyard. I run around to the back, and see Mrs Lewis standing in front of their open barbecue pit. There is a fire burning in it. She is bunching paper into balls and then throwing it into the fire.

She turns slowly toward me. 'Hello,' she says evenly, as though it is perfectly normal to greet me in the middle of the night. Her eyes are glassy, and she turns and picks up each piece of paper as though her body is moving through thick liquid. Sometimes I've seen her like this in the morning. She takes pills to sleep, and if she takes them late in the night, the effect doesn't wear off until the afternoon of the next day.

The papers she is throwing into the fire are letters. There is a pile of them on the garden table next to her. There are also cards, books, a scarf, a viewmaster that she usually keeps on top of her dresser. When you look through the twin eyepieces you see a miniature scene of white cliffs, and red fishing boats on a blue bay.

'What are you doing?' I ask her.

Mrs Lewis scoops up the rest of the letters and throws them into the fire. 'Getting rid of garbage,' she says, and takes the scarf from the pile. It is silk, and has a maze pattern of trees and flowered gardens on it. She takes a pair of scissors from the table and cuts the scarf into small squares, and then tosses them into the fire. I look at the books. One is the *Arabian Nights*. It has gold-leaf lettering and gilded camels on its cover. 'Are you going to burn this?' I ask her.

'Yes,' she answers shortly, and starts to take it from me.

'Can . . . I have it?'

She hesitates, her fingers resting on its cover. Then she takes it from me. She reads something that is written on the first page and then crumples it up and throws it in the fire. She hands the book back to me. 'Take it. Go back to sleep, Haddie. It is late.' She turns back to her pile of things. Picks up another book and starts ripping pages out of it, and tossing them into the pit.

When I get home, I sit down in our library with the book. There are pictures of amazing lapis lazuli skies and emerald seas; giant onyx rocs and amethyst sea monsters and gold tigers with black stripes; a maharajah with a gold turban and a silver saber. As I turn the pages, they suddenly flip open toward the back. There is a small cream-colored card placed there with 'MONTGOMERY L. MONROE' printed in raised black letters. On the back is a sentence written in French, ending in a question mark. It is hard to read – the handwriting is awkward – as though written by someone who is left-handed. I look closer. '*On revient toujours a ses premiers amours?*' The same phrase that was inscribed on Mrs Lewis's fleur-de-lis ring. Was Mr Monroe Mrs Lewis's first love? Were they planning on 'returning' to one another?

Our English teacher told us that a love poem often has similar cadences to that of elegies, because true love creates a loss – a loss of yourself and the other person – which can create a divine insanity. Did Mr Monroe commit suicide because of Mrs Lewis? Did she say: 'No, I cannot . . .' or, 'No, I will never . . .' or, 'No, do not speak of it ever again' and these were the last words in Mr Monroe's mind as his car plunged off the bridge? Love songs and love poems are always using the word 'forevermore'. But that is a word that doesn't seem to fit what Leonora calls this big old round world that was just born to be blue.

The glabella is the space between your eyebrows where the sense of the future and the imagination reside. The philtrum is the vertical indentation between your nose and mouth. Leonora told me that, before you are born, you know all the secrets of heaven and earth, but as you are getting ready to come into the world, an angel comes down and presses a finger to your lips, saying 'shh' to keep all the secrets inside. I close my eyes, and rub my philtrum with my little finger, whispering 'shh . . . shh . . .' Leonora taught me to keep secrets this way. It is an old ritual that keeps your lips sealed.

On page 690, Professor Weltschmerz talks about meeting a marquis who is engaged in studies about the Influence of geological Strata on the Morphology of the unique Mammals of the dark Continent, and Weltschmerz journeys with him to the land of the ibis and zebu to measure the Lamarckian neck of the camelopard and the humped back of the dromedary. However, once encamped there, Weltschmerz learns that the marquis's motto is '*in vino veritas*', and spends his hours brewing an elixir of Spirits in the beakers and flasks of their distillation Apparatus, which leads him to vulgar Caprice, odious Vice, and a feckless Laxity of Principles that would have shamed Trimalchio of the *Satyricon*. Many pages later, Weltschmerz encounters a river-dragon, and the marquis, who held the pistils upon his person, and whose erratic Gait was usually of the Cambrian slowness of Geology, forthwith betook himself with the sprightliness of the Springbok to the highest branch of a distant tree. Weltschmerz finally escapes by zigzagging across the open Savannah, but soon after collapses from undulant brain fever, and has to be carried home on a palanquin by a cortège of natives whose basal ganglia is disposed to a scrofulous Distemper due to the large quantity of aquae vitae left behind by the long-vanished iniquitous and depraved marquis.

LIST OF SURVIVAL TACTICS: Dip a bezoar stone in your glass of wine to check for poison. Do not walk blindly into the desert. Keep small pebbles in your mouth to relieve thirst. Remove the legs of grasshoppers before eating them. Do not tease or corner gila monsters. Do not underestimate the strength of a person in a state of panic in deep water. Do not stand near seals – a killer whale will mistake you for one. Grab seabirds that have settled on your raft from exhaustion. Suck water from the eyes of large fish. Give jellyfish a wide berth. Wear a mask on the back of your head to confuse tigers. Avoid icebergs. Avoid polar bears. Avoid the presidential palace in Namibia. Do not put on boots before checking for scorpions. Do not drink salt water. Do not swim directly away from a shark. Do not wander into Iraq by mistake. Do not eat hemlock, locoweeds or larkspur. Do not eat fish that puff up and have humanoid teeth. Do not criticize the Thai Royal Family. Do not sleep under a palm tree – falling coconuts kill. Do not get out of the Land Rover. Do not panic.

Santorio Santorio, the inventor of the thermometer, sat for days on a huge scale over a bonfire in an effort to weigh his soul. Galvani wired a dozen frogs to his roof so that lightning would strike them and make their legs twitch with electricity. Pasteur carried a microscope under his cloak to dinner parties to check for germs. Pascal drew secret parallelograms on his bedroom floor. Tycho Brahe lived in a sky palace on the island of Hven with his jester Jepp who possessed second sight. Newton practiced alchemy. Alexander Graham Bell and his assistant wore special metal helmets so Edison couldn't steal any of the ideas that leaked out of their heads.

Louis and I have been performing *Gedanken* experiments. And we have been recording how our thinking process changes under different circumstances – walking in the rain, while walking backwards, up as opposed to down stairs, while wearing hats, under the influence of water torture, while jumping from the high branch of a tree, while staring at one thing for hours, while repeating every single action three times in a row.

Last week we experimented with how our thought processes changed while being imaginary invalids. We lounged against pillows and coughed delicately into lace handkerchiefs and rang a little silver bell next to the bed for our nonexistent houseboy. And we suffered *mal à la tête* and attacks of the liver, but mainly from Spleen and *le cafard* – the black cockroach of depression. This was remedied by drinking cough medicine straight out of the bottle until the outlines of my body went hazy and the birds outside the window were speaking to me of something in code. Louis would rouse me from my stupor with smelling salts and read to me about the canopies of purple trees in Africa, and of bazaars and jewels and giantesses. It all came to a halt when Louis started mixing us infirmary cocktails of three parts E-Z Rest Fizz to one part Vicks 44, with chasers of Nyquil. And afterwards, when Mrs Lewis urged us down to dinner, I collapsed face down into my bowl of bouillon.

'Is this yours?' I hold my hand out to the bachelor. He is sitting at a table in his backyard. I have been carrying his medal around in my pocket all week, trying to think of how to give it back to him. I took it from Louis's chest of stolen goods in the woods. The bachelor stares at it. 'I found it . . . in the woods . . . near your house . . .' I wave vaguely over at the ravine. 'I thought it might be yours.'

'How very odd.' He shakes his head and takes the medal from me, holding it by the tips of his fingers. 'But, actually, this is quite uncanny.' He sweeps his hands out at the tarot cards lying on the table in front of him.

'Leonora – she's staying with me while my parents are away – she can tell your future with those.' I point to the cards. 'She also uses galloping dominoes. And she can read stones and footprints. She can even figure out what's going to happen next by watching the way a cat jumps. She learned it all from her daddy.'

'Yes?' The bachelor lifts an eyebrow. 'I learned this hobby from my father as well.' He gathers the cards into a pile. 'Toward the end of his life he became a bit eccentric.' He shuffles the cards like a Mississippi gambler and places them back on the table. 'Maybe even senile. He was a scientist and a farmer. Not a mystic. But now I wonder.' He spreads the cards out in a fan and then gathers them together again, tapping the edge of the pack against the table.

'Did any of his predictions come true?'

'Some did. I believe that he mainly liked the process. He was dissatisfied with the laws of science.'

'Leonora taught me how to read people's fingernails.'

'Yes? Can you read mine?'

'Are you right-handed or left-handed?'

He holds out his right hand and I look at his nails. They are neat, cut short, squared at the edges. There are faint half-moons at the base. I love the word for these – lunulas. On his ring finger are three white flecks. 'See these?' I point to them. 'These mean you are ripe for love. A deep and abiding love will enter your life if it hasn't already. This finger is connected to your heart. If you only had one fleck, it would mean the future will bring you loneliness. Two means you have a false love. But three means true love. The one fleck is you, the second is your lover, and the third is the spirit which blesses it.' I start to look at his other fingernails but he pulls his hand away and looks at his ring finger.

'Baby, where *are* you?' Leonora's voice echoes through the neighborhood.

'I guess I've got to go,' I say, turning to leave.

'Yes. Yes,' the bachelor says, but doesn't seem to be talking to me. His eyes are bright bronze and copper. His feet are still moving back and forth and he's all jazzy-jittery, as if any minute he might start snapping his fingers and break into a razzmatazz soft-shoe.

Later, I ask Leonora if she ever read my sister's fortune. She gets a very serious look on her face. 'She wouldn't let me. Not just because she didn't believe in fortunetelling, and what she called "old wives' tales and superstitions".' Leonora looks over my shoulder, with sadness in her eyes. 'She said she knew that she wasn't going to live a long life, and that she didn't need any black magic cards or lines on her palms to tell her so.' Leonora gazes intently at my face. 'On the outside, you look like your sister, but on the inside' – she points to my chest – 'you are different. On the outside, she was a young child, but on the inside – she was old – older than me, seemed even older than old Methuselah.'

HOW TO DIVINE THE FUTURE BY THE MOON: On a night of the full moon, find a clearing in a wood where the moon shines brightly. Make a large circle with nine white stones. In the center of the circle place a silver bowl full of water. Walk nine times clockwise around the circle, chanting: 'Old moon, new moon, moon of sorrow, bring me now a new tomorrow.' Pick up a white stone and toss it into the bowl of water, in which the moon is reflected. The rippling impressions on the water will foretell the future.

According to Newton, if he were given, in minute detail, the state of the universe at its creation, he would be able to figure out mathematically the entire history of any given particle within it. He also said that attraction at a distance explains just about everything.

We are practicing the tried and trusted rituals of keeping tears at bay and anger restrained – which includes pinching the palm of your opposite hand, counting to one hundred, remembering compliments paid to you in the past, and humming a jolly tune such as '*Che sera sera*'. 'Nothing breaks the magic spell of the pleasant atmosphere of a social gathering more than an emotional outburst of tears or rage,' Mrs Lewis is saying.

Weltschmerz wrote that the ancients believed that anger could be a form of art. One time I saw Mrs Lewis run outside Muffy Madigan's, a dress shop in town, in just her slip to talk to her husband who was standing on the sidewalk. You could tell she was angry by the way she was standing. And my grandmother once threw a priceless Ming vase at my grandfather, and it missed him, hitting the wall instead. She has a piece of it, set in gold, that she wears on a chain around her neck. She says she wears it to remind her whenever she misses him. Leonora told me that any time you mix up a man and a woman all you get is dog heart madness. Which is certainly the case in romance novels: the hero and the heroine are basically furious with each other from beginning to end. First he hates her and she loves him, and then she hates him and he loves her, then she hates him and he hates her, on and on *ad infinitum*. And then there is, of course, the added conflict that arises from the Man Who Could Destroy Them Both.

First of all, the hero might lightly finger a loose tendril of the heroine's hair, and she is puzzled by new thoughts. Then she is careful not to let his fingers touch hers, and his fingers brush her collarbone, lingering there too long to be an accident. So she throws her hands over her face, he slams his hand down on the table in front of him, she snatches her arm away and sits down, with his powerful hands he yanks her to her feet, he turns on his heel and strides to the door, she swallows hard and squares her shoulders, he moves closer, her defenses begin to subside, he says words with the certainty of a man who could never be satisfied with just a dream, she bites her lip and looks away, he shows no sign of relenting, his expression darkens, she gasps and with a pang realizes, he gives her a narrow glinting glance – a silken thread of warning – not so her heart whispers back, his face closes as if guarding a secret, every fiber of her body warns her against him, his curt voice lashes at her, she stares at him in haughty rebuke, his face twists with anger, she turns a vivid scarlet.

Trout Hammer, one of the football players at school, called Louis a 'French fag', and then said: 'Do you fuck your mother?' Trout was taken to the hospital afterward to be treated for concussion, multiple contusions, a broken arm and several ribs. Later, no one could quite believe what they had seen. It was as if Louis had suddenly been transformed into a wild beast. Apparently, he had gotten a hold of a rock and was bashing the side of Trout's head with it. Practically the whole football team had to drag him off Trout. One of them said that if they hadn't, Louis would have killed him. So now everyone at school gives Louis wide berth, they are all a little afraid of him.

If space is curved, then if you had the most powerful telescope, would the furthest point you would be able to see be yourself? When you walk, holding a pair of binoculars up to your eyes, you are here and there at the same time. Actually more 'there' than 'here'. Einstein said there is no such thing as 'here'. Because everything is moving so fast that you are already 'there' before you can even say 'here'.

I come to a clearing in the ravine and focus the binoculars up at the sky. There is a bright spot that might be Venus. I still think of it as the Female Love Planet, ruled by Zsa Zsa Gabor, Queen of Outer Space. She starred in a fifties interplanetary adventure movie I saw one afternoon when I was in bed, sick with the mumps, at an impressionable age.

What makes rocks in space obey laws? What makes planets travel in ellipses, set on their course? Laws have that tumde-tumdedumdum certainty of Chinese proverbs: All falling bodies gain speed at exactly the same rate. Every particle in the universe attracts every other particle according to its mass and the inverse square of the distance between them. The action of heat makes substances combine. To every action, there is an opposed and opposite reaction. I wonder if nature has gotten better at what it does, if things are going more smoothly now, after its billions of years of practice.

Our science teacher at school wears pressed pants and a white belt, and a huge watch on his wrist that tells the time in Greenwich, whether he is facing north, south, east or west, and the temperature of the air in Fahrenheit and Celsius. Louis Lewis says he has the green complexion of a homunculus bred in a petri dish. He uses a large monogrammed handkerchief to wipe at his continually running nose, and his nerves seem too delicately spun to bear the rude shocks of this transitory world. And he reads while walking, and if asked will recite one thousand and one decimal places of pi, the numbers singing at the top of his suffering sinuses.

My grandmother says that your right side is mystical and your left side is rational. So you have a mystical leg, and a rational leg. An Eastern eye and a Western eye. I look to the right through the binoculars. It's like spying through a keyhole. I see the needles of a pine, amber sap oozing on its bark, then the black eye of a crow sitting on one of its branches. It has the strychnine stare of pure poison. It makes you wonder what it sees with those eyes. Moving further right, I see a blur of leaves, and then the sun on the stream, watercress on the banks, bluebottles, nettles, the wet roots of trees. I turn left. A wall of gray stone and then a window. A blue ceiling and a chandelier. The shadow of a cloud passes back and forth along the ceiling. I lower the glasses and realize I am looking into Mrs Dimmer's window, the one who lives alone and hates the word 'succulence'. Her house backs up to the ravine. I raise the glasses again. Another window. Inside, tables and chairs. Then a rain-stained ledge, a sparrow hopping, a drain-pipe rusting, a gray flagstone path, marigolds in a stone urn, a ginger cat, rotting pears under a tree – then the small bronze-green statue of a satyr in Mr Lodge's garden. And the gate that creaked whenever we were dared to run inside and touch the statue's lichened foot.

I've only been in that house once, in a sitting room that is curtained and carpeted a rich fez red. But that is the room where I imagined Jane Eyre being locked up after her temper tantrum, and where Tess confesses her secret seduction to Angel and where Emma Bovary died, stretched out on its cardinal window seat, her priest's long black soutane trailing behind him on the floor. And I looked through its windows at the fog of Bleak House, and at the gaunt, stunted firs of Wuthering Heights. The lunar apparition of a male servant stood on the reeling red staircase, and up in Nurse Hammond's room, eagle-eyrie high, was Bertha Rochester, and Dorian Gray's aging portrait, and the window at which the ghost of Catherine knocked, awakening Lockwood in the middle of the night.

Further right is the Russian's house. I see a white flicker at the window, then another. I've never been inside. Legend has it that there are black satin sheets on all the beds, that he applies vermouth to his martinis with an eyedropper, and serves perfect Pink Squirrels to his lady friends. And that he once tied a cravat around his mistress's head, and played blindman's-bluff in the buff with her in the woods, and that she wandered off, never finding him, and no one ever found her. Someone once told me that 'love' and 'blood' rhyme in Russian.

I turn my binoculars to the left and suddenly I see two winged-tip black shoes. A low branch sways in front of my binoculars, and then I see a woman's foot encased in suede pumps. The leaves swim across my lenses again, and when the current of wind lifts them away, the shoes are gone. I find a pile of rocks a few feet away and climb up on it, checking my footing, as they are loose and seesaw back and forth a bit. Several brown sparrows flutter around me, there are hundreds of them gathered in a gooseberry bush next to the rocks – so many that it is hard to tell the leaves from the sparrows. I raise the binoculars to the left again and scan across the woods. I see a clearing between trees, with high grass, so fluorescent the air above it seems green. Mrs Lewis told me that in Paris there used to be *l'heure verte* – the green hour – which was when everyone drank *'tremblement de terre'* – a hallucinogenic mixture of cognac and absinthe. I lower my lenses back down again, and pan across the grass, and suddenly see the bachelor in his black suit, and Mrs Lewis in a linen summer dress. They seem so close that I back up on my teetering rocks and almost fall off. When I regain my balance, I focus in on them again.

The bachelor is pointing to something in the grass. Mrs Lewis is nodding and holding her hair back with one hand. The bachelor looks odd in his formal suit. One of Mrs Lewis's linen straps slides off her shoulder and she pulls it back up, touching, by accident, the bachelor's arm. He turns to her, he moves closer, the trees sway, her strap falls. He leans toward her, his mouth opens, speaks the shape of 'who' or 'you'. Her eyes half close, the lids are violet, a black tear falls down her face, his finger brushes it away, she steps back, his arms fall to his sides. The wind blows his hair, his tie tosses over his shoulder, he speaks to his hands spread out in front of him. Mrs Lewis steps toward him, she takes his hand, her ring flashes in the stormy light.

There is a loud clap of thunder which makes me jump and I lose my balance and fall off the rocks. The binoculars slip out of my hands and clatter against the stone. All the sparrows whoosh out of the gooseberry bush and hover above me, and then take flight through the trees. I grab the binoculars and limp back up onto the rocks and when I find the bachelor and Mrs Lewis again the sparrows are surrounding them, alighting on her gold-green hair, his black shoulder, her fallen straps. They are laughing. Their teeth flash in the electric light. And then he kisses her, his arms are around her, her hands in his hair. A huge gust of wind blows up and Mrs Lewis's hair covers both of their faces. A big raindrop falls on my lenses and the trees turn to floating seaweed, the bachelor and Mrs Lewis become smudges. I wipe the lens with my shirt, but it has fogged over. Then I hear a scuffling of leaves and when I look below I see Mrs Lewis half running along the path. I jump off the rocks and hide behind them, afraid she might see me, and watch her as she disappears behind the pines.

I stand up and the floating sensation comes over me. I think of that man in Jack London's story, whose feet and hands are frostbitten, and when he stands up he feel separated from the earth, and he has to look down to locate his hands, and when he finds them hanging at the ends of his arms, he thinks how curious it is to use his eyes to find out where his hands are.

Nothing can be proven. Every proof requires a proof, which requires a proof, which requires a proof. This continues endlessly backward, as there is no proof that can be proven that does not need a proof.

An ATOM is the smallest unit into which matter can be divided, and is composed largely of empty space. No one has seen the atom. Only by detecting light reflecting from a surface can we know an object's position. Yet photons of light possess momentum, and when they strike small particles they alter their momentum. Thus, the position of the smallest bits of matter cannot be ascertained without imparting an unpredictable amount of momentum to them. This is called the Uncertainty Principle.

Close your left eye and point at something and then close your right eye, and you will find you are not pointing at the same thing. Being that you change the world just by looking at it. And not being able to go by appearance even though being is only being when it is being perceived.

I keep seeing this scene in my mind, from *A Place in the Sun*, when Elizabeth Taylor first sees Montgomery Clift. She walks past an open door and sees him sink a couple of balls in an amazing pool shot. She looks at him, says, 'Wow.' That look. That shot. That 'wow'. And you know immediately that she is in love with him.

'What is it, Haddie?' Mrs Lewis asks me. We are in the car. I realize I am gaping at her. It might be my imagination, but there is this sexiness about her, clinging like an expensive scent behind her ears, at the base of her throat, warm and redolent at all pulse points. And all her movements, reaching for her purse, turning the steering wheel, arching her neck to look in the rear-view mirror, are lazy and languid, as if she's just emerged from a week-long bath.

'Behind the smallest of gestures lies the greatest of principles,'

Mrs Woods says. She and Mrs Lewis are showing us which chairs to pick in a room, according to our height and weight. Those with uncomely short legs are at an extreme disadvantage as most sofas will throw them into unlovely attitudes. It is best to avoid the Turkish trap of the modern chaise. If you know in advance that your hostess is a fan of Bauhaus, lounging pajamas and jewelry kept to a bare minimum are the smart choice. We should remember that a girl shouldn't fade into the background, but neither should she stick out like a rough-hewn sculpture.

In the middle of the room is a low-slung couch. Mrs Lewis enters the room from the right, and walks toward it. Her hips sway and she seems to be feeling every outline of her body as she moves, every bit of her slides smoothly together. She turns with style and sits, statuesque, the toe of one foot drawn up to the instep of the other, knees close together. And the eyes of a dozen girls and Mrs Woods stare, saucer-eyed and thunderstruck.

Weltschmerz says a philosopher named Kant wrote that our minds structure everything according to time and space, which are like spectacles we can never remove. Light moves at 186,000 miles per hour. Our brain waves travel at 150 miles per hour. So isn't it possible we are seeing everything at the wrong speed? Or maybe sometimes the time in your mind and the space in your mind aren't coinciding, and this is what causes the sensation of having just walked through a door and suddenly underneath you there is no floor.

There will probably have to be all sorts of new rules of etiquette invented if everyone starts journeying into space. And you can just imagine the novel and bizarre *faux pas* that will be committed if we start traveling at the speed of light.

*

'I looked old enough to vote by the time I was nine years old,' Leonora says when I ask her about her love life, 'so the pots were on pretty early between me and men. The first man I was with was so mean he was scared of himself. He had a smile like a knife, and every time you answered one of his questions it was like walking over the backs of sleeping alligators. And he was an ugly creature. His feet were big as fiddle cases. But he had big catnap eyes and I loved him so much my mind ached.'

'He's the type of man I call the Old Snagger Tooth. Your life is like a song, you're just following the notes all the way home until some Snaggly Tooth comes along, blowing his raggy do re mis, tearing your tune to tatters. And before you know it you've got a deep-down monotone depression, and the days start stretching and you're listening to the last bubbles of your Canada Dry sighing.

'Of course,' she sighs, 'it's not really Snagger Tooth's fault. It's right here.' She points to her forehead. 'This is what makes you head for suffering. It makes you think Snaggly's going to lead you off somewhere else, and instead you loop de loop back into yourself. Or that he's going to mean something, when all he is is just somebody, who doesn't *mean* anything. No one does. They just *are*.'

Something bright and gold is shining on the side of the Monroe house, next to the front door. I've been gazing at that house, thinking about the bachelor, and Mrs Lewis, not knowing what to think. I wander across the street, drawn almost hypnotically toward it, and whatever it is that is gold, and glinting in the sunlight. As I get close to the door, I hear the bachelor's voice behind me. 'Are you looking at the inscription?' he asks. Then he passes in front of me, to the front door. I follow him. He points to a square brass plaque. 'It was covered in ivy, and the brass was black. I cleaned it off.'

I step up and look at it. '1955' is engraved in heavy black lettering. Below it: 'THE MONTGOMERY LOUIS MONROE FAMILY'. Montgomery Louis . . . Montgomery Louis . . . Louis? The bachelor takes my hand – I hear him saying from far away that I should sit down, but instead I mumble that I am all right, and run across the street to my house. When I get inside, I go to my room and take the photograph of my sister and Mr Monroe out of my top dresser drawer. I sit on my bed and look at it. Mr Monroe's hair, the line of it at his temples. His nose. His chin. His hands. They are familiar. I grab a magnifying glass off my desk and hold it up to the photograph. There is a hazy blue vein running along his left temple. I swallow. His eyes. Something about his eyes. I focus the magnifying glass on them. His right eye is looking straight at the camera. But his left eye is wandering off. Montgomery Louis. He has a wandering eye. Louis. He is Louis's father.

It is strange to think of how we see through a thin film of sea water by the light of a huge star that is pushing us around. I look up at the dark sky and see a bright point. Still. Occupying a space equal to itself. Even if it is a position or a location from which an infinite number of lines may be drawn which are made up of an infinite number of points. Although in drawing the line you are not necessarily moving, but actually at rest at each point in the process of drawing. Never being able to finish the infinite. Or place that part of your mind when someone asks you the time. Or know for certain if you would believe because it is impossible that the truth of a theorem would still exist after the universe had disappeared.

Weltschmerz ended his book with this long poem about how he must take flight from the lapidary laws of reason because he feels lyric reveries pounding on his Promethean pulse, transporting him back again to the golden dales of Arcady.

ADYTUM is what the Greeks called a secret hiding place. I am sitting under a huge pine tree in the ravine. There is a smell of sap and the branches dip down to the ground on all sides, casting long dark shadows. I always come here to read poetry. The light falling through the needles is the light of daydreams. If secrets had a color they would probably be this same deep marine, shot through with visionary gleams.

My grandmother says that the world is made up of ten thousand things – each of which calls out precisely nothing. And that all Japanese words end in one of five vowels because they are yielding to emptiness, where moments are vast as centuries.

My head is full with secrets, weighing me down. Did Mr Monroe know that Louis was his son? Leonora said Mr Monroe was always plotting something, just like Louis. I imagine their faces superimposed – the high brow, the straight nose, the look of insolence. I wonder if Mr Monroe's hair had a green smell to it, like Louis's, like the stem of a plant freshly broken. 'Nobody really knows his own father,' said Odysseus's son. The uncanny is the familiar that we cannot bear to recognize.

'What are you reading?' a voice says, but all I see is this stream of light. I blink. 'Wordsworth's "Prelude",' I say, and as my eyes adjust I see it is the bachelor, who has lifted up a branch of the tree and is looking in at me. I get up and duck under the branch. The bachelor hands me the notebook he is carrying and takes my book of poetry and looks through it. He stops at a page and reads.

'I never read poetry,' he says. 'I never understood it. I don't know. Poets always seem to know something that I don't. And they're holding their cards close to their chest. I suppose I've always dealt better with facts, I prefer the feel of them. Facts are dense and hard. The best ones fit in your palm as perfect as a baseball thwacks into a glove.' He stands awkwardly, and I suddenly realize he isn't wearing his black suit. I must not have noticed before because my eyes were dazzled from the sudden light. He's wearing tan chinos and a cotton golf shirt. He looks collegiate, wide awake and ready for his morning class.

'How's your book going?' I ask.

'Not much progress. I've been trying to remember.' He looks out through the branches of the trees as though he's lost something there. 'I am uncertain about how to describe – Do you know of the explorer Peary? The one who reached the North Pole?' I nod. 'When he reached the Pole, his compass turned from north to south. North, east and west vanished. Disappeared completely. Up there, one day and one night constitute a year. One thousand days a century.'

'Keats said uncertainty is the best part of poetry. Because it describes things you cannot measure. Maybe if you tried writing a poem about your trip, it might get you unstuck. If you are unsure . . . You could think about how it felt rather than what it meant . . . the moon – it actually inspired a lot of poets.'

'Yes.' The bachelor rolls his notebook into a thin scroll, then unrolls it. 'Calliope,' he says. 'I remember reading somewhere . . . yes, I believe the name is Calliope. One of the Greek muses of poetry. May I call you Calliope?'

I nod slowly, testing the name in my mind. Calliope. My name is Calliope. I love it. 'Yes,' I say out loud. 'Calliope. Yes. Call me Calliope.' I feel something I've never felt before, a light, rushing motion throughout my body.

'Okay, Calliope,' the bachelor says, smiling, and the name rings like a silver bell.

I say the name under my breath and its sound fits inside me. I hear someone calling 'Calliope!' and I know that they are calling for me.

Due to their peevish temper, pernicious influence, lack of nuance in gesture, and inclination to expose to the public the inner recesses of their lives, poets are not a safe guide to mannerly conduct and etiquette.

Aristotle thought poetry was higher than history in showing life's true intentions, because it describes the universal instead of the particular. Words in poems are different from words in everyday life. For example, the word purple in real life is a Crayola crayon, my father's deep purple leather chair, the ink they stamp on fresh meat. Purple in a poem sounds like it comes from some other place, far away from crayons and grapes, somewhere where it exists on its own, purely purple, without having to inhabit an object.

'Now that has a seesaw rhythm to it,' Leonora says when I tell her my new name. 'One that deserves to be sung by a skat-singing soprano.' She crosses her arms in front of her, presses her lips together and nods her head, as if in time to 'Calliope' being sung in skippity high notes. 'Now you've got a title to your story, Morning Glory.' She gently chucks a forefinger under my chin. 'One long appellation with a definite sound of destination.'

'I am Calliope,' I say, while looking into the full-length mirror on my bedroom wall. 'I am Calliope.' My face seems to change slightly, each time I say it. ATAI is the mirror soul. When you stare at your face in the mirror, the changes that take place in it are all the faces that you've had in past lives. 'I am Calliope.' I feel as though I am facing two opposite directions at the same time. Like I am both at the beginning of something and at the end of something. Is truth in the beginning, or the ending of things? There isn't a word for something which is both a beginning and an ending at the same time.

ANTITHESIS is an opposition of ideas placed in sharp juxta-position and tension. The German philosopher Hegel saw antithesis as the essential counterpoint to his thesis in his dialectical system of philosophy. Out of the opposition of antithesis and thesis comes a synthesis. Counter to this synthesis will be another antithesis. This process, according to Hegel, will continue until the Absolute Idea is reached, which constitutes the whole of reality. Hegel describes the World Historical Individual as the heroic type, that helps to reveal to all the Universal Mind and Absolute Spirit, and who embodies the very nature of the transition toward the Absolute Idea.

On the same page is ANTIMATTER, a particle in which the electrical charge is opposite to that of the usual matter in our universe. Matter and antimatter cannot coexist at close range for more than a fraction of a second, because they annihilate each other, which results in their masses being turned into pure energy and their consequent simultaneous disappearance.

I got Einstein's autobiography *The World as I See It* out of the library. If anyone could tell you if what you see you can believe, it would have to be Einstein. He has a section called 'The Meaning of Life'. My palms get all sweaty just trying to find the page where it starts. It is only a paragraph. Einstein asks, 'What is the meaning of human life and organic life altogether?' I don't quite understand his answer but he says something about the extraordinary situation of mortals and our brief sojourn. I get this sinking feeling. It's like seeing those exhibits in the reptile houses at zoos. There is a huge glass case with an official-looking card in front that says, 'The Zebra-Striped Iridescent Frenzical South American Long-Tongued Lizard' and when you look inside, no matter from what angle you position yourself, all you see is a big stick and a piece of wilted lettuce.

Einstein discovered that a falling body is both at rest and in motion.

ALIENATION is a state of estrangement between the self and the objective world, which can create the feeling that one's destiny is not under one's control, but determined by external agents, luck or fate, and thus lead to a loss of overall meaning or comprehensibility. 'Apollo! Apollo!' being what the alienated Cassandra cried in *Agamemnon*. 'Where, where have you brought me? How shall I tell of the end? Soon, very soon it will fall.'

'Ah, the omens drear of the macabre Pillage of Charnel,' says Louis, wrapping me into the black velvet cape that he is wearing.

'Give it a rest, Louis,' I say, unwrapping myself from the cape. 'This is your inane idea.' Louis says he won't call me Calliope until he has christened me. And the perfect place for me to be baptized is on the grave of my sister, at midnight. This way her evil *Doppelgänger* will be laid to rest at the same time I am initiated into my new name. We've told Leonora and Louis's mother that we are sleeping out in the woods tonight. The moon's light pulses along the gravestones and high clumps of grass. The branches of a huge dead buckeye in the middle of the graveyard casts shadows along all the tombs. An owl hoots from high in one of the trees, and Louis pulls a gun out from under his cape and points it around wildly.

'Louis, what the hell are you doing with that?' I point to my grandmother's gun, the one he stole. The jade handle glows in the moonlight.

'It's my transitional object,' Louis says, tucking it back into his belt. 'I've found that teddy bears and blankets no longer grant me a real sense of security.' The owl hoots again and a flock of bats fly low over the graves and then up to sit on the small fieldstone chapel.

Louis puts his hand up to his ear. 'Hark! The ennui bird in its nest of melancholia!'

'Louis, do you believe in fortunetelling?' I watch the bats, hunched in their wings, sitting in a row on the roof.

'Sure.' Louis pulls me toward him. 'Mammomancy. The bumps of benevolence and amorousness.' He slides his hands up under my shirt. 'They give me a correct vision of the future.'

'Yes, well, I see great pain looming on your horizon,' I say, sticking my knee between his legs.

'You', he says, tossing one edge of the cape over his shoulder, 'should become more aware of your vernal impulses. I'll introduce you to zee organ of nature's zelf-revelation. *My* chief organ of sentiment –'

'Louis, let go,' I say, struggling to get out of his cape. 'You're hurting me – and this is a cemetery for chrissakes –'

'The Divine Marquis said we need both pleasure and pain so the natural balance is maintained,' Louis says, pulling me in tighter, 'and the cemetery is the perfect place for *mort douce, non?* Eros and Thanatos.' I stamp on his foot.

He walks off in a huff ahead of me to my sister's grave. The little bronze angel is turning green, and lichen covers the stone in patches. 'I don't know,' I murmur to Louis, and turn away from the grave. I feel like I am inside this hollow drum someone is pounding and pounding. 'Maybe . . . we shouldn't . . .' But he takes my shoulders and gently pulls me toward the ground, placing a cool hand on my forehead. In his black flowing cape and with his wild blond hair he looks like a high soul full of sublime longing, a wandering outlaw.

'You are suffering from excessive sensibility.' Louis unclasps his cape and wraps it around me. 'Close your eyes. Think of the most beautiful words in the English language. Lullaby. Silver moon. Listen to the elegiac meter of their sphery syllables.' I breathe deeply and say the words to myself, and in a few minutes I have a soft swaying feeling. It must be all the 'l's and the 'o's. I wonder if each letter of the alphabet creates its own particular sentiment.

'Okay,' Louis says. 'Strip.'

'What?' I wrap the cape tighter around me.

'Get naked. Like the day you were born. I am going to *baptize* you.'

'No way, Louis.' I get up and start to walk back down the path. This is just another one of his games to get off with me.

'Stop.' Louis grabs my arm. 'Okay, I'll compromise. Take off your clothes but leave on the cape. You do want me to call you Calliope, don't you?' He crosses his arms in front of him. 'We have to follow a set form,' he says firmly.

I can see the little pieces of quartz shining in the path. I stomp off to the side of the buckeye tree where he can't see me. Then I take off my clothes, wrap the cape back around me and walk stiffly past Louis.

I lie down on Haddie's grave. The moon is cold and blue. I feel the ground falling away beneath me and I dig my hands into the dirt to hold on. Louis takes my hand in his. He cups my one palm on top of the other, holding them in one of his palms. He draws circles with his thumb in my uppermost open palm, around and around and around, and then lays my hands on my chest. I feel his wet fingertips on my forehead. He is whispering. I cannot hear everything he says – '. . . knock and it shall be opened . . . ye must be born again . . .' His fingertips are on my forehead again, drawing looping lines across it, over and over and over. He is writing the name Calliope. 'Calliope,' he says out loud. The name hums on my tongue, against my teeth, at the base of my throat.

I blink open my eyes. The moon is bright. Louis is stroking my hair, murmuring something. Then I hear the words. 'You do not know yourself, but I do. I know the places that you can't see. The nape of your neck. The shape of your back. How you look at yourself in the mirror. I know the space between your eyes, and the hollow behind your ears.' Suddenly he draws back, leans against an opposite gravestone. 'Just forget . . .' He draws his fingers through his hair. 'I didn't mean – just – forget it.'

I sit up and look at him. I remember once how he squeezed my hand when he was excited about something – I can still feel his fingers cutting sharp between mine. Another time when we were lying in the sun, he took off his watch, and I remember the band of white skin around his wrist. When I read something after I have been with him, it is his voice that is saying the words on the page. I know the sound of his footsteps – whether he is wearing moccasins or boots. He seems forever off to somewhere else, forever leaving.

I creep over to him. I take his hands and feel the large bones and veins in them, his unbuttoned cuff, the flash of his watchface in the moonlight makes something unfurl in my stomach. I look at his face, the shadowed indentation between his eye and nose, the strange, familiar swell of skin at the sides of his mouth. I kiss the place where his hair meets his temple and smell his hair. I feel his eyelashes against my cheek, his tongue under my chin. I want to press my whole body up against him like a cat, into all his curves and hollows. I rub my nose against his chin, collarbone, Adam's apple. He grabs my hair, runs his fingers through it, tangling it, pulling at the roots. Then his tongue is in my mouth, twirling around mine. I unbutton his shirt and pull it away from his shoulders. He unclasps the cape and it falls about my hips. I rub my breasts against his chest and run my tongue along the crease between his chest and armpit. His hands are on my breasts – I rock my pelvis against his, I can't stop moving – I run my hands down his chest, feel the bones of his pelvis. I unbutton his jeans. 'Wait,' Louis says, out of breath. He kicks off his shoes, unzips his jeans, lifts his hips up and pulls them off. His penis lies large and swollen against his stomach. I lean over and lick the long incurving line of his pelvis, suck at the long dip running between his hip and stomach. I run my hands along his inner thighs and his legs tense as if he is about to leap; his hands run long strokes down my back. I kiss the tip of his penis. I put it in my mouth, his skin slides like eyelids.

'Come here,' Louis whispers, lifting me from his lap to face him. He kisses my forehead, my eyelids, my neck, my shoulders. He strokes me between my legs and I move in circles, Louis presses me hard against him, and then his penis is inside me – I move up and down, circle around on his lap, feel his thighs against my bottom. I hear Louis mumble, then he suddenly stops moving. I press myself down into his lap, circling my hips. 'Stop,' Louis says sharply. His penis has slipped out of me. I feel for it. It is soft and small. 'Stop it.' Louis slaps my hand away. 'Let go.' He grabs my other wrist and flips my hand from his shoulder. His whole body is stiff. He gropes on the ground around me, finds the cape and flings it at me while pushing me off him. 'Get dressed.' He's pulling on his jeans, he grabs his shirt up from the ground and it cracks in the air like a whip. 'What . . .' I ask, pulling the cape around me.

'I can't . . . How can you expect me to . . .' Louis is yelling at me, chopping his hands in the air as if he might hit me. 'Where the fuck are my shoes?' He glares at me as if I've hidden them from him. I point to them. My insides feel as though they are slithering out of me. Louis is cursing under his breath while shuffling his feet into his shoes. 'You're too young. Haddie.' He stresses the syllables, hard and blunt. 'You don't know. You don't know anything.' His voice trembles. 'You aren't a woman yet . . . You don't even smell like a woman yet – you're a little girl –' He turns and stalks off down the path to the road.

I stare after him. My mouth is dry and my mind won't stop humming. I don't know what I did wrong. I don't know where to move to.

When I finally cross the path to get my clothes from behind the buckeye tree, I see Louis standing in the road under a street light. His hands hang at his sides. He is looking off somewhere. Like the wind has just picked him up and set him down nowhere. He reminds me of one of those distant dark figures in the paintings of Chinese mountains on my grandmother's walls, standing in some lost corner with huge volumes of space boxing their ears on all sides. He seems to see me, starts to walk toward me, then abruptly he changes direction and walks off down the road.

'Why must this persistent fear beat its wings so ceaselessly and so close against my manic heart?' cries the chorus in *Agamemnon*. '. . . Against one's will comes wisdom . . .'

The ARCHAIC SMILE is the expression that characteristically appears on the faces of Greek kouroi statues. Several critics have interpreted the strange smile on these figures as signifying the birth of human consciousness. I think the smile looks bittersweet. A curve of uncertainty about whether we really want to know.

When I look up at the sky, I always wonder whether there is an end, or no end. And which is more frightening. AZURE is the last word in Book A of the encyclopedia. 'How far they are in their azure . . . how far,' a Greek chorus laments about the gods when yet another person is tragically struck down. Of course, we all have a bad ending. 'We die because we cannot join our beginning to our end,' said one of the ancients.

When I get home I see that Leonora's car isn't in the driveway. She must be staying at one of her boyfriends' since she thought I was sleeping out tonight. I let myself in. Everything is still – the tables, chairs, vases, piano. I keep walking from one room to another. I go into my father's study and look at his bookshelf. I need something to distract me. If you have a row of fifteen books and start changing their order, one change a minute, it would take you two and a half million years to place them in every conceivable order. A likely impossibility being always preferable to an unconvincing possibility. I take down the dictionary. A book is a book. Something being most true at the cost of saying nothing. Maybe if I look up each word in the paradox 'this sentence is false' it will suddenly be clear to me. And my head will stop spinning. And I will be able to put this night out of my mind and go to sleep.

I look up the definitions of each word in the sentence and get this:

> One, unnamed, approaching
> A group of words
> Which exists
> Unreal.

Suddenly I hear the back screen door open and then slam closed. I open the shutters of the library and look out at the drive. My heart starts beating in my throat. I look around my father's desk for something, something sharp, his letter opener – but there is nothing but pens and pads of paper. I tiptoe out into the hall and look into the living room, waiting for my eyes to adjust to the dark. The furniture is in humped black herds, quiet, as if holding its breath. A shadow sways against the farthest wall, moving forward, stretching out to a tip, then receding back into itself. I look to the french doors and see it is a shadow of a tall tree. The stairway is dark. The telephone sits on the entryway table, remote and inscrutable.

I tiptoe toward the telephone. Suddenly our grandfather clock chimes from an upper hallway and when it stops the whole house seems suspended in formaldehyde. I move closer to the phone. A shadow on the wall next to the mirror slow-dissolves, then looms larger – the shape of a head and shoulders. I lunge for the phone but just as I pick it up someone clamps their hand over my mouth and slams the phone back down on the table. 'It's me,' I hear Louis whisper in my ear.

His hand is trembling and cold. He lets go.

'What –' I start to say, turning to him, but he cuts me off.

'Where's Leonora?' His voice is quivering, his whole body is shaking, as if he's just been rescued from a frozen river.

'She's out. What's wrong –?' His face is so pale that in the dark it seems to be floating above the rest of his body.

I reach out to turn on the lamp on the entryway table but Louis's hand grabs mine before I can reach it. 'Don't,' he says, letting go of my hand and falling into a chair opposite the table. He picks up a glass sculpture of a leopard and holds it in both hands, rubbing his thumbs along its arched back. He is saying something softly that I cannot hear. I put my palm on his forehead to see if he has a fever. He whips his head away so violently that I jump back. 'Don't touch me *ever*, ever touch me *ever*!' His teeth flash white.

'Louis, what's wrong with you –' Now I am trembling; my eyes are filling with tears.

'*Wrong* – what's *wrong* – with *me*?' He glares at me. 'SHIT!' Louis yells and then throws the leopard across the room and it strikes the mirror and they both shatter.

'Maybe you should go home, Louis,' I say as firmly as I can.

Louis jumps up. He pounds the fist of one hand into the palm of the other. '*Go home*! I *have* no *home*!' He pulls wildly at his shirt, bunching it in his hands, twisting it from side to side. 'She was *fucking* him – in the bedroom – *fucking* –' He puts his fingers up to his temples, the forefingers curled upward like horns, he makes a ramming movement like a bull, then slams his fist into the wall, crumbling the plaster. 'She was fucking him.' He starts pounding on the wall, kicking it, and then he abruptly marches off down the hallway.

I follow him to my father's bar. He's flinging open the refrigerator, opening cabinets, and when he finds a glass he fills it with whiskey. He drinks half of it and then slams the glass on the counter. He has turned on the light and I can see him now – there are blotches of red on his chest, cheeks, forehead. His eyes are bloodshot. His hair is wet at the edges. His fist is bleeding.

'Louis,' I say, trying to sound calm, 'your mother . . . it was no one . . . nobody . . .'

'*Nobody – No one –*' He gives a funny laugh and drinks the rest of the whiskey. He pours himself another glass and brushes past me out of the room. I follow him to the library. He looks out the window. 'Him.' He points his finger toward the bachelor's house. His finger is shaking. 'He – is *no one*?' As he drinks, the glass spills whiskey down his shirt.

'Louis.' I turn to him. He is drinking steadily until the glass is empty. 'Your mother loves you, she wouldn't –' Louis swipes his arm along my father's desk, sending everything crashing. He grabs books from the shelves and throws them to the floor, their pages flung open. He sinks down to the floor, sitting on a pile of open books, and suddenly everything is silent. Outside it is dark, but I see movement on the street, a man turning into the bachelor's drive. It is him. 'It's him,' I say out loud, without really meaning to. Louis cocks his head toward me, alert. 'He's gone home.' I point out the window to the bachelor's house. 'Go home, Louis.'

He clenches and unclenches his hands. 'Yes,' he says, chopping a stiff hand down into the upturned palm of the other. His nostrils are white. 'Yes,' he says again and leaves the room. A moment later I hear the front door slam closed.

I kneel down and start closing all the books, putting them in piles. The words blur into black squiggles because my eyes keep filling with water. I wipe my face with my shaking hand. The sun will rise soon.

I go outside. The sky has turned that gray of hesitation before sleep. But the trees, houses, bushes, stones are still dark as deep water, as if enclosed in their impenetrable souls, filled with stillness to the brim. I sit down on the porch. Nothing is ever really still. Your weight is your movement. If something became completely still, instead of the mute and motionless beauty of a statue, there would be absolutely nothing, a void. It would dissolve, and vanish.

I hear the clicking of heels on pavement, and make out a figure walking toward me through the mist. It comes closer. It is Mrs Lewis.

'Haddie,' she says before she reaches me. 'Have you seen Louis?' She doesn't look at me directly. She is uptight, her voice is coiled and hard. It gives me a tense feeling at the back of my neck.

'He went . . .' I begin to say 'home', but I trail off, because over her shoulder I see the door of the bachelor's house open, and someone walks out onto the front porch, across the drive and onto the lawn. Mist is rising from the grass. I can't tell who it is, but I don't think it is the bachelor. In the odd indigo light it seems to be made of smoke, looks as though, if you were close enough to touch it, your hand would pass straight through it. The figure stops and stands still facing the street, as if waiting for someone, something, a message. It is Louis. His long arms hang at his sides. His head is at an odd angle. The door stands open behind him.

'Louis!' Mrs Lewis calls out to him. The word echoes on the empty, early-morning street. Louis doesn't move. His arms and legs seem detached from him, they don't match up, they are bent askew, as if he has fractured all the bones in them. Mrs Lewis and I run toward him.

When we reach him I see he is holding the gun in his hand. Mrs Lewis starts shaking him by the shoulders. 'What did you do? What did you do?' she asks over and over, in this strange, pleading voice. Louis just stares at her.

'What did you do?' she keeps asking, her voice getting louder and higher, starting to lose control. I stare at the gun in Louis's hand. It looks like a toy gun, the sort that leaves the smell of burned carbon in the air. I hear a loud slap.

'Tell me!' Mrs Lewis shouts. There is a long red mark on Louis's cheek. 'Tell me!' she screams, raising her arm. He grabs her wrist before she can slap him again. She struggles to get out of his grip, but he holds her tight. Then he twists her wrist behind her back, pulling her close. He dips his head in close to her face, and kisses her, his tongue thrusting deep inside her mouth.

'Is that what you wanted?' Louis whispers, while pulling his face back from his mother's, his mouth wet and red, tilted up in a strange, sick smile. 'You always pretended you wanted me – but it was him, all along. I knew one day he would return. But now he's gone –' Louis waves the gun casually in the direction of the Monroe house.

'You're crazy! You are mad!' Mrs Lewis screams at him. She starts hitting him with her free hand.

Louis thrusts the gun up under her chin. 'Stop it,' he says coldly, in a voice not his own. I try to speak, but nothing comes out of my mouth. I try to move, but everything is whirling. I close my eyes.

'Go ahead,' I hear Mrs Lewis say softly. I open my eyes. Her head is thrown back. Her neck is long and white. 'My life ended when you were born.'

Louis lets go of her and stumbles backward a few steps. Mrs Lewis strides toward him and hits his chest with the heel of her hand. 'End it. I want it to be over,' she says, crying now. 'I will never be rid of him, because of you, reminding me.'

'What? Who?' Louis stutters, shaking his head.

'Your father, you idiot! It was not *him*!' She waves wildly at the house behind us. 'It was Monroe. I should have known you would be just like him,' she says, throwing her hands up over her face. 'There's no end.' She sinks to the ground, sobbing. 'It was horrible . . . horrible . . .' she says over and over, 'horrible.' She looks up at Louis. There are tears streaming down her face. 'It was an accident. You must believe me – it was an accident. Monroe was – sick. He was touching her –' Mrs Lewis tries to take Louis's hand but he tosses it off him. 'He was kissing her – I hit him – Haddie was in the way.' She lets out a sob. 'On the edge . . . she lost her balance . . .' Mrs Lewis starts to rock back and forth. 'I had her by the arm, the hand, her bracelet broke – I saw her eyes – she fell –'

'No . . . no . . .' Louis says, shaking his head.

'Do you remember – anything?' Mrs Lewis asks him, trying to take his hand again, but he pulls roughly away from her. 'You were here,' Mrs Lewis says softly, 'below, on the path.'

'Shut up!' Louis shouts, covering his ears with his hands. 'Shut up! I don't want to know –' He turns from us and runs.

I run after him, into the ravine. It is still dark here, and I lose sight of him. Then I see a flicker of blue between the trees. Branches rush and stab at me as I run. I lose sight of Louis, but I know where he is going. I jump over the stream and run alongside it. Dark leaves slap at my face, and then suddenly everything is bright with light. The woods have ended. We are at the Bottomless Lake. Louis is standing at the edge, looking across it.

The lake seems to be on fire, glittering with sharp points of light.

'Wait,' Louis says, looking through me. He walks into the lake until the water is up to his hips. He dives under and I lose sight of him. Then I see something black, moving, far, far out. 'Louis,' I call. A black dot on the water. I squint my eyes. A still, small, black point. Is the point going? Or coming? 'Louis,' I call louder. A wind blows over the water, through the trees. 'Louis?' Still water. Still trees. Soundless. Out of the corner of my eye I see a black silhouette, darting into the ravine. I turn my head to look, but it is gone.

The body falls slowly. The arms are flung outward, the head thrown back. A school of minnows swims toward it, then flashes, in a quick V, away again. A bright shaft of light breaks through the water, illuminating the blue shirt and the ribbon of magenta flowing from the head. Then the body is swept into a strong current, it is pulled down faster now. The water is olive green, then brown. The light is gone. The body will keep falling. The bottom of the lake has never been sounded.

INDEX

126–127, *see* forgetting, nostalgia
mind, and Anaxagoras 14; and fear 98–99;
    in heart 98; light of 122; and falling
    183–184; Descartes on 222–224, 234,
    255; and coquettes 255; Leonora on
    268, *see* body, knowledge
miracles, Louis Lewis on 196
mirrors, and soul 59; and memories 88–
    89; in convent school 144, *see* atai
moon, goddess of 27; viewing 38; weight
    and speed of 136; distance of 147; and
    medieval virgins 158; bachelor on 211;
    pull of 221; etymology of word 235;
    list of 235–236; Leonora on 236;
    fortunetelling by 276
movement, and thinking 14; Parmenides
    and 16; of stones 17; paradox of 19,
    62, 74, 206, 216, 249; backwards 30;
    glamorous 35; proving 38–39;
    childhood list of 41; and illusion 42;
    and mind 63; romantic forms 63; good
    and evil 73; and Aristotle 90; of
    communists 108; of missing persons
    118; in koan 125; of soul 154; and
    Gallileo 241; apoplexy and 259, *see*
    paradox, speed, thought
murder, and glamorous deaths 87–88;
    Robert Walker on 117; belladonna and
    119; Mafia and 119, 195–196, *see* death

names, Louis Lewis on 18; and
    anonymous 18; forgetting 26–27;
    turning upside-down 32; and *The
    Third Man* 81–82; Leonora on 96;
    sound of 96–97, 289; of cats 97; and
    fame 129; like doors 134; in movies
    135; changing to Innocent 148;
    meditation on 189; bachelor on 227;
    Leonora on 289; and beginnings and
    endings 290, *see* self
Newton, Isaac 242, 276, *see* gravity
nostalgia 129, 236, *see* memory
numbers, and future 7; zero 13, 20;

infinity of 122–123; as adjectives 123,
    see arithomania, fortunetelling, Plato
nymphs 250

Odysseus 27, 28, 60, 61, 82, 86, 150, son
    on 287, *see* heroes
Odyssey, The 29, 39, 82, *see* heroes,
    Odysseus, nostalgia
ololuge 113, *see* sacrifice
ontalagia 265, *see* being, self

Pan, and Artemis 27; looking for 48–51,
    see gods
Paradox, as a cure 16; of Achilles and
    tortoise 19; of arrow 34, 74, 249, 252;
    and proving movement 38–39, 42; of
    crossing field 62; Sophist 65; Third
    Man 84; and aporia 105; of numbers
    122; of truth in saying nothing 127; of
    parts to whole 152; Augustine's
    paradox of mind 166; of arrow in
    space 206; of proof 282; of drawing
    lines 286; of false sentence 298
Parmenides 16, 34, 39, *see* Paradox
Pascal, Blaise 273
Pasteur, Louis 273
perception, of animus 46–47; of sounds
    171–172; and reason 248; and arrow
    paradox 249, 252; list of sensations
    259–260; and cause 260, *see* sight,
    smell
philosophy, of stones 17, 157; and
    fragments 32; and Greek philosophers
    48; and Academy 59; and walking 73;
    and senses 248, 252; dialectical 290
philtrum 271, *see* secrets
photosynthesis, feeling of 42; and
    evolution of brain 146
Plato 59, 73, 80, and universal forms 84;
    and love 86, 120; and memory 88; and
    names 96; Louis Lewis on 105–106,
    see Academy, anamnesis, knowledge,
    love, Socrates, truth

speed, of thought 9; earth 9, 62; of gravity-less body 9; of light 134; of moon 136; of soul 154; of falling through center of earth 184; of brain waves 284, *see* movement

stealing, Louis Lewis on 20–22

stillness, of stones 17; paradox and 34, 74, 249, 252, 286; and fear 127; of God 215; of dark 301, *see* movement, paradox, Parmenides

stones 17, 124, *see* alchemy, immortality, memory, philosophy, stillness

superstition 37, list of 89; of evil eye 109, *see* death

survival tactics, list of 272–273

Swedenborg, Emmanuel 147, *see* visions

tanha 65

Telemachus 30, 287

termine 191, *see* Leonardo, space

thought, listening to 13–14; and geraniums 90; and fear 98; and seeing 104–105; and trees 122; while falling 182–183; in limbo 194; of God 204–205; Descartes on 221–223, 237; and haki-maki 243; feeling of 244; experiments 273–274, *see* body, mind, perception

time, and magic 30; paradox of 62; and being 84; and eternity 108; how to lose sense of 122; Augustine on 164–165; list of 166; of angels 171–172, 194; paradox of 216; and third eye 223; smell of 258; and Kant 284, *see* paradox, space

Torchlusspanik 242, *see* abyss

tragedy, Aeschylus and 5; Greek philosophers and 47; and anagnorisis 86, tragic flaws 87; and the French 230, *see* fate

trees 26, 28, 39, 41, Louis Lewis and 42; and truth 122

trombipulation 253, *see* etiquette

truth, Grandmother and 13; Plato on 86, 88, 106; Augustine on 136; of dervishes 161; and falling 188; endings and 290, *see* beauty

vertigo, and disappearing 3; and facts 6, 11; and hokey-pokey 10; and body 11; French expressions for 11; and questions 11–12; cures for 16, 30, 76; and trees 122; of light 141; of religious vision 142–143; of looking at others 152; of Disneyland 154; of large numbers 173; of the abyss 182, 242; of wonder 184; from looking at paintings 186; of angels 194; of time and space colliding 284, *see* body, mind, perception, thought, truth

visions, Leonora and 142–143; Buddhist 160; of whirling dervishes 161; bachelor and 212, *see* knowledge, light, truth

Wandervogeling 253

words 6, Greek 13; in dictionaries 73; and gravity 78; on beginnings and endings 91, 290; divine 136; medieval 146; eating 146; evil 159; in Garden of Eden 165; and Abelard 173; copying from books 193–194; and smoting devils 194; Oriental 221; Leonora on 235; of smells 254–259; Japanese 287; in poems 289; beautiful 293, endless definitions of 298, *see* beginnings, definitions, dictionaries, doors, endings, evil, good, names, perception

yawning 19, *see* etiquette

Zen 13, and dialogue 80; Louis Lewis on 106; monks 107; koans 125, 159, *see* Buddhism

zero 13, *see* numbers

Zeus 29, *see* death, gods, sex